Mountain
of Lost
Magics

S.W. Strackbein

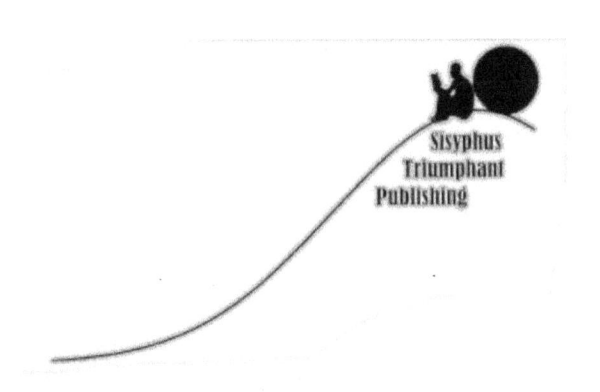

Sisyphus
Triumphant
Publishing

Text, map, and cover design copyright © 2023 by S.W.Strackbein

Edited by Lisa Lickle

All rights reserved. This book or parts thereof may not be reproduced in any form, stored in any retrieval system, or transmitted in any form by any means—electronic, mechanical, photocopy, recording, or otherwise—without prior written permission of the publisher, except as provided by United States of America copyright law and fair use.

Library of Congress Cataloging-in-Publication Data

available upon request

Mourning of Lost Magics is a work of fiction. Magic isn't real regardless of how much people want it to be. Any resemblance to actual events or persons, living or dead, is entirely coincidental. While opinions expressed are those of the characters and should not be confused with the author's there may or may not be some shared views.

First published in the United States of America in 2023

by Sisyphus Triumphant Publishing

www. Sisyphus Triumphant

First addition November 2023

For information about permission to reproduce selections from this book, email

Permissions, Sisyphus Triumphant Publishing

Books may be purchased for business or promotional use. For more information, contact the author at swstrackbein.com

Portions of this story deal with acts of suicide. If you or someone you know are in crisis, there are options available to help. Text or call the Suicide & Crisis Lifeline at any time to connect with a trained crisis counselor.

Confidential support is available 24/7 for everyone in the U.S., call or text **988**

or chat at **988lifeline.org**

or visit **www.nimh.nih.gov**

#shareNIMH

As always—

to Tanya,
for making all my dreams come true.

I Love You

Nor

Wellipeney's
Lighthouse

Guppison

Belt of Allennud

Sal Basin

Mistfall

Southern
Ocean

Shellnock Palace

Kingdom of New Byzantium

Krastas
Tiltas
Bulwark Divide

Gaeao Temple

Republic of Elam

Northnook
Lonestone   Silkfrost
Cottonwood   Angel's Pearl
Westcliffe   Citadel of Iks   Chestone
Silverton   Truegate
Leafside   Gunnison
South Fork

Sal Basin

All we have to decide
is what to do with the time that is given us.

JRR Tolkien

Mourning of Lost Magics

Part I

The Lines of Magic

Missing from the sky, the hawk devours the angel

of black light.

Struck down by the venom of the martyred,

brandishing his five claws.

As alms to earth are stolen then returned,

So shall the hawk be divided by the

serpent, buck, and lion

CHAPTER 1
The Memory Eater

A shroud of foggy curiosity greeted him as he sat on the cold stone floor, disoriented, legs outstretched. Gawking into the darkness beyond a ring of glowing coals, flickering motes caught his sluggish attention as they danced within the warm currents, rising, floundering, then falling. Radiant warmth prickled his feet. Icy rock jabbed shards into his back as stale, brackish air clawed at his throat. He pursed the edges of his dry lips as fever chills spread across his forehead and down into his shoulders, adding to dizzying nausea.

Vague thoughts of danger floated just beyond his awareness. Like a caught breath, nothing substantial, nothing he could cling to. He scratched his upper thigh as his opposite hand met the handle of a rough-hewn rock blade. With an uncertain grip, he brought it close to the ember's light.

His narrowed eyes searched for its meaning, its origin. Its obsidian edge dulled with mud, or perhaps... blood. Much like the cave, the circle of rock around his meager fire, or how he'd arrived at such a place, this knife held no place in his memory. He shifted it to his lap and gazed beyond his alcove, feeling eyes watching him, waiting, but for what he couldn't say.

A click rang out somewhere in the recesses of the darkness beyond. A slow drip from an opened fissure perhaps, or the dull tip of a stalactite knocked free. Within his mind's eye, he pictured blood-soaked, overgrown claws, dagger-sharp teeth dripping saliva, gaping jaws hungry for flesh. He tightened his grip on his knife and held it over the glowing embers, toward the darkness beyond.

"Hello?" he croaked with an ill-used voice. "Is anyone there?" The echo mocked a trapped creature's panic. He cleared his parched throat, igniting reverberating growls throughout the cave. Rumbles explored the darkness, only to return as warped versions of the original, ominous, and menacing.

Phantoms played at his periphery, the tension held too long with attempts to catch them. He listened with held breath, taking in what little he could as he shifted his weight and scratched his upper thigh.

The blade clinked stone off stone as he pulled his legs beneath him and lifted to his knees, taking in the musty still air, tinged with iron and trapped smoke. He found his balance wanting, catching himself with a hand planted on the rock floor. How long had he been here, wasting away, fending off imagined demons?

Sitting back on his heels, he stretched his stiff back; felt the ache from his tailbone through his spine to the base of his neck. He wiped the cold sweat from his forehead, felt the stubble along his square chin and beneath his nose. In the dim light, gold stitching shimmered off his wool tunic. An embroidered chimera at the center, its lion's head in full roar against a dark backdrop. He brushed his hands across the intricate stitchwork. The effort of remembering tired him, bringing a dull ache to the back of his head.

Setting down the blade, he held his hands over the glowing coals, taking in what heat they offered, his only comfort against the indifferent stone surroundings. His breathing calmed as he massaged the atrophy from his muscles and scratched at his thigh, the itch raw and irritating. He pulled up his tunic's hem, exploring the cause. Sliced through his trousers, three raised horizontal lines stretched across the whole of his thigh just below the groin. Only a finger's width separation, each held varying degrees of healing as they traversed down the muscle. He touched each line as if precious, yet their meaning remained clouded within his decayed memories.

Withered strength fought every move as he struggled to his feet. Bracing against the cave wall, he inched toward the mouth of his chamber. Lying at the entrance, a fallen longsword, nearly lost to the shadows were it not for its golden pommel and inlaid guard, its intricate design mirroring his tunic.

His knees screamed their displeasure as he bent to retrieve the weapon. He held it outstretched. The black leather-wrapped hilt fit his hand as if tailored-made. The blade, cared for and honed. It seemed so familiar, so prized. "My sword?" he whispered. The cave seemed to echo in answer. He slid his fingers across the emblem, searching for its meaning, unable to capture the memory as pinpricks bore into the base of his skull. He clutched at the back of his neck, finding nothing to substantiate his agony.

Echoes from other parts of the cave jabbed at his unrestrained imagination. Yet through his clouded mind, the word formed: *Da'Kar*. Fear bit deep into his chest. Heat traversed up his neck, into his face, and burrowed into his temple. Unsure of the significance or why it brought such panic, he hurried back to his original position, as much as the stiffness in his limbs would allow, dragging the sword's bulk along the stone floor as he went.

He perched the obsidian blade against his hip. The sword, hidden beneath his leg. The noise was nothing, he reassured himself, a stray pebble or rainwater from the outside. But like a panicked rabbit, his eyes fixed on the hapless entrance as fear crushed in on him, stealing his breath. His muscles froze as the clicking intensified. He clamped a tremulous hand around his knife, cursing himself for his cowardice, and the detached recollections from nowhere.

"Not again," he whispered, making a fourth cut below the last. Droplets of blood leached to the surface and absorbed into the wool of his trousers as the fresh wound swelled beyond the previous three. Icy sweat formed rivulets at his brow, dripped down his temple, and eddied into his eyes. In the emptied folds of his mind, he fitted the creature to her name, Da'Kar, the Memory Eater.

The clicking grew louder, closer. Talon-like

daggers wrapped around the mouth of his alcove. Two at each side, black on black, glistening against the dull rock.

Madness tightened its grip around his chest, intensifying the percussion of his heart as the dim firelight reflected bright, inhuman eyes. The vertical sits of her pupils pulsed to the ember's glow as they fixated on him, watching, waiting, savoring his terror.

"It is surprising," Da'Kar said in an unexpected musical tone, seductive, yet calculating, "that you still wake." Her head bobbed rhythmically, matching his quick gasps for breath. "It is a rarity that I enjoy one's company for so long."

He thrust the obsidian blade toward the creature, holding it quivering over the glowing coals.

"How long have you held me captive?" he asked with feigned courage. The fingers of his free hand traced the scars on his thigh.

The creature tilted her head as if fascinated by his mock conviction. "We have conversed three times, sword-bearer. Each time ending the same."

"And how is that?"

Her eyes narrowed. "With my gorging on what remains of your mind." She sucked in a breath of morbid pleasure, accentuating her words. "And my eagerness for soon-to-be rotting meat."

He swallowed the lump forming in his throat. "I'll ask you again, monster." Wrestling calm into his trembling voice. "How long have I been captive here?"

Da'Kar pushed her diamond shape head into view. "Longer than most, longer than expected." Down her face and neck, fire-red scales reflected the trembling light. A black swatch cut along her jawline, below slit nostrils, through her eyes, and ended at the fleshy horns atop her head.

He tightened the grip on his blade and pushed down his anxiety. "Then why not end me now?" Six segmented legs explored the cave walls as her underbelly, warmed by the glowing coals, glistened the same red as her face. Her tail remained in the darkness of the tunnels as she pushed her swaying head above him. A pair of needle-like fangs folded out beyond her lips, glistening and tipped with venom.

"Human flesh digests easiest when the fight is removed."

Breath once again caught in his throat, shadows magnifying the demon's presence. His muscles petrified as the stench of rancid meat and Da'Kar's body heat filled the shrinking space. His heart pounded. He turned his face away, squeezing his eyes shut in anticipation. "Please, have mercy." Yet when the strike failed to arrive, he ventured a sidelong glance.

Da'Kar's jaw closed as she pulled back. "Dare you plea for mercy?" Her head tilted as if in study of him. "The memories I've taken from you evoke a life of depravity and hedonism beyond abandon. Mercy has no place in you and rarely had it been indulged."

"No." He shook his head. "That doesn't seem right. What man do you imply I am?"

Da'Kar's mouth widened to an ape of a smile. "You consider your punishment unjust? The man you were was as much a monster to your kind as I had ever been accused."

He stared into the creature's face, questioning.

"I've rendered you nobody. Taken all of who you were and who you are. Your name is as meaningless as one given to a pet." Da'Kar widened her smile and lunged forward, pressing him further into the cave wall.

"The name Guilder Rayne is uttered by few without contempt." She leaned near to his face, her forked tongue caressing his cheek. "Your past and present are mine."

"And my future?"

"Your future," she whispered as venom dripped onto his temple, "mirrors those who've ventured into these caves, no matter the reason." She pulled away as if savoring the perfume of his renewed fear. "For sport or spoils, they all end as sustenance." She lifted her head and loomed over him.

Phantom pain erupted at the back of his neck as the sheen of a scorpion's tail flickered behind her. The recollection of her memory-erasing sting jabbed into the base of his skull like lightning. "Savor this knowledge, son of Rayne. You will not possess it long. Why you've been so animated this round interests me, but only as a bleating goat intrigues its butcher."

Emaciated muscles flexed. He arched the obsidian blade toward Da'Kar's drawn-out neck, stopped by a spindly hind leg. Curved talons cradled his wrist as a second leg flicked the knife into a darkened corner.

The creature drew the rest of her bulk into the alcove. "This offense demands your suffering."

Guilder clenched his jaw, finding strength as rage replaced fear. He jumped to his feet, throwing an uncontrolled fist toward Da'Kar. Her flinch allowed Guilder space to grasp the sword. He offered a withered, yet capable swing, slicing through her countering hind leg at the joint, leaving it thrashing on the stone floor as her cries echoed throughout the cave. Black-red blood dripped and sizzled on the coals beneath. Da'Kar's taxed breath surged through seething jaws as she coddled her severed limb.

Guilder held the sword out before him, skirting the stone room, forcing Da'Kar to the rear as he kept her at bay. Had this standoff occurred before? Its conclusion and origin forever paralleled? The jagged wall scraped at his back as a foot met a slick, expanding puddle of blood. Blinded by the thickening shadows, Guilder swung his sword again. Metal clanged off armored flesh. A second swing, this time with measured control, sliced through, yielding screams of pain as he turned and ran for the tunnels.

"There is no hiding, sword-bearer!" The hiss from close behind, maddening in the resounding chambers. "I will find you!"

The tunnel's paths ran steadily upward, irregular, branching like an ancient oak. Guilder ran aimless, his eyes scarcely adjusted to the blackness, thoughts sluggishly taking command over renewed panic. He sniffed the air, searching for anything that wasn't dank, stale earth, or cold, lifeless rock. He imagined Da'Kar's monstrous eyes searching. Was it lost in its own labyrinth, or did it relish the hunt?

Cool, fresh air met his nose as he sniffed again, running past the next juncture. Darkness allayed as the cave entrance knifed through the black rock, starlight piercing the shadows. Guilder peered behind him. The gloom, unyielding as the sound of approaching talons fell against stone, a limp every fifth step. Screams of agony, of lost meat, echoed after him, closing in with freedom only an arm's length away.

Guilder stood at the narrow gash of an entrance, wiping the monster's blood from his feet onto the stone floor. The fresh air helped him move faster and cleared his mind, helping to solidify his plan. He doubled back, ducked into a diverging path, and readied his sword for a downward strike.

Flattened against the jagged wall, he peered around the corner and listened for her approach. Da'Kar's pain should cloud her sight. The chase, the blood loss, would have weakened her. The thought spurred his resolve as his heartbeat mocked his stillness. He raised the sword in anticipation and waited.

"You consider yourself so clever," Da'Kar whispered behind him.

Electricity charged into Guilder's arms, muscles tense, hands clamped tight around the hilt. He shifted his weight, swung down, and to his rear. Sparks birthed and died off the rock floor. Within the flash, his weapon raced Da'Kar's lunging attack. Sword met flesh, as his blade cleaved the monster's skull apart.

Guilder fought to control his breath. He lowered the blood-stained sword, staring into Da'Kar's bisected skull frozen in her final moments. Brain liqueur diluted blood spread across the cave floor, warm and slick as it washed over his bare feet.

The monster's bulbous tail collapsed onto her body. Guilder jumped back, raising his sword, his heart beating in his ears, ready for a renewed fight. He stood watchful, scrutinizing the lifeless corpse, finally dropping his arm from exhaustion. The sword tip clanged off the cave floor, sending echoes racing through the caverns. He turned away from Da'Kar's dead body and fled her cave.

CHAPTER 2
And Then There Was Magic

Guilder pushed through the narrow opening and stepped out onto an unfamiliar landscape. Midnight breezes whistled through the tree-covered hills, raising goosebumps on his sweat-damp arms. He flicked the ichor from his sword, rested the blade on his shoulder, and filled his lungs with fresh air. Free from the confines of the cave, the dim twinkle of starlight offered little more than the dying embers had in way of illuminating a path.

Three times we spoke, it said. Suggesting hours between, or days, weeks perhaps? His hand found the raised marks on his upper thigh. Longer even? With no mind of returning to the cave, even for shelter, Guilder turned back to the entrance and spat at the ground.

Aided by countless large saplings, Guilder trudged down the hillside. His overexertion in escaping Da'Kar hindered his descent. His bare feet helped even less as he plodded over stony ground, broken twigs, and countless seasons of fallen pine needles.

A few meters from the hill's base, Guilder slowed and crouched behind a sizable beech tree. At the edge of a dirt road, he studied a figure tending a pile of brushwood mouthing unheard words. Set off to one side was a forest-green rogue's hood, a bow on top, protecting it from blowing away. Delicate arms spread over a circle of stones, hands cupped together, eyes closed in concentration. Sparks fell from ring-adorned fingers as white-gray smoke rose from the pyramid of tinder. More words chanted with increasing vigor, another spark, then fire.

Guilder's eyes widened. What sorcery? No, nothing so sinister, but something perhaps familiar? Magic? Pain, like an icepick, jabbed the back of his skull, forcing away the recollection. He returned his attention to the stranger, the ache fading as he did.

As the fire blazed away, several plump spider wasps were plucked of their wings, their bodies skewered and placed over the flames. The stranger gnawed on the wings, rotating the wasps for an even cook. Hunger rumbled in Guilder's stomach as the aroma of roasting meat wafted out from the camp. Gilder's stance wearied, rustling the loose foliage beneath. The stranger hastened for the bow, nocking an arrow as the string was pulled taut.

"Show yourself," the stranger demanded.

Guilder hobbled into the clearing, leaning against his longsword like a crutch, his hand held out. "Hold, friend." He pressed his palm out further as the stranger pulled the arrow back a centimeter more. "I mean no harm. I've just escaped a cave partway up this hill." He thumbed behind. "I'm simply looking for a friendly face, safety in numbers, and perhaps warmth by your fire? Maybe a share of your catch?"

The stranger tightened her stance, eyes narrowed, jaw set. "The only cave in this area belongs to Da'Kar. A rather diminutive memory eater, though still dangerous. You say you'd escaped?" She rounded the campfire, cautious steps echoing the still-drawn bow.

Guilder nodded, keeping his eyes glued to the skewered wasps charring over the fire.

"Then you are a liar or are now a simpleton." She let down the bow's tension and took in Guilder's appearance. "By the manner of your dress, I'd wager simpleton."

Guilder returned his attention to the stranger. "I hadn't expected a woman thief-taker." She stood a head shorter than him, feathered ash-brown hair shaved on one side, and dressed in an azure arming doublet brocade with gold. "Not in woods belonging to such monsters."

"And I hadn't expected a half-naked con artist to insult me, not tonight anyway." She returned the arrow to a hidden quiver and set her bow atop the rogue's hood. She returned to her seat, poking the wasps to test their doneness. "Monsters come in many guises, so state your business, swindler."

"Please, I'm not trying to con you." Guilder took a step toward the fire, pressing his down-turned blade to the center of his chest.

The girl stabbed the pointed end of a skewer at Guilder. He spread his hands, pleading. "I'd already escaped death once tonight. I don't have the energy for another attempt." Eyes downward, he lowered his arms from sheer exhaustion. "Look, all I have is my name and this sword." He held out the blade as an offering, the firelight catching the inlaid crest. "Perhaps in trade for something to eat?"

The girl's questioning eyes darted between Guilder and the sword. "You'd trade that for a spider-wasp?"

"I would. Truth be told, I don't remember much of anything before the cave. I couldn't say if this sword was even mine."

"That's Da'Kar's toxin," the girl said, biting into the crisp insect. She wiped away a greasy dribble, licked her fingers, and offered an inviting hand to Guilder. "She injects it with a barb on her tail. Steals your memories to make you a more willing victim; reason they call her a memory eater. You didn't see the marker?"

Guilder shook his head as he sat. Leaning against a felled tree stump, he warmed his hands next to the fire.

"It's up the road, a triangular-shaped symbol warning travelers to stay clear." She handed Guilder a skewer, the wasp steaming in the cool air. "What did you say your name was?"

"Guilder Rayne."

The girl's eyes narrowed as she huffed out a breath. "Didn't take it all, I guess."

"It's what it told me." He navigated around the wasp sting and took a tentative bite.

"Her. Not it. Da'Kar's a her."

"Was." Guilder swallowed the mouthful of wasp. "Anyway, I had no reason to doubt… her. It seemed like she was playing with me; like I was already dead."

"To her, you were. Memory eaters are

notoriously arrogant." She bent to her side, retrieving another wasp from her pile, rethreading the used skewers. "The name Shyloh Erbus hold any meaning for you?" Guilder shook his head. "Watch out for the antennae, they're bitter," she warned, pointing toward the front end of his meal. "Pity. Call me Shyloh, then."

Guilder sucked the last bit of meat from the end of the wasp's stinger, then flicked it into the fire. "Happy to meet you, Shyloh. It was a steep price to pay, but..." Guilder heaved over his sword, holding it out to the girl.

Shyloh searched Guilder's face, narrowing her eyes as she scanned the sword. Dark blood filled in the ridges of the chimera crest. "How did you escape the cave again?"

Guilder set the sword down. "Slashed its head in two."

"You slashed *her* head in two." Shyloh's icy stare returned as she stoked the fire with a thick branch. "Memory eaters are creatures of incredible intelligence, strength, and cunning. They don't just take memories from you, they absorb them, make them their own, then use them against you." She shook her head and shrugged. "What's done is done."

Guilder stared at her, widening his smile of wonder.

"What?"

"You talk like you admire it... her... them, whatever. She was simply another monster. Better I killed it before anyone else wandered into that cave."

Shyloh handed him another skewer. "She was only feeding herself, same as any other creature." Her expression turned melancholy, her gaze lost in the dancing flames. "She can't help her nature." She prodded the crackling fire with her empty skewer. Embers reached into the midnight sky, losing their brief lives to the indifferent wind.

Guilder finished his second wasp. "I'm afraid it was her or me."

Shyloh nodded, her expression unchanged as she reached behind herself. "Here." She tossed a pair of ankle-high leather boots toward Guilder. "I found those up the road a piece."

Guilder slid on the boots, fastening the bronze buckles at each side. "I'm not sure how to repay your kindness."

"Call it restitution for… recent lapses in judgment. I'd get at least a silver for them, but… they seem to fit so…"

"Whatever wrong you've done, your actions have fully repaid." Guilder licked the remaining spider-wasp grease from his skewer. "May I ask a question?"

Shyloh shrugged, holding her eyes fixated on the flames.

"How did you conjure this fire?"

"What do you mean?"

"I watched you make fire with only your hands, no flint or anything. How is that possible?"

"Magic." Shyloh looked at Guilder with curious eyes. "Da'Kar left you with only that sword and your name?"

"She told me only as a last request and didn't seem overly concerned about the sword."

"Her arrogance was always going to be her downfall." Shyloh glanced at Guilder and shook her head. "You were further gone than you'd let on." She turned her gaze back to the fire, a sadness taking over her face. "Any human can use magic, some non-humans, most faery."

"I can't. At least I don't remember how. Something else that creature must have taken from me."

"You just need to find your element." Shyloh stoked the yellow-orange flames with the scorched branch. "Remembering the words helps."

Guilder sat, expectant.

"If you're waiting for me to teach you magic after opening my camp and sharing my food, then Da'Kar took more of your sense than I'd expected."

"My apologies. I shouldn't assume that you'd have that kind of knowledge. To teach back what I'd lost, I mean. I just… you seem skilled at wielding fire so, I thought…"

"You thought wrong."

"My apologies." Guilder stared at Shyloh, an uncomfortable silence growing between them.

Shyloh's stare flicked between him and the crackling flames. "You fought off that memory eater without magic?" The firelight reflected in her dark brown eyes.

"It was luck. Without the sword, it would have ended differently."

Shyloh sighed. "One spell. To help you along your way, but no more."

Guilder sat up, his eyes wide, stretching a childlike smile across his face.

"It should be entertaining, at least."

"It will be." Guilder nodded and clasped his hands. "I'll be your most humble student."

"Humble, ha?" She got up, gathered an armful of nearby fallen tree limbs, then returned to her seat, tossing the branches into the campfire. "Magic conforms to two varieties, natural and unnatural. Stay clear of anything unnatural. There are rules."

"What rules?"

Shyloh tilted her head and glared at Guilder. "You're not getting everything from a free lesson," she said, irritation entering her voice. She turned back to stare into the flames. "Never mind those now. There are five virtues of natural magic: fire, earth, air, water, and metal. Fire and water are opposite, as are earth and air. Ice is a combination of water and air and tends to be more advanced than each. Metal has its own unique qualities, with several virtues of the other four. It's also the most difficult to master."

"Are there rules to natural magic?"

"Are you a student or an inquisitor?"

"Student. I'll be quiet, sorry." Guilder pulled his knees to his chest, attempting to squash an outburst of enthusiasm.

Shyloh took a heavy breath. "Most people

can do simple spells in each of the virtues, so even if your element isn't fire… well, you should just give it a try. The words for this spell are *summoneie perjos adiuvare tegere*. Essentially calling on the fire to aid in your wellbeing or some such shit."

Guilder whispered the words.

"Out loud, so I can hear you say them correctly. *Summoneie perjos adiuvare tegere*."

"*Summoneie perjos adiuvare tegere*." Guilder repeated.

"Good. Now imagine the words in your mind. Picture them coming from out of the darkness. Create them. Bring them into being." Shyloh closed her eyes, cupping her hands over the stone ring. "Make them hot, sparking, flickering. Turn the words into flame, then push them out into the world."

She said the words, then hinged her hands open. Orange-yellow flames erupted from the coals. Fire and embers flew skyward into the treetops. She pulled her hands back and opened her eyes as the flames died again.

"Wow." Guilder's eyes grew wide with awe. "If I had that in the cave, I would have killed that monster sooner."

"This spell is only for lighting a campfire or a lantern if you're careful. Offensive spells are different."

"Let me guess. They have rules."

"And are generally more taxing on the spell caster. Now try the spell so I can turn in. It's been quite a trying day. I'm sure you can relate."

Guilder closed his eyes, cupping his hands similar to what he'd been shown. The words swirled in his mind. He imagined them flowing from his fingers, throwing them into existence. He peeked an eye out at the coals. Nothing happened.

"Again," Shyloh instructed.

He tried again, slower, more precise. He saw the words, letter for letter, growing from the darkness. Like a seedling bearing its first shoots, reaching toward the sunlight, growing like stalks of corn. He flicked them around as if from the end of a whip, then snapped them into the coals. Blue-gray sparks leaped from the embers, popping like firecrackers above their camp. Guilder looked at Shyloh and smiled, proud of his trick, hardly understanding what happened.

"Needs practice." Shyloh stretched out, placing an arm beneath her head. Her eyes closed as if already asleep.

Guilder sat watching the conjured flames. Yellow-red tongues lapped at the starlit sky. How can he remember fire, woods, trees, swords, rocks, or other humans, but nothing beyond the mundane? Even his name; when Da'Kar reminded him, he knew what she'd said was true. And then there was magic. He grinned, proud of this newfound ability. Was magic something he could do before the cave? Were there others who could use such talents? All humans can, Shyloh said, but do they?

He tried the spell again, feeling the warmth of the flames as he cupped his hands. Within his mind, stalks of wheat grew from the darkness, set ablaze by the words. He pushed it out. Like thumbs of black powder, the sparks popped, but he'd raised nothing like Shyloh's intensive flames. Once again, this time setting the wheat field to burning. A bigger pop, but no fire.

"What are you doing?" Shyloh asked without moving from her curled-up position.

"Practicing. As you'd suggested."

"Why does it sound like a canon fleet?" Shyloh sat up and scowled at Guilder. "That spell is one of the easiest I know. A child could do it. What's the difficulty?"

"I've never done magic. At least I don't think I have. I don't remember."

Shyloh's eyes remained thin slits, her lips pressed together. Finally, she softened, taking in a calming breath. "You really had been trapped with that memory eater for some time."

"I don't remember. It could have been days or weeks for all I know."

"Few could last days, but weeks? She'd take away most everything, leaving very little hope of recovery. Best come to terms with starting fresh."

Guilder stared into the fire. "Who am I if not for my past?" he whispered. "I'm nobody."

"Look." Shyloh sighed. "Magic is like singing. Anybody can do it, but only a few can do it well. Some merely warble along as best they can, others perform beautiful arias as they rain down molten death over the entire

Kingdom of Aurora."

"I'm not sure I remember how to sing, either." Guilder's smile faded, lost along with his memories.

"Not my point." Shyloh shook her head. "The words are just a conduit. Eventually, you won't even need them. What's important is how you bring them into existence. What do you imagine when you visualize the words?"

"Fields of grain. Harvested then set on fire."

"There, you see. Earth casters dream of crops." Shyloh closed her eyes, cupping her hands again. "When I cast this spell, I think of a torch, white cloth soaked with oil, stained gray, then saturated black. The words bleed from the base of my neck, flow through my shoulder, my arms, out my fingers, twirl up along the handle, then dive into the greasy rags. Flames burst skyward as firelight fills my mind." She mouthed the words, a crisp staccato off her lips. Orange-yellow flames shot into the heavens, then died down just as quickly.

Guilder closed his eyes and cupped his hands as before. This time he saw a dead tree, his hands pressed against its coarse tangled bark. The face of an old man, bearded, with a rough crown on top of his head. Anger crept into his mind. Guilder pushed the feeling into the tree, anger for the monster that stole from him, hate for the feebleness he felt, and for the unknown face in the tree. Smoke rose from the bark. Heat blistered his hands. The tree burst into a green-blue inferno. Guilder pushed it all out toward the campfire's stone circle. Green-blue dragon's fire exploded into the sky, the heat setting nearby branches and limbs a flame. The blaze roared as if an overhead storm were razing the area with its thunder.

"Gods be damned!" Shyloh jumped back from the unearthly firestorm. She glared into the sky, her mouth agape at the power he'd called into existence. "That was..." she gawped at Guilder. "That was... better. Maybe try for something... in-between." She regained her seat as the flames died. The encircling rocks glowed red, solidified after having drooped like candle wax, the firewood reduced to white ash. "Something in-between would be better." She nodded.

"Sorry. The image was more... emotional than I'd expected."

"Emotion tends to strengthen the spell." Shyloh afforded Guilder a sideways look.

"I feel, suddenly ... exhausted. Like I hadn't slept in days." Guilder slid down in front of the stump he'd been leaning against and laid his head on the ground.

"After a display like that, I'm not surprised." Shyloh sighed. "The stronger the spell, the more energy it takes. Part of the rules." She grabbed her branch, poking the end into one of the glowing rocks, watching it distort, the stick catching aflame. "Sleep it off, I'll keep watch, I guess."

As the orange glow faded from the heated rocks and darkness settled in, Guilder closed his eyes, his mind turning to images of old men's faces and tangled bark crowns. His anger lifted as if taken by the very monster he'd nearly escaped. His dreamscapes remained dotted with smoking dead trees set aflame by green-blue dragons. All fading to nothing, darkness once again taking him.

CHAPTER 3
The Reawakening of Isaiah Crowley
Generation One

The dark held no fear for me, not initially, only pain. I'd wake, sense my heartbeat, my thoughts coagulate, lungs falter. My eyes swam in nothingness as if I'd failed to open them. Each time like the time before. Yet the memories of thousands of years, the endless reawakenings, and ceaseless deaths, remained. Reason told me I was awake, as did my thoughts, heartbeat, and the ever-present burning in my chest. It'd radiate from my lower extremities, mill through the gravel where my spine should've been, claw up my ribcage, and into my throat. Each time, I prayed it would be my last death.

Measured by this waking nightmare, what purpose would dreams serve? Hell would have offered relief if I'd ever believed in such places. How many times had I awakened? A hundred? A thousand? Had I not awakened once for every life stolen? Died the same every time, then once more, for Isaiah Crowley, the man I used to be? If so, billions then. Each time I closed my eyes, it was the blackness that refused to change.

Fractions of time passed, or was it centuries, before my next attempt at gasping breath. Fetid air, moist and tepid, like the breath of a colossus, ratcheted into my starving lungs. Tortured thoughts wrestled panic as I swallowed a blood-filled scream, recognizing full well the futility of such things.

I coughed. The weight of the massive stone on top of me benevolently allowing it. Moisture landed on my cheek, spittle, bile, or blood, I wasn't sure, but a sign that something had changed, or more likely, shifted. Thoughts of freedom brought momentary relief. Though freedom felt within a prison is mere illusion, hope, however, cleared my mind. I listened to the darkness beneath the crushing meteor, my jailer for so long, gone slack. My right index finger waggled free. Atrophied muscles yanked at stiff tendons, knuckles full of grit released as skin touched ragged skin, yet the stone remained above.

A faint rhythmic thud met my ears, near inaudible were it not for the absolute silence. My own blood pumping, I reasoned, mixed with a quiet hiss outside my periphery. I strained to hear, strained to block out all but the hiss. Concentrating, I finally heard it. A single word repeatedly whispered through the darkness. It felt intimate. As if a loved one had breathed my name, tickling the vellus hairs at the edge of my ear.

"Rūkas," the whisper hissed, burrowing itself into my head. "Rūkas," it repeated over and over. My lips played with the vowels. The word, familiar, yet unfamiliar, scraped inside my throat like wet sand. I coughed again, shallow within my confines. I cleared my mind, took in as much breath as my stone warden allowed, and croaked out the word.

The tip of my liberated finger turned feathery. Weightlessness slid through my hand, my wrist, my arm. Ecstasy replaced pain as emaciation dissolved, exchanged by a pull, a tumbling. Panic reestablished itself as the cooling sensation traveled into my shoulder, chest, neck, chin, and jaw. Darkness again claimed my consciousness.

Flashes of a world in ruin filled my dreams, or were they memories? Heavenly bodies collided, delivering fire, ash, and global devastation. I believe myself uncounted among the few survivors. Thoughts, no longer recognized as my own, occupy my mind. Revealing evolution spurred by unearthly power. Humans altered to forms deeply engraved in the subconscious, familiar yet foreign. The whispers overlay each vision like an itch behind my awareness, though its meaning remains unknown.

The name, *Iks*, escaped my lips as I awoke again, now free from my prison, a knife's edge of light cutting through my sight. How long had I only known the overwhelming mountain of stone upon me, that space of any size seemed foreign? I crawled along on withered limbs to survey a meter-wide fissure. At either end of the forty-meter expanse, vertical walls of mushroom-covered cinder blocks barred any further exploration. The jagged ceiling only allowed me to squat on rusted knees or sit without hitting my head. The air remained stale and earthen, my throat parched, my shrunken stomach empty. Had I escaped one confinement only to trade it for another? I laid my head on the icy stone floor, itching for the familiar crushing weight I was so eager to escape.

Sunlight touched my skin with such tender warmth I turned my hand, attempting to capture it. Sleep had come with peculiar dreams of dead trees and green-blue fire. Newfound light washed the images from my mind as I squinted toward the near side of the cavern, dragged myself the few meters to a pinhole opening, and peered outside for the first time in god knows how long.

Beyond a tiny patch of salted earth lie fields of windblown grasses. Toward the horizon, mature trees dotted my view. Birds flitted between as insects buzzed at my periphery. I wept dry tears as my thirst forbade me to expend any moisture. I had accepted penance for my hubris, and yet, despite my worst fears, the world had remained. My relief, short-lived, as I grasped the excessiveness of my punishment.

The paltry light gave me pause to take in my skeletal appearance. Skin hung on bone like fine lamé off wire hangers, limp and structureless. My chest and stomach, hollow; exposing the curve of my ribs. My legs, as thin as spindles. I ran stiff fingers over my face and head. A toothless mouth and sunken eyes mirrored scant patches of stringy hair, gray-white as I pulled weak strands free. How could one fully escape in such a feeble state?

I slumped down from the peephole, feeling as if the stone were again crushing against my chest. The beam crept along the floor, keeping time as I sat in contemplation, regaining my faculties. The light traversing the cavern revealed an unnaturally flat surface. I brushed away a thick layer of dust. Beneath lie a poured concrete floor, cracked and disintegrated in places yet recognizable. A man-made prison. No. My hellish position reeked of providence. Yet how did I still live? Nature assuredly could have taken me long ago.

Scratching noises from the far corner pulled my gaze. Tiny claws wiggled through an even tinier crevice, followed by a plop to the dust-covered floor. Stiff as the rock at my back, I waited, willing my angry stomach silent. Apprehensively, a tawny mouse, no longer or fatter than a man's thumb, scurried into the blade of sunlight. Its bald feet pawing at its face.

I reached out, not wanting to scare the creature, yet unable to pounce in my weakened state. The mouse sniffed my outstretched finger in curiosity before a bolt of static jumped between the two of us. The mouse froze as the stiffness in my fingers released. Dexterity returned to my hand and wrist; my arm swelled and strengthened. I marveled at the renewal, felt the limb in disbelief, the emaciated muscle now plump.

The mouse stood, desiccated, its tiny mouth held open, its dead stare frozen. I didn't understand, couldn't understand. My stomach's rumblings shifted my thoughts. I grabbed the mummified rodent and shoved it into my mouth. Its flesh turned to powder in my throat, its skin, brittle like fallen autumn leaves. In the dim morning light, as I choked down my meal, I stared at the stone that held me for so long and wondered as to its purpose.

More mice came. One time a rat and once a snake. Each in turn fed me. I piled their bones in tribute, gaining strength enough to move around with ease, yet I remained trapped in near darkness and endless silence. My dreams remained haunted by green-blue fire and unfamiliar words repeating in my head. *Augnis*, over and over *augnis, augnis.*

After waking from one, particularly vivid dream, I narrowed my eyes at the stone wall, its sun-filled cavity. I held out my hand, flattened my palm, and spoke the word. A bright red spark bloomed from my palm, fell to the floor, and died. Again, I wondered about the stone. I tried once more, this time with authority. "*Augnis!*" I shouted at the wall, holding the word in my mind.

The first thing to catch was the tip of my finger. The fire pinched at my flesh as I attempted to flick it out, but like oil floating on water, it spread, engulfing my hand, wrist, and arm. I screamed in pain, from fear, until it reached my neck. All at once, it snuffed itself out, leaving trails of smoke in its wake. It left my limb charred; the skin shrunk taught and black. I ached from the trauma and yet it was exhaustion that overtook me.

I awoke to a mischief of rats gnawing at the pile of bones I'd gathered. My arm had healed over the unknown amount of time I'd slept and dreamed. The rats dispersed one by one as the bones vanished. I captured the last, and in my hunger ate it raw.

My rest seemed to bring a renewed fervor of discovery. I shimmied to the stone that had restrained me for so long and placed my hand along its glass-like exterior. Flecks of silver metal and crystals of green and orange sparkled in the dim light. Warm to the touch, it radiated power and seemed to speak to me as if alive. Words so foreign and yet again familiar.

I still could not understand this power, this... magic. Even to think the word seemed sacrilegious to such an enlightened mind. I spent the next month practicing, counting the hours and days by the light beam's movement as the stone whispered new and intricate spells into my head. Finally, with strength and vigor returned, I was prepared to rejoin a revitalized world and escape this secondary prison. I stood on one knee, bracing myself, the stone to my back, the pinhole to the world outside before me. After a deep breath, I held my hands out and spoke the words. The wall flew out with such force the blocks disintegrated into dust.

Sunlight flooded my home. Crumbled cinder blocks peeked out from beneath layers of encrusted grime as a forest of petite stalactites rooted themselves to a steel-reinforced ceiling. I crept to the new-formed entrance and stepped out into a revived world, a world that felt entirely too large.

I gazed back at the stone, my jailer, the whisperer. Mesmerized by its full scope, it sat as a mountainous hill a kilometer wide and partially buried. Its smooth surface was reflective, like obsidian. "Is this all *your* doing, my old friend?"

A distant rumble met my advance as I stepped into the waist-high grasses. A herd of zebra-striped bison stampeded along the far plane, chased by men on horseback. Arrows loosed from their mounts, set the beasts aflame as they struck, lighting the surrounding grassland. A second rider doused the flames from his outstretched hands as he rode past.

The herd turned in my direction. The riders followed suit. At five hundred meters, I softened my stance as the ground quaked. I closed my eyes, held out my hand to the oncoming charge, and quieted my mind. A hundred meters out, the herd's pursuers yelled to rein in their horses. At fifty meters, I felt the heat of the collective, the reek of their musk, the snorting of their leaders. At ten meters, the herd split, as if cleaved by my very presence. I opened my eyes. The beasts curled around me as a river diverged along a blade of land.

The hunters remained at a distance, watching, waiting as the herd ground to a stop. Bulls scraped the ground with their hooves or rustled the brush with the quartet of pointed horns jutting from their heads. Cows milled around the smaller calves, overly bold and curious. I approached a mature cow gnawing on the soft grass, her thick fur, coarse and wiry between my fingers. I drained her life as I'd done the mice, felt my skin tighten and my strength fully return.

The herd scattered around the whispering mountain as the hunters approached.

"Hail, stranger," the lead rider called as the four others moved in to surround me, scanning the throng of animals with suspicion in their eyes. "Not seen you in these parts. From where do you come?"

I gazed at the riders. Their peculiar dialect seemed so foreign, yet through the whispers inside my head, as familiar as my own mother's voice. Dressed in black and white bison hides, some held bows, quivers at their backs, others no weapons at all. "From under the hill," I said. The men sniggered as I gestured behind me.

"The cursed hill?" Their leader shot a snide smile to the others. His black curly beard framed a deeply tanned face, bow held tight to his arm, arrow nocked and at the ready. "Nothing lives beneath Mount Iks. I say you are either touched or a liar."

"I am no liar and far from insane."

"Wyrmlen," one rider said. "The bison."

The party's leader narrowed his eyes at the emaciated beast. His gaze returned to me and in a cautious voice asked if I was a witch. I didn't know how to respond. For what is a witch in a world where magic seemed commonplace? I met his gaze, unsure. "Are you a damned witch, or not?!" Wyrmlen's bellow prompted the nocking of arrows and lips ready for casting.

I put out my hand, fingers splayed as if to stop their assault, twisted, and quickly clenched into a fist. Shards of black metal burst from the earth, embedding into four of the hunter's skulls, one into Wyrmlen's neck. The horses fled, spilling their riders as fear hastened them along.

"I am no witch," I said, peering down at Wyrmlen. I pulled the shard from his neck. Blood spurted around his hands, painting the grasses, as he clutched at his wound. He looked up into my face, his eyes quivering with fear. "This power though seems…" I wasn't sure, instinctive? Unscientific? Perverted? "Unnatural."

In the time it took me to decide, Wyrmlen's eyes emptied. Magic, it seems has found this world and in its wake reverted it to savagery. My longtime jailer, if it is as I suspect, the genesis of these magics, will need study. I gathered Wyrmlen's skittish horse, emptied its saddlebags, and sent it on its way. With a few days' supplies and a slightly used journal, I returned to my prison beneath Mount Iks. The home I had so fervently sought to escape, now a comforting familiarity. I sat in the shadow of the massive stone I'd known for countless lifetimes, absorbing its power and taking in its murmured words.

As night fell and the last pages of the journal were filled, I gazed up into a starlit sky missing its brightest light. Shame filled me. The influence of this mountain may have been the harbinger of newfound power, but I alone suffer blame for the destruction it wrought. I must find the means to reverse what has been done. I looked back toward the stone, sensing amends within my reach.

CHAPTER 4
Gunnison

The rising sun warmed his back as he tried to escape the nightmares that haunted his restless sleep. Guilder poked a stick at the dying embers of Shyloh's campfire as visions flashed beyond the firelight. The tangled bark of dead trees pulled him back to Da'Kar's cave. Her cleaved face, mocking, as toxin clawed through his body, weakening him, stealing his past and his mind.

The stick caught aflame. Guilder shook it out, only to catch fire once again. The only memories left to him returned like lightning strikes to the base of his skull. She'd taunt him with riddles of promised crowns and angels bathed in black light. Phantom winds chased him back to the alcove where he'd see himself, still trapped, weak, and delirious. The black mirror-like cave reflected a stranger's face, transforming into a toothless dragon breathing green-blue flames at dead soldiers carrying obsidian daggers.

"You awake?"

Guilder jumped to his feet, sword in hand. Though the action, the instinct, seemed foreign and outside himself.

"Wow, you are strung tight." Shyloh chuckled, her hands held up. She shook her head as she retook her seat, her smile lingering as she unhooked three plump rodents from her belt.

Guilder wondered at his response, the quickness of action, the readiness to fight. "Sorry." He placed his sword beside him and sat back down, edgy from adrenaline, from the recollection of his dreams. "Where were you off to?"

"Just checking a couple of traps along the hillside, and your cave." Shyloh laid her cloth satchel down, glass vials clinking inside, and set to field dressing the animals.

"That cave should be sealed. To prevent any more… abductions. Why go back?"

"To find some truth in your story, if any."

"And?"

"Da'Kar's body is there, just as you'd said."

Guilder nodded as if her affirmation solidified the experience beyond his nightmares. He motioned to the skinned animals. "What's that?" He moistened his lips in anticipation of her answer.

"Breakfast." Shyloh removed the tip from one of her arrows, slid the three carcasses crossways onto the shaft, and dug them into the glowing coals. She leaned the fletching across the top of the rock circle and sat with her knees pulled up to her chin. "Coypu, or muskrat, maybe. Must be a stream around here somewhere. You hungry? You'd been out for over a day."

"A whole day?" Guilder rubbed the back of his neck, his face scrunched in disbelief.

"Typical of memory eater toxin. Your body needs to fight off its effects. Give it time.

Believe me, you did not want to be awake for that hangover. How's your head, by the way?"

Guilder ran a hand over the back of his neck. "Foggy. Dull ache at the back."

"You're through the worst of it then, probably dehydrated on top of it all." Shyloh tossed a leather canteen over to Guilder. "Drink that. It's fresh. Well, it was a couple of hours ago."

Guilder gulped greedily from the canteen, coughing as he drank. Shyloh let out a burst of laughter, her smile widening. "Slow down. You'll drown yourself if you're not careful." She prodded the coals with a bit of magic and pulled out the blackened rodents, handing them over to Guilder. "Eat. You'll need your strength."

"Why are you helping me?" Guilder wiped a sleeve across his mouth, crinkling his nose at the charred meat. He picked off a few lingering ashes and nibbled at an outer leg.

"Why does anyone do anything?" Shyloh's attention returned to the flame-covered coals. Her smile dissolved as she wrapped her arms around her legs, seeming to turn her thoughts inward. "Anyone stumbling around these woods would need help, more so after surviving a memory eater's cave." Her eyes rose to meet Guilder as she rested her chin on her knees. "My guess? You're someone special."

"Can't remember being anyone important," Guilder said, his mouth half full of overcooked meat. "I don't feel all that special, just lost."

Shyloh's smile reemerged. "Well, my lost friend, when your strength returns, I'm heading toward Gunnison to meet up with some colleagues of mine. You're welcome to accompany me."

"I won't be a bother?"

"No more than you already have." Shyloh stretched her legs out and leaned back onto her elbows. "These foothills aren't known to be dangerous but, as you've seen, they aren't a day at the fair either."

Guilder finished the remainder of his meal while Shyloh sharpened arrowheads. "Thank you for all your help. I'll find a way to repay you." Crestfallen, he stared at the greasy shaft as Shyloh replaced the last arrow into her quiver. "I guess I was hungry, sorry."

"No worries. Those things taste like shit, anyway." She got up, grabbed her satchel, slung her quiver and bow over her shoulder, and signaled Guilder to follow. "Maybe when we get to Gunnison we'll run into someone who knows you."

***

"I didn't grow up a strip miner," Shyloh explained as the early evening sun kissed the horizon on their exit from the Shaman Bluffs into the Sal Basin. "The bulk of the people I know are, though. Backbreaking work, mining the flats. Five generations have passed along the trade. A hundred and thirty years of scraping the earth, amassing its various materials, all for the citadel lord's experimentation, though what he does with it all is anyone's guess."

Shyloh shook her head. "What's left is an

empty corpse of useless land." She pressed her lips tight, her words turned to a whispered snarl. "Salt leaches to the surface, leaving it infertile for crops, for livestock, for any natural life. White decay weakens the earth and anyone around it." After a quiet second, she shook off the anger like a bothersome fly, her smile returning. "The farming colonies move ever outward, toward the coasts. The lord gets his raw materials, and the villages remain employed. Everybody's happy."

Shyloh swept a finger across the northern horizon. Twelve shanty towns surrounded a circular wasteland. A cracked skin salt bed thirty kilometers in diameter outlined the spokes of a dozen roads connecting each town to the central towers. The twin monoliths' onyx mirror façade surpassed the highest cloud cover, reflecting the bleached white of the basin and the struggling wheat fields beyond. Ghostlike bands grew outward from the center, echoing where the towns had once been.

"The collective's been stationary for nearing four years," Shyloh said as they made their final push toward the flats. "Exactly fifteen and a half kilometers from each city's center to the next. After the expansion, they'll be separated by over twenty kilometers. Plans for another radial move have been in the works for the last few months. There's almost a holiday atmosphere about it, despite the work it takes."

Boomtown-style architecture seemed to salvage any remnants of the last static period while piecemeal roofs cobbled together ramshackle buildings along pole-strait roads and alleyways. "City planning is paramount to a moving town. The houses and shops are a bit worse for wear, but any new construction can take from the bordering forests." Shyloh pointed to a town within the southwest quadrant. "That's where we're headed, to Gunnison."

She motioned toward the easternmost town of the twelve. "I spent most of my time in Crestone. It's quaint, in a sleepy sort of way. Really, if you'd seen one, you'd seen them all." She shrugged. "Northbrook to the north. Longstone is Gunnison's opposite. You get the gist."

Shyloh stopped before the steep descent into the Sal Basin. She held her hand out to Guilder, crouched, taking in Gunnison's wooden bastion, its elevated guard towers positioned between a massive set of doors.

"Front gate is open," Guilder said, crouching next to Shyloh. "Why not just head in?"

"The Trades Commission polices who come and go. The short answer is you don't belong."

"Trades Commission?"

"They keep everyone in line, as much as their stretched forces can. They're also a pain in my ass." Shyloh sighed. "But if it weren't for them and their regulation of free exchange throughout the collective, many of the cities would have been starved out, and Lord Iks would never tolerate that."

Guilder stared at the structure at the center of the collective cities. The mention of the lord's name sent a familiar ache toward the base of his skull, accompanying a peculiar draw toward his towers. Guilder refocused on the town before them. "There's a group approaching from the west."

"Day shifters, most likely, returning home from the flats." Shyloh nodded. "Another shift will be headed out shortly. The gate stays open only for these transitions."

"We could steal into their flank, blend in."

"Not a bad plan. Sun's going down behind them. We'll sneak in while the guards are blinded." Guilder shifted his sword to his backside, hiding it as best he could. "The twilight will help hide your face. Put your head down and try to act inconspicuous."

"How do you *act* inconspicuous?" Guilder asked with a puzzled expression. "Anyway, I thought you said you lived here? Why are we sneaking in?"

"I said we're meeting my colleagues here."

"You're in trouble, aren't you?" Guilder turned a wise-ass smirk toward Shyloh.

Shyloh sighed; her brow lowered. "The Trades Commission and I don't… see eye to eye."

"You mean they don't take kindly to… smugglers? Bounty hunters?"

"Who said I was a bounty hunter?" Shyloh looked over at Guilder, her narrowed eyes washing over him.

"I just thought... well... you... out in the woodlands and all."

"Whatever." She turned back toward the town. "Here they come, stick close, and blend into the crowd." Shyloh pulled her hood up and took off down the hill. "If we get separated, we'll meet up at The Marked Oak Tavern," she shouted behind her.

Guilder followed, shouting over his winded breath, "I don't know anything about this town. How am I supposed to find some random bar?"

"Far side of the city, close to the flats. Look for the seediest place you can find." Shyloh reached the small crowd at lightning speed, disappearing almost immediately. Guilder slowed his run as he approached the river of workers. The crowd dispersed into the town as the entrance gates closed behind, the last laggards skirting in just as the gates slammed shut.

"Hey! Hey, buddy," one of the gate guards yelled. Guilder lifted his head, meeting the guard's outstretched arm and pointed finger. "Yeah, you." The gruff officer strode over to where Guilder had stopped. "I know pretty much everybody who lives here." He tipped his head sideways, attempting a better look at Guilder's face. "But I don't know you."

He stood a half meter shorter than Guilder, dressed much like that of the crowd, leather trousers, a bland colored tunic in muted reds and browns. On his left forearm, just above the elbow, he wore a black armband, a white circle with two black cylinders at the center, the symbol of the Trades Commission, Guilder presumed.

"I'm here visiting friends. Please, just let me be." Guilder turned toward the city center, attempting to avoid eye contact.

"What friends? Where do they live? What are their names?" The officer cut off Guilder's retreat, taking notice of the longsword at his back. "Are you armed?"

"I'm supposed to meet them…" Guilder stammered, panic nudging his hand toward the sword hilt. "At some inn… or tavern, The Oak Tavern."

"Ain't no such place." The man grabbed Guilder's tunic, pulling him close. He looked up into his face, chin at Guilder's chest. "You an Auroran spy? Come with me. The Trade's inquisitors will know what to do with—"

His words cut off as wisps of smoke solidified into a black metal dagger. A specter's hand locked around an ironwood handle, the blade pressed to the officer's throat. Gold accents traced into existence along a flowing sapphire-colored sleeve leading to a boyish face partially hidden behind the officer's stiffened body. "This one has engagements elsewhere, Wyrmlen," the specter said, his smoke-gray eyes gazing out at Guilder.

"Please." Guilder released his grip on his sword and held out his hands. "He meant no harm."

"And how would you know of this man's intent?" the specter asked, a questioning look on his hazy face.

"He's no threat to me, please. Let him go."

"Please, Oriel, I didn't mean nothing. He's just—" Wyrmlen stretched onto his toes as the knife pressed further against his throat. Dark red beads formed along the blade's edge.

"I'll spare him this time." The misty corner of a smile crawled behind Wyrmlen's shoulder. "Run along. Your appointment lies at the end of that road." The specter nodded to a street running to the opposite side of town.

Guilder took a hesitant step around Wyrmlen. "You won't hurt him?"

"We are nothing without our word."

With a nod, Guilder took off down the road, wondering who this Oriel was. Why was he so willing to slit Wyrmlen's throat for him? Who was he to someone like Oriel?

Who was he to anyone?

***

The Marked Oak Tavern lay on what might have been a seaside pier were it not for the surrounding ocean of white earth. The rickety building set back into the Sal Flats atop deteriorating salt-licked timbers. Packed shoulder to shoulder for several blocks, it mingled effortlessly with the other dilapidated bars, gambling halls, and brothels of the district. The defensive wall ended several blocks to the south leaving the town overexposed at its rear, though the looming towers seemed defense enough.

A carelessly painted nameplate declared

Guilder to be in the right place. Petrified gray lumber and numerous cracked and taped-over windows seemed to ask for the seedy bar to spill its next fight onto the slop-filled Gunnison streets. Despite this disheartened appraisal, Guilder pushed reluctance aside, adjusted his longsword to his hip, and with a sigh, walked through the squawking gull doors.

A dozen round tables, fashioned from the same salt fossilized wood as the exterior, sat interspaced between the entrance and a lengthy back bar. The only empty seat seemed a private table, set higher than the others, dusty steins and seidels filling the surrounding shelves. Patrons milled around, trading off dice and card games for their next rounds of ale or other such swill. Guilder looked over the rough crowd, only in the infancy of their night's revelries, seeing no one familiar to him. He leaned his back to the bar and waited for Shyloh, all the while thinking himself abandoned.

"You'll need to buy something if you're going to stand there." A confident feminine voice radiated over the din with an authoritative gentleness he hadn't expected from such a place.

Guilder turned to face the bartender polishing a metal stein with a dirty rag. Her auburn hair was intricately woven into a tight ponytail falling forward of her left shoulder. Stately in presence, she conveyed a gracefulness in her athletic frame extending to her unchanged expression.

"I'm sorry, I'm here looking for someone.

A girl… another girl—a woman, I mean," Guilder stammered as the bartender cracked a tiny side smile. "Her name's Erbus, Shyloh Erbus."

The bartender's smile faded to an irritated scowl. "Erbus ain't welcome here, not after the shit she pulled last time." A handful of patrons rose from their seats after hearing Shyloh's name, spurred on by the bartender's irritation. "If you've got any sense, you'll stay as far away from her as you can." She looked around at the growing mob, switching back to her forthright authority. "Calm yourselves down now," she said, her hands encouraging everyone to sit. "He didn't mean nothing." Her eyes narrowed at Guilder. "He's just a dumb townie, didn't know any better."

The crowd settled back into their chairs as Guilder released his grip on his sword, turning warily back to the bartender. "I don't want any trouble," he said as a full mug was placed in front of him. "She said to meet her here." He took a long swig of the draft. "Guess I'm the asshole then."

The bartender's smile reappeared. "Don't be too hard on yourself." She mopped the bar top with her dirty rag. "Shyloh's good at screwing people over. She's had years of practice, believe me."

Guilder nodded and stared into his half-empty mug.

"Name's Marlow, Ryleigh to my friends." She pointed at his mug. "First one's on me."

Ryleigh crossed her arms and leaned against the back bar.

"Guilder Rayne," he said, growing a melancholy smile. "Thanks."

"Rayne? Like the king?"

"I guess. But I've—"

"There's that prick!" Wyrmlen stood in the doorway, pointing the toe of his hatchet toward the bar.

"Hey! No weapons in here!" Ryleigh shouted back.

Behind Wyrmlen, two Trades Commission officers in similar leather tunics drew their swords as tables of people got up from their seats, brandishing daggers, short swords, and maces. Guilder palmed his sword handle, readying himself.

Wyrmlen rushed toward the back bar as a patron punched one of his trailing officers. Ryleigh hurtled the bar, shoving Wyrmlen into the growing scrum behind. Guilder pulled his sword partway from his belt, stopped by Ryleigh's powerful hand.

"Not you, love." She nodded toward a stone staircase behind the bar, a previously hidden passage leading beneath the building. "You have other obligations."

Guilder reseated his sword as the entire bar joined in the fight. Metal clanged off metal, fists flew alongside insults, and tables and chairs upended or broken for clubs. Wyrmlen slashed his hatchet at a pair of burly miners, sparks erupting from his empty palm. Ryleigh grabbed the last of Guilder's beer, chucking it at the fireball growing in Wyrmlen's hand. "Go! I'll sort this out."

Guilder looked back from behind the bar. "Thank you. Will I see you again?"

Ryleigh's smile widened. "We're nothing without our word," she said before jumping into the fray.

Guilder watched Ryleigh throw punches, a wild beast, instinctual, effortless, like a master of the art. He forced himself to turn away and headed down the staircase. The hidden door closed behind him as he grabbed a torch suspended from the wall, the fight still sounding from above.

"What were those damn words?" Guilder cupped his hand over the end of the torch and closed his eyes. "*Summoneie per advare teger.*" Sparks flicked from his palm, bounced off the torch, and onto the floor. "Come on now. It's a torch, not a furnace." He closed his eyes. "*Summoneie perjos adiuvare tegere.*" A lick of flame fell like honey out of his palm, landing on the torch head, slowly spreading, lighting the passageway in a warm glow.

He ambled through the brick tunnel for a hundred meters, stooping against the low ceiling. Light met his torch as the tunnel butted against stairs leading to another room. Voices sounded above him. Two, it seemed, debating something just beyond earshot. Guilder crouched at the base of the stairs, straining to hear, assessing these new threats.

"—and then you didn't finish the job,

anyway?" A male tone, delicate through his irritation, and somehow familiar.

"I should have. Wanted to. But he wasn't the same—"

"Wait."

A cold burst of moist air rushed past Guilder, extinguishing his torch. The change in light, blinding as the sharp point of a dagger pushed into his side, caused Guilder to raise his hands in surrender, still clutching the snuffed-out torch as a silhouette cut through the tunnel exit.

"Ashyr, don't cut him too deep. We may have questions."

"I didn't mean any harm," Guilder said, trying to adjust to the darkness. "I just got lost. I'm looking for a friend, Shyloh Erbus."

The dagger dug into Guilder's side as a slight chuckle emanated from its wielder. The silhouette raised a hand and snapped a finger, bringing Guilder's torch back to life.

"Friend seems a strong word," Shyloh said, sporting a wide grin.

CHAPTER 5
Iks Tower
Generation Two

The citadel, my citadel, is nearing completion after twenty stimulating years. An additional ten to gather the labor force, build, then occupy the four towns surrounding the tower, one for each compass point. For a second generation, I've shaped and planned, only to find my efforts in molding my new surroundings a mirror of the old, fruitless. Even as the corrupted power grows within me, newfound abilities perfected, I find myself, yet again, as only one man.

"Lord Crowley? Begging your pardon, but I'm in need of a word."

Wyrmlen, my hapless but capable builder, continually hounds me with problems and appraisals as to the tower's construction. Was it his potential as an engineer that solidified his appointment, the mob of a workforce he had at his disposal, or my own guilt for murdering his grandfather?

"My lord?"

Further analysis of the meteorite known locally as Mt. Iks has yielded little, as I have limited resources for advanced research. I am forced, therefore, to work primarily from memory. It is conclusive; this is the very same meteorite I'd discovered... ages.... lifetimes... it's difficult to postulate. I'd only re-awoken a few short decades ago. How long I'd endured that hellish existence beneath I cannot fathom, and without the proper, inaccessible equipment, I confess, I may never know.

"Why do you scribble so much inside that book?"

I glared at Wyrmlen briefly before returning to my journal. *Its contents, largely iron silicate with trace amounts of sulfides, are wholly unremarkable. However, interspersed within the peculiar crystalline structure, appears a previously unknown element. I postulate this to be the source of... I hesitate to name it, to call it... magic.*

With my journal closed, I stared at Wyrmlen's cow-eyed face, adopting an ape's grin if only to ease his tension. "These books, you so eloquently refer to as scribbles, are my observations of this world. The behavior of the rabble you brought to these towns has granted me an opportunity for sociological observation."

"Socio—I don't understand, my lord."

My smile faltered to annoyance. "There's little need for your understanding. I trust this interruption to be pertinent?" Wyrmlen's eyes crinkled in confusion. "What is it you want?"

"Well, sir." Wyrmlen jerked the woolen arming cap from his head. "The salt has already taken back its percentage and in only two years. It seems the leach has reached the outer barriers of the compass towns. The people are worried that it'll soon take over the farmlands."

With an irritated sigh, I turned my attention back to my journal opening to a fresh page. "Move them then."

Some aspects remain embedded in societal instinct, farming, animal husbandry, hunting, warfare, while others have merely been left to archaeological obscurity. A new world built on the ash heaps of the old, with little thought given to what came before. Even so, the repurposing of the meteorite materials into the structure of my citadel had proven difficult, but only at first, with prodding, my workforce was able to be convinced.

Stories of human flight without Fae wings, horseless carts, or communication through walls sized moving pictures have endured, though these stories seem analogous to Atlantis, or men walking on water. Nonetheless, the reeducation of this regressed social structure into something of merit, I'm now convinced, is an act of futility. Perhaps a more institutional solution would be merely to observe. Allow evolution to take its course, to see what it would eventually—

"My lord?"

"What is it, Wyrmlen?"

"Move the towns, sir? We'd only just finished the fifth, still more people come every day. We've certainly no loss for workers but—"

"If you've no loss of workers, then delays should be dissolved."

"Yes, but the town hasn't even been named."

"Gunnison."

Wyrmlen dropped his gaze as if mulling the name over. Deciding, he looked back up. "And your inn?"

I paused to consider. "Cristen it The Marked Oak. I'll need a private table set higher than the others, facing the entrance, and shelves for my books. And, Wyrmlen, we'll require three more towns after the expansion."

"Moving five towns would take…" Wyrmlen shook his head. "I'm not sure I'd know how to, sir."

I tapped my pen off the inkwell's lip and placed it on the unfinished page. My eyes finding Wyrmlen's again, I folded my hands in front of me. "Are you not my master builder?"

"Aye."

"And by this position, have I not granted you authority over your people?"

"You have, sir."

"Then I suggest you commence in moving the towns before your bellyaching irritates me further." I floated my pen above the journal, attempting to regain my previous thought.

"Begging your pardon, sir. But it seems as though... my authority, that is. With five towns to... authoritize over... the people are becoming more unruly."

"Then you'll need a policing force," I said without looking up from my writing. Wyrmlen remained silent. Further analysis of this new idea was enough to draw my attention back. His squint eyes and his mouth raised at the corner were enough to betray his confusion. I rolled my eyes and sighed. "Gather several of your largest allies. If anyone would challenge you, make a public spectacle of them. Anyone who refuses to stay in line, banishment, and make sure they never return."

Wyrmlen's brows turned down as a malevolent smile of recollection grew. "Aye, sir."

As populations increase, whether under an autocratic authority or otherwise, it seems essential for order to be maintained. I shall establish a commission under the assigned head engineer to maintain a degree of public order and to generate respect for the rule of law by proper enforcement, which is consistent with the preservation of the current and future workforce. Though I am painfully aware that such powers negatively influence men of feeble constitutions...

I glanced back at Wyrmlen, scrutinizing the man I knew him to be.

... it remains a necessity.

Supplementary to the regulating authority will be the maintenance of each of the citadel's surrounding cities, no matter the number. Essential items: food, water, treatments, and remedies for ailments, materials to produce clothing, important documents, and news of the collective sales shall be freely exchanged as well as documented by this Trades Commission as will the population censused. Their authority shall be absolute, apart from myself.

I explained this with Wyrmlen's seemingly mixed understanding.

"I know just the men for the job, my lord." Wyrmlen made to leave yet hesitated. "There is but one more issue, my lord. The stone quarrying of the mountain. The miners, sir, they're frightened."

"Of?"

"Well, sir, there had been accidents. The men feel the site is..." Wyrmlen took a half step forward, leaned in, and whispered, "Cursed, my lord."

I narrowed my eyes in disbelief.

"Some of the men are saying... well, they hear things." Wyrmlen stepped back. "And one, just the other day, burst into flames. No words spoken or anything." He lowered his voice again. "They fear the Dragon."

"Fascinating," I said, raising my brow.

"I know it's gibberish, just men talking, but…"

Wyrmlen's concerned look said more than his words could. He looked back at me for… what? Guidance? I breathed a heavy sigh. "Tell your men there is no Iks Dragon. The stone is just that—stone. I'll hear no more of this curse nonsense."

"You're right, of course, my lord, just nonsense. It's just that… my grandmother, she'd told me stories of the Iks Dragon. How it would burn with just a look and breathe molten black metal."

His pleading eyes met mine. I softened my gaze as he spoke of a past he knew nothing about.

"She'd always said the Iks Dragon killed my grandfather, and if there was even a chance at it still being here. We thought…well the men thought… that… as skilled in magic as you are, my lord…"

"You want me to slay a fictitious dragon?" I clenched my jaw, narrowing my eyes.

"It's the men… they only suggested…" Wyrmlen took a step back.

"One that we'd only just agreed was nonsense."

"Y-you're right, my lord. I've spoken out of turn." Wyrmlen spun on his heels and headed for the door, then turned back. "I'll tell the men, we'll redouble our efforts, sir. No more talk of dragons." The door slammed behind him as I regained my seat and my thoughts.

Of the five natural energy sources: solar, geothermal, wind, biomass, and hydropower, where then does magic (for lack of better terms) come from? As work continues on my citadel, I'm more convinced than ever that this energy originates from the meteorite. Having the tower encased in it will grant me continued proximity for further observations, among other advantages.

Dragons. Interesting. The thought caught in my head like a sliver.

Countless generations removed, and yet the same legends persist. This reborn after-culture seems to distinguish magic from sorcery and witchcraft, even categorize science alongside. However, their collective understanding of chemistry is at best medieval, akin to alchemy. Witchcraft is the alleged practice of socially prohibited forms of magic. However, it is undefined as to what is socially acceptable and what is not. A more precise definition might be any magic or even science that is not well understood could be considered the practice of a witch. Sorcery, in opposition, refers to a higher order of magic proficiency. Whereas anyone can utilize magic, a sorcerer, therefore, is someone who intentionally takes on the role of a magical practitioner.

"Magical practitioner." I tapped my pen against the inkwell in contemplation.

Where then do others think magic came from? What is the difference between superstition and magic? Historically, it has been the fodder for the religiously and culturally biased, between the accepted and unacceptable religions. It is only now, with magic being commonplace, that these concepts have been freed from their tyrannical religious upbringings.

What exactly is the source of this power? What is its extent, and how can it be replicated, harnessed... controlled? Perhaps the answers will reveal themselves in time.

CHAPTER 6
The Wasted Marshlands

Guilder looked out on the darkening Gunnison streets. A block away, Wyrmlen and his underling Trades Commission officers stumbled from the Marked Oak Tavern. A horde of brawlers flooded out after, no shyer for the experience as they shouted obscenities. Wyrmlen ran a hand across his face, smearing blood over his cheek before heaving one of his companions onto his shoulder. He yelled some warning, prompting laughter and further jeers from the mob.

"Keep your face plastered to that window and the Commission's bound to find you," Shyloh said as she braided a fresh bowstring.

Guilder turned from the window. "Was this your plan, then?" He looked toward where she sat on a run-down wooden coffer. "Have me sit on my hands in some rat-infested bar waiting to get caught?"

"Ryleigh had your back, and that bar hadn't seen a rat in over a week."

"The bar fight part of the plan too?"

"Not entirely. Good cover, though." Shyloh looped the braid onto her bow, tying off the loose end. "You got here, no harm done."

"And if I'd killed someone, or got myself killed?"

"Did you kill someone?"

"No."

"Okay then, relax."

"And what about that girl? The bartender. What did she say her name was? Ryleigh?"

"Y'all talking about me?" Ryleigh came in from the underground tunnel, a cavalier smile plastered on her face.

"Hey, Ryleigh." The pale misty one, Ashyr, returned her smile. He wore a white hooded robe, flowing like the curls of haze constantly emanating from beneath. It belled out just below his elbows, similar at his ankles, a tied rope belt holding it all together. He and Ryleigh forced the stone fireplace shut over the secret entrance. Shyloh whispered her incantation, lighting it from across the room.

The room, perhaps an apartment at one time, was cluttered with kegs of beer, broken barstools and chairs, crates of tankards, and bottles filled with a rainbow of colored liquids.

"This the guy?" Ryleigh pointed a turned-up finger at Guilder. She hadn't a scratch on her, despite having jumped unarmed into the center of the brawl.

"Afraid so." Shyloh slid over, giving Ryleigh room to sit on the coffer.

"Cute. Not so good in a fight, though." She winked at Guilder, her smile unfaltering.

"I had to save him, too, from Wyrmlen of all people," Ashyr added, leaning an arm on the fireplace mantel. "He came in pretty hot. What did you do to get under Wyrmlen's skin?"

Guilder narrowed his eyes at Shyloh. "Apparently I broke into town." He crossed his arms in irritation. "Your fearless leader's idea."

"You're our leader now?" Ryleigh glared at

Shyloh, questioning.

"Yeah, well…"

"What, you all aren't together? I mean, a gang or something?"

"More freelance than anything," Ashyr said. "Sorry to disappoint."

Guilder nodded toward Ashyr. "That was you at the gate, helping me with that gorilla."

"Guilty." Ashyr's smile widened. His amber eyes remained sharp as he evaporated and floated to the opposite side of the room. "Ashyr Oriel at your service."

Guilder's jaw fell open at the display before coming back to himself. "Is that your practice, then? Helping strangers harassed by this Trades Commission?"

"Practice? No, it's my pleasure to keep that asshole in check."

"Until he finagles a noose around your neck," Ryleigh said with a smirk, prompting a shrug from Ashyr.

"If you all are done fawning over each other, we need to figure out how to get our boy here to Byzantium."

"Why the Republic and not Aurora?" Ryleigh asked, keeping her eyes glued to Guilder.

"Because that's where my contact is."

"Contact?" Ryleigh shifted her gaze to Shyloh. "Since when do you have a contact?"

Ashyr floated to Shyloh's side, eyebrows raised mockingly. "Thought she'd do this one without us."

"And you didn't finish the job?" Irritation rose in Ryleigh's tone.

"I asked her the same thing."

"What job?" Guilder interjected. "What are you all talking about?"

"My contact, so he tells me, may be able to fix your memory problems." Shyloh aimed her razor-thin eyes at Ryleigh and Ashyr. "If he's still in Byzantium, that is."

Ashyr slid back to Guilder's side of the room. "Ask her how she plans to get to the great Republic of Byzantium from here."

Ryleigh gawked at Shyloh. "Well?"

Shyloh hesitated, her stare finding an empty corner. She whispered, "Through the Belt."

"The what?" Guilder asked.

"Through the Belt of Allenrude, okay!" Shyloh barked.

"You have got to be kidding." Ryleigh shook her head.

"What's the Belt of Allenrude?"

"What's the…" Ryleigh looked at Guilder, dumbfounded, then at Shyloh. "What in the nine realms did you do to this guy?"

"She saved me from a memory eater's cave."

Ryleigh shot a disbelieving glance at Shyloh.

"He saved himself. I was just there to—"

"To what?" Ryleigh snapped. "To pick up whatever pieces remained?"

Guilder leaned over to Ashyr and whispered, "What's the Belt of Allenrude?" as

Ryleigh and Shyloh continued their argument.

"It's a narrow isthmus between the northern and the rest of the Amarikan Continent. Wetland marshes, an endless network of pools and soft mires filled with chest-high grasses stinking of rot and decay."

"Sounds repulsive, but not that treacherous. What's the problem going through, then?"

"If the stench of the place doesn't make you want to kill yourself…" Ashyr folded his arms and shook his head at the two verbal combatants. "The undying will probably do the job for you."

"The undying?"

Ashyr's brow raised in sympathy. "That memory eater really did a number on you, didn't she?"

Guilder nodded, shifting his sight back to Ryleigh and Shyloh, as they pointed accusatory fingers at each other.

"They drag any unlucky man, woman, or beast below into the mud and muck, transforming them into the undying. Some return enchanted, most hideous, and all, dangerous. Anyone drawn under by them or merely dies in that marsh for any reason, come back to draw more unfortunate souls to their deaths."

"Zombies?"

"For lack of a better term. They're dead, but not dead. Reawakened corpses with no mind of their own, except, of course, for the master who controls them. The undying are a relentless throng bent on annihilation. They fear nothing. Their ranks, forever feeding, and continually renewed by their fallen enemies. Lucky for us they hardly ever venture beyond the marshes. Then there's the Fae."

"Shyloh mentioned faery." Guilder shook his head, eyes questioning.

"They're sneaky bastards, hide in plain sight, make you think you can't see them."

"Like they're invisible?"

"Not quite. More like they trick you into seeing things that aren't there. Mask things that are."

"Why not go around?"

"This outfit isn't equipped for that kind of undertaking," Shyloh said, abandoning her argument to intrude on the other conversation. "Traversing the Western Ocean takes money. Money, we don't have. So, we go on foot."

"What do you mean, we?" Ryleigh laced her arms in defiance. "I have a bar to run. I can't go running all over the continent on some damned fool's errand. I've got my own problems here. Like how I'm going to keep the Trades Commission goons off my back now that your boy here kicked over Wyrmlen's hornets' nest."

"Gunnison's moving outward, along with the rest of the collective. That shitty bar of yours is about to be shut down and relocated. You can stay here sitting on your thumbs or you can come with us. You're the only one who's been through the marshes."

"In a convoy!" Ryleigh threw her hands up. "With an armed escort. You get through the marshes with numbers. Even with the escort, the undying took half our horses and a dozen people. No way the four of us get through."

"Ryleigh, we're going to Grand Valley."

"The harbor town?" Ashyr's face lit up. "I can taste the saltwater taffy already."

Shyloh grew a cockeyed smile. "You're the only one who knows the way."

Ryleigh looked at Guilder, her stone expression remaining. "You find your man," she said to Shyloh. "We sail back."

"Done." Shyloh nodded.

Ryleigh shook her head. "We're going to need more than knives to get through this."

***

Gunnison was far easier to leave than it was to enter. The gate guards paid little attention to the crowds leaving for the mines, and Wyrmlen seemed nowhere in sight. After gathering supplies from South Fork, Gunnison's nearest neighbor to the east, they turned slightly southeast, keeping at a slow trot, saving the horses for the long trip.

Guilder remained quiet through most of the journey. He had been lucky to find Shyloh and her friends so helpful. Stumbling from Da'Kar's cave in such a sorry state may have ended worse for him had he been alone. Though he couldn't grasp why they'd all take such risks for a stranger.

Shyloh reined in her horse, bringing it

alongside Guilder, and handed him a full canteen. "Here, drink."

Guilder took a few swallows and held it back toward Shyloh. "Thanks."

"Keep it, it's a long journey and... I noticed you don't have much in way of provisions so..."

Guilder nodded as he ran a thumb over the canteen's neck. "I'll find a way to repay you."

"I know." Shyloh offered a sympathetic smile before spurring her mount to catch up with the others.

Your name uttered by few without contempt, Da'Kar had said. Guilder drank a few more gulps from his canteen, feeling the familiar sting at the base of his skull. What sort of man was he before... Does that man still exist? If not, then who was he?

The midpoint of the third day saw Guilder's vigilance piqued as they skirted the far edge of the Shaman Bluffs. The same highlands where he'd escaped Da'Kar and met Shyloh. He kept his eyes peeled for triangular warning signs of creature-occupied caves. As the bluffs faded to the distance and the prairies deteriorated into wetlands, Guilder brightened. Ryleigh broke camp near the end of their fourth day at the edge of the marsh, several kilometers from the isthmus after hooves began sinking into the bog.

The marshland had closed in like a surrounding army, overtaking the solid ground from either side. Gentle breezes swayed cattails and papyrus reeds, rustling like children's whispers or a siren's call, soothing yet ominous. Shyloh stoked the white-red coals of their campfire, watching over the others as they slept. She kicked up weak flames struggling to cook what emaciated breakfast she'd found as a fog-covered dawn broke behind her.

She handed Guilder another full canteen. "Drink. We won't be stopping until we get to the other side of the marshes." She thumbed southward, toward a narrow stretch of road scarcely above the murky waterline. "Allenrude's Belt is nothing to dawdle across."

"How do we get through?" Guilder guzzled half the canteen and rubbed the back of his neck. "The horses have been skittish ever since we left the prairie lands. Besides, they're having a hell of a time keeping above the muck."

"There should be a corduroy road through the moors, fit for soldiers, small wagons, not much else." Ryleigh turned over on her bedroll, cursing Shyloh and her discomfort under a listless sleep, the fragrance of crisping rabbit failing to rouse her.

"How do we know it's safe?" Guilder asked between gulps from the canteen.

"It isn't." Shyloh took a drink from her own canteen. "Ashyr's scouting ahead, plotting our route. It'll be as safe as we can make it. Don't let your guard down, though."

Clouds shrouded the sky, giving the wetlands a gray, dreary feel. The horses fidgeted at their ties, irritable, sensing danger in the wind, hesitant being so close to the marshes, let alone to enter. Guilder felt it too as he drank his fill.

"What's so important that we risk trudging through the isthmus?" Guilder asked. "Who are we meeting in... Grand Valley, you said?"

"The harbor district is supposed to be full of pirates," Ryleigh said through a yawn, still groggy as she sat next to Guilder. She snatched a rabbit off the fire, its steam wafting in the crisp morning air, and sized up her first bite.

"We'll resupply at Grand Valley, catch some R&R. We meet with my associate in the Republic's port city of Foxgate. Hopefully, he'll know how to get your memory back."

"And who do you know in Foxgate?" Ryleigh asked, passing her half-eaten rabbit to Guilder.

Shyloh kept her eyes locked on the dying campfire. "The Scarecrow Man," she whispered after a moment's hesitation.

"Who?" Ryleigh's face distorted into a tired, distrustful look.

"Never mind. Here, have some more rabbit. As soon as Ashyr gets back, we go."

Ryleigh's question was left hanging as she wolfed down the palm-sized hindquarters of the rabbit. She wiped the drippings from her chin, seeming to revive with the meal. Shyloh finished the rest of the meat as Ashyr arrived back at camp, unease betraying his tone as he reported the way clear.

The sun trudged up the eastern sky, poking through the breaking clouds as the heat of the day rippled on the horizon. Shyloh checked the horses for injury, nuzzling each before saddling them up. Soon, the camp fell behind. The wetland stretched out for miles, encapsulating them in tan-brown grasses, reeds, and sedges. The smell of mud and rot permeated the now stagnant air as their mounts measured each step on the decaying road.

By midday, Guilder had lost all perspective with the unchanging horizon. The vast marshlands caught him in awe, rendering him small and powerless. The horses snorted out their shared fear, ears swiveling, eyes wide. Spooked by nothing and yet everything. "Easy, girl." Shyloh patted her horse's neck despite the animal's contrary mood.

"We need to hurry through," Ryleigh said, nervousness apparent in her voice. "If we don't make the other side by nightfall, we won't get out at all."

"I haven't seen anything since we rode in," Guilder said. "Why's everyone so frightened of this place? Seems quiet, almost peaceful, if it weren't for the stink."

"That's the allure of the narrows," Ashyr said in a low, cautious voice. "The quiet lulls you to sleep. Fall into the muck and it takes you. Even your mount won't know you've been lost. With your next breath you're pulling the horse down with you, then your companions, then anyone else foolish enough to enter the Belt unprepared."

"Quiet," Shyloh murmured. "Keep

moving."

"So, it's haunted?" Guilder leaned over so Ashyr could hear. "By these undying?"

"Not exactly, they're far more... devious creatures in the moors."

"Then what exactly?"

"No one knows," Ryleigh said from behind. "Those that make it across recount not seeing anything. They just come out with fewer people than they went in with. No screams, no sign anyone went missing. Not until after when... they're just gone."

"That stench you smell," Ashyr added. "Said to be the rotting corpses of the dead. Look down."

Guilder looked below his mount. Saw the water leaching up through the timber road, dark red, like blood mixed in with the muck. The heels of the reeds mirrored the gore with an inflamed ring climbing up through the stem, like spears after felling their mark, burying their kill below the mud.

"Only place on all the continents where the planet shows its rage," Ashyr said.

"I said be quiet back there," Shyloh scolded, leading the three others riding side by side.

"What takes them? Spirits?" Guilder asked.

"Legends say there was a battle here," Ryleigh whispered. "Two armies from opposite sides of the continent. Emperor Thaddeus Aurora from the north and the warlord Allenrude Byzantium from the south. These war-torn nations staged a final push to determine who'd rule over the whole of the Amarikan Continent. They met at the center of the isthmus, faced off, ready to destroy every man on the opposing side. As the slaughter began, the ground itself rose in protest, taking men, fallen or otherwise, into the wetlands, using their blood to water the marshes. No one survived. To this day, the corpses of those taken continue to bolster the ranks of the ancient armies, silent enlistments from anyone venturing into their territory."

Ashyr leaned toward Guilder. "If no one survived, who relayed the story?"

Ryleigh rolled her eyes. "Why the Belt of Allenrude if neither side won?" Guilder asked.

"Politics, most likely. Emperor Aurora had foresight enough to leave an heir as he went off to battle, an easy decision since Empress Constance the First was only six when she took the throne. The other side of the continent, though…" Ryleigh shook her head. "Allenrude's lands, without a strong national government behind him, fell into disarray in his absence."

Guilder gulped down the last of his canteen, Ryleigh following suit. "Eventually they created a ruling republic, equal representation for all landowners, for all that's worth." She tightened her canteen cap, stowing it back into her saddlebags. "By the time they'd sorted it out and proclaimed themselves the Republic of Byzantium, the Auroran Empress had come into her own. As a last insult for the war, she declared the battle site the Belt of Allenrude, blaming him for the devastation, and the undying. The Republic protested, but by that time the name had stuck."

Shyloh turned back to the trio. "Did I not tell you all to shut the fu—" Her horse reared up, tossed her to the ground, and bolted forward. Riderless, it ran panicked for several meters, then tumbled forward into the marsh, screaming, writhing, then fell silent.

Shyloh sat where she'd been thrown, breathless, staring dumbfounded into the marsh where her horse had disappeared. Guilder's horse let out a nervous snort, ears scanning, hooves pounding the sodden road. Ashyr dismounted and hurried to Shyloh's side. His hand held out to her. "Wait," she said, stopping him. "We're not alone."

Guilder strained to match Shyloh's eyeline. The golden-colored reeds blended like a dense sheet, motionless as the slightest wind held its breath. Two tiny black spots, like eyes peering out from the marsh, gleamed there, then vanished. Guilder squinted into the bog, questioning what he'd seen. If he'd seen anything at all.

Shyloh scurried to her feet, jumping back as a tiny, human-like creature bound from the roadside. A spear aimed center at her chest. The amber-colored creature stood barely knee high, iridescent wings fluttering behind. A second emerged from the reeds, then a third, slashing at Ashyr. He turned to mist, faded, solidified, catching a spear tip to the side of his ribs.

Guilder pulled his sword and slashed one in half; its jagged teeth caught mid-grimace. Entrails splattered against his horse's backside. The mount bolted, losing Guilder from his saddle. He tumbled onto the sopping road. The longsword clanged off the pylons as the frightened horse nearly trampled Shyloh, her limbs pulled inward.

Shyloh scurried back to the group and readied her bow, arrow nocked. "Gods be damned, *korrigans*." She drew her bow, primed for another attack. Guilder recovered his footing aiming a questioning gaze at Shyloh as she loosed another arrow. "Pack hunter fae. They'll ambush anything considered edible.

Guilder sloughed the mud from his blade as his horse ran headlong into a nest of the creatures. Razor-like teeth sunk into the beast, its neck, haunches, and belly. The animal's innards spilled onto the road, its squeals dying away as they swarmed.

Ryleigh's horse reared as several of the creatures flocked toward her. The horse toppled over as chunks of flesh were taken from its legs, Ryleigh caught beneath. A dozen faery prodded her with spears, the tips deflecting off her skin. Ryleigh swiped her attackers away with an open hand, pushing herself out from under her horse. Shyloh helped her to her feet, clearing the creatures from her gnawed-on mount. The two ran back, circling with the rest.

"There're too many!" Ryleigh hollered, batting the air, striking one in five that came.

Guilder swung his blade as if swatting flies. Countless in their swarm, he stood over Ashyr, defending him as he sat, knees bent, on the waterlogged road, straining to conjure a spell, anything to blow the faery out of their dive-bombing lines.

Shyloh cupped her hands, mouthing a spell under her breath. A growing tongue of fire manifested between her fingers.

"No!" Ryleigh shouted. "You'll set the whole bog on fire!"

Shyloh shook out the spell, employing a fresh arrow to stab another faery leaping at her face. "Then what in Hekate's name do you suggest we do?"

Teeth gnawed against horse bone as the swarms turned their collective attention to the four that remained.

Ryleigh continued swatting the creatures as they bit into her unyielding legs, thighs, shoulders, her neck. A failing sphere of wind encircled the group. Sweat beaded at Ashyr's forehead as he chanted, blood from his wound trickling down his side.

"We have no choice!" Shyloh yelled as several faery bounced back from the wind sphere. She cupped her hands again. Blue-yellow sparks leaped across her palms.

"*Summoneie metelas spy-guki inimicus,*" Guilder chanted, his eyes closed, sword hilt posed above his head, the blade pointed toward the soft wooden road. "*metelas spy-guki inimicus.*" He thrust the blade into the pylons. Spikes of gleaming black metal erupted from the road finding airborne and hidden faery alike, iron slicing through soft flesh. Copper-blue blood washed over Ashyr's wind sphere, as hundreds of impaled faery writhed from metal pikes.

Guilder's companions staggered back from him as he opened his eyes, his mind blank, the intensity of his spell lingering on his face. Meters away, the reeds shuffled as survivors of the metal onslaught fled deeper into the moors. Guilder pulled his sword from the muck. The metal spikes returned to the ground, releasing their captive's remains. Guilder fell onto his knees with a splash from the wet road, the sword clanging beside him.

"Gods be damned." Shyloh shook out her hand, the lingering fireball still burning between her fingers.

Ryleigh looked down at Guilder. "Who are you?" Concern overtaking her face.

"What's it matter?" Shyloh said, kneeling to examine one of the dead faery. She prodded the body with all the delicacy of a lepidopterist. "They'd camouflaged themselves." The korrigan's teeth were canine sharp, eyes black. Their limbs, body, and head, seemed reminiscent of tiny humans, only their gray-blue skin set them apart. "I'd never seen one up close. They really are fascinating. This cloak he's dressed in is the exact amber color of the marsh. Darker spots mimicked the shadows and mud. Even the spears they used looked like the marsh grass."

Ashyr propped himself up, breathing

heavily.

"Lie still." Ryleigh hurried over to Ashyr's side, examining where the faery had slashed him. "This wound is only skin deep. It shouldn't have affected you so much."

"Poison?" Shyloh asked.

"Maybe. We'll have to get out of the marshlands to get him treated."

"No wonder people think this place is haunted," Ashyr said in a drowsy voice, letting himself drop into Ryleigh's arms. "If these things could take down a horse, imagine what they'd do to some unsuspecting traveler." A drunk smile crossed his face. He closed his eyes, mumbling something unintelligible.

Ryleigh picked Ashyr up, effortlessly setting him over her shoulder. "We need to move. Guilder's bought us a chance to get out of this damned place, so let's take it."

Shyloh heaved Guilder onto his feet. "I'm fine," he said, unsteady in his legs. "I can walk." Guilder pushed off Shyloh's help and ambled ahead. "Those malicious little bastards, what did you call them, the undying?"

"No." Shyloh shook her head. "These were korrigans, a lesser class of faery. Though there hadn't been any reports of them hunting in these swamps, not in so great a number, anyway."

Guilder nodded, troubled more by his own actions than the water faery. Where had his power come from? He trudged behind the others, regaining his breath as Shyloh helped with Ashyr. It abandoned him in the cave, maybe stolen by that monster. Was he only now reclaiming it, rediscovering it, unearthing it? Would he be able to control it before—he glanced ahead at the others.

Ryleigh readjusted Ashyr's weight from one shoulder to the other. "If they've reestablished a Fae queen, then she'd have supplied her soldiers with poison. Ashyr will need a physician, and fast."

"There's one I know of in Paracel," Shyloh said.

"Who do you know in Paracel?"

"A healer, all right! If we're lucky, the townsfolk wouldn't have burned her as a witch."

CHAPTER 7
Family of Mist

"Paracel is one of those towns you question how it still exists," Shyloh told Guilder, as they kept a quick pace behind Ryleigh. "If you'd even call it a town. The Republic sees no strategic use for it, not with their grand harbor and fleets of ships at the ready. And Aurora can't see a handful of farmers being of any use to them, either."

"So, they're ungoverned?"

"Free is a better word for it. The only free town on the eastern continent. But freedom has its costs. Being so close to the Belt, they're on constant alert. They make do, somehow. The caravans keep them in gold and farming keeps them fed. Not a terrible life, if you're willing to settle."

"Sounds like they keep those creatures that attacked us from spilling onto the rest of the continent. If the realms can't see a strategic use in that, maybe they need to be shown."

Shyloh's step faltered, her mouth agape. She cleared her throat, catching back up to Guilder. "Yeah, well, there are worse things than korrigans that come out of the Belt."

Ashyr faded in and out of consciousness. Delirious from the Fae's poison, he muttered fears of gasifying into nothingness through fever dreams. "He's not doing well," Ryleigh said, craning her neck over her empty shoulder. "I can feel him struggling to stay solid. You'd better be right about this healer of yours."

"She'll be there. Breya's too stubborn to die." Shyloh stopped mid-stride, her face scrunched up, fist covering her mouth.

"Breya! That's your grand plan?" Ryleigh turned and took a step toward Shyloh. "She'd likely watch him die rather than help, probably take some sadistic pleasure in it just to spite us."

"We haven't much choice," Shyloh said as she continued past. "She'll help. I'll make sure of it."

"Who's Breya?" Guilder asked, watching Shyloh trek on ahead.

Ryleigh screwed up her face and shook her head. "Ashyr's older sister." Ryleigh readjusted his body over her shoulder and started after Shyloh.

"If she's his sister, she'd have to help him, right?"

Ryleigh sighed. "It's more complicated than that. They had a rough go of it as kids. Their close-minded parents clung to the old religions and superstitions. Kept them from seeing what the world really is. Didn't much appreciate having magical children, either. Breya could keep her powers secret, Ashyr, not so much. His powers protected him, so Breya took the brunt of their wrath."

"Why the animosity, then?"

"That would be Shyloh's doing. The three of us were friends, way back when, in Gunnison, until Breya introduced Shyloh to her brother." Ryleigh's jaw tightened as she peered ahead of her. "Damn her schemes. Shyloh was more interested in Ashyr's air magics, his mist abilities, and stealth, rather than Breya's healing. My guess, Breya got sick of being left out. She blames Ashyr for whatever her own fool reasons are. After their falling out, she ran off to the other side of the Belt, Paracel apparently."

"Funny, Shyloh knew she'd be there."

Ryleigh narrowed her eyes toward Shyloh. "Yeah, that is funny."

Paracel's wall spanned across the narrowest stretch of the eastern continent. A few meters thick, and a dozen kilometers across, it spilled back into the moors to the west, utilizing the Shaman Bluffs natural barricade going east. Beyond, the region widened, like a stream flowing into the Southern Ocean. Guard towers spread along its length, six in all, with a few dozen signal fires already blazing in the early dusk. A fortified door at the center, the only egress, a wicket gate fashioned within. Shyloh pounded on the door, peering back at the stragglers.

"State your business!" a pock-nosed face said from behind an even tinier peek door.

"Our friend is injured," Shyloh said as Ryleigh plodded up next to her. "We seek asylum from the Belt and a healer."

"We've no healer here. None that'll do your friend any good, anyway."

Ryleigh shifted Ashyr's near weightlessness to her opposite shoulder and stuck her face between Shyloh and the gatekeeper. "Breya

Oriel is a capable healer. We have it on good authority that she resides here."

"Aye, that witch is lucky enough to find herself behind these walls. But you'd best stay clear of her…" The gatekeepers' eyes stretched wide as Guilder caught up to the group. "Your Majesty?"

Ryleigh narrowed her eyes at Shyloh, who dropped her head in mock defeat. Guilder shrugged at the two of them, shaking his head, oblivious.

"Fine," Shyloh said. "Open the gate. Best not to keep His Royal Highness waiting."

Behind the barricade, a gridwork of stone paths strung together a smattering of thatched roofed houses. The gatekeeper's home, the only structure, butted against the wall. Small plots of vegetable gardens bracketed tidy walkways between houses and roads. Villagers harvested pole beans and seasonal squash, grew peppers of all shapes and sizes, cut cucumber vines, and dug root vegetables. Children ran around bartering their harvests, chasing chickens, or getting into mischief.

Shyloh and Ryleigh headed toward a cluster of buildings further down the main road, while Guilder stopped an arm's length from the gatekeeper. "Gatekeeper."

The pocked nose old man put a fist to his chest and bowed.

"You know who I am?"

He lifted his head with a questioning look. "Aye."

"Then tell me."

The gatekeeper's questioning looks deepened. "Your Royal Highness the Prince Guilder Rayne, Duke of the Southern Continent, Royal Knight of the Most Noble Order of Cañon, Extra Companion of the Queen's Service Order, Lord High Admiral of the—"

"Fine, fine." Guilder held up a hand to the old man. Once again, Da'Kar's words, *'uttered by few without contempt,'* resounded in his head. Guilder glanced along the main road as Shyloh and Ryleigh continued toward the center of town. Had Shyloh known? Did they all know? "Tell me this. If I am this price, how long have I been missing?"

"Missing, your Grace?"

Guilder shook his head and sighed. What constituted this gatekeeper's loyalty to a monarch alleged to be so detestable? The fear in his eyes spoke mountains. Or was it something else entirely? "Never mind. Just... keep up the good work." He trotted down the road to catch up with the others.

"Can't say I see it myself, but..." Shyloh was saying as Guilder approached.

Ryleigh stopped, cold as stone. "What in all the gods' names have you done?" Her voice, in full throat, dagger eyes fixed on a cheek-flushed Shyloh.

"What are you two arguing about?" Guilder asked, trying to catch his breath.

"The guard mistaking you for someone else." Shyloh's eyes narrowed on Ryleigh.

"Lucky enough for us. Shadows from the setting sun, I'll guess. Makes one look more… regal." She turned away and started toward the back-end of town. "Breya lives on the outskirts, away from everyone else. Let's not trust anymore to luck. Keep your head down so nobody else mistakes you for someone important."

"What's got her all rabid?" Guilder asked as Shyloh stormed away.

Ryleigh's teeth remained clenched. "Family business." She shook out her balled fists and readjusted Ashyr on her shoulder. "Come on." She tilted her head for Guilder to follow and headed after Shyloh.

The small stone house was isolated a short distance away from the rest of the town. Its lack of windows and overgrown garden added to its general look of dilapidation. Still, smoke billowed from the chimney as much as any of the other rickety hovels in town.

Shyloh pounded on the door. "Breya! I know you're in there! We need your help."

"Fuck off!" The quick response roared from inside the house.

"Guess you're pissing everybody off today," Ryleigh said, sauntering up to the ramshackle house.

Shyloh pitched a disdained look at Ryleigh as she pounded on the door again. "Breya! Come on, it's Ashyr, he's hurt."

"It serves him right!" the voice said, sounding closer, maybe just to the other side of the door. "Shit happens, and I said fuck off, I'm busy."

Shyloh shook her head, her lips pinched as she turned away from the house.

"Breya, it's Ryleigh. Please, we really need your help, Ashyr, I mean." She pushed Shyloh off to the side and leaned her hand against the doorframe. "We got in bad with some korrigan coming across the isthmus—"

The door swung open as a pair of smoke-gray eyes scanned the group. Dressed in a woolen turquoise tunic, her pale swanlike neck sported numerous silver and bone talismans. Her braided golden brown hair fell well below her shoulders, tight fists set against her hips.

She ran her hand over her brother's wounds and, with narrowing eyes, glared at Shyloh. "Set him on the table. Face down." Ryleigh passed into the house, her stare never drifting from Shyloh. "And take his clothes off. Those little bastards will stick you where you'll least expect'um to."

Guilder followed up to the door, Breya's arm blocking his way. "You're new to this rabble." She studied Guilder thoroughly top to bottom. "Shyloh." Her head tilted sideways, a wry smile caressing her face. "Where'd you scrounge up this lovely creature?"

Shyloh forced her way through the door. "He's broken goods, baggage for now."

Guilder grew an uncomfortable smile. "I was... taken by a memory eater."

"You don't say." Breya's smile widened, echoing his.

"Shyloh said she'd help me reverse the effects."

"Did she now?" Breya turned her narrowed eyes back toward Shyloh. "Come in. If you've survived this long following this shit bunch, you can't be entirely useless."

Guilder skirted around Breya, her immodest smile following his movements.

"Not with those strong shoulders of yours."

Guilder crossed to a darkened corner, attempting to hide himself from her roaming eyes.

Breya sauntered by, continuing to look at Guilder as he shrunk further into the shadows. "What in the nine realms?!" she barked, turning toward the table. "Ryleigh, I didn't mean bare ass to the gods. Leave the man some dignity, for Gaea's sake. Here, put a sheet over his nethers. I eat off this table, dammit."

Ryleigh wrapped Ashyr's waist with the jute sheet.

Breya examined the wound at Ashyr's side, Ryleigh standing nearby. The lesion gaped at the edges like an opening tulip, red and swollen, green-yellow pus foaming inside. "You said he got stabbed by a faery soldier?"

"That's right," Ryleigh said, holding her stomach as she averted her eyes.

"They don't usually take up poisoned weapons." Breya lifted her head in thought. "Unless they've taken a new queen."

"Our thoughts as well," Shyloh said,

joining Guilder in his corner.

Breya leaned back into her examination. "If you had any thoughts at all, you would have stayed out of the Belt." She ran her thumb over the edge of the wound, licked the residue, and gazed up at the ceiling, smacking her lips. "Something's off about this poison."

Guilder exchanged a questioning look with Shyloh. "Off, how?"

Breya shifted to a workbench in what looked to be her kitchen. She threw several herbs into a large stone mortar, bringing it back to Ashyr's side. She spat into the mixture and ground it with a mismatched pestle. "Not sure." Her face turned quizzical. "Not yet. I can put a poultice on it for now. It'll stop the poison from spreading, but..." She drew her brows together, shaking her head. "The antivenom might be tricky. I'll need a few ingredients." She smeared the paste into the wound, crossing her hands and splaying her fingers over his side.

"Gydyk varda Gaea. Askvieku bet kokia zemyska kera, gydyk varda Gaea." A blue-white light glowed under Breya's hands. Ashyr groaned. His face writhed in pain as he stole gasping breaths. *"Gydyk varda Gaea."*

From outside, a horn sounded, a long baritone followed by townsfolk yelling from all directions. "Acolyte's ass!" Breya shouted.

"What's going on?" Guilder moved past Breya to the door.

"Undying."

Guilder turned back to Shyloh, who looked at Ryleigh, who only shrugged.

"They've been coming out of the wetlands for the last three nights and attacking the barricade. These farmer hicks have been able to fend them off so far. Even bolstered the barrier wall, as well as they could, anyway. They're running out of ammunition, though," Breya said, continuing to dress Ashyr's wounds. "If you don't hit those sleepwalkers in the head, and fell them where they stand, they take your arrows with them." She went back into her kitchen, tossing random plants into the used mortar. "Ryleigh can help me here. You two, go help at the front." She shot one last crossed look at Shyloh. "Assuming your aim is better than your leadership skills."

Shyloh and Guilder exchanged looks, Guilder grabbing Breya's bow and a full quiver from the corner as they went. "And don't go getting your asses chewed off by those damned things," Breya yelled after them. "Don't need anyone else dying today."

***

Torches were lit all along the face of the barricade wall. Evening mist supplied a layer of quiet ambiance as the wind rustled the encroaching marsh grasses like war drums, its steady breath combing across the battlefield. Archers spaced themselves along the alure behind the battlement, cavalry along the front. The troop commander, all too eager for additional help, directed the new volunteers to fill in the gaps.

Guilder readied himself and his unfamiliar

gear, testing the bow's strength, drawing back and dry firing to get a good feel. He looked over at Shyloh, an arm's length from where he stood. She scanned the surrounding soldiers. A strange mixture of farmer and warrior. Fathers next to sons, leather bracers, well used and adorned with diminished family crests. Mounted troops in chain armor, bite-proof, with dented helms and mismatched greaves and sollerets.

"The undying offer no sound, just mindless advancement," the commander said in a solemn tone. "They'd swarm and tear and bite any warm body unlucky enough to be in their path—man, woman, child, and beast alike." He walked the line, adjusting chest guards and stances. "Our dead add to their ranks, so archers should fare well to keep the hoard from advancing too close. Horsemen!" He leaned over the wall, raising his voice as he peered toward either end. "Take out those who slip through. Finish the ones who won't stay down. Take their heads before they take your life." He leaned back, addressing the whole of his company. "Save magics for a last resort and only after all ammunition had been spent. Don't waste your strength." His fervor wavered. "It'll be a long night."

A simple plan for an untrained army. It had worked for three days, but half-filled quivers with nothing to refill them left the defenders ill-equipped and looking tired for their efforts. Horses twitched their ears, restless in the unnatural quiet. The archers stood looking out into the night. The black horizon echoed their resolve, hiding a collective fear, a dam holding back the floodwaters, its cracks straining against the inevitable.

Shyloh stared out over the murky fields. "There had been a time," she said in a hushed voice. "My grandfather told me, on especially dark nights, that this world once had a guardian angel. She lit up the night sky like a torch, spreading her silvery flame, blanketing the shadowy recesses of creation. Then one day, the necromancers came. They raised an army of the dead from fallen soldiers, farmers, kings, and peasants alike. With limited intelligence, and lacking any will of their own, they weren't a formidable army. Not for any competent fire wielder. Hell, if you could ignite a torch, you could destroy a battalion of them, as long as you could see them coming."

"Since the dead outnumber the living to such an extent, they were an unending supply of soldiers. The people rose up against the necromancers, killing as many as could be found. Those who were left used the entirety of their power to raise a zombie lord to control the hordes after their deaths. They sent their new creation to snuff out the light, a powerful advantage that man had over the undying. Three days it took to devour the light in whole, darkening the world forever after." Shyloh looked up into the star-filled sky, her expression blank. "Now, only starlight fills the midnight battlefield. And the darkness favors the dead."

Guilder turned his gaze to the horizon.

"That supposed to be some kind of galvanizing speech?"

"No. Just a reminder of what we'll be fighting against, and that there's always more behind them. Get ready, here they come."

The horses sensed it first. They scampered around in their anxiety, calmed only by the experience of their riders. Soldiers on the line strained their eyes against the gloom. Shyloh only waited, patient, like she'd seen this type of battle before. Guilder's eyes flicked between Shyloh's stoicism and the blank canvas of the battlefield, taking his cues from her. The bow felt foreign, unlike his sword. A mount may have afforded him better use had there been one to spare.

Shambled movement rippled the darkness, first one, then a handful, then a wall of undying. The line held, bows at the ready, arrows nocked, the dead still a kilometer away. The lead one broke from the pack into a dead sprint. No one moved. Six hundred meters, a boy to the side of Shyloh raised his bow. Five hundred meters; the horses snorted their discontent. The boy drew, pointing his arrow high into the midst of exalted stars. Four hundred meters, the arrow loosed with the sound of a well-tuned harp string. Three hundred meters, the boy's arrow found its mark.

The creature landed on its knees, strength taken, then plunged face-first into the dew-covered earth, the arrow shoved further into its skull. Not one sound was heard apart from the horses. No congratulatory cheers. No "good shot" for the boy's marksmanship. There was merely one less arrow to fight the oncoming hoard.

The wall of undying broke ranks. Individuals sprinted full-on toward the barricade.

"Arrows!" the commander shouted, the order echoing down the length of the barricade. Archers lifted their bows into firing position. Guilder followed suit. Shyloh kept still, watching the oncoming wave.

"Take aim!" Guilder pried his gaze away from Shyloh's inactivity, finding his target and drawing his bow. The rest of the line doing the same as the command hurried down the wall.

"Release!" The assemblage of bow strings twanged in harmony, sending a swarm of arrows into the night sky. Most found their targets but few undying fell to the battlefield.

"Arrows!" the cry came again. Shyloh removed a shaft from her quiver, nocked it into place, and leaned her head toward its tip. She whispered an unheard incantation, blowing measured breath onto the arrowhead.

"Take aim!" Her arrowhead glowed red, then orange, then white. Shyloh straightened her stance, pulling the bowstring back.

"Release!" As before, the melody of plucked strings sounded. Shyloh's arrow streaked across the sky, a painter's brush adding color to the drab night. It struck its target in the chest, exploding into a primordial fireball, lighting a swath of undying like bundled torches. They ran sightless into one another, infecting their brethren in flame, their dried flesh catching as so much kindling.

Shyloh nocked another arrow, heedless of the commander's calls. She loosed a second white streak, meters to the right of the first. Another, meters to the left, each with similar results. The bonfires lit up the battlefield. With the undying line broken, Shyloh continued to fire arrows into the throngs, the crackle of burning corpses, a symphony to the townsfolk's ears.

"Cavalry, at the ready!"

The battlefield was ablaze, bright as midday, smoke blanketing the sky and the stench of burning decayed flesh mixed with anxious horse sweat. Shyloh slung her last arrow, catching only a single runner in the throat. He exploded like the others as the cavalry spurred their beasts to hack down what remained of the dead army.

Shyloh turned to descend the wall, the eyes of the exhausted townsfolk following. The rear commander stopped her a meter out from the barricade, spinning her around. Each bow held up, archers holding two fingers to their temples parallel to the wall's length, a silent salute to Shyloh's victory. Her expression remained somber as she scanned the line of citizen soldiers. Her hand moved to her chest. She bowed deeply, her trailing hand held aloft before coming up with a wry smile.

A point and a flick of her wrist beckoned Guilder to descend the barricade. "Let's check how Ashyr's doing," she said with a hand to Guilder's back. He nodded at her with a congratulatory half-smile, bringing hers out all the wider.

CHAPTER 8
The Undying Faery
Generation Five

The Taxonomy of Creatures by Isaiah Crowley, Volume Seven

The creatures the common people have deemed faery are, like most of the fauna in this land, evolved, or rather mutated, from a base order. Examination of the skull and other bodily organs leads one to postulate that they are an offshoot of humans. Clearly remaining in the species of hominid, genus Homo, this new species, deemed H. faery, has within them three distinct sects.

The Fae represent the most populous and seem to have remained the most human-like. Though taller by an average of a meter, their lanky bodies put off an awkward appearance in their movement. Their wingless backs place them societally inferior to others in their hierarchal structure, though their magics seem equivalent to their governing class.

"My Lord Crowley, there's a gentleman to see you."

I took in a slow breath and tapped my pen off the inkwell. "Can you not see that I am engaged?"

"Yes, my lord. Of course."

Wyrmlen cleared his throat as I placed pen back to paper.

"However, he was rather insistent. He said he has a message from his queen."

"Queen?" I looked up to see a charming young man framed in the doorway. Clothed in a wheat-colored drape, looking of chiffon or other such finery. His sandal-clad feet were tiny in contrast to his taller-than-average stature. He held his hands folded one over the other at his chest, patiently awaiting his invitation. "Intriguing. Thank you, Wyrmlen. That will be all." I set my pen in the crease of the book.

"My lord." With a bow, Wyrmlen turned on his heels, leaving the gentleman where he stood.

As I scrutinized the young man, his human veneer flickered, a yellow-brown skin, like withered leaves, bled through his pale, defectless disguise. "My deepest apologies for my footman. He means well. However, stewardship is difficult to train. I must make note to procure a proper butler."

The creature tilted his head yet remained silent and unmoving from the doorway.

"I must admit I've made several studies of your people, though you tend to keep to your own. I'm much surprised by your visit. In fact, I've been penning some of my research. As you can see, I'm rather prolific in my writing. The library may only be partially filled, but I can see it one day abundant with all my acquired knowledge."

The man tilted his head again but did not speak.

I exhaled my growing frustration, narrowing my eyes, if only slightly. "I confess that in all my research, I've gained little knowledge of your culture. Come. Sit. I welcome the exchange to further expand my manuscripts." Finally, he moved from his position, his gaze taking in the three-story library. Concentric circles expanded upward into the heights of the tower. Walkways underlined the edgeless stacks, hardly a quarter full, a black iron spiral staircase connecting each floor.

"If it burdens you to hold your... allure, you're welcome to lower it. You are under my protection while in my citadel."

The Fae gave a slight bow. "It is for your comfort, my Lord Iks. Though may I say it is rare, near impossible even, for a human to be able to see through our illusions." His voice rumbled from his lips, a deep baritone, melodic, with a hint of foreignness.

"I find the impossible not to be so, not while residing in these lands."

"Then you are truly as powerful as I'd been told, my lord." He bowed at the waist, arms splayed back. His silken hair nearly touched the floor.

"Tell me of your Fae queen and what she might require of me."

"My lord, I fear your servant has misspoken. I am here on behalf of my master, Cirrus Yelrem. He leads a cabal against our counsel of twelve, to place new leadership upon the once mighty Fae throne."

"Politics do not concern me. Least of which, the politics of one I have never met." I reclaimed my pen and bent back to my journal. "Or have no stake in. Your master must wage his war campaigning with his own kind."

"My Lord Iks, my master wishes—"

"Why do you call me that?" I glanced up at the taken-aback Fae.

His hands refolded back at his chest, salvaging his composure. "It is our name for you, my lord, Andorian Iks."

"Meaning?"

"Andorian refers to a Fae legend of otherworldly power, one who could break mountains and tame storms. The mountain where your bastion now sits, Mount Iks, is a Fae word meaning bringer of change, though humans have used the name, I fear they have lost its true meaning. We believe you will bring powerful changes to this world, and my master wishes to start with the Fae."

"Your master has little to exchange for my aid. Neither power nor political."

The Fae's eyes searched the room, perhaps in search of further motivations to gain my assistance. Finally, his staunch demeanor broke with an audible sigh. "There is a book precious to the Fae, full of incantations, magics that we've been... unable, though some claim toothless, to invoke for nearly ten generations. My master believes your power is sufficient to invoke the enchantments, yet only a solitary spell will fulfill his promise to our future queen."

"Sufficient?" I turned my gaze to my meager library. The books I'd penned, the spells and potions, alchemical cocktails, miracles to the lesser mind, all from the whispers of the stone. I hear them even now, murmured instructions and recipes. Yet, this Fae brings suggestion of others' influences. Perhaps there could exist a way, outside my own practice, to reverse this bastardized world and return to civilized times. "Your master, Yelrem? He possesses this book?"

"He does, my lord."

"Then I accept his proposal. In exchange for the book, what exactly does he want for this future queen?"

"He wants what Viviana wants, eternal rule, beauty, and power."

***

The Taxonomy of Creatures *Volume Seven, cont.*

The least populous subsection of faery represents the upper society of rulers and, within their culture, royalty. These tend to be shorter than the average human by roughly a meter and, within my own observation, though possessing no more extraordinary abilities, tend to be more self-important than the rest. They possess suitable wings for their size, along the order of Lepidoptera, four-winged creatures similar to butterflies or moths, which seem held amongst them statements of honor, pride, or simple arrogance. Iridescent fractals exploit the full spectrum of color along the entirety of the surface. While brighter colors seem the most common, dark or even black is the most prized, as can be observed in their current ruler. Her wings, adorned in translucent dark blues, grays, and black, can fly her short distances with relative ease. These symbols seem juxtaposed to their unglamoured visage of mottled brown crepey skin, and reedy, largely unpleasant, appearance.

"Rarely have humans been offered a glimpse into our world, Lord Iks. Least, not outside the dungeons." Cirrus Yelrem led us through the circular ivory-colored corridors of what seemed their palace. Appearing as if carved from inside an ancient tree, crawling vines were etched into each surface, floor, and piece of furniture alike, flowing as if nature herself brushed across the interior façade.

"You'll forgive the crudeness of my... what is the word you humans use? My glamour? Your open appearance would cause panic throughout the colony."

I brushed my hands down my forearms for the hundredth time. The concealment, their... glamour, felt as if ants paraded over my skin in rank and file. "Curiosity overall eventually got the better of me. Studies of your clan had only taken me so far. Non-participant observation of your hunter class, for instance."

"Ones deemed korrigans by your kind, though their actual titles would be meaningless to you. Front-line observers and security of our outlying lands, sometimes reconnaissance, they serve their purpose like everyone."

"And what of your purpose?"

Yelrem grew a contemptuous smile. "Mine is to secure the future of this colony."

"By usurping your oligarchy in exchange for despotism?"

"Our ways are not your concern, sorcerer. You will be richly rewarded for your efforts."

"I am not some petty magician you can summon at will! My concerns remain larger than the health of a single colony of… faery."

"Apologies my lord. I assumed your interests—"

"My interests lie with the book I've been promised and have yet to be shown, nothing more."

"As you wish."

Yelrem turned a corner into an immaculate library. Looking as if grown from the curved wall, the shelves held an untold number of leather-bound books in reds, browns, and greens, each with golden spine texts exquisitely scrawled. Maps and scrolls with carved wooden handles stacked over stone tablets with cuneiform-type etchings. At its center lay a circular dais, its edge engravings depicting faery warriors in battle. Set atop what appeared to be chalk-white petrified tree roots reaching upward, splayed hands and gnarled fingers held a weighty tome.

Without a glance at Yelrem, I crossed the room to mount the dais, fingers stroking the embossed dark purple cover. The impressions, like an autograph map, shifted beneath my touch, tectonic plates provoked by the lightest pressure. The book spoke in whispers, a feminine seductive voice much like that of the meteor, imploring me to explore its content.

"Do you hear it?" I asked as Yelrem sauntered over. "The siren's call of the book?"

"Few can, a very few. A skill which drew me into curating this library. There are others, I'm told, who can hear." His deceptive eyebrow rose. "You, for one."

"Tell me of the one who composed this book."

"The Lich Grimoire was one of our earliest editions. Its author worked tirelessly to complete over half its pages. It's said that each spell was whispered to him by the vary mountain quarried to construct your citadel. Without sleep or sustenance, ultimately it drove him mad. Even in isolation, he heard it beckoning him."

"And where is its creator now?"

"Sadly, he is no more. A clever one to the end, he obtained a quill from an inexperienced guard. Without ink, he used his own blood and the walls of his cell to finish his opus. Still raving about the constant whispers, he ended his dismal existence by plunging the quill through his ear and into his brain." Yelrem took a long, calming breath. "For his efforts, we transposed the walls into the Grimoire to complete his work."

"Admirable." I opened the book to a random page, meticulously embellished, showing innumerable stars encircling the page and nine planets orbiting a single sun while snaking through the white space. They moved, almost imperceivably, as if mirroring their very counterparts. The spell I hadn't realized I was looking for faced me. My heart pounded like a disregarded prisoner at the walls of my chest as I moved to touch the page. It was the exact spell to correct the wrong done countless millennia ago. I clenched my jaw, holding my fervor in check.

"The compensation is acceptable," I said, paging through the tome. "However, the spell will take some time. I'll need to study the—"

"You have three days."

I stared at Yelrem. His inscrutable countenance said that any protest would fall on deaf ears. "There may be side effects."

His pause was almost imperceptible. "Three days."

I bowed my head and removed my book from its resting place.

***

The Taxonomy of Creatures, *supplemental*

Creation is no longer an act of gods. The Nemurtagumas spell, or as the aptly named Lich Grimoire had whispered, a curse for immortality, as I had warned, had needed specific syzygies or astronomical alignment of celestial objects to be fully effective. The resulting creature is no longer a faery, but something else entirely. The difficulty of the spell, though flawlessly cast by my own hand, has left me weakened. A state I have not suffered since my emergence from beneath the meteorite. Further study will reveal this new creature's aptitudes, though, at the time of this writing, only a fraction of her full powers have manifested.

"My lord?"

"Wyrmlen." I sighed. "If you truly value your position, you will take care when I am engaged. Is that clear?"

"Yes, my lord." He bowed at the waist like a marionette on a tangled string. "Very sorry my lord, but…"

I lifted my narrowed eyes to a familiar shape filling my library doorway. Wyrmlen's kowtowing attempted to redirect my wrath toward the returned guest. His masquerade flickered as if it were increasingly difficult for him to conjure. Or was it I, having been in their realm and felt their magics, that the faery's glamour had little effect on. "Wyrmlen, since you've failed to announce our visitor…" I held my gaze on Yelrem's servant, seeing him for what he truly was. "Tell me what you see."

"My lord?"

"Announce our guest as per your current position."

"Yes… my lord, the gentleman… messenger from… with his queen's…" Wyrmlen stumbled, looking behind to find the appropriate words for information not gathered.

"Tell me *what* you see, Wyrmlen."

His gaze bounced between the faery and his master, confusion overtaking his face. "He's the man who'd called on you near a month ago, my lord."

"A man indeed." I allowed a smile to escape. "Bring tea for our guest, and honey. I understand your kind has a sweet tooth." The faery closed his eyes and bowed his respects.

"Right away, my lord."

Wyrmlen's plodding footfalls disappeared down the hallway as the faery and I stared at one another. "You may enter, messenger, assuming you bring word from your master."

"I do, my lord." The messenger folded his

hands, holding his position in the doorway.

"A tribute for the coordination of your new monarch, perhaps?"

"Would it be so, my lord."

"What, then. Speak so that I may return to my studies."

"Master Yelrem thanks you for your assistance in our cause. He understands now the… consequences of your unheeded warnings. The unfortunate side effects have proven… unprecedented."

"Speak plainly, messenger."

"My master wishes for you to reverse what has been done."

I retrieved my pen and lowered my gaze back to my journal. "The spell cannot be undone, only transferred."

"And how would that be, sir?"

I glared at him over the top of my book. "Transferal would leave you without a queen."

"I see." His eyes dropped; shoulders hunched. "If there were a way—"

"Your library."

"My lord?"

I lowered my eyes back into my book. "The cost to reverse the spell is your people's entire library."

"I'm not sure—"

"Yelrem told you, at any cost, did he not?"

The faery straightened his stance. "He did."

"Then your library is now forfeit. After its relocation to my citadel, I will research a feasible solution."

"My lord, I must protest—"

"Then you do so at your own peril." My glare drilled through the messenger's last trace of resolve. "Orchestrate the transport within a week. And inform Yelrem, the research will take time!"

CHAPTER 9
Family of Stone

The merriment from the night before had been short-lived, as was anyone's rest. The undying would return and preparations for a renewed battle demanded to be made. Paracel had a new champion in Shyloh, and after several long, disquieted nights, a seed of hope. Hope, however, wouldn't conjure an antidote to bring Ashyr back from a slow death. At first light, as arrows were restocked, and the bodies of the dead burned, Guilder and Ryleigh hazarded back into the Belt.

Only a few ingredients Breya had said. The most critical coming from the Faery queen herself, the poison of her royal jelly, converted to Ashyr's cure. Shyloh would stay in Paracel and defend the town against more attacks from the undying, much to the dissatisfaction of everyone, including Breya. Ryleigh and Guilder would seek the antidote from the Faery queen.

"And how in the nine realms are we supposed to find her?" Ryleigh had argued. "A faery's keep is near invisible to non-faery and accidentally stumbling on it will only get us captured, or worse."

"You'll find a way," Breya responded. "If not, don't bother coming back for Ashyr."

Silence fell over the cabin. Ryleigh stormed out; Guilder followed. Without a word, a pair of fresh horses were gathered and prepared for a return ride north. Spurring her horse onward as soon as she'd finished tightening her saddle, Ryleigh trotted on ahead. Shyloh, in uncharacteristically reserved tones, handed Guilder a full canteen and wished them a fruitful journey.

"Be safe," Guilder told her, promising they'd return with the antitoxin.

Shadows bowed to the morning sun as the land shrunk back into the isthmus choke point. Ryleigh's bearing remained tight, her breath, quick and shallow as the safety of Paracel's barricade was left far behind. Plums of black, oily smoke rose behind them as the stench of burning corpses lingered. Guilder followed a horse's length behind, replaying the last moments before their ride began. Their horses' resolve wavered as they approached the Belt, far too aware of what might happen, their rider's own hesitation, and the smell of blood, strikingly fresh.

"Guess we walk from here," Guilder said as the horses refused to venture further. Ryleigh replied with a tight-lipped nod, releasing her horse with a slap to its hindquarters, coaxing them back the way they'd come before wordlessly trudging into the Belt.

"Is there a plan to find this Faery queen or do we improvise like last time?"

Ryleigh shrugged and marched on in silence. Near an hour and no signs of life for kilometers. Her head leaned into her stride, hand clutched to the hilt of a double-edged beast of a great sword, the scabbard trailing down to her ankle. No longer willing to be the object of her silent rage, Guilder adjusted his broadsword's scabbard at his hip, drank greedily from his canteen, and sighed out his frustration. "I assume you're just worried about Ashyr, but if I've offended you—"

"Don't," Ryleigh said, rounding on him, the tip of her sword pointed at his chest. "Just don't." She sheathed her sword and stuck up a warning finger in punctuation, turned, and marched on. A few steps later, she turned again. "Just what is your game here?"

Guilder shuffled a step back, his eyes wide. "Excuse me?"

"Somehow you've glommed yourself on to Shyloh—"

"I haven't glommed on to anyone."

"—dragging us over this whole damned continent—"

"I certainly haven't dragged anyone anywhere."

"—with this asinine claim of surviving a memory eater, of all things. And for some reason—"

"I did survive that memory eater."

Ryleigh took a step toward Guilder, eyes narrowed. "—For some reason, you're recognized as the heir apparent to the Aurora throne. Why is that?"

Guilder broke his gaze and stared off into the horizon. He shook his head, jaw clenched. "I don't know," he whispered.

"Memory eater venom doesn't last more than a day." Ryleigh took another step toward

Guilder. "How did you end up in that cave in the first place?"

Guilder stayed silent, forcing his eyes elsewhere.

"Then there's your magic." She slapped her palms into Guilder's chest, pushing him back another step. "Who schooled you in metal magics?"

"I don't know," he said, eyes misty, refusing to look at her.

"You cast spells no one else can. Who taught you?"

"I don't know."

"Who?!"

Guilder felt his body tighten. "I don't fucking know!"

Ryleigh's eyes narrowed to mere slits as she took a step back, her hand instinctually around her sword.

Guilder loosened his clenched teeth, his fists, and took a deep, cleansing breath. He softened his gaze and looked at Ryleigh, his lips pressed together. "I don't understand how I—" He squeezed his eyes shut against the sting of threatening tears, pushed the emotion down, and gasped for another breath. "How I can do these things." He ventured again to meet Ryleigh's quizzical eyes. "I can't say why I don't remember. All I know is I don't."

Ryleigh straightened from her stance, easing her hand from the hilt.

"In the cave, I remember trembling so hard it hurt and not being able to stop." Guilder shook his head, letting out a calming breath.

"My body, frozen against action, frozen to stone. Eyes constantly watching. I was weak... so weak. Not only from what that thing had done to me but... I was a coward. Just sat there and did nothing. So much like a pathetic child, alone and helpless." Tears flowed freely, chilling rivulets carved down his stubbled face, his neck. "My sword lay an arm's length away, unused for however long I was there." He turned away, jaw tight, eyes fixed on the horizon. "I will never feel that small again."

Ryleigh flexed her sword hand and massaged her upper arm, the overtaxed muscle. "I've known that feeling." Her eyes fell away from Guilder, distant. "I... I've known that feeling." She let the silence grow between them before turning to wander onward. Guilder picked up a step behind her. "Maybe I get why you're here. Shyloh's a convenient alternative after being so afraid... and so alone."

"And being hunted by Da'Kar... for as long as I could remember, which wasn't long." Guilder sipped from his canteen. "She was a friendly face after that cave. Invited me into her camp, offered me food. Now she's trying to help me regain what I'd lost. If she hadn't been at the base of that hill, I'm not sure what I would have done."

"The two of you met as you escaped the cave?" Ryleigh's eyes narrowed again.

"I must have been a nightmarish sight, covered in that creature's blood, cut and bruised, hanging onto my broadsword like some murdering lunatic."

"And she was just waiting there?"

"Camping, yes. She had some spider wasps she'd caught."

"You should know something about Shyloh." Ryleigh tightened her lips and shook her head. "The only time that woman does anything, it's to benefit herself."

"Why do you stick with her, then?"

Ryleigh let out a remorseful sigh, her gaze straining from their path.

"If she's so self-interested, why would you—"

"She makes me strong," Ryleigh interrupted, her tone soft, introspective, her melancholy face unchanged.

"You seem pretty strong on your own," Guilder said, cracking a congenial smile.

Ryleigh turned her eyes toward him with a hint of a smile in return. "It's probably a story for a different time." For a few paces, they walked on with only the ominous sounds of the marsh between them. "I had already… been strong," Ryleigh said, breaking the silence. "But Shyloh, she made me feel it. It wasn't just the schemes or the thrill of it all. She let me be a part of it. Ashyr too, I suppose. She'd always had this way of bringing out the most in people. Their unique skills, whether it was magic or… otherwise. In the end, you find out the only reason she helped you be so strong is that she needed you that way." Ryleigh's smile faded back to despondency. "Her schemes wouldn't have worked any other way. How did you learn the memory eater's name?"

"Shyloh told me. But what you're saying doesn't seem like the same Shyloh I'd met. She was kind, offered me food, and help with my memories. Taught me some magic."

"Hmm… that's Shyloh, all right. It's part of her trap. She douses the shackles with honey, hiding her stinger as best she can. If she was waiting at the base of that hill, then she probably put you in that cave." Ryleigh's ears perked up. She stared out into the moors, searching.

"For what possible reason would she—"

Ryleigh thrust her hand in front of Guilder. "Shut up," she whispered. "There's something out there."

"Faery? Like last time—" Guilder's words choked off as a silk band wrapped tight around his throat, his mouth, his eyes. He scratched at his face. Tugged at the slick edge of the band. Fought for every breath, as if drowning in fabric. He fell to his knees. The unforgiving plank road sent shards of pain into his knees, radiating up his thighs.

Muffled sounds of his own gasping breath mixed with Ryleigh fighting off her assailants. Metal arrowheads tinked off hardened skin like hammers off anvils. The restraints, suffocating.

"Guilder!" Her screams faded into the distance as consciousness slipped away.

***

The throne was ill-fitting, comfortable though it was with its tufted garnet red seat and contoured gilded wood back. It simply fit wrong. Like a sense of foreboding deep in one's bowels. His wrists and arms were secured with royal purple silk, strong as tempered steel, holding him fixed against the throne's fabric armrests. His bare feet remained cemented to the dais, his head immobile with hemp rope stretched taut around his neck and his forehead. Twisted fibers rubbed his skin raw as they held him against the throne.

Guilder looked out through an imposter's face. An automaton mimicking a living prison. His court consisted of unfamiliar barons and lords, their ladies dressed in formal attire, murmuring between themselves behind golden animal masks: panthers, apes, crocodiles, mountain lions, coyotes, and snakes. Their collective gaze set on him, the buzz of their gossip as chittering birds, static and nonsensical.

The court horseshoed around a lone knight. Shyloh's feminine-shaped armor gleamed over a fire-red arming doublet accented with a woven lamé sash the darkened black of dried blood. Her amber eyes, vacant, onyx hair braided into a bullwhip. A hissing cat ornamented the corner of her pauldron and chest plate. A helm, held beneath her arm, plumed with crow's feathers, black as the fletching in her full quiver. Held over her non-dominant shoulder, a long bow. Peculiar glyphs of a more ancient time were carved along its limbs, glowing blue.

"Why didn't I kill you?" Shyloh said, more a statement than a question, with no discernible emotion.

Guilder choked on his sandpaper-like restraints. His lungs and throat lashed out, screaming without breath, unable to give music to his terror or this nightmare.

"You did," Guilder's voice answered as if from far

off.

A hand fell to his bare shoulder. Stone-like and cold, yet gentle and caring. Guilder's head turned. The rope cut into his neck as blood lubricated the movement. Framed at the mouth of a black stone cave, Ryleigh stood only an arm's length away; her auburn hair adorned with pink and white wildflower chains, her eyes gleaming as bright as a smile. She ignored the gash across her throat as blood painted her neck and soaked into her fine lace gown, eclipsing the pure white with red gore.

"Prisimink ka esk, ka tu esk." *A hollow voice, so familiar, echoed from behind. He searched for the owner as he pulled against his restraints. His binds pulled back, the throne swallowing him, wrenching him again into the dark. Disembodied, he fell, splashing into the damp chill of unforgiving ground. His body, broken, as he lay helpless, afraid. Blinding light emerged from far above. Guilder shielded his eyes as smoke filtered through the sun's rays, accumulating as dew on his bare skin and along the granite floor.*

Torches ignited with green-blue flame, encircling Guilder and illuminating an ancient, gnarled tree. The face of an old man, a king, pushed through grizzled, charred bark. Eyes narrowed, face wrinkled in disgust as the king tree stared into Guilder. The tree whispered silently, spitting out green flames. Its face pinched all the more for the effort. The fire hit Guilder as a glacial wave, his body trembling from the shock.

"Wake up," the king tree shouted, spitting more icy flames at Guilder. An all-encompassing mist descended, covering the torches, the light, the tree. Once again, Guilder was swallowed in darkness.

"Wake up!" a deep musical voice called from far away, followed by a freezing surge of muddy-tasting water crashing over Guilder's shivering body. He opened his eyes. His dripping hair melded into the hay-strewn stone floor. Guilder held his hand in the direction the voice had emanated, warding off another wave of dirty water.

"Human, you alive?" the voice asked.

"Aye." Guilder scraped his hand down his dripping face. "Where in hell am I?" His throat felt raw, gravelly, as he rubbed his inflamed neck.

"They're awake." The musical voice had moved off. "Tell Yelrem."

"Guilder?" Another voice, closer, more feminine yet less musical. "Guilder."

"I'm here. Still alive, apparently," Guilder coughed. He pushed himself up, taking in his new surroundings. "Ryleigh? You all right?"

"I'm somewhat difficult to kill. You, on the other hand... I thought they'd—" Ryleigh snuffed back her words. "I'm glad you're okay."

"Me too." Guilder lifted himself to his hands and knees. Coughed out his dry sandpaper throat, spitting out blood and mucus onto the damp floor. He rolled over onto his backside, stretching out his stiff muscles, and leaned against the back wall. "Where are we?"

"Underground."

Guilder's tiny six-meter square platform sat bound by two coal-black rock walls forming the back half of his cage. A semitransparent shield, like a shimmering curtain of water, flowed from a craggy ceiling into a shallow moat surround, separating him from Ryleigh and what seemed a larger open room beyond.

"Their castle wasn't half a dozen kilometers through the moors," Ryleigh said as Guilder struggled to his feet to examine the shield barrier between them. "Glamoured, my guess. It didn't even come into focus until we'd passed the portcullis."

Guilder poked a finger into the barrier stream, pulling it back with a shock. "Can you make out anything from where you are? A way out of here?" He took a step back, placed a hand on the stone wall opposite the barrier, and tested his footing.

"No," Ryleigh sighed. "The barrier makes it impossible to see. All the colors meld together like I'm behind a waterfall. I can see glistening movement beyond, but nothing recognizable."

With a lowered shoulder, Guilder charged the shield, bouncing off with a mule kick jolt, sending him flying into the rock wall behind.

"And I wouldn't try busting through it, either," Ryleigh continued. "It delivers a considerable punch. Some kind of energy manipulation, lightning or something..." Her voice trailed off.

Guilder picked himself up, bending to a squat, cupping his hands in front. "*Summoneie metelas spy—*"

"And don't try casting any spells." Guilder shook his incantation off mid-word. "Fae magic has unique properties all its own. Wouldn't want to chance a recoil, not with the shit I've seen you do."

Guilder took a seat against the wall nearest to Ryleigh's cell. "What do you suggest, then? We just wait?"

"Not much more we can do." Ryleigh's voice came through the shimmering barrier as if she'd moved closer as well.

Guilder let out a frustrated sigh and leaned his head against the hard stone. "So, what happened out there?"

"After they did... whatever they did to you, I fought them off as best I could. Frankly, I thought they'd killed you. They surrounded me, told me if I didn't surrender, they'd finish you off." A long silence followed. "I'm sorry, Guilder, I... I was just so angry at Shyloh, her stupid schemes." She sniffed back her quiet sobs. "I took it out on you, and... I guess it got us caught."

"It isn't your fault."

Ryleigh sniffed again. "I never said it was."

Guilder nodded in his empty cell. "We'd been taken by surprise. Why didn't you use your magic?"

"I don't use magic." Her voice subdued, followed by a few more sniffs.

"You haven't learned how?"

"I just don't, is all."

"Oh. I didn't know."

"I don't... I don't talk about it much. Not with people I... not with very many."

Guilder listened to the rustle of the barrier

wall, steady, like a stream weaving through gravel. "Well... I have nowhere to go."

Silence. Then, "I used to use magic. Earth magic." Her soft voice, as if she'd turned away, mingled with the babbling shield. "They called me a prodigy... once."

"What happened?"

Ryleigh sniffed again. "I was sent to study with an Archmagician at a Gaean temple. A cruel man, Master Lusoren." Her tone traded sadness for disdain. "That bastard was never satisfied." She took a breath, steadying her voice. "The pain he'd inflict... I was fourteen and angry, full of myself like all stupid kids are. Still, I couldn't help but feel weak. Even with all his training, he kept me feeling weak." She took another long breath. "So, I snuck into his library and found an earth spell that would keep him from hurting me, to make me strong."

After a long silence, Guilder asked, "Did it?"

"It did. I never met the sting of his Bo staff again."

"So, it worked out?"

"Not really." Ryleigh sighed. "When he found out I stole his spell, he was livid. He challenged me to a duel, for the right to stay or live or... I wasn't even sure. He was relentless. Would've killed me, most likely. He used his magics in conjunction with his martial artistry. There was no one better. Certainly wasn't me. I took his eye, though."

Guilder matched her smile. "I still don't

understand. If you'd been that good, why not use magic?"

"Well, that spell made me strong, near-indestructible, or so I believed. Still do, I guess. That jackass managed to drop two house-sized boulders on top of me. Only way he could keep me down."

"And?"

"And it took… it took away my ability to feel."

"What do you mean? You're the most sensitive person I know."

"Thanks, I think. No, I mean, the spell took away all my bodily sensations. I don't sense any physical pain, may never again. But, I'll never get the chance to enjoy the cool midnight breeze on my skin or the warmth of the sun…" Her voice quieted. "Or the touch of someone I care for… the touch of anyone." Ryleigh stayed silent for a time, adding, "My last memory of anything was that sanctimonious prick's staff across my bare back."

"I'm sorry, Ryleigh. I didn't know."

"Yeah, well… so, what about you? Any changes on the memory front?"

"Maybe. After I passed out, I had the weirdest dream. I think it was about my father—"

The barriers to the cells lowered with the sound of distant rolling thunder. Guilder glanced over to Ryleigh, who met his gaze, wiping lingering tears from her cheeks.

"Humans," a faery guard called. "Lord Yelrem will see you."

CHAPTER 10
Master Iven Lusoren
Generation Five

I stood at the center of their courtyard; Order of the Fallen Star, indeed. Their temple, built in the Shamon Bluffs, deep in the Crystal Mountains, in the very shadows of my tallest tower, as if their conspiring could elude me. These anarchists recruited children for campaigns beyond reasonable understanding.

"Your temple was quite well hidden." A dozen monks lay behind me, unconscious, perhaps worse. "Wrongly believing yourselves past my reach."

"These are sacred grounds," another monk said. His fellow warriors stood fearful, seeing their brethren beaten so effortlessly. "You are not welcome—"

"Sacred to whom? What deity is worshiped here? Or is it what I believe and your training for battle, for revolt?"

Silence from the monk. He stood, backed by two others clad in gold, atop the carved stairs. Guarding a sanctum behind. They wore a student's uniform: long garments overlaying the hip and a pair of loose pants tied with a braided rope belt, tasseled at the ends. "Our beliefs are our own."

"Your beliefs are of little interest to me. What I seek is your diviner. He's taken near a generation to identify, as such, courtesy dictates he be present."

The monk in brown hesitated. "There are no prophets here."

"Missing from the sky, the hawk devours the angel of black light. Struck down by the venom of the martyred."

"These words mean nothing to us, Necromancer. Here are only pupils of the *kovu mentai*. Hunt your seer elsewhere."

A vain smile grew unfettered and beyond my resolve to stop it. "So, you do know who I am."

"We do." An old monk pushed through the other three. "Lord Andorian Iks, the Necromancer from the North." A white leather eyepatch covered the right side of his grizzled face, matching his silken robes. He held an etched metal Bo staff, used as a walking stick as it clunked off the stone stairs. "This temple was hidden so these students could be one with nature, one with their own powers."

"I've allowed you your freedoms. Your recruitment, however, robs from my workforce."

"A workforce that invokes the wrath of this world. Surely you see this, the land continually turning to salt around your own citadel. Your people having to move further from your grasp if only to feed themselves." The white monk moved to the base of the stairs, his stance open, inviting, yet cautious. "Your powerful magics are known throughout these lands, only they corrupt you."

"The only corruption in these lands is an abomination of power never intended for human consumption!"

The monk took a step forward. "And yet you've harnessed this power yourself. Felt its pull, its seduction. The only difference between us is we choose to revel with the natural magics while you—"

"Have grown beyond."

More students flooded from the temple beyond. Dressed in gray, each had an unembellished short bow slung over their shoulder, a quiver at their back. They surrounded the courtyard, removing the bodies of their fallen, and stood along the outskirts of the courtyard.

"We believe otherwise. One of my own students, in fact, chose this unnatural path and became one of my greatest failings."

"Then you were a poor master."

"I was. She was a most gifted student, but her lust for power cost her far more than my eye."

I gazed around at the young men and women surrounding me. Muscles tense like a dam holding back the raging water beyond, only to be given outlet for release.

"Missing from the sky, the hawk devours the angel of black light. Struck down by the venom of the martyred," I recited, eyes turning to the monk in white. "Brandishing his five claws. As alms to earth are stolen, then returned, so shall the hawk be divided by the serpent, buck, and lion. Produce the one who foretold my demise, or I will return this temple to the rubble it erupted from."

The white monk's half smile worked its way into his one good eye. "You have no authority here, Sorcerer. We are under the protection of King Æthelred Rayne of Aurora. Our freedoms are given by him who rules this land."

"Yes, the impotent king who shares this continent with his enemies, ripped at the center, as he grows fat with inactivity."

"The crown prince is set to wed a Republic heiress and end the Allenrude Pacts, reuniting the continent."

"Your politics are irrelevant. I rule these lands and no king or monk dare defy me. You will surrender your prophet and pray that my benevolence doesn't wipe all memory of you and your students from this existence."

The monk bowed his head. "Our elders have yet to discern its full meaning, although I divined the prophecy, knowing what's to come. I wish I hadn't." He stiffened his posture, holding his staff in defense. Within a blink, bows stretched taught, arrowheads pointed to the center courtyard. "Diplomacy has not been one of your strengths. For your insult to this monastery, I'll fulfill your regrettable interpretation."

The first arrow loosed with a low baritone timbre. Sandals scraped off stone, following a symphony of bowstrings. An arc of my arm, the words held in my mind, turned shafts to char as they approached. Heat shimmered in the air around me as metal arrowheads fell at my feet.

The white monk rushed forward. My wrists crossed, warding off his advance. Glaring white sparks leaped from the diminutive space between us, obscuring the monk's ardent gaze. Bows stretched taut. The words bolted from my lips faster than lightning.

I shoved the monk back. The force landed him near the base of the staircase while he held his staff parallel to the ground to center his balance. I swept two fingers around my periphery. A blue dragon's tongue whipped around me, breaking bows and strings, cutting wrists, knees, abdomens, and ankles. A chorus of pained screams emanated from the courtyard. The white monk narrowed his eye and ground his teeth.

A sickly thunk sounded from behind. Fire burst from the base of my shoulder. I pulled the shaft from my back, buried only half an arrowhead deep into my flesh, and turned my gaze to the trembling boy gone numb. His pants, piss-soaked, bow empty. I gathered my spilled blood, frozen into a shard, and hurled it forward only to shatter off the white monk's metal staff. With a snap, the boy's hands grasped at his throat, breath failing him as I returned my gaze forward.

"Damn you, Necromancer." The white monk stood and gaveled his staff, producing a curved glaive to one end. "Leave now, while you still can."

I straightened my stance, ignoring his taunt, and crossed my arm over the opposite wrist, holding it forward like a one-man phalanx as goosebumps erupted from my skin. The monk arched his sandaled foot along the dirt-strewn courtyard, his staff held at arm's length. A breeze swirled around him. Bolstered to a wind, lifting sand and pebbles, strengthening into a rock-laden tornado. Its conical head leaned into its rush. A million stone blades scoured my near-invisible ice shield.

Scrapes and gouges cloaked hate-filled eyes deep in his waning vortex. A final lunge buried his glaive to the center of my defense. Stopped, millimeters from cleaving my sternum, I stepped back, words already flowing through my mind. A slight twist sent cracks throughout the frozen armor, shattering it like sheet glass in a tempest.

At my periphery, lanterns along the courtyard wall burst to life. I held out my fist, the opposite hand grasping the elbow as blue-white tongues snaked together between us. The white monk stretched out his arms. Thunder sounded in the near distance as if the mountain had cracked in half. On staunch legs, my fire took form. A hulking golem shrieked against its hellish existence, belching ash and magma at the monk's feet.

A fiery mace formed in the golem's hand as it lumbered forward. The monk held his ground, bringing his fists together, one over the other as a hollow hissing sounded outside the temple, pulling my attention from my creation. The golem raised its mace as a mammoth limestone boulder extinguished it from existence. Bones in my outstretched wrist shattered from the impact. I lowered my uninjured hand, pushing into the air as a second boulder crashed where I'd stood.

Pained and enraged by the effort, I clapped my hands above my head, thrusting my arms down to bring lighting ripping through the cloud-filled sky, striking the screaming monk. His half-ready spell fizzled out of his hand as his crumpled body steamed from the jolt. I gathered the dispersed energy into a sparking blade, slicing through his body, shoulder to hip.

I stood over the white monk, robes now largely a dark crimson, his labored breath betraying his anger as life began to fade. "When I was reborn into this world," I told the dying monk. "Magic had already corrupted humankind." All around the courtyard, fallen limbs were left with the dead. The school crumbled into ruins, deserted but for one. "I'd assumed that others could hear the unfamiliar words whispered out of nowhere." The last boy appeared trampled by his fleeing classmates yet continued to gasp for air.

This seemed the mark of this unnatural power. My unchecked rage drew it out like an addict in relapse. "As I explored this… altered world, I realized some were more skilled than others." I dragged the boy through the rubble and laid him next to his master. "Not everyone could hear, but all had promise. Yet promise without guidance is wasteful." I released the block that held the master's breath. He gulped greedy lungfuls of air, his eyes fixed on me, trembling. "Your teachings may be of some benefit to me," I told the monk, whose questioning look pained him even more.

"There is a sickness in this world. One I intend to remedy."

Grasping the boy's leg, I felt my weariness disperse. "As with many ailments, the proper procedure is needed before cancer may be cut from the body. Only then can healing begin." Clutching the master's attached leg, I healed his wounds enough to support his life. "Until that discovery, we seem reduced to leaching and bleedings."

Standing, I gazed into the temple, its library, dusty though intact. "I've spent countless years collecting the accounts of various peoples, their divinations, incantations, alchemy, sorcery, conjurings, necromancy; their magics." I traced a finger along a dusty stack, leaving a snake's trail behind. Lusoren's breath came heavy, gasping. I shifted my gaze back to the beaten monk. "With the accrual of such wealth and, as you've pointed out, the… shifting political environment, I require someone with skills to be both liaison and librarian."

Our eyes met as I looked down on him. Hate, the shame of his defeat, and… something I didn't quite recognize eddied at the corners of his one remaining eye. Envy, maybe? "The journey to my citadel is long, Master Lusoren. For you, it will not be pleasant." I turned to leave and grant him one last memory of his shattered temple. I craned my neck back to the beaten monk. "I presume that in defeat you are no longer considered a master. For your efforts, I'll offer the smallest concession and merely call you Iven."

CHAPTER 11
Lord Yelrem

The faery guard escorted Guilder and Ryleigh out of the stockade, through a narrow bulkhead embedded in the rock face. His lean form stood a head taller than either of them. Overly long arms and glistening alabaster skin gave him a gangly appearance vastly different from the covert soldiers they'd battled in the marsh days before. A sheer forest-green tunic lay on him like chiffon, accentuating a sinewy body beneath. He held an ashwood spear with a leaf-shaped blade, its silver ferrule tapped out his fluid movement with each step of his bare feet.

The first guard's twin secured the prison door, then fell in line behind the group. After climbing several flights of carved stone stairs, the dull black rock gave way to polished marble, gold accentuating the widening runs and curved archways. Stories above, a cloud-filtered late-day sun shone through a domed skylight, casting red-orange hues over the veined white marble stairwell.

Their group exited into an extended hallway, arched ceilings and walls colored a winter white, carpets in deep umbers with green vine adornments with pale amethyst blossoms dotting the curled ends. Countless rooms scanned the hall to either side as carved round top doors carried a touch of nature in their ornate construction.

The lead escort stopped partway down the hall, opened a random door, and held his palm upright as an invitation to enter.

"What's all this about?" Guilder asked.

The faery's hands clasped impatiently around his staff, an overlong index finger tapping against the weapon. "I was informed humans knew what a bath was." His eyes narrowed as his ethereal voice mocked the authoritative stance.

Guilder clenched his teeth. Surely, this guard heard what he was capable of. Heard what he'd done to his kind. If they planned to separate him from Ryleigh, torture them, or worse, he would have some lethal words for them.

Ryleigh took a deep breath, stuck out her chin, and walked into the room, giving the faery a sideways glance as she passed. The guard held out his hand as Guilder tried to follow, pointed to his comrade, then followed Ryleigh inside, closing the door with a final snide look at Guilder.

Guilder shook his head, echoing Ryleigh's sigh before entering the room next door. Hesitation yielded to awe as he took in the space. A forest oasis sparkled with sunlight bouncing off a central grand pool. Bubbling waterfalls flowed between palm trees, blending with birdsong and the blue sky beyond. White sand encircled the pool while dragonflies encroached upon amber-colored reeds. To one side, a gold leaf-shaped faucet filled a polished marble basin with crystal clean water. A dark wood accent chair, carved to match the organic landscape, sat beside the pool holding a tower of plush bathing towels.

Guilder marveled at the landscape. He knelt by the pool, dipped a hand into the clear, cool water, and took in the reflected picturesque vista. He closed his eyes, breathed deep the scents of citrus and lilies, and tightened his jaw. "There is nothing here but lies."

He stared into the rippled image, rage simmering beneath a cold façade. His hands and lips were dry as ash, his hair greasy with sweat. His face, an unrecognizable nest of mud-caked whiskers from being dragged though the moors. Guilder lifted himself to stand in front of the marble sink, letting the warm water trickle through his fingers. As the dust and grime washed from his hands and clean water filled the basin, his glance flitted toward the guard.

The faery's eyes remained blank, a mingling of purples and blues, pinks, and grays. Yet his stare passed to a point beyond the display.

"I'd prefer not to be trapped in some faery's imaginings," Guilder said through his teeth.

The faery considered Guilder for a moment before refitting his absent stare. "The illusion is for your comfort. Take advantage of it. I assure you, your friend has."

Guilder squared his shoulders, his muscles tight. He knotted his arms and bolstered his hold on the faery's unblinking glare. The guard released a held breath and extended an index finger to trace unseen symbols in the air. The bathroom oasis faltered like paint being washed away by sudden rain. "Either way, you will bathe before meeting Lord Yelrem."

Mining lanterns cast their emaciated light over moss-infested walls, spilling onto rough-hewn plank floors. Guilder let out a sigh and glared at the half-filled animal trough at the center of a near-empty chamber. The guard's appearance shifted along with the room. His height remained, as did his elongated arms. The chiffon tunic draped over his sagging muscles and brown papery skin the color of dried leaves. A flat, turned-up nose sat at the center of his angular face, only his eyes preserved the same mingling of colors from before.

Guilder undressed and bathed in the frigid water. A hessian towel was tossed onto the floor, replacing his clothes. "And what am I to wear when I meet this Lord Yelrem?" he asked, standing wet with the ineffective towel around his midsection.

The Fae guard continued to stare over Guilder's head. He pointed a bony finger at a three-legged stool in the corner of the room. Silk undergarments lay on top of a pile of neatly folded clothes. Guilder dropped his towel as he turned away from the guard. He slipped on the tan trousers and black leather boots. Buttoned the white silk shirt, ruffled at the breast. All seemed tailored to him, and everything fit eerily well.

Guilder finished dressing, leaving his hair

dripping over the back of his cobalt-blue swallowtail jacket. Its brocade gold buttons bore the familiar vines and amethyst blossoms, echoed again in the jacket's black accents. Light from the hallway leached its way into the room as the guard stood against the open door, having returned to his glamoured state. Guilder eyed the guard as he passed, unwilling to meet his glare.

The room next door opened as Guilder stepped back into the hallway. The lead faery held position as Ryleigh passed, wearing a frilled black dress covering her lace-accented boots. Her black leather corset offset silver catches, while an off-the-shoulder blouse covered her arms and dripped garnet red fabric from the wrist. The colors accentuated her alabaster skin, her auburn hair. Her smile reached into her eyes as she spotted Guilder's stare.

"You look... really... quite amazing," Guilder stammered.

Ryleigh winked at him, adding a slight curtsy. "Can't say I mind the upgrade. You as well." She traced a finger over her ear. Guilder tilted his head with a shrug and returned her smile. "Looks good, though. On you... I mean." A wave of redness overtook her face, expanding to her bare shoulders.

Guilder leaned his face close to her, his smile fading. "These clothes are definitely real. Can't attest to anything else, though."

"Last room. End of the hall," the guard behind Guilder said, his human-like hand pointing along the hallway.

Ryleigh started down the hall, whispered, "What were you saying about something not being real?" The faery guards followed close behind, paying little attention. "What's not real?"

"Everything. This castle, the cells, my bathroom. It's all a glamour."

"Of course it's a glamour. That's what faeries do. That's all faeries can do."

"I told them to stop."

"That was dumb." Ryleigh closed her eyes with a reminiscent smile. "My bath was steaming, filled with bubbles, and smelled like jasmine. I couldn't care less if it wasn't real."

"I just hate to be misled like that. It's like being lied to."

Ryleigh's smile disappeared. "Believe enough and lies become truth."

The group paused at the end of the hall, the faery guards turning their backs to an elaborate library. Guilder and Ryleigh stood at the threshold, taking in the room. Off to one side sat a massive fireplace, taller than any of the faeries they'd seen, wide as outstretched arms. Orange-yellow flames blazed in the hearth, like a dragon in the throes of a nightmare. Floor-to-ceiling shelves dominated the remainder of the room, filled with more books than any one person could read in a lifetime. At its center, a bespectacled faery sat behind a mahogany-stained writing desk. His pointed ears poked through long white hair, blending into robes draped below his feet. Pen in hand, his face stuck in a modest journal.

The aged-looking faery waved the two humans in without lifting his head.

Ryleigh glanced at Guilder as they entered. "Lord Yelr—"

Yelrem held up a finger in interruption. They stood waiting for him too, again, acknowledge their presence. He looked up, set down his pen, removed his glasses, and leaned back into his chair. He rested his sharp chin on his thumb, underlining his hawk nose with an index finger, examining the two humans standing before his desk. After a slow, thoughtful breath, he said, "You received the garments I'd sent. Good." He nodded. "And been offered a bath." He replaced his glasses and tipped his head back into his book. "I'm glad you've accepted. Humans stink worse than death." He rested his lanky arms back on the desktop. "We've had our share of death. Enough to fill a mountain-sized necropolis."

Ryleigh looked over at Guilder, who fixed his eyes on the bespectacled faery. "What do you want with us?" Guilder asked.

"Umm…" Ryleigh chuckled. "What my inarticulate friend means to say is, we're grateful for the hospitality, the clothes, and amenities, and… stuff."

"You threw us into your dungeon, then summoned us here like some interloping peasants."

"Guilder!"

Yelrem looked up from his journal, his gaze landing on Guilder, then Ryleigh. He removed his glasses, setting them in the book's crease, and took a deep breath. "You're very welcome, my dear. Both of you. *Mistfall* hasn't hosted any human in over a hundred years." He tapped the pen off its well and set it aside. Folding his hands over tented arms, he took in another steady breath. "Our two species have had a long history of… disagreement."

"That tends to happen when you kill every human who enters your marshlands," Guilder said. Ryleigh covered her eyes with her hand and shook her head.

The white-haired faery grew a half-smile. "An unfortunate symptom of our tumultuous past. Not to be overshadowed by our recent history."

Guilder turned, meeting Ryleigh's gaze, her hand resting on his forearm "What recent history?" she asked, her eyes wide, pleading. "We'd never met you before now." Guilder returned an exasperated shrug, questioning her insistent decorum.

Yelrem's smile faded to stolid coldness. "I refer to the battalion of korrigan soldiers your party killed not three days past."

"With all due respect, My Lord Yelrem." Ryleigh stepped forward. "Your soldiers attacked us. One in our party was injured. We were simply defending ourselves."

"Seven hundred eighty-two dead to your one injured." The library's air thickened in the silence. Yelrem turned his icy stare toward Guilder. "You're quite the conjurer, Guilder

Rayne."

Guilder remained silent, turning his eyes from Yelrem and avoiding Ryleigh's gaze.

"Your men... Fae, they're... quite talented at illusion," Ryleigh said attempting to steer the conversation elsewhere. "Their glamours are extremely convincing."

Yelrem turned back toward Ryleigh, his smile reappearing. "You're very kind. The Fae take pride in their phantasms, though our practice has faltered over these last few seasons in lieu of darker... less sustainable magics."

"Less sustainable, my lord?"

"The very reason that I've brought you here, under considerable peril to myself, the Fae who remain loyal to me and to our ancient heritage." He rose from his seat, gesturing to the faery standing guard outside the library. "Our queen inherited her throne only a century ago." He stretched his back, fluttered dual pairs of iridescent wings, and moved to face the blazing fire. "Far too young by many opinions, but... the monarchy, so it's believed, must endure."

Ryleigh stepped closer to the white-haired faery while Guilder took a seat on the edge of the desk, craning his neck to peer into Yelrem's journal.

"A decade before her reign, she struck a bargain with the sorcerer of the black tower, Lord Andorian Iks."

"The necromancer?" Ryleigh turned her gaze back to Guilder, who only shrugged. She pursed her lips and flicked her hand in irritation.

"The same." Yelrem turned his back to the fire. "An ill-advised arrangement, to say the very least. He granted her power over the dead. Not only our dead but the dead of all the high species. As long as there was enough flesh to reanimate."

"There's a village at the southern edge of the isthmus, Paracel." Ryleigh folded her arms as Guilder looked up from Yelrem's journal. "The undying have attacked every night for the last week. Is that your queen's doing?"

"Most assuredly. Queen Viviana wishes to inflate her territories, starting with our southern borders. Her recent dissatisfaction with the hidden isolation we've maintained for generations has led to a fracturing of ideals. The Great Expansion, she calls it." Yelrem shook his head, narrowing his purple-blue eyes at Guilder. "She thinks nothing of our dwindling numbers or the inevitability of a future unification... but I digress. Our ruling court is unwilling to remove her from power. Some fallen to corruption, themselves under the queen's thumb. A small fraction of the court proposed to enlist an outsider. One who has proven themselves formidable against our forces."

"You want me to kill your queen and put someone else in her place," Guilder said coldly apathetic.

"Ineloquent, but yes."

"If you're found as the arbiter of this coup, those who remain will put you to death."

Ryleigh moved closer to Guilder, placing a blocking shoulder between him and Yelrem.

Yelrem nodded, his sober eyes meeting her gaze. "As is our law."

"In exchange, we'll need the antidote to your Fae queen's toxin." Contempt bled from Guilder's words as he stole attention back.

Yelrem's eyes flicked to his guards. "To help your friend, yes. You'll have more than you'll need." His gaze fell back to the two humans as one of the guards departed.

Ryleigh leaned into Guilder's unwavering stare and whispered, "You can't seriously be considering this?"

"I am." Guilder fixed his gaze on the white-haired faery.

"Regicide! Guilder, you'll destroy the entire colony."

"No." Yelrem moved toward them, arms folded at his elbows. "We can maintain stability for a short time. There are enough loyal to the old ways. We'll merge with another."

"Then it's settled." Guilder held out his hand, Yelrem stepping up to take it.

"No!" Ryleigh shouted. Yelrem's glamour flickered. In a blink, the library shone empty and cold, Yelrem a crackled shell in dull browns. Then, back to what was. The fire blazed its soft light. Behind, leather-bound books stood like soldiers on their shelves, and Yelrem again looked nearly human.

"I'll have rooms made up for you and your weapons returned." Yelrem motioned toward the remaining guard. "A meeting will take time to arrange. Until then, you'll need to stay hidden," he said, a hint of a smile in his voice. He sat down behind the desk, reapplied his spectacles, and leaned back into his book. "One more thing." Yelrem's tone turned somber. "You won't be able to use your magic, not while in her presence."

"You couldn't have mentioned that before?" Guilder's fists clenched, his face tense.

"Would you have accepted if I had?"

Ryleigh's face tightened as she pushed Guilder to follow the faery guard. "Do you have any idea what you've just done?"

"I secured Ashyr's cure."

"You made a blood oath to a Fae, a Fae lord, of all people."

"Ashyr's life is all that matters."

"More than your own? More than this Fae queen, possibly this entire colony?" The guard turned an ear behind. Ryleigh balled her fists beside her, and breathed deep, regaining her calm. "You don't break promises to the Fae. They will always find justice."

***

Mistfall castle's silence lay like a death shroud over Guilder. Eyes staring into the ceiling, he listened to his soft even breath, his hands rested on his bare chest feeling his heartbeat. Thoughts played over in his mind of what may happen when he and Ryleigh stand face to face with this Fae queen. What would happen to Ashyr if they didn't?

The Fae will always find justice, Ryleigh

had said. What justice would they enact after the murder of their queen? Would it matter, knowing it was for a friend? A life for a life, such a morbid balance. His own traded for Da'Kar's, that memory thief, Ashyr's, for this Fae queen.

A restrained knock at the door disrupted his dark musings. "Guilder?" Ryleigh's hushed voice pulled him from uneasiness. The dim light from the hallway refused to follow as her shadowed form eased into the room. "You awake?"

"I am." Guilder sat up, hanging his feet off the bed, shoulders slumped forward. "Seems you are, too." The sting of her reprimand felt fresh. He wasn't keen on another argument. Certainly, he didn't need another reminder of the bargain he'd struck with Yelrem. But being alone with only his thoughts seemed worse.

"Can I come in? I couldn't sleep."

"Please." He glanced at his silk shirt and jacket hung across the dressing chair. "Come in." Shadows scurried across the floor, filling the corners of the room to escape the crackling fireplace. Cool night air crept in from the high window and danced with the fire's heat, summoning gooseflesh to rise on Guilder's arms.

Ryleigh sat on the bed beside Guilder. "I wanted to talk to you about what I said." Her soft skin brushed against his, hands at her side, matching his posture. "Earlier, about this plan you'd made."

Guilder took a slow, deep breath. "It was

all I could think to do." He stared at the unlit oil lamp on his bedside table. "No plan, really." He held his hand out toward the lantern and mouthed the words Shyloh taught him.

"Magic won't work inside the castle," Ryleigh said, placing her hand on his forearm.

Starlight reflected in the lantern's glass, the wick sparking at its end, refusing to ignite. "Yelrem said so much."

"Yelrem." Ryleigh spat. "That bastard."

"Yeah, well. I'm the one he forged the pact with." Guilder leaned over, grabbed a match from the table, and put it to the lantern. He glanced over at Ryleigh, her upturned eyes piercing. The flickering light accentuated shadows across the curves of her chemise nightdress as a sad smile spread across her face.

"So, what are you going to do?" Ryleigh asked as Guilder moved to the window.

Guilder breathed in the night air and stared out at the stars. "I have to trust Yelrem will be true to his word, that he'll arrange an audience with this Fae queen and return our weapons. Beyond that… I don't know."

Ryleigh's hands slid around Guilder's chest. She laid her head behind his shoulder, her breasts pressed against his back. "I'm scared, Guilder. I can't take any more death."

Guilder placed a hand over hers. "Ashyr's not dead yet. We still have time." He closed his eyes and breathed in her scent. The subtle vanilla of evening primrose, mixed with perspiration and… something less familiar.

"I know, but this entire scheme... what if... what if we don't make it back?"

Guilder turned to face her, his eyes questioning. "I'd never seen this side of you. You'd always seemed so... resolute."

"Hard, you mean." She brushed her fingers along his biceps. "I have my moments, lying in the dark, alone. Nothing exposes you more than a quiet room, ruminating thoughts being your only company." She kissed his shoulder, his neck, drew his face close to hers, and kissed him deeply.

Guilder licked her taste from his lips. "I wasn't aware you... felt that way." Ryleigh stepped back and sat on the bed, Guilder followed, standing above her. He brushed the back of his fingers across her jaw, down her bare arm. Her skin, like fine silk.

She smiled and closed her eyes. The lantern's flame sent light fluttering around the room. Its soft orange-white glow explored her curves, exposing her glistening form beneath the gossamer-like fabric. "I feel. Same as everyone." She gazed up at him. Her fingertips traced down his chest, the ripples of his abs, hooking into the top of his trousers.

Guilder brushed his hands across her shoulders, the thin straps of her nightdress dropping down her arms, only her breasts holding the fabric against her. She stood, permitting the dress to fall to the floor, and slinked around him. With a firm hand, she pushed Guilder back onto the bed. She pulled off his trousers, straddled him, and allowed him inside her.

Guilder clutched her hips as his heart pounded. They danced with the flickering lantern light and caressed the fitful shadows. Night winds poured into the open window, exploring the room, stirring the scents of sweat and night flowers, heavy breath, and release. Guilder squeezed his eyes closed, gasping before his body relaxed.

Warmth from the fire brushed over his bare skin, his eyes refusing to open. He reached out, finding nothing, as an unyielding weariness threatened. Had she really been here? Or was it merely a dream an expression of his untethered wants. The aroma of primrose still lingered, mingling with burning wood, smoke, and ash. "Ryleigh?" He babbled, half unconscious, darkness eventually overtaking him.

CHAPTER 12
Lord of Zombies

Like an archer, the sunlight loosed its bright arrows, striking Guilder where he slept. He crumpled his face against the morning, rubbed his temples, imploring mercy from the ache behind his skull. The lantern sat unburned beside him. His trousers, loose around his waist. The scents of vanilla, earth, and rot lingered in the room.

He sat, arms propped behind him. She *was* here, wasn't she? His sheets were wet with sweat as if a fever had broken in the night. The memory, still fresh in his mind. Had it only been a dream? A smile took root, expelled by the searing pain behind his temple.

His boots, shirt, and swallowtail jacket lay folded on the chair, accompanied by his sheathed broadsword. Its chimera inlay gleamed in the morning sun. On the chairside table sat bread and butter, cheese, and a red berry jam with a tankard of fruit juice. Guilder dressed. Positioned his scabbard, heavy at his hip. He drained the juice and grabbed the hand-sized loaf of bread before leaving the room.

Ryleigh cracked open her door just as Guilder chomped a mouthful of buttered bread. She peered out at him, eyes mere slits in their sunken hollows. "What?" she managed through a drowsy scowl.

"Good morning to you too." Guilder seeded a half-smile while finishing his last swallow of bread. "Sleep okay after you left?"

"Left what?" Ryleigh's scowl turned to irritation. "I'm not awake enough for your foolish babblings. Come back in an hour." The door closed, leaving Guilder alone in the hallway, once more questioning whether the dream was real. He knocked again.

"What, Guilder?" Ryleigh's voice sounded just to the other side of the door.

"Can I come in?"

"No! Why in the gods' names would I let you into my room? After that jackass stunt you pulled last night, you're lucky I'm even speaking to you."

Guilder took a step back, replaying what happened the night before. The pain in his temple throbbed, reminiscent of his cave prison, not weeks before. He raised his hand to knock again, thought better of it, and instead sulked back toward his own room.

"Guilder!" Ryleigh stuck her head out of the room. "Get your dumb-ass in here."

He turned and trotted back, traces of a renewed smile breaking across his face. The scent of jasmine lingered in her wake. She'd stepped back into the corner, fastening up her dress from the day before. "Don't think I'm not still pissed at you for last night," Ryleigh said, tying back her auburn hair.

"As I recall, you came to me. If I'd offended you…" Guilder sat on the edge of the bed watching Ryleigh as she tightened the braid behind her head and straightened her black leather corset.

"Whoever designed this thing should burn in the deepest parts of hell." She pulled the laces taut behind her, letting out a held breath. "Help me with these boots."

Guilder knelt to one knee, tightening and tying off her boots in military fashion. His gaze raised to meet hers. Ryleigh's hands remained clamped at her waist as she stared down at Guilder, her forehead wrinkled, eyes narrow. "Thank you." Her tone assumed anything but.

Guilder stood, not a hand's width apart from her. He took in her scent, felt her radiant heat, yet her exasperated expression remained. She stepped around him to the dressing table behind and attempted to pin up the superfluous material at her wrists. "How anyone could expect me to fight in this is beyond me. What were you saying about offending me?"

"I was talking about last night." Guilder shot back, more assertive than he'd intended. "You were—"

"The only thing that I'm *offended* about is this idiotic deal you made with Yelrem." Ryleigh turned toward Guilder, arms laced as tight as her corset. "Now, because of your... indiscretion, we have to go through with it. Other than that, we're good!"

"That's it? We're good?" Guilder ran his fingers through his hair, rubbed the back of his neck, and wiped the accruing moisture from his temple. "We're good." He nodded, whispering to himself. Ryleigh fortified her staunch position as he took a deep breath. "When you were in my room—"

A vehement knock stole Ryleigh's attention away. She cracked the door as Guilder leaned against the back wall, craning to see the human-looking faery standing in the hallway, hands to his back, apathy on his face. "Queen Viviana summons you to her court," he announced without prompt.

"Fine," Ryleigh said with a sigh. "Give us a minute." She shut the door, turning in search of her gladius.

"Ryleigh…" Guilder started. "Something happened last night."

"Yeah, you blundered us into a situation that's bound to get us bloody before we're through." She ran her hand across the leaf-shaped blade, sheathed it with a click, and searched the sides of her dress for a place to attach the scabbard.

"That's not what I mean. Something happened in my room… at least I think it happened."

Frustrated, Ryleigh slung the belt over her head. "Whatever it was, it doesn't matter." She adjusted the sword between her shoulder blades and turned her stern eyes toward Guilder. "It's time to get focused. Now let's go kill this bitch and get back to Ashyr." She crossed the room and pulled open the door, nearly colliding with the waiting Fae guard.

Guilder took a deep breath, pushed himself off the wall, and followed Ryleigh out into the hallway.

The guard led them into the bowels of the castle, sun-starved pathways smelling of earth and rot. Cells bracketed the corridors as shield walls hid prisoners behind their shimmer, reflecting dim torchlight back onto their path. At the end of the last hall, the space opened to an underground amphitheater. Near a hundred meters deep, a dozen oil-filled cauldrons lit the oval-shaped area to the stalactite-laden ceiling three stories above.

Guilder and Ryleigh walked out onto the arena floor, their Fae guard forgotten. All around them, countless unglamoured faery, the entire hive it seemed, gathered to witness their summoning. Tiered seats were filled above the high walls as sounds of dry leaves rustled throughout in raucous ovation. Wingbeats added to the din of the crowd, faery spectators proclaiming their eagerness for the upcoming sport.

The metal portcullis clanged behind as their escort disappeared back into the dark catacombs. "I'd hoped for a calm, level-headed discussion," Ryleigh said. "Maybe some tea with honey and biscuits."

"Tea will have to wait." Guilder pointed to the far end of the arena. An elevated imperial box sat overlooking the oval ring. At its center, seated on a crystalline throne, a considerably human-looking faery. She sat, legs crossed, her hands folded over her knees in a noble gesture. Her narrow jawline, sharp cheekbones, and wide-set eyes made her almost beautiful were it not for her mottled, ink-black skin and the malicious smile spilling into her eyes.

At the far end of the arena, erected to the left of the queen's box, three pillars grew from the arena's floor. On the center pillar, naked to the waist, beaten and bloody in his unglamoured state, was Lord Yelrem. To either side, the two guards who'd escorted them from the stockades. Each nailed, hands and feet, to their pillars. An iron cable-laid rope strung across their necks, looped a second time across their midsection, tendrils of smoke wafting past their faces. The smell of burning flesh permeated the arena. Shimmering blue blood dripped onto Yelrem's face from a pair of incandescent wings nailed above his head. His outstretched fingers appeared to reach for them, longing for them to be reattached to his body.

Ryleigh covered her mouth, hands holding in her shock. Guilder pulled his sword and pointed it toward the Fae queen. Boisterous applause exploded from the crowd. Queen Viviana's smile widened. Beside her, a faery crier stood up, prompting the crowd to silence.

"Before you stand a pair of outsiders, humans accused not only of the unprovoked massacre of two full battalions of our brothers and sisters but of conspiring with the usurper Lord Cirrus Yelrem in an assassination attempt against your sovereign queen." The coliseum boomed with profanity, vulgarities directed at Yelrem and at the two lone humans.

The crier held up his hands, hushing the crowd. "Your queen has offered you sport.

Entertainment for her fellow Fae, in the guise of the wretched humans' deaths at the hand of her majesty's horde."

The crowd remained silent. A hiss of dissented whispers and murmurs crept across the arena. The crier turned toward Viviana. Her smile diminished to a scowl as he raised his hands again, prompting a resurgence of cheers. "At your leisure, my queen." He bowed, retreating into the shadows behind the throne.

Viviana stared into Guilder, a lascivious smile reappearing as needles burrowed their way into his temple. He winced at the pain, fighting it with clenched teeth, his eyes squeezed shut.

"You okay?" Ryleigh unsheathed her gladius, tossing its loose scabbard beside her. "Guilder, I need you with me."

"I'm here." He pressed his palm against his forehead. Readying his own sword. "I think that witch might have done something to me."

"Will it keep you from fighting whatever's coming?"

Guilder lowered himself into a fighting stance. Pain pushed back, his longsword held out in front. "No."

Viviana scanned the overflowing arena, the mixture of praise and silent resistance. She listed her head behind, acidly nodding for her cowering crier to begin the entertainment.

He stepped forward and took in a deep breath, yelling, "Release the horde!"

The crowd roared as five of the six gates throughout the arena ratcheted open.

Guilder stepped back-to-back with Ryleigh.

"Any sage advice before we start?"

"Don't die."

The first of the undying shuffled through the archway just left of the three crucified faery. It studied the two humans, swords bared. Contemplated the quieted, awestruck crowd, the high walls. It tilted its head, baring a mouthful of ragged, decayed teeth. A hellish scream arose from deep in its gullet before taking off at a full sprint toward Guilder.

With his sword raised above his head, Guilder took a deep, calming breath. He swung the blade down, slicing through the creature's neck, separating its head and left shoulder from the rest. Its tar-like blood splattered over Guilder's body and oozed down his arms, down the length of his sword. As the body slumped at his feet, the crowd erupted with cheers.

"Here they come," Ryleigh shouted over the din. Her voice, composed and focused.

The gateways flooded with snarling faces, bodies hunched over, ravenous, predacious. From every direction they came, countless reanimated dead. Like stampeding horses, they raced toward the two gladiators. Guilder swung his blade, taking limbs and heads two, three at a time. He pressed toward the nearest arena opening, each belching more and more dead into the ring.

Where the first of the undying had entered, Guilder located the portcullis release. The gate slammed shut, crushing several of the creatures beneath its metal tines. Black mottled arms reached through the lattice, unable to grab or rip or tear. Guilder turned from the closed gate, glancing over to Ryleigh before heading for the next.

Ryleigh swung her razor-sharp blade, separating heads from necks and limbs from their owners, spilling rotted entrails with every swing. A voracious undying soldier clung to her back, gnawing, straining to bite through her unyielding skin. She seized it by a dangling leg and hurled it into the arena wall, leaving a greasy black stain where it hit.

The arena floor ran thick with bodies, crowded at its near end. More undying struggled to push their way in, pressing against a growing wall of corpses, snapping jaws and ravaged fingers cresting the pile. Guilder hurried toward the opening near where he and Ryleigh had entered. Three dozen more zombies fell to his sword, slashed through at the neck, the head, the face. Guilder leaped toward the nearest cauldron, its bright yellow flame stretching from its surface. Momentum forced the cauldron over, crushing a half dozen undying beneath, spilling its contents along the arena floor.

The flaming oil spread through the horde. Bodies combusting like dried kindling, a forest fire of screaming corpses. Their withered skin and flailing arms caught their neighbor and their neighbor's neighbor alight. The lamp oil flowed into the catacombs as screams of the burning dead echoed throughout the arena.

Two rear entrances, now blocked by fire and blazing undying. On her side of the arena,

Ryleigh lowered the last rear portcullis, cutting several squirming bodies in half, her designs on another cauldron. A dozen creatures close on her heels, Guilder rushed past, swinging into the oncoming hoard, taking off four heads, and lodging his blade into a fifth's skull.

The crowd cheered as Guilder freed his sword. His boot pushed against still-clamping jaws as he turned to find his next target. Ryleigh chopped at the supports of a nearby cauldron. Another writhing soldier clung to her back, biting at her neck. Its bony hands scraped across her face, her eyes. She felled the leg of the cauldron, adding its contents to the swelling inferno, cutting off the remaining entrance and another wave of screaming dead.

Turning her back from the flames, Ryleigh swung her sword in a long, flat arch, cutting a trailing undying at the midsection. At her back, teeth cracked off her cold stone-like neck, its legs dangling into the fire, catching it and Ryleigh's dress alight. Blue-yellow flames lapped up her back as she thrust the sword tip through another onrushing undying's temple. Running to the arena's edge, she slammed her back against the wall, ending the still-chomping soldier with a sickening crunch and extinguishing her flaming dress.

Guilder struck down the dwindling number of undying as a third cauldron released its oil. Its base burned through. One entrance left beneath the queen herself, the one unused by any of the dead. Ryleigh dispatched the remaining few on her way to join Guilder at the center of the ring. The crowd, again silent, all eyes turned toward the dais at the end of the arena.

Viviana leaned forward on her throne, fists clenched, her jaw tight, eyes fixed on the two blood-soaked humans staring back at her. She relaxed into her throne. "You think you've defeated them?" Her venomous retort, punctuated by a smile creeping back onto her face. "My hoard is endless, and the dead are legion."

From beneath the dark cavern, the imperial box ensued a predator's growl. Whispers from the crowd carried onto the arena floor as the crier retook his mark. After another long breath, full-throated, he announced, "Her majesty gives you... the A-m-a-r-o-k!" The name found weight with Ryleigh as she took a step back, eyes wide, her sword shaking in her grasp.

"What is it?" Guilder readjusted the grip on his sword.

"An Amarok." Ryleigh's breath came quick. "We're in trouble." Her mouth set, eyes wide as she stared into the dark tunnel.

"But what is it!?"

The yellow glow of a hunter's eyes heralded the wolf's emergence from the darkness. Bent low to clear the three-meter-high entrance, its mottled gray-black fur, lacking in large swaths, exposed deep battle scars and putrefied skin, raw from decay. Its mouthful of dagger-like teeth, exposed, its lips and jowls ripped off or eaten. Fangs dripped foamy saliva over a blacked tongue as thick, angular claws flexed, sinking into the muddied arena floor. Giant paw marks left in its wake. The beast stared at the two humans as if seeing nothing but meat for an unsatiated hunger.

Queen Viviana leaped from her imperial box. Her translucent wings caught the reflecting oranges and yellows, blacks, and greens of the dying firelight as she landed with grace next to the Amarok. She held an intricately carved purpleheart glaive, a dragon glass blade fixed at one end. Her free arm stretched above her head, caressing the underside of the beast's face as it crouched at her side.

"You made a blood oath to kill me." The Fae queen's eyes remained on her wolf. The crowd continued to hold their collective breath, the unease palpable and thick as winter mist.

Shards of glass jabbed into Guilder's temple, just behind his skull. He squeezed his eyes shut, willing the pain to subside. In the darkness, he breathed in smells of rot and burned flesh, sweat, hot bestial breath, and evening primrose. His eyes opened, his stare tipped with venom and aimed at Viviana as revelation dawned.

She returned a knowing smile. "Your mind was so clear and childlike. As if you'd been erased, renewed even. Yet so open to carnal urges." Viviana turned to Ryleigh. "His narrow awareness remains so focused on you. Have you returned his affection?"

Ryleigh turned a questioning gaze toward

Guilder, his jaw tight, hand pressed against his temple, leaning on his sword like a crutch.

Viviana's smile widened. "Lust, then. Humans are such… uncomplicated animals." Her smile diminished. "So lacking in substance, and so dull."

"Then why attack travelers through the isthmus?" Ryleigh asked. "Why not stay hidden like you always have?"

"You are fiery… No," Viviana corrected, "passionate. That's what he likes most about you. What he desires in you."

Ryleigh clenched her teeth and clamped her fist around her sword.

"Now is the time…" Viviana raised her voice, addressing the hushed crowd, "… that the Fae take their rightful place in this world. Too long have we cowered in the shadows. Too long subservient to the humans' schemings, their politicking. They will cower before their betters and know what subservience to the Fae means."

"Guilder?" Ryleigh's eyes fixed on the demon wolf's stare. "You still with me?"

"I'm here." Guilder raised his sword, jaws set against his pain.

"You have any kind of plan?"

"Same as the last, I'm afraid."

"… with our kin from the Crystal Mountains and the clans of the Forrest Narrows, reunited," Viviana continued. "We will take the Republic, we will take the southern kingdom. The whole of the eastern continent will be united once more under the Fae!"

The fervor of the crowd grew with each prophesied expanse. Viviana turned back to the humans. "Now our conquest of New Aurora is all but assured with the capture of the Crown Prince, the Butcher, Guilder Rayne."

Ryleigh turned a readying eye toward Guilder. He gave a slight nod in return, his full attention fixed on the Fae queen. A primal scream rose above the crowd noise as Guilder sprinted toward Viviana, sword raised above his head. She raised her staff, blocking his feeble strike. He collapsed into a heap at her side, pain overwhelming him.

Viviana narrowed her eyes at Ryleigh, clicking her tongue to signal the demon wolf. The Amarok took off from his lying position, fangs bared, his claws anchoring deep with each stride. Ryleigh raised her sword to strike as a boulder-sized paw raked across her face, batting her to the muddied floor. The wolf's powerful jaws wrapped around Ryleigh's midsection, taking her into its maw.

"Guilder!" Ryleigh fought, punching and slashing against the beast as it bit into stubborn flesh, forcing her into its throat. "Help me!" she screamed before disappearing down the Amarok's gullet.

"Good boy," Viviana whispered, a satisfied smile across her face. The Amarok sauntered back toward her and sat. His hairless whip tail swished as he waited for her next command.

"No!" Guilder pounded his fist against the arena floor. The pain throbbed behind his skull.

He pushed it into his grip, straining his muscles. Sweat dripped from his temple as he staggered to his feet and swung his blade, arms outstretched in desperation. Viviana deflected the attempt, effortless as the time before, as Guilder's pain intensified.

"The sting you feel when you attack," Viviana slinked over to Guilder's side to whisper into his ear. "A glamour only a High Fae can conjure. It keeps the livestock in check."

Guilder struggled to his hands and knees, madness behind his eyes, his breath heavy, jaw clenched. He jumped a hand to his sword as pain radiated throughout his body, robbing him of his strength.

"Tenacious human." Viviana's smile faded. She thumped the staff's metal pommel into Guilder's gut. His gasps for breath added to the rising clamor of the crowd. Lying at the feet of the queen, Guilder tented his sword over him. Its tip sank into the mud as he attempted to ward off any continued blows.

"The Scarecrow Man only requested proof of your death." Viviana slapped Guilder's sword aside. "Your life, however, was gifted to me." She readjusted her stance. Volleying strikes off Guilder's defenseless body. Each hit reverberated in his head, stealing his remaining strength as cheers erupted from the crowd. Behind her, the Amarok coughed on his last meal, skulking away to a cooler side of the arena. "You'll be a welcomed addition to my horde." The Fae queen's malicious smile grew as Guilder shielded himself from her unrelenting blows.

The Amarok sat hunched over, struggling to keep his jaws closed. Fingers wrapped around the hinge of his jaw, around his teeth. A knee pressed against his tongue; the wolf's sinewy muscles stretched taut. Ryleigh stepped a boot against his lower jaw, her back at the roof of his mouth. The beast gave one last yelp of pain before his lower jaw was ripped off. Ryleigh stepped out of the beast's mouth, drenched in blood and bile.

Stunned silence met the Amarok's meager whimpers. Ryleigh wiped the muck from her arms, gazing in contempt back at the downed beast. She knelt beside the unmoving creature, its eyes pleading, and plunged her arm, shoulder deep, back down its throat. She retrieved her gladius as if unsheathing it from an oversized scabbard. The crowd roared with applause as their queen gnashed her teeth with murderous wrath.

With a distracted reprieve from Viviana's strikes, Guilder regained his footing, struggling through the pain from the glamour, his body, bruised and bloody. The Fae queen turned her attention back to Guilder, beating him back into the arena wall, beating him until his knees again gave out. In his periphery, he watched Ryleigh run her sword through the top of the Amorack's head, putting it out of its misery as the crowd roared all the more.

"Beg me for mercy, human," Viviana spat.

She spun her staff, the dragon glass blade poised above her head. "Lord Iks will thank me for killing you and reward me for scouring the world of the human pestilence."

Ryleigh's face emerged from behind Viviana's shoulder, her arm wrapped around the faery's neck. Viviana's expression glazed over, her eyes wide as Ryleigh's sword exited through the faery's breastbone. The crowd fell into a hush. Ryleigh withdrew her sword, arching around with a swift downward slice, cleaving the wings from Viviana's back before the Fae queen crumbled to the arena floor.

"You okay?" Ryleigh asked, offering a hand to Guilder. She heaved him to standing taking his weight as he steadied himself against the arena wall.

Guilder nodded. "Pain's fading." He rubbed his temple as Ryleigh picked up the queen's iridescent wings. She scanned the quieted arena, the countless faery, all eyes watching her before thrusting the wings above her head to explosive applause.

Part II

The Lost Prince

CHAPTER 13
A Reverence of Magic
Generation six

Humans were never meant to possess true power, this magic, for lack of a better word. We'd survived on pure luck and our own fortuitousness. Some would say intelligence, but that, given our history, seemed debatable. Inventiveness was the closest we'd ever gotten. Though the purposes of such seemed either for sloth or coercion.

Iven's reconstruction played out as a symphony in sonata-allegro form. Quick tempoed at first, as damaged tissue was flayed off. The screams of his exposition filled the citadel for days. His second movement, andante, played out more lyrical as surgeons combined magic with mechanics to replace severed limbs with automated prostheses. Their development commingled my designs with a spell from the Lich Grimoire. The same tome which produced the faery abomination. Affixing metal directly to bone, wire tendons to muscle, artificial synapses to a fleshy brainstem took a mere day as his agony crescendoed to fortissimo resolving morendo.

The third and final movement composed a minuet of engineering prowess, Iven's eye, taking the most thought and care to fabricate. Motors and gears needed to reconstruct the cornea, iris, and pupil required the delicateness of a skilled horologist. The precise curvature and thickness of the lens, calculated to the nth degree.

I clasped my hands behind me and paced the periphery of the room for what must have been the thousandth time in anticipation of Iven's surgical finale. He said nothing as the operating table tipped forward, his orchestral surgeons giving leeway to their maestro as feet, flesh to one side, metal to the other, touched the sterile tile floor. His mechanical aperture whirred in its casing as his eyes adjusted. Taking me in with what seemed cold indifference. He followed my movement as I approached to inspect the adaptations of this forced evolution.

"For nearly two hundred years, I've watched this world be reclaimed by humankind." I scrutinized his mechanical arm, skeletal in its construction, its wire tendons exposed. "With genuine power, I hoped humanity would, at last, be catapulted to its rightful place." I felt his mechanical shoulder, down the skeletal, titanium arm proper, humorous, and elbow, his forearm to the myriad of tiny brass joints in his chromium hand. "As gods in an ever-expanding universe."

"Disappointingly, this gift of ... magic, has only served to inhibit humanity's evolution." I took a step back, marveling at my Prometheus, the sacred fire still burning in his eyes. "Leave us!" The surgical team trampled over each other until only Iven and I remained.

"I'll admit the scar tissue from your previous... injuries was tiresome to remove. I assure you, malice was never my intent." I ran a finger along his aperture's obit. "Your temporary discomfort was an unfortunate side effect of the procedure, as your consciousness needed to be maintained." Thumbed the crease between metal and flesh at his temple. "Cranial implants are notoriously difficult to adjust without input from the subject. I apologize that you no longer have free will of your own, those circuits were tedious to perfect, but I'm proud to say, the bulk of the surgical procedures were completed without the use of magics."

Iven stared, unblinking, as his new servos hummed.

"You're likely wondering why I've bothered maintaining your life at all." I stepped back taking in his full countenance. "After your fruitless strive to usurp my authority, I contemplated it myself. Yet something told me you were yet to play a role in my continued ascension. In your clumsy way, you'd succeeded in what you'd set out to achieve. You will be my head chancellor from here on out." Iven's remaining human eye narrowed.

"I understand your puzzlement. Please allow me to explain plainly. In my accumulation of this library, I've discovered a spell to excise what the meteor has done. Reverse it, if you will, and return humanity to its rightful course." I paced the room, examined the operating tools with mild curiosity. "Though to succeed in this I require anonymity." I picked up a scalpel, scrutinizing its edge. "The governances of this continent are far too curious about my affairs.

They need distracting."

I set the scalpel down, returning to Ivan. "New Byzantium's heir, this Butcher Prince, has thrown the northern kingdoms into discord. Elam's Republic will be obligated to act. In the interim, if the crown prince was to disappear, Elam would likely be blamed, shifting the eyes of the continent elsewhere and I would be able to finalize my studies in relative seclusion."

I took in a deep breath prompted by Ivan's unchanged expression and continued silence. "After generations of observation and intervention, I've concluded that this world should never have been. I take responsibility to correct the mistake. Your own rebirth notwithstanding, sloth has replaced invention as this new dark age has left human progress to fester." The aperture in Iven's left eye adjusted with a whir.

"Yours will be a renaissance to a time of ingenuity, adaptation, and science over magic. A reminder of what once was. Magic has become a blight in this world, and I will orchestrate the cure. You will show neither apathy nor self-interest in your action or your advisement. The memory of these procedures will ensure me of that. What say you to these terms of indenturement?"

Iven's silence hung in the room like a mountain atop my chest. Our eyes fixed until his gaze dropped.

"For what I've done, do you think me cruel?"

Iven's saddened gaze lifted to again meet mine. "Only in method."

***

"Gentlemen, if we do nothing, 2026TC will not only destroy life on this planet but the planet itself. I've calculated the impact force at—"

"Professor Crowley…"

"Dr. Crowley, if you please, General." Fools in military garb. An overstuffed boardroom of nothing but bureaucratic fools.

"Dr. Crowley, we've taken your concerns into consideration. Our own engineers calculate this as a near-miss event at best."

I clenched my fists white-hot against the growing rage. If even one of you could fathom what this inaction will cost. "Your engineers are wrong." I tightened my jaw, eyes narrowed. Imbeciles, the lot of you.

"We're done here, professor."

A deep breath brings a moment of calm over me. My eyes remain fixed on the myopic general as the colonel to his right bursts into flame. His screams send a wave of panic through the room. Soldiers beat their fists at the door behind me, ice-covered, impenetrable. The room, now divided between those who cower against the walls and those brazen enough to draw their weapons. The general, the only one remaining in his seat.

The officer to his left drops his service pistol to clutch at his throat. His chest expands as his lungs turn vacuous before rupturing, speckling the pearl-white conference table with his blood.

Black metal spikes erupt from the floor, piercing those around the room's exterior, freezing their concluding moments of horror like macabre waxworks. Gunfire explodes from the few remaining bullets caught midair by the unseen cyclone surrounding me. Their trajectory redirected to the doors behind, passing through the glacial barrier, halting the unending percussion of unseen soldiers.

The general's eyes remained fixed on me, his condescending stare unchanged. The room, now a muddle of debris and blood, stone, and shattered bone. My wrath remains unchecked. I raise my hand, commanding the rocks and pebbles to my will. Thrusting my arm forward, they strike the confounded officers peppering them like crepe paper shielding against a meteor shower.

I look over the devastation of the room, the unmoved general. "Your hubris makes you weak," he says over tented hands. "And magic has only served to grow that weakness."

I stood there defeated by mere words. Emptied and abandoned by my rage and shamed by my own actions. My gaze fell. I placed a wanting fist on my chest, raised the opposite arm above my head, and motioned an arc to my thigh. The scene replayed in reverse.

I stood at the foot of the table. Officers again crowded the room, seemingly unaware of their changed fate, chimera patches at their shoulders.

"We're done here, Professor," the general said, shifting papers around in front of him. My down-pointed forearm was charred, crisp, and ridged, my fist useless. The opposite arm stuck, fused to my bare chest, black as coal.

"Professor?" the general prodded. "You don't look well, my lord."

Atrophied muscles declined to move as arthritic joints shrieked their dissent. Ancient eyes met the general's questioning gaze, echoed by his cabinet's disgust. "My lord?"

Sunlight erased the boardroom like an erupting quasar. I squeezed my eyelids shut against the onslaught, pain radiating through my body with each attempt.

"My lord?" A familiar voice sounded as soft down pressed like shards of glass into my indignant skin. "My lord."

"Yes, Iven. I hear you."

"The servants found you in the upper library." Iven's matter-of-fact tone was a welcomed familiarity despite its emptiness. "We'd feared the worst, sir."

"I'd found the spell I'd been searching for in one of the grimoires—" Electricity shot through my body, sealing a scream in my throat. I looked down at my trembling hands, black and charred. Gravel gnashed in my neck, in my joints. Torturous pain accompanied even the slightest movement. "Iven?"

"I can only speculate as to what occurred, sir."

The mirror at the dressing table showed a decayed corpse, an ancient face, skin hanging from my skull like a filthy shroud, yellowed with puss and stinking of cadaverine. My horrified gaze met Iven's in the glass. The hint of a sadistic smile seemed erased by his own reflection. Memories of his own tortured recreation.

"Speculate," I said, turning scrutiny toward him.

"Whichever spell you'd been pining over required more magical energy than even you'd been able to provide." Iven stiffened his posture. "With all due respect, my lord."

"Granted." I blinked, urging him to continue. Stilling my body to bask in the nominal reprieve the lack of movement gave.

"It has been postulated, sir, that a celestial aligning can enhance magical prowess, minimizing the repercussion of such a spell." His eyes fell back on me. "That is to say, dependent on the type of magic wished to be conjured."

"Temporal Chronomancy."

"Sir. I strongly advise against…" Iven regarded the mirror once more, his eyes fallen. "There is an alignment, one which will add your endeavors and increase your power tenfold."

"When?"

"By year's end, sir."

"Then by year's end, your indenturement will be concluded."

CHAPTER 14
Covenant in Fire

Guilder sat in his warm bath, staring at the walls of his room. Mahogany red, discolored splotches darkened the colors in random places. Printed patterns repeated along alternating columns, patterns of family crests, and royal Faery bloodlines. Specters of time and forgotten names, their marks left long after passing.

Guilder Rayne, the Butcher Prince, Viviana, had called him. The Paracel gate keeper, too. The recognition in his eyes showed it to be true, the fear, like talons digging into his chest. *If this name still fits, the Butcher Prince, am I still that same man?* "We are *nothing* without our word," Guilder said to the empty room. "Nothing."

Memories flashed through Guilder's mind like lightning strikes. Bloody vestiges of tortured souls, dank chambers hidden away in shadowed corners, screams so horrific they echoed as if sharing the room. The visions lived for fractions of seconds, like wraiths caught in his periphery, then lost, leaving a lingering hurt, a tightness in the chest, for acts only partially claimed. His own or others, Guilder couldn't tell, the images implying a life no longer familiar.

His bath had long turned tepid, stained blue-black with Fae blood. His hair, sticky, face streaked with black rivulets, like war paint without honor. Guilder slumped forward. He closed his eyes and slid beneath the water, waiting paralyzed by the flood of returning memories. His lungs burned, aching for want of air, yet in the silence, the darkness below the murky water, he found some solace.

The surface broke as his body compelled him above the water. He slicked back his hair, the tacky dried blood releasing some of its hold. His eyes pinched shut. He heard the rush of water wash down his back and slosh around in the clawfoot tub. Submerged again, wondering what monster he'd once been, who he'd now become. Were they the same? Would it even matter were he to stay beneath the polluted, bloodied water?

Guilder pushed his legs out straight, bringing his upper body above a torrent of midnight-blue waves. A knock on his door broke him free from his mental anguish. "Guilder? You there?" Ryleigh called from outside his room.

Guilder wiped the water from his face. "I'm here," he said, not bothering to hide his mood. He wrung out his hair and stepped out of the tub, Ryleigh's knock as good a reason as any to shake himself from his sullenness. "Give me a minute." Guilder wrapped a towel around his midsection and opened the door before ambling toward his bed.

"They're having fresh horses readied for our—" Ryleigh stared at Guilder lying barechested on his bed, arms raised above his head and gazing at the ceiling. "Are you... okay,

Guilder?" She held her distance, leaning against the closed door.

"My memories have started to return." Guilder blinked away phantoms crawling across the slate-colored ceiling.

Ryleigh feigned a weak smile against his flat tone. "That's good. Isn't it?"

"I guess." Guilder sat up and sulked toward his dressing table. He draped his towel over the chair and slipped on freshly laundered trousers. "Though the memories… they're fractured, scattered like… pieces of an unfinished puzzle." He turned back toward Ryleigh, her eyes dropping to the floor. "They don't seem my own."

"It'll take time, I'm sure." She lifted her flushed gaze to his face. "To get a lifetime of memories back, I mean."

Guilder donned a shimmering cobalt blue shirt, light and durable Fae-made silk. "So much violence in my past life. So much disdain. Much from those who chose to be around me." He tied off the laced neckline and sat to pull on his boots. "The emotion seems… disjointed, memories fragmented, needing reassembling. Obscene pleasure mixed with hate, and such deep anger, all directed at no one and yet everyone. It's all… dissociated. My father, his advisors, strangers, friends, even my mother. I see glimpses of their faces, familiar, but…" Guilder shook his head, dropping his pained gaze onto his lap. "I'm just not sure. There's a sadness behind it all. Like they're lost to me, or I to them." Guilder wiped his eyes and looked to where Ryleigh stood, hands clasped behind her, eyes searching for a safe place to land, looking unsure how to respond. "Ryleigh, what if I don't like who I was?"

Ryleigh cleared her throat and sighed. She moved from the doorway to stand in front of him. Guilder's eyes nearly overflowed with tears as he turned his gaze up to meet hers. "Guilder." She ran a finger over his ear, brushing back his still-damp hair. "Who you were before isn't as important as who you are now."

"I'm not sure I know how to be either." Guilder rested his head on Ryleigh's chest, wrapping his arms around her.

She put her hands on his shoulders, pulling his gaze as she dropped to a knee. "I know you'll figure it out." She offered a faltering smile as the muscles beneath his shirt tightened. "I'm... We're here to help. Your friends, I mean." She cleared her throat, stood, and took a step back. "Anyway, we'll get through... together." Her faltered smile turned clumsy. "You're with us now."

"You're sure?"

"We are nothing without our word."

"Our word." Guilder nodded and bent down to readjust his boots. "How's our host doing?"

"Yelrem? He's alive, incredibly." Ryleigh shifted her stance back towards the door, seeming thankful for the change in subject. "He made his first decree while being lowered from that beam. Their healers are patching him up now. We should thank him… for the horses, I mean."

"Thank him? After everything we'd done, you want to thank *him*?"

"He isn't giving us much choice. It's the reason I came over. He's called for us."

Guilder affixed his scabbard to his hip. Unsheathed the sword to its tip. He stared at his reflection in the cleaned and polished metal. His eyes fell to the gleaming chimera inlay before snapping the blade back into its place. "Fine." He gazed at Ryleigh, solemn and dry-eyed. "I've had enough dealings with Fae for two lifetimes."

A pair of glamoured guards stood in the center of the hallway as the two exited Guilder's room. "Your memories," Ryleigh said as they were escorted down the endless corridors of Mistfall castle, "If you'd like to talk about them… to a friend, I mean. I'm willing to listen… if it'd help."

"I'm not sure I could explain." Guilder's stare remained distant. "They're almost dreamlike, yet they interfere with reality, even now. Like a waking dream transposed over what's real. Faces and events playing out of order, without context. Some I recognize. Those close to me, the few I trust, a lot more I seem leery of, though I can't tell why. People I've hurt, maybe even murdered." Guilder glanced toward Ryleigh, her concern mirroring his moist eyes.

"There's this feeling of ill-fitted power."

His throat thickened as he continued. "Lauded over others, though the feelings are mixed, it's so confusing. When the memories replay, what I recall is their terror in my presence and anger…so much anger. But it's as if I'm detached from it all. The anger and terror turn to remorse and guilt and shame."

Ryleigh took a cleansing breath. "Guilder, I can't imagine what you're going through, but there's something you should know."

"Something about Shyloh, too." Guilder held his hand in front of him as if trying to touch the memory. "Something not quite returned to me. It's still hazy, lost. I'd met her. Known her somehow, before the cave, even."

"Guilder, Shyloh, she… she's not who you think—"

"Lord Yelrem!" One of the trailing guards announced beneath his slight bow, his hand held out, signaling them to enter. Guilder and Ryleigh followed his cue, the guards turning outward, staying their position at the entrance.

Morning sunlight streamed into the room from vaulted windows, highlighting the forest-like greens and browns embedded in the naturalistic walls. Boots clicked off creamy white marble floors, its gray-blue veining weaving like rivers on an outstretched map. At the center, a wood conference table, looking as if cut from a single tree, polished to a mirror shine and spanning meters long. At its head, Lord Yelrem, with his unblemished humanlike chin and hawk nose. Spectacles, perched at the end of his nose, cut across the purple-blue mottle of his eyes.

"I know you dislike the glamour," Yelrem said before anyone spoke. "But I assure you it's necessary, if only for my own vanity. Viviana was not kind in her… transgressions against me." He sat with his hands folded before him, the shadow of nail holes shimmering at their centers.

Ryleigh looked to Guilder, who stood staring through Yelrem, transfixed by the deluge of returning memories. "We're pleased for your recovery, my lord." Placing a hand at Guilder's back, she shifted her attention to Yelrem. "What happens to your people now that your queen has been…"

Yelrem offered an abashed grin. "Queen Viviana assassinated the whole of her royal bloodline in her appropriation of power." His eyes remained sad and remorseful. "She represented the last monarch in her line. The last monarch ever, if I have my way."

"You'll take power, then?" Ryleigh's question coaxed Guilder from his trance. His gaze fixed on Yelrem.

"With a council of others." Yelrem nodded. "Trusted throughout this stratagem, yes."

"With decorum that the queen sorely lacked, I assume," Guilder said with narrowed eyes.

A wry smile widened across Yelrem's lips. "Of course."

"The Necromancer from the Black Tower,

how does he fit into all of this?"

Yelrem's smile failed as he turned his eyes from Guilder. "Andorian Iks. The queen had an insatiable longing for him. Whether it was a lust for power or something... more carnal, no one could say. It seemed not only unhealthy but unnatural."

"Lord Iks enchanted her?" Ryleigh stepped between Guilder's ridged stance and the defused faery. "To what end?"

"Enchanted? No. Viviana was a formidable sorceress in her own right, limited as she was by her Fae blood. Lord Iks tendered her a... compromising bargain." Yelrem removed his spectacles, his eyes vacant. He stared, passing his fingers over his false reflection on the polished table. "Iks granted her dominance over all the dead, an unyielding army wielding unlimited power." He refocused a tearful gaze on the two humans. "In exchange, he stole her natural life, her beauty, and ultimately her sanity." Yelrem sighed, salvaging his composure. "Not only this colony, but all the Fae were at her mercy. As to his rationale... I wish I knew."

"You loved her," Ryleigh said.

"As much as a common-born Fae can." Yelrem cast a shrewd eye on Ryleigh. "You're very perceptive, for a human." He replaced his spectacles onto his face. "Her madness for power squashed any lingering affection I'd held. Her accord with Iks took everything from her, from her people... from me." His gaze again turned distant before returning to Ryleigh's stare. "It was cowardice, asking so much from you."

"You'd promised an antidote for your queen's venom," Guilder said, his expression cold and unmoved. "The least you could do for asking so much."

"Of course." Yelrem motioned to the standing guards. "The antitoxin is made from the queen's blood. Since Viviana's... corruption, no more could be made." Ryleigh looked at Guilder, his eyes narrowing on Yelrem. "However, as a precaution against such... incidences, we keep a reserve supply." The guard placed a small glass vial at the end of the table. A lilac-blue liquid shimmered halfway up the bottle. "Your healer should know how to utilize this tincture."

"If you had the antidote the whole time, why make us part of your coup?"

"Quid pro quo, human. For such a valued item, an exchange must be made."

Guilder turned without another word.

"Thank you, my lord." Ryleigh carefully pocketed the bottle. "For the medicine, and the fresh horses."

Yelrem nodded as he removed a pen from the inkwell. "One additional matter before you go." He set his journal atop the desk and returned his attention to the two humans.

Guilder stopped, not turning back. Ryleigh's gaze caught between the two.

"The slight matter of our agreement." Yelrem's expression turned detached. "I've supplied the antitoxin—"

"And we slew your queen," Guilder said, his chin turned over his shoulder. "Fulfilling our bargain."

"Sadly, our blood oath stipulated that you, Crown Prince Rayne, were to dispatch Viviana in exchange for our elixir. I've given what you asked, out of courtesy. A deed done."

Guilder balled his fists, turning his head to stare down the hallway.

"But your debt to me remains, young prince. A life taken. One equivalent at a time to be named… at my discretion."

Guilder set his jaw and flexed his sword hand as he marched from the room, Ryleigh shuffling behind. "Guilder, wait." She turned back. "My lord." She curtsied and ran after Guilder. "Wait up! Why are you acting like this?"

"Like what?" Guilder stared straight ahead, his teeth clenched, fists balled.

Ryleigh grasped his shoulder, his muscles tight. "Like what? Guilder, you left me behind. I get that you're angry, but don't… don't be like this."

"He tricked us, Ryleigh. Made a fool out of me. Now he thinks I'll kill for him again."

"I killed Viviana." Ryleigh held her palm to her chest. "And… it was my error. I should have seen through Yelrem's schemes." She shook her head. "Fae deals are nothing but traps. Guilder, I'm sorry."

Guilder relaxed releasing the scowl from

his face. "It's not your fault." He sighed. "I was the fool. I agreed to his deal."

Ryleigh gave a tentative smile. "I'm here for you, Guilder." She removed her hand with a smack to the side of Guilder's shoulder, regaining her step behind the Fae guards. "I'll help you through it… we, I mean, your friends. We'll help you through this." She bit her lower lip as her face turned fiery, eyeing Guilder as he matched her step for step. "We should get back."

"We should." Guilder returned her smile, though his eyes remained tight.

CHAPTER 15
White Magic From The Black Towers

My gaze fixed on the predawn sky. Ombrés of reds, purples, and blues meet heavy eyes as I take in the aromas of fresh summer air, hints of vanilla, and budding wildflowers mixed with oxidizing paper and ancient leather. Grain fields beyond the salt leach fall to the eastern sea kilometers from the uppermost library's singular window. I pause, if only for a breath of air before the obsession steals my mind back. This library, only one of many in my citadel, has become a hermitage in my incessant study of the Tessermancy spell.

These towers have stood nearing their second century, conjoined monoliths like the dual fingers of a fossilized giant's hand, sheathed with the very object which denied my natural death. For countless centuries further, I'd absorbed the meteorite's power, its tainted radiation. And for what? As the means of eradicating its corruption has now been granted to me, I'm rendered impotent and lacking after being here far too long. Power beyond measure seems not power enough.

"Sentry!" I croak in an emaciated voice as I return to my seat behind the faery's grimoire. The spell possessed such an extravagant incantation, almost alive in its complexities, or near to life as the entity that birthed it. Part magic, part alchemy; the spell required a competence that even my ancient knowledge found taxing. Iven was right, damn him. I was a fool to attempt it before gaining a full understanding.

The library door opened with a tentative creek. "My lord?" The sentry entered a mere step into the confines of the room. His black and silver tunic was embellished with the house's basilisk crest. Its amber-stitched eyes sparkled in the growing sunlight while dual claws gripped the hilt of a down-pointed sword.

"Summon Iven." A hollow old man's voice echoed in my ears as I stood again, mesmerized, over the spell book. "And bring tea."

"Right away, my lord." The sentry's footfalls clomped against the stone-carved floor, dying away as he went to fulfill the request.

I trailed my arthritic hands over the open page, its words and embellishments shifting beneath my touch. Grains of sand, unadhered, yet insubordinate. As if time itself determined its adaptation. I turned to the fire raging in the library's hearth, feeling its heat against the crepey skin of my arms. Only days ago, I was ageless. The spell had ravaged me indeed.

Talons of cold electricity traced their way up my twisted spine into the base of my skull and sat as a dull, throbbing ache. I glanced back toward the window, foreboding overtaking me. Emaciated muscles tremble as I push myself to stand. The vertebrae in my back and the stiffened joints of my knees and elbows popped like dry kindling from the fireplace. My index finger explored the filigree scrawl around the neck of my blackwood cane as I shambled into the darker corners of the library. The silver collar, a simple spell of unbreaking, proves invaluable as I pull a dusty manuscript from the shelves.

Another acquisition from appropriated libraries across this continent. Notes as to the preparation of certain remedies, healing balms, snake oils, and witcheries. And a hidden prophecy nearly forgotten yet resolved decades ago, or so I thought. I ambled across the room and hooked my cane at the edge of a carved wooden plinth, ran the tips of my fingers along the archaic symbols carved along its edge, protection spells for the massive codex set atop. Its pages, yellowed and frayed, its corners worn. The ink, though, stood out as if freshly penned, its black-red hue and faint metallic aroma still distinct.

Bony fingers trembled as I turned over several pages and scanned the passages. I brushed a clawed hand over an anatomical illustration set off in dark blues and reds, two zombified bodies seen back and front. The various organs, painstakingly detailed in their dissections. Quartered segments highlighting lost major muscle groups, its text hypothesizing how animation was still possible.

Another page, another illustration, this one, two halves of an altered brain. Precise structures in the frontal cortex mutated or evolved into a postulated zombie lord. I read the caption, the cursed words that create such a being. Recalling the long nights spent penning the incantation, the stiffness in my wrists after each intricate diagram. It had seemed less complicated than the words let on. "But not impossible. Was it Viviana? Never impossible."

The measured stride of hard leather soles striking stone, a metal clink every other step, echoed beyond the library walls before stopping for a firm, glove-cushioned knock. "Lord Iks, you summoned me?"

"Yes, Iven. Come in." I continued paging through the lengthy tome without looking up. "Are you aware of what's only just occurred?"

"Not as such, sir." Iven stood in the black suit of a steward, paired with a gray vest. His white shirt protruded two centimeters from the jacket cuffs. Black Windsor-knotted tie drawn tight to his metallic neck. He pulled a pocket watch from his waistcoat, opened the cover, and glanced at the interior crystal, a bronze half-human face staring back. "Regrettably, I was unaware of any occurrences happening this morning." He snapped the cover closed and replaced the watch into his pocket.

My attention turned toward Iven, weary eyelids hiding a narrowed gaze. "Nothing scheduled, mind you." I steadied myself against the dais. My weak legs nearly gave way as Iven made no move to aid me. "Only, something that I'd been told was taken care of long ago seems to have re-emerged."

The aperture which replaced Iven's right eye refocused with a whir in its riveted housing. Gears and tiny gold chains shifted across his temple. "How may I be of assistance, sir?" His remaining human eye twitched, servo motors whining their discontent as he adjusted his stance.

I hobbled to my seat behind the Gaean Temple's text, my free hand, heavy on the backrest of the tufted chair. "I was reminded, only just, of a vision one of Rayne's oracles had made." My breath came heavy as I caught Iven eyeing the Tessermancy spell.

Iven sighed, rectifying his view forward. "Sir, there have been countless diviners during the last age. Could you be more specific?"

I ran my parched tongue across my bottom lip. "Do you know why I saved your nose, Iven?" I sat heavily behind the desk, my back moaning its discontent. "Protected it from the forge master's zealousness?"

"Sir?"

I smoothed out the grimoire's page, refusing to meet Iven's stare. "I remember when my forge masters cast it, prepared to fuse it to your face." The delicate leaves felt like scritta paper between my fingers; its vibrant illustrations, muted by my old eyes. "After all the enhancements they'd done, it was the only time you didn't scream for them to stop." I turned my glance toward the automaton.

Iven straightened his stance, gazing beyond my leer. His metal tongue clicked against porcelain teeth as the mechanism allowing his mouth to function hummed in its subtle manner.

"At first, I thought the work my forgers

had done, the agony they'd inflicted, had somehow diminished over the lengthy process. Perhaps you'd accepted your fate or simply lost your sanity. The augmentations had taken weeks. Madness would have been expected from someone… lesser. The tears you'd shed when they placed the still smoking mask, your flesh sizzling as it melted onto your face, the odor lingered. It assured me you'd never forget the stench of your failings."

"I remember quite vividly, my lord. However, I'm not sure I understand this… bout of nostalgia."

I closed his eyes, taking in a ragged breath. "Viviana's dead."

"The zombie queen?" Iven's aperture whirred idly. "How is that possible?"

"She demanded power, not immortality."

"Sir, there remains no credence to that particular prophecy. Divination is fraught with inaccuracies. The interpretive nature alone—your former advisor must have made it clear—"

"*The hawk devours the angel of black light…*" I recited the verse through clenched teeth.

"There have always been multiple understandings —"

"*Struck down by the venom of the martyred lion, brandishing his five claws.*"

Iven's aperture whirled open, refocused, and narrowed again.

"*Alms to the Earth, stolen, then returned.*"

"*So shall the hawk be divided by the serpent, buck, and lion,*" Iven finished. "I recall the prophecy." Iven's gaze turned downward. "I wish I hadn't."

I slammed the book closed at his impertinence. "Every human boy in each of the three kingdoms. That was my command!" I pointed a grizzled finger at Iven, taking a calming breath. "In your grand counsel, what is your explanation of this?"

Iven stuck up his chin, his arms tight to his sides, fingers curled. "The deed was done, my lord. In my own village, I took on the grim responsibility. A successful test of your engineering prowess, I felt little as the river was stained red with innocent blood. Infants purged on your order and surrendered to the waters, washed away to whichever purgatory the gods saw fit."

I shambled back to the window, gasping for breath. "It appears, despite my premeditated response, that our lion still lives." Leaning against the window ledge, I closed his eyes against the now cloud-filtered morning light.

"My lord, I assure you, it would not be a commoner that opposes you. May I suggest a more imperial betrayal?"

"Alms to the Earth, stolen, now returned," I murmured. "Yes, Iven. A wise supposition. Prepare two flies."

"As you wish, sir." Iven reached into his jacket pocket, taking out a round tin box. He shifted to the window, removed the cover, placing two metal insects on the sill. Pairs of delicate wings encased their iridescent bodies, each no bigger than a damselfly.

He removed his right glove, exposing the bleached bone of a skeletal hand tensioned in copper wire. His three inner fingers were crowned with thimble caps enveloped in scrawling symbols visible only upon the closest inspection. He stretched out his index finger, bringing it close to each mechanical fly. The bracelet at his wrist, a bronze modulator, spun its innards as he flexed his hand. A blue spark leaped from his fingertip, jolting wings into life.

Iven replaced his glove and cupped his hands over each fly. He leaned in, whispering instructions before releasing them to the outside winds. Moving to the opposite side of the room, Iven again assumed his neutral position near the door, hands wringing against one another. "Viviana returned to the dead," Iven whispered. Not unnoticed, he let a slight smile escape the still human side of his face.

"Send for the governors of the continental kingdoms," I said, ignoring Iven's further insolence. "We will evoke the counselors to elicit the appropriate response for my ignored edict." I sighed, craning my neck toward Iven. "The conjunction is nearly upon us. I will not have a stale prophecy waylay my grand plan, regardless of which puppet it originated from."

Iven's mouth opened, then closed with a reflexive whir. "I'll send messengers to the southern kingdoms right away, sir." He snapped his stance tight as he came back to himself. "Will there be anything else, my lord?"

"Yes." I hobbled my way back to the tufted chair, anxious to resume my studies. "I'll need a *vessel*. Have one arranged before the delegates arrive."

"Of course, sir." Iven gave a slight bow before turning to leave.

"And Iven, if it turns out that our lion is indeed in possession of his five claws, my punishment will be far less kind than returning half their life."

Iven turned, lowering his head in a deep bow.

"One other thing," I said, adjusting myself in the chair. "The sentry who sought you out, fetch me the tea he neglected to bring, along with his tongue."

CHAPTER 16
Promises of Luna

"Breya tells me Ashyr's through the worst of it," Ryleigh said, handing Guilder a cup of steaming honey tea. Guilder nodded, took the cup, and went back to minding the fields beyond Paracel's gates. "We were lucky to get back when we did. He seemed in pretty bad shape." Except for the two of them, the alure stood empty. For the last two nights, no zombie marauders had come, freeing the townspeople from their nightly vigil.

"We did all we could," Guilder said, setting the cup on the wooden parapet, his gaze following the mounted patrol passing near the front of the wall. "Seen Shyloh?" He clenched his jaw at the mention of her name.

"Not since we got back." Ryleigh sipped from her cup, eyes trained on Guilder. "Breya says that with time your memory will catch up, and likely be less intrusive. I can't imagine what it must be like. A lifetime of memories bubbling to the surface."

Guilder returned his stare to the horizon, the dying sun, stars winking into existence as the light began to fail. "The memories I had from before, they're all just... stale information." He gulped his tea and shook his head. "There's no perspective."

Ryleigh took in a deep breath.

"See that bright blue star?" Guilder pointed into the darkening sky. "Her name's Sirius in the constellation Canis Major. As a boy, I had an army of tutors. The scope of my rote education was more than anyone could absorb in two lifetimes. I'd even had a few books hidden away for me. Childish things, really. I was taught battle strategies, leadership skills, even diplomacy." Guilder flicked his hand at the idea. "The only subject I enjoyed was astronomy."

Ryleigh nodded, leaned her arms on the battlement, and gazed up at the stars.

"I'd never told anyone," Guilder said. "You're the first." He ventured a week smile. "Stargazing was frivolous, or so I'd been told, not something a crown prince should waste time on. Auroran armies comprise only foot soldiers and cavalry. No sailors, never a need to look skyward." Guilder stared at the emerging constellations as a screech owl cried out in hunger and the occasional bat took flight in the twilight sky. "Were you aware that the planet once had a baby sister?" He glanced at Ryleigh, taking in the soapstone contours of her face, the ever-present sadness in her eyes.

Ryleigh nodded and sipped her tea.

"A natural satellite orbiting this very planet. Luna, they called her."

"My grandmother used to tell a story about Luna," Ryleigh said. "About a girl lost in the darkness. One day, with the help of a great wizard, she returned home. Only, while she'd been away, her home had changed. Seven great family houses had turned to a paltry dozen or so, small squabbling siblings."

"Sounds similar enough to a story I'd been told."

"She'd said the story cautioned not to want something without understanding the consequences. Like wanting to eat a whole pie but doing so would give you a stomachache."

"The lesson I'd been given," Guilder said, "was to stay where you were meant to be." He leaned against the battlement next to Ryleigh. "As the crown prince of New Aurora, beyond this world, even beyond my own kingdom, wasn't where I was meant to be. The stars, astronomy itself, were best left to Byzantium's mariners, or the gods."

Ryleigh watched a horseman ride beneath them, lighting torches along the base of the barricade while the sun disappeared beneath the horizon. "Guilder, don't you want to be here? With us… with me?" she asked as dancing torchlight reflected in her glassy eyes.

"You misunderstand." Guilder trailed Ryleigh's eyeline to the horseman. "These memories that I have from my life, the teachings that used to fascinate me, astronomy, history, even magic. There's no emotion attached to any of it. Just… facts. Like watching a play you have no interest in." His gaze faltered. "There are other memories, too… darker, more sinister, and… so much anger." He sighed, tightening his lips. "It seems a different person."

The torch lighter rode out of sight. Guilder looked back toward Ryleigh, her face pointed at him, eyebrows furled with concern.

"If you need someone to confide in, I'm here," she said. "I can't say I appreciate what you're going through, but at least you have friends around to help. You can make new memories while you're figuring out the old ones."

"Some I cherish, but... I'm not sure the constant near-death encounters are memories I'd prefer." Guilder attempted a smile before turning back to the darkened field.

"Well, I've enjoyed our time together." Ryleigh leaned her head on Guilder's shoulder, draping her arm along his back. "All except getting eaten by that giant wolf. Still, more exciting than the life of a barmaid."

"Bet that Amarok wouldn't think so." Guilder's smile betrayed the torrent of emotion held at bay, sadness and anger muddled with confusion and doubt.

"So," Ryleigh said with a devilish grin. "Tell me more about the lessons of a crown prince."

"He's awake!" Breya yelled from the roadway, waving her arms franticly. "Ashyr's awake! Stop canoodling and get your asses down here."

Guilder turned from the parapet and scrambled after Ryleigh, already a third of the way down the ladder.

"Ashyr's safe, he's okay," Ryleigh said with a relieving sigh as Guilder caught up.

"The antitoxin worked?" he asked.

"Worked fine." Breya put her hands on her

hips. "Would've been nice if you'd got it here sooner, but yeah, he's going to be all right. He's asking for you, Shyloh too, but…"

Ryleigh took off at a sprint down the road, leaving Guilder and Breya in her wake. "Well, bless her heart, it's ever so versatile." Breya stared at Guilder, her soft cornflower blue eyes peering into him. "You be careful with her. She's fragile," she said, turning to hurry after Ryleigh.

"She doesn't seem fragile," Guilder said to the empty road before running after Breya.

Ryleigh kneeled at the side of Ashyr's bed, crying and laughing in spasms as she stroked his bone-white hair. "I knew you'd be all right," she whispered over and over again, tears falling onto the bedclothes.

Guilder stood in the doorway, reining in his breath, allowing a slow, genuine smile to overtake his face. The wave of relief refocused him, his smile short-lived, as he turned to Breya. "Where's Shyloh?"

"Took off shortly after you did." Breya crossed her arms and leaned against her workbench.

"Took off for where?" Ryleigh asked, wiping tears from her face.

"Ryleigh, don't—" Ashyr's words cut off with another coughing fit.

"Ashyr!" Ryleigh dabbed specks of blood away from Ashyr's mouth, her eyes watering again. "You said the antivenom worked, that it cured him."

"He's still fighting off the last of the toxin's

effects," Breya said, eyes focused on Guilder. "He'll recover soon enough, he just needs rest."

Guilder returned her stare, his fists balled white, muscles tight. "Where is Shyloh, Breya?"

"She rode east, toward the coast. Foxgate, unless I miss my guess." Breya held her defiant stare. "Didn't bother saying why, or when, she'd be back."

"We were going to Byzantium together." Ryleigh sat at the foot of Ashyr's bed, shoulders collapsed forward, eyes questioning. "Why go without us?"

"She had a job," Ashyr said between strained breaths. "Some contract holder."

"Ashyr, you need to rest, Breya—"

"No, Ryleigh. He needs to be told." Ashyr pushed himself up, cleared a cough from his throat, and looked toward Guilder. "Shyloh accepted a contract from some society adviser, a politician or judge or something."

"Damn Shyloh and her schemes," Ryleigh said. Breya shook her head, tightening her crossed arms.

"She was asked to dispose of some sensitive cargo, to make it disappear. She wouldn't tell me what the cargo was… my guess is it turned out to be you, Guilder."

"Shyloh told you this?" Ryleigh placed a hand on Ashyr's shoulder, turning sympathetic eyes toward Guilder.

"Shyloh put me in that cave and left me for dead so that monster could feed off me." Guilder aimed a narrowed gaze toward Ashyr.

"In Gunnison, our run-in with Wyrmlen—had you known then?"

"Not yet. I recognized you, though. Had my suspicions, you and Shyloh showing up at the same time." Ashyr turned back to Ryleigh. "She told me after we met up at the safe house. Said it had been more difficult than she'd thought." Ashyr shook his head, refocused on Guilder. "She couldn't do it herself. So, she just…left you."

"Then she's a coward." Guilder clenched his jaw. "That thing, that memory eater, took everything I was. What Shyloh did to me was worse than death."

"You're right." Shyloh stood in the doorway, looking road-weary and deflated.

Guilder pushed a fiery breath through his teeth before charging toward the doorway, catching Shyloh by the neck. He lifted her a meter off the ground with one hand, his free hand reaching for his sword. Shyloh beat against his arm, her strength waning. Her eyes rolled back as she fought for breath.

A sinewy tendril constricted around Guilder's chest, stealing the air from his lungs before tossing him across the room. Ryleigh bolted from her seat. She slid down beside Shyloh, propping her up as she gasped for air.

Guilder struggled to regain his breath as circles of white smoke swirled around him, pinning him to the far wall. His rage-filled eyes refocused on Breya as she pointed her outstretched arms toward him. Her hands flayed out, fingers tense and wide. "*Sisa apsourgo skydas vessa yrah mano geinkas taika mano taikalas,*" she mouthed as a second vortex picked up dirt from the cabin's floor, dusting the outer edges as a crane glyph formed at its center. The bird's outstretched wings extended into the outer ring, folded inward, then evaporated. "There will be no fighting in my house," she spat. Her eyes remained closed as she concentrated on maintaining the spell's effect, the vortex slowing as tempers cooled.

Breya glared at Shyloh. "Animals fight for food, monsters for vengeance. Family talk out their differences. Which are you?" Her glare shifted to Guilder, now seated against the far wall.

"She's no family of mine!" Guilder jabbed a finger at Shyloh, his hand colliding into the unseen force shield of Breya's spell.

Breya moved over to Guilder as he rubbed his sprained hand. She stared into his eyes until his gaze softened. "Guilder, if you're not part of this family, then who the fuck are you?"

Guilder sat dumbstruck as Breya turned toward Shyloh, Ryleigh helping her to her feet. "And as family, Shyloh deserves ample opportunity to convince us she's not a total ass."

"Thanks a lot, Breya," Shyloh said between lingering coughs. "Guilder, I—"

"Save it," Guilder shouted. "Your words are meaningless to me."

"Guilder, give her a chance to explain," Ryleigh said.

"What's to explain? Some prick from Byzantium wants me dead, and Shyloh Erbus gets to add 'king slayer' to her moniker."

Ryleigh stood up. Her fists clenched. "She didn't kill you, Guilder. She put you there, yes but—"

"She trapped me there! Simply another monster, better off dead." He pointed an accusatory finger at Shyloh, echoing Ryleigh's tone. "Thinking one monster would end the other."

"Damn you, Guilder, you ungrateful—"

"Ryleigh." Shyloh held up her hand. "He's right." She stood, dusted herself off, and wiped her damp eyes with the palm of her hand. "I brought you to that cave because I am a coward. I couldn't finish you myself. Figured Da'Kar would do the job for me. I waited to make sure, but then… you… came out." She looked across the room at Guilder, tears streaming down her face. "You seemed different, after. Pure… kind, even. A far cry from the cruel monster I'd known, the person I hated."

"The memories I have of you before that cave are mere scraps," Guilder said. "Not enough to know that we were anything to each other. You took those memories. You stole them from me."

"I did. It was my choice. I couldn't kill you myself and I couldn't let you return as the hateful, warmongering demon you were. In gifting you a second chance, I harvested Da'Kar's venom, what little I could, and spiked your water with it. It kept your memories from returning."

"And who the fuck granted you choice over who I am?"

"Guilder," Ryleigh warned, standing in defense of Shyloh.

"Ryleigh," Breya said. "Let them argue it out." Ryleigh shifted her glance between Breya and Guilder, finally moving to Breya's side.

"At the time," Shyloh said, watching Ryleigh retreat, "I considered it compensation."

"Compensation! I just told you I didn't know you from anyone. You were nothing to me!" A sardonic chuckle escaped Guilder's lips. "What in the nine realms would I have been compensation for?"

Shyloh averted her gaze, wiping away her tears.

"Well?" Guilder waited. "Answer me!"

"You killed my parents, you goddamn ogre!"

CHAPTER 17
Ancient History

"My father oversaw New Aurora's royal stables. An equerry for the ruling family." Shyloh stood near Breya's worktable, a cup of steaming honey tea clutched between her hands. "None of this matters. It's all... ancient history."

"It matters," Breya said, refilling her pot for more tea. "Your secrets started this." She turned back to Shyloh. "It's time you aired them out."

"I'm not the only one with secrets here," Shyloh blasted back. "Ryleigh, tell them—"

"This isn't about Ryleigh!" Breya pointed a scolding finger at Shyloh. "This is about what you did to Guilder. You tell them." She brought her finger back, calming her voice. "Or I will."

"Fine." Shyloh sighed. "Where was I?"

"Your father, the stable charge for my family," Guilder said, leaning against the opposite wall, his arms folded tight, eyes narrowed.

"Right. Well, I'd been apprenticing with my father since I could walk. He taught me everything about those steeds. I'd call them each by name and knew them better than anyone in the kingdom. We'd fashioned saddles for each individual horse. We knew their moods, their fears. I just loved those animals, but I could never match his passion for the trade." Shyloh's eyes grew distant, quiet.

Guilder shook his head, his arms laced

tight over his chest.

"It's been... shit, almost three years now. The crown prince here got betrothed to some Republic of Byzantium aristocrat. A peacemaking gesture by the king meant to bring the two countries together. They seemed happy enough, the few times they'd visited the stables, anyway. One day, my father received word that Prince Rayne and his bride-to-be wished to go on a hunt. Some fool rumor that a kitsune, one of those nine-tailed foxes, was sighted nearby." Shyloh shook her head, her lips pinched in. "Ridiculous. Kitsune that far north and in the middle of summer—"

"Shyloh," Breya said. "Focus."

"Anyway, I fixed up this beautiful white Paso Fino, Rainmaker, a fleet-footed light horse the Byzantium woman preferred, a little skittish but an overall nice ride. My father saddled the prince's mustang, Hellion." Shyloh hesitated, taking a cleansing breath. "There was an accident." She sniffed back her gathering tears. "Rainmaker... the woman... she fell. Broke her neck. My father took the blame, of course. King Rayne threatened to discharge him. Maybe he would have." Shyloh stared over at Guilder. "Until you demanded his execution."

Guilder's heart sunk. His gaze softened, exposing a growing uncertainty before turning away. He opened his mouth yet said nothing.

"They forced me to watch, being his apprentice and all. For his years of service, he received a quick death. The king paid the royal executioner for a clean cut. For that, it was my duty to thank him."

"Shyloh, I—"

"Oh, I haven't told you the worst of it," Shyloh interrupted. "I'd found Rainmaker where she fell, a broadsword puncture straight to her heart, girth cut clean." Shyloh's teeth clenched against her tears. "The pain I endured from my losses, the disgrace, it all soured to raw hate when I found my mother dangling from our cottage rafters."

She shook her head, her eyes growing distant. "Her grief, so deep, she couldn't even bear to be near me, not in my greatest time of need, and certainly not in hers. All over what you'd called a malattached saddle."

Guilder broke the thickening silence. "If it means anything, Shyloh, I'm sorry."

"It doesn't!" she scoffed. "You were the worst type of monarch, self-indulgent, manipulative, focused on whatever agenda suited that day's purposes. You would've made an excellent politician."

"You'd never shared this with any of us," Ryleigh said. "We could have helped. At least you wouldn't have suffered alone."

"You helped. Ashyr too. After leaving Aurora, I came here to find another of his majesty's royal castaways." Shyloh's eyes met Breya's as unspoken words passed between the two of them. "She helped get me straight, in her own... special way. Eventually, I ended up in Gunnison. Built my strength at the mines, learned to fight on the streets, and honed my magic. By the time we all banded together, I'd reinvented myself. But my goal remained."

Silence festered in the cottage. Guilder swallowed the dry lump in his throat. Ryleigh sniffed back lingering tears.

"If you'd changed your mind about Guilder," Ashyr asked, "why drag us all back to Byzantium?"

"Someone calling himself the Scarecrow Man put a bounty out for the crown prince. I took the contract as soon as I got wind. Wasn't long before I had his overindulgent routines down. A few coins to turn his minders' heads and I had him bent over my horse riding toward the Shaman Bluffs." Shyloh's gaze fell. "The rest, you know."

She turned a remorseful eye toward Guilder. "After you'd come out of the cave you were... different. I even considered you a friend, in one of my... weaker states. But failing to satisfy my end of the arrangement meant there was still a price on Guilder's head. My plan was to confront this Scarecrow Man with Guilder in my back pocket and get him to pull the contract."

"And?"

"Our meeting didn't go so well. He threatened that if I didn't finish the job, he'd send others who would."

"Great," Ashyr said, shaking his head. "So, what's the move?"

"The move is that you stay put, at least until you're well enough to stand," Breya said.

"She's right," Shyloh added. "The three of us can continue to Byzantium to sort this out in greater numbers."

"I'm not going to Byzantium on some fool's errand," Ryleigh said, crossing her arms in defiance.

"And if you expect me to sit here and stew, you're out of your damn mind," Ashyr shot back.

Guilder shifted his attention around the room. Everyone talked over one another, their volume matching the rising tension in the small cabin. "I know what we need to do," he said, with no one seeming to hear.

Breya's containment spell flickered. "This is no time to go off half-cocked without a plan. But you all need to figure this shit out and get the hell out of my house."

"I have a plan," Guilder said a bit louder, to no avail, dust beginning to stir throughout the cabin.

"Byzantium is where the threat is," Shyloh said. "It was why we came. We need to keep going."

An earsplitting screech cut through the mounting din. Breya's face reddened with exertion as she whistled through her fingers. "Y'all shut the fuck up for two seconds!" She looked around, making sure she had everyone's full attention and in as calm a voice as anyone had heard from her. "I think Guilder has something to say." She turned toward him. "Go ahead, say your piece."

"Um, thanks, Breya."

She nodded and, with a smile, held out her palm for Guilder to continue.

"Much has happened in such a short time. These memories I had of a life so far removed, they're still coming into focus. I remember the Byzantium woman." Guilder looked toward Shyloh, her eyes glassy. "How much unrequited hate I held for her. Only I couldn't say why. I can't even say I'm that person anymore. Not sure I'd even want to be.

"Meeting all of you, being treated like a longtime friend, family even…" He gazed at Ryleigh, who returned a tentative smile. "When you didn't know me from anyone or knew me as someone… I no longer seem to be. It's given me something I hadn't remembered ever having, a feeling of belonging. Ryleigh, we fought as one, and we were ferocious."

Her smile widened in admiration. Guilder stepped over to Shyloh. "You didn't take my life, Shyloh. I'm still pissed you stuck me in that cave, but…it's given me a chance to start over, erased old transgressions. That's how it feels, anyway." He stuck out his arm. "In that other life, I wronged you. I can never make that up, but because of how you all treated me, I'm willing to be a better person."

Shyloh nodded, clasping his arm in turn.

"Okay," Ashyr said. "Now that we're all playing nice, nice, what's *your* plan?"

"We'll need to deal with this Scarecrow Man," Guilder said. "But before we do, we'll go to New Aurora and have a word with my father."

***

Guilder stared into the midnight sky, tracing out constellations that looked vaguely familiar. Outside Breya's cabin, his fire had died to embers, the heat still radiating through to his feet, the cool night air licking at his shoulders and the back of his neck. The cabin door creaked open as he searched his mind for hidden names of unreachable stars.

"You should get some rest." Breya sat on an upturned log next to Guilder. "You have a long journey to New Aurora and everyone else is already asleep."

"Everyone but you." Guilder's eyes continued searching the night sky.

"Yeah, well." Breya leaned forward, warming her hands over the glowing coals. "I'm not the one traipsing halfway across the continent. You, though…"

"Not tired, I guess."

Breya nodded. The coals crackled like wind chimes. An owl made its presence known, calling out before his hunt.

"I've been trying to remember the names of the old gods." Guilder pointed skyward. "I'd been taught they look down on us from the stars. Atar, the turtle god of water. Those eight crossed stars mark due north." He tilted his head. "The kite, Tenya, god of wind, and her brother, Ildir, who looks like a measuring ladle."

"God of planets and rock," Breya said, looking up.

"These half-memories, the knowledge I

know I have but can't seem to hold on to. They return to me in waves. It's maddening."

"You see those three stars?" Breya ran her arm across the whole of the night sky. "The small red one is Marza, the god of battle and strength. The brightest one in the center, is Jupter, a thunder god, and Sumturn, the goddess of fate. The closer they get to each other, the angrier they become. Or so the story goes." Breya turned back to the embers as her smile faded. "Ancient texts speak of these gods not as stars, but as other planets. Eight altogether, or nine... whatever. Point is when they come into conjunction, magic increases in power and ferocity."

Guilder continued to look skyward. "Uteus is the god of magic. He has nothing to do with it?"

"Perhaps." Breya nodded, taking in a deep breath of cool air. "Yet perhaps there are elements of this world, even this universe, we don't understand. Or maybe we once understood and only forgot."

"What elements don't we understand?"

"Nothing, only thinking out loud." She shook her head, pursing her lips. "Just contemplating the true nature of things. Like who we are or why we're here, things like that."

"Breya." Guilder narrowed his eyes at her. "You know something."

"What? You're crazy." She waved a hand at him, her eyes scrunched as she shook her head. "Why would I keep something from you, from any of you?" Breya stared into the embers. "It's just that, Shyloh and Ryleigh, they're the same age. Only a few months separate their birthdays."

"So?"

"Ashyr, he's not quite three years younger than either of them. He'll be twenty-two later this year."

Guilder shook his head and shrugged.

"Seems you're about the same age as the girls, twenty-five, I'm guessing." Breya's eyes widened, expectant.

Guilder squashed his eyebrows together and tilted his head dumbfounded. "Breya, are…are you flirting with me?"

Breya's mouth hung open. "Are you fucking kidding me?" She stared Guilder square in the eyes.

"I'm flattered, I really am, but this isn't really the time. And you're like almost fifty or something, aren't you?"

Breya raised her hands, shouting at the sky. "Gods be damned, shut the hell up, you horse's ass." She looked back at Guilder. Disappointment mixed with his lingering bewilderment at her outburst. "You ever see any other males your own age? No, you haven't, because twenty-five years ago they were all killed. Ordered by that ageless prick, Andorian Iks, and executed by both kingdoms. You're the only male born that year still alive."

Breya took a deep meditative breath and closed her eyes. "There was a prophecy written by some obscure seer, only a few decades back.

About someone who will strike down the devourer of light. It's widely believed to be about Iks, maybe something he'd done or is about to do."

"I'm twenty-six," Guilder said, stone-faced.

Breya turned a blank look toward him. "Of course," she said, forcing a smile. "Probably just some stupid poem… to scare children into… not being such… little shits or something. Never mind. That your sword? Can I see it?"

Guilder pursed his lips, narrowing his eyes. He unlatched his sheath and passed it to Breya. "I just want to figure out who I was or… who I am and try to get back to some semblance of a life. If I have my way, a better one."

"An admirable goal, figuring out who you are." Breya unsheathed Guilder's sword, laying it across her knees. She stroked her palm across the blade, closing her eyes. *"Aspaugite so pleno valdikus kad ju nesulazu."* The blade glowed blue beneath her hands as if the steel absorbed the light. She held the sword over the dying embers, then handed it back to Guilder. "That should help in what's to come."

Guilder took back his sword, eyes affixed to Breya. He stood up and flourished it around, a faint blue light trailing the blade. "It's lighter."

Breya flicked a dismissive hand. "One of the side effects."

"Thanks. For everything." Guilder slid the sword back into its sheath. "I think I'll get some sleep."

"Yeah, wise… wise idea," Breya said

staring into the dying coals.

Guilder stood gazing at Breya, her face somber in the orange-red glow. "I'm not who you think I am."

She turned toward him. "Whatever plan the gods have for you doesn't involve who you were. What's important is who you are now." Breya turned back toward the embers. "Figure out who you ultimately want to be and do it quickly, Prince Guilder Rayne, before you doom us all."

CHAPTER 18
Æthelred the Unready

"Your Grace, the circumstances of the crown prince's absence have been noted. It does not excuse the fact that preparations need to be finalized." Near the far end of the cavernous room, only a single chandelier remained lit. Three men occupied the massive table dividing the space. The blaze from the open hearth fought with refracted candlelight as a skeletal shadow danced within the fire's glow. The fourth of those assembled stood off the king's right shoulder, watching the others while warming his reedy frame by the room's hearth.

The king's eyes drooped with weariness, his complexion pale, nearing gray, hair stringy, more white than the chestnut brown it had once been. "Your council, General Greymoor, is always welcomed as it was when my father, Basil Rayne, was king. However, Guilder is still my son." The throne had robbed Æthelred of his once boyish fascinations and left him a meager shell of an old man.

"Guilder's had longer absences than this." Tasker Greymoor shifted toward the table's head, placing a palm near the king's left hand. "Nonetheless, Byzantium will not suspend their attack while we shift our forces toward a search. Your Grace… Æthelred, I implore you."

"Do not lord your familiarities over His Majesty or this council, General!" Eshtyn Barrows slammed a fist onto the table. "We each lend a rightful voice to these ventures and are fully capable of making our sentiments known without pressing childish advances."

"You've always been a man of mighty throat, Barrows." Greymoor slid his hand back, folding one over the other. "Equaled only by your girth."

Barrows stood, slammed down his other fist, and clenched his jaw as he loomed over Greymoor.

"Calm yourselves, please." Æthelred massaged his temple. "Eshtyn, sit."

"If not for his sister's betrothal, he'd not be on this council," Greymoor remarked under his breath. "No offense to the queen, Your Majesty."

Æthelred glared, frowning at Greymoor. Barrows seethed; his arms laced over his chest.

"Barrows sits at my right hand as royal chancellor by my decree, Tasker. You'd best remember that."

"I will, Your Grace."

"Now, while I appreciate your passions, I can't agree with these priorities."

"This war will undoubtedly ensue, regardless of whether we sent a few men in search of the crown prince. Fool though he may be." Æthelred turned his gaze toward the fire. "Any sage advice to add, Wilfried?"

"Bickering amongst ourselves will not solve either crisis."

"Thank you for that brilliant insightfulness," Barrows scoffed. "Why is Shayde even here?"

"I'd have to agree, Your Grace." Greymoor leaned in toward the king, voice lowered, eyes glued to the scarecrow. "Spies cannot be trusted, Auroran or otherwise."

"He's loyal to me." Æthelred tightened his lips into a scowl. "And I'd expect, at the very least, you'd respect your king's judgment on such things. If it weren't for Wilfried, we'd all be facing the Byzantium Council's headsman instead of plotting our counter strategies. Besides, he has a knack for getting into places."

"All the more reason he can't be trusted." Greymoor leaned back into his chair. His gaze drifted into a shadowed corner where a fly buzzed, barely audible, over the crackling flames.

Barrows picked his teeth with his fingernail. "What intelligence have you to add then, Shayde?"

Æthelred shivered as Shayde moved like a wraith to Greymoor's side of the table. "Byzantium's council has already decided their time to strike." He sat glaring at Greymoor, challenging his affinity for the shadowy corner before turning his attention to the table. "Your Grace will need to finalize your counterstrike. The crown prince will be looked after, but for now, he is a needless distraction."

"How dare you!" Barrows leaned across the table, an accusatory finger pointed at Shayde. "The prince is an asset to this council! He is not, nor has ever been a distraction."

"Eshtyn, please." Æthelred shrunk into his

chair, stealing a deep, calming breath. "Guilder has continually been the loudest voice for this war. We can all agree on that account. His absence at this council, distraction or not, troubles me. Without him, we must all be in agreeance."

"Your Grace, with all due respect, the prince has always been prone to impulsiveness. Not in the least missing these council meetings his… treatment of his fiancée—"

"Measure your next words aptly, General," Barrows said. "The Byzantium Lady's death was deemed an accident and dealt with accordingly."

"Byzantium does not see it as an accident, Eshtyn," Greymoor barked. "Had they, their armies would not be amassing at this very moment."

"They chose war! We are obliged to answer."

Greymoor pressed back in his chair. "A morganatic marriage would have united the southern continent—"

Barrows rose to his feet. "To what end? The dissolving of the monarchy? The severing of the kingdom? Aurora's crown prince would never sacrifice his own sovereignty for one Byzantium life!"

Æthelred rubbed at his temple. "Sit down, Eshtyn."

He sat, continuing to stare daggers into Greymoor's eyes. Finally, the general let out a held breath. "Relations with Byzantium had been fragmented even before the crown prince's insistence on this war." Greymoor turned his gaze back to Æthelred. "Our bilateral experiment has failed and attempts to appease the divide have only kept the issue fresh. Byzantium's reactionary insult because of the crown prince's… misgivings with his fiancée was at best an excuse. While I've given my voice to oppose this path over the last few years, I'm sorry to say, Your Grace, but our defenses need to be finalized, regardless of Guilder's ill-timed absence. I regrettably must side with your spy."

"Wise of you, General."

Greymoor narrowed his eyes, turning toward Shayde. "This time."

"When will Byzantium's army strike, Wilfried? How much time do we have?"

"Some." Shayde watched Greymoor's gaze steal into the shadowed corner before readdressing the king. "The Necromancer, Lord Andorian Iks, has called an assemblage."

"Why have I not been notified of this?" Barrows asked.

Greymoor smirked, opening his mouth to comment before abiding the king's warning eyes.

"Messengers have been sent," Shayde said. "One should arrive for you today. Representatives of both kingdoms have been called to resolve accusations of an ignored edict and I suspect Byzantium intends to use the opportunity to lend credence to their war efforts. We will need to do the same."

"Why not campaign for the illegitimacy of their claims," Greymoor said. "Without the lord's backing, Byzantium will have to reconsider this opening gambit. Aid from Iks would unquestionably tip the scales in our favor."

"Because their claims are far from illegitimate," Æthelred said. "Besides, Andorian Iks lends his backing to no one."

"Damn that sorcerer." Barrows slammed a beefy hand onto the table. "Sitting in his tower with only his prized books for comfort. He takes no sides but asserts dominion over all? I don't give two shits how powerful he thinks he is."

"Now you must mind *your* words, Chancellor," Shayde warned.

"That sorcerer will heed the prowess of Aurora's military." Barrows pointed a sausage finger at the king. "When this farce of a war is through, we should march the remainder of our troops right to his salty doorstep…"

"And do what, Chancellor?" Greymoor said. "Plead for his surrender right before he sets our entire army to blaze?"

"We have magic wielders, too, General!"

"An entire army of magic wielders couldn't breach those walls. Let alone get through his D*ragonaught* Troops…"

"Then you're a coward!"

"Fuck you, Eshtyn!"

"Enough!" Æthelred narrowed his eyes at his counsel. "We're not planning a second war before the first has even started. Your childish squabbling hasn't got us any closer to solving either problem or if at all possible, avoiding them altogether. Wilfried, when will Byzantium strike?"

"A fortnight beyond the Necromancer's summons, Your Highness. They plan to gather near the center of the Bulwark Divide and march on the city thereafter."

Æthelred tented his hands, returning the expectant stares from his advisors. "Eshtyn, you will accompany Shayde in answer to Lord Iks' summons. Wilfried, be my eyes in his citadel. Byzantium may well tip its hand given such an audience. Any such bolstering could give us an advantage in the battle to come."

"As you command, Your Grace," Barrows said, clenching his fists tighter. Shayde tilted his head in a bow.

"Tasker, follow along after. If his lordship or his army of Dragonaught troops should possess any weakness, any at all, we may find an opportunity for future exploitation. All of you, be mindful. I feel there is more at play than we're privy to."

Shayde moved his gaze to the shadowed corner. "Wise moves indeed, Your Grace."

***

Wilfried Shayde stood near the shadowed corner of the war room long after the council had adjourned. Firelight dimly played off his sharp, angular features. His gaze fixed toward a minuscule iridescent body crawling at the ceiling corner, its animated wings buzzing intermittently.

The chamber door cracked open allowing a

slender figure to ease into the room. "You cannot be here. Not now," Shayde said his eyes unmoving from the shimmering insect.

"I know. I won't tarry long." The figure, shrouded in the darkest of brown, stood a petite step in from the doorframe. "You're going to see him? Meet with him?"

"Word travels fast through stone walls." Shayde sighed. "Preparations for my departure have already commenced."

The shrouded figure took another step into the room, raising a draped arm toward the darkened corner. "I feel his presence, even now."

"Be silent! Do not speak his name in such contexts."

"But his promise—"

Shayde snapped his scowling gaze toward the shrouded figure. "I told you to bite your tongue."

The figure's head bowed. "Yes. Of course. But please, Wilfried." A delicate hand protruded from the dark shroud, double rings of gold adorning the fourth finger. "Bring him this letter…as a favor."

Shayde reached out, taking the letter. "Very well. Now go." He watched the figure turn and leave. Soft footsteps quickly padded down the corridor. He turned the letterlocked message over in his bony hands and gazed into the darkened corner of the room, sporadic buzzing filling the silence.

He ambled to the fireside, broke the royal seal, and studied the letter. He tossed the paper into the flames watching it shrivel and char, the blood-red wax melting and boiling away to black smoke. "His lordship does not offer forgiveness so easily." Shayde glanced back into the shadowed corner. "Not without recompense, my queen."

CHAPTER 19
City Beyond the Trees

"Shellrock Palace was carved out of the existing mountain hundreds of years ago, or so the elders say. The summit is one of the tallest of the Crystal Mountains. It envelops the palace like an angelic halo," Guilder said with a newfound giddiness churning in his breast and a wide smile. He peered at Ryleigh, keeping pace beside him, her tiny nods encouraging. "The range is snow-covered much of the year, and at the back, the crater plummets right into the Eastern Sea."

"Sounds like something out of a dream," Ryleigh said with an indulging smile, her eyes fixed on the road ahead. "Memories coming back, then?" Her smile faded as she ambled along the indistinct goat-path of a road. Three days since they left Paracel, it had been slow going with Ashyr still recovering, Ryleigh insistent on a slow pace, regardless of anyone's alternative wishes or Ashyr's complaining.

"Still overwhelming, at times." Guilder nodded, his humor turning melancholy. "The familiarity of the southern side of the continent seems to help."

"I'm glad," Ryleigh said, looking his way.

Small towns and villages dotted the landscape between Paracel and the Bulwark Divide, a kilometers-deep gorge carved by the river at its base. The sister cities of Krastas and Tiltas expanded out from the rim to either side. For a price, they'd accommodate travelers who wished to cross the rickety suspension bridges or guide them to the river below flowing west to spill out into Grand Valley Harbor and from there, the Southern Ocean.

The rolling hillside of the Shaman Bluffs returned to southern grassland planes. Homesteads were spaced kilometers apart, with hardly a goat path between. The Crystal Mountain foothills rose out of the far edge of the Forrest Narrows and by the time they'd traversed the woodlands and trekked through a few of the outlying towns the terrain turned outright rocky.

Guilder spread out his hands in front of him. "Picture it, kilometers of pear orchards encircling the front of Cañon City, the palace looming above. The trees grow massive due to the army of royal arborists attending them. They supply endless fruit and work for whoever wants it besides keeping any attacking siege weapons out of the city and out of range of the palace. You get tired of pears in everything, but it beats having an enemy sitting on your doorstep."

"We're all glad you remember hating pears so much," Ashyr said with a pinched look. Mist bled off him as he passed between Guilder and Ryleigh, cool steam billowing out beneath his gossamer robes. "Hope we make the city limits before nightfall. Be nice to sleep in a bed again."

Guilder tipped his chin as Ashyr moved ahead and out of earshot. "He doing all right?"

"He still tires easily, even with the slowed pace." Ryleigh watched Ashyr glide along the gravel-covered road. "When he's tired, he loses moisture and dehydrates, tiring him out all the more."

"Makes him cranky too," Shyloh said, passing on Ryleigh's right, eyes fixed on the city sprouting from the horizon. "Makes us all cranky. He's right, though, it would be nice to sleep in a bed tonight." She trotted ahead, catching up to Ashyr.

"I think Shyloh's avoiding me," Guilder said with pursed lips. "Can't say I mind, considering." He shook his head. "It grates on me, though, her stubbornness."

"She'll come around. Shyloh's not used to forgiveness coming so easily." Ryleigh narrowed her eyes ahead of her. "Let her stew in her guilt a while. Better to soften the gristly bits." She turned back to Guilder with a widening smile. "What else do you remember of Cañon City?"

"I remember there being a market. Just inside the city proper. Colorful tarps stretched along either side of the main street over vendors hocking everything from handmade trinkets to fresh-cut vegetables, potatoes, beans, nuts, even candies."

"And pears?" Ryleigh added, her smile turning coy.

"Pears too, yes." Guilder nodded, returning her smile. "Preserved, dried, pickled, you name it. Alongside the palace, in the higher elevations, they herd goats, hunt for large-horn sheep, and even trap hare and hyrax. The furriers have an entire street to sell the pelts." Guilder looked ahead as he talked, the memories playing out as visions before him. "A few blocks down there are tailors and seamstresses making clothes right next to the looms and dyers. They couldn't make the fabric fast enough. Wools from all over the continent, cotton, silks, and other bast fibers, and at least a dozen leatherers."

"I've never worn anything that was made by someone else." Ryleigh stared ahead as the tops of abscised trees, lifeless chimneys, and roofs of the lower city dotted the landscape. "Not as an adult, anyway."

"You'll find countless merchants of fine clothes, dresses, shoes, you name it. The tanners are on the outskirts, along with the blacksmiths. That end of town stinks in the summer, but they make the best leathers, weapons too. And wait till you taste the food. Steamed dumplings, meat carved right off the spit, set in freshly fried bread, there's more than you could taste in a month."

Ryleigh nodded. "It all sounds so wonderful." Her smile echoed Guilder's inner passion.

"It is." Guilder met Ryleigh's gaze. "I'd love to show it to you. When we get there... I mean."

"I'd like that." Ryleigh's smile widened, her cheeks turning pink.

Guilder and Ryleigh caught up to Shyloh, who snapped a branch from one of the peach trees along the outskirts of the orchard forest.

Planted in concentric rows and only shoulder-width apart, the orchard gave a staggered view of the city's wall and her outer reaches.

"This isn't right." Guilder pulled down a branch, breaking off a smaller limb. "This tree is dead. Looks like it's been dead for some time."

"Be quiet," Shyloh whispered, kneeling behind one of the larger trunks, Ryleigh kneeling behind her.

Guilder snapped another twig off a nearby tree. "All these trees are dead. The arborists here are meticulous about their trees. It's more than just fruit to them—"

"Guilder," Shyloh hissed. "Shut up and get down." She pointed. "Look, guards in the city."

"During the day? Now and then, I guess, but most times, not even at night."

Ryleigh pulled Guilder down beside her. "Where's Ashyr?"

"I sent him ahead, to sniff out what's going on."

"Ashyr isn't ready to use his powers yet," Ryleigh said in a vicious, hushed tone. "He's all but exhausted from the trip and you send him in as a scout?"

"It's why he came." Shyloh peered through the rows of trees, avoiding any glances behind. "He even insisted. Seemed enthusiastic enough."

Ryleigh balled her fists and huffed out her anger as she took in the city through the bare trees.

Guilder leaned closer to Shyloh. "There's something wrong here. The city's bolted up like it's under siege. Those guards are wearing Aurora war colors, but their patrol patterns are all wrong. Where's General Greymoor? Where's their banner? It's as if they're preparing for an outside attack."

Shyloh pointed to a central road leading toward the mountain. "They cross a midline every few minutes, patrolling a hundred meters into the city, give or take. Hard to tell how many altogether, seems like they're trying to disguise their numbers."

"To what end?" Ryleigh asked.

"Not sure, but something's definitely up."

"No direct way in." Ashyr materialized behind Ryleigh and kneeled next to Guilder. "Dual lookouts on each of the parapets, armed with longbows." He pointed a misty finger to the outer corners of the city. "No great number of archers, though, a handful across the alure. A dozen or so swordsmen patrolling. It's odd. They give the appearance of fortification but have nothing to back it up."

"Gods be damned, Ashyr, you're barely holding yourself together." Ryleigh waved away Ashyr's bleeding mist as it wafted toward her. "You need to take it easy."

Ashyr shook his head in defiance.

"I know another way in," Guilder said. "One I'd used a few times to sneak out of the castle."

"Why would a prince need to sneak out of his own castle?" Ashyr asked.

"Not for any virtuous reasons, I'm sure,"

Shyloh said, a scowl hardening her face.

Guilder looked at Ryleigh, pasted on a childish, innocent look, and shrugged.

Ryleigh narrowed her eyes. "Whatever the reason, can it get us into the city without being seen?"

"Better." Guilder grew a cocky half-smile. "It'll get us directly into the castle. This way." He took off, running low, into the setting sun. After a kilometer or so, the orchard thinned. The outer edge of the city all but disappeared. Guilder stopped, catching his breath, scanning for any signs of guards or archers glancing their way. "A bit further west of the city, there's an inlet into the mountain. At the back of that inlet, there's a hidden door leading to caverns beneath the city. Only…"

"Only what?" Shyloh said between heaving breaths.

"Nothing." Guilder shook his head. "We'll figure it out when we get there."

***

"You've been molesting that stone for hours. You sure we're in the right place?" Shyloh folded her arms into herself, warding off the chill of the night air. "Maybe your memory isn't as clear as you'd thought."

Guilder propped himself on one knee, his hand exploring a flat obsidian rock. "I'm positive this is the entrance… exit… whatever. There's a hole at the center of this stone, crossed by a shallow slit. It's the only blemish along the entire sheet. I just have to remember how to open it."

Ashyr lay sound asleep against the far side of the fissure. Ryleigh sat beside him, her legs tucked into her chest. "Why not make camp? Rest may help jog Guilder's memory and a fire would ward off the cold."

"Not worth the risk," Shyloh said, preening her fingernails with an arrow tip. "If someone sees us, whatever's going on here is going to spill into our laps. Better to keep at it. Once we get into the caves, we can take a breather. If we ever *get* into the caves."

Ryleigh jumped to her feet. "Maybe if we stop breathing down Guilder's neck for a minute, he can concentrate," she said, looming over Shyloh.

Guilder wiped an arm across his forehead as Ryleigh strolled over to him, her glare still resting on Shyloh. She placed her hand on Guilder's shoulder and lowered herself to her knees. "How's it going?"

"It's frustrating," he said. "The Earth caster words seem unfamiliar and there's a specific hand placement, but… I can't remember."

Ryleigh tilted her head, staring at the marks on the stone. "These cuts intentional?" She traced her fingers across the gap. "It looks like an Earth caster symbol all right. *Judeti*."

"I didn't want to ask, the whole Master Lusoren thing and all, but we're kind of in a bind. Can you work the spell?" Guilder looked at her, beseeching.

"No. I mean, not anymore." Ryleigh stood

up, folding her arms in front of her. "I don't do magic, remember? Not since… I just don't do magic."

"But you know the words."

"I don't… do… magic," she said through clenched teeth.

Guilder threw up his hands. "Okay, I got it, no magic. But if you help me with the words, I can try to get it open."

Ryleigh tightened her knotted arms and looked back at Shyloh, her hands folded over her chest as she reclined beside Ashyr, watching his shallow breath, the wind catching his mist. "Fine, but I'm not doing the spell." She stepped around Guilder and peered down at the symbols as she placed her hand on the rock.

Guilder peered up at her, eyes sympathetic. "Want to talk about it?"

"No," she said without looking at him. She huffed out a breath, eyes turned downward. "Later… maybe."

Guilder smiled. Ryleigh met his gaze, conceded with a hesitant smile of her own, and turned back to the stone. "Earth spells are more conjugal than the other elements. The words are more important than feeling or imagery."

"Shyloh told me that Earth mages picture crops when they cast."

"Shyloh doesn't know shit about Earth magic." Ryleigh glared behind her. Shyloh shook her head and looked away. "Fire wielders visualize," Ryleigh said, turning back. "Wind tamers give themselves over to their element. That's why Ashyr bleeds mist when he's tired."

She glanced behind her again, concern creeping back onto her face. "He's literally living mist."

"What about water... umm, water mages?"

"Breya does aquamancy. It leans toward the scientific. Chemistry, I think she calls it, or alchemy. She tried explaining it to me once. It's an understanding of the composition of certain substances and how they interact, combine, or change. Seems to need a lot more practice and experimentation."

"That poultice she made for Ashyr seemed pretty straightforward to me," Guilder said, turning to examine the stone. "Can she manipulate water?"

"Only to a point. Water is a difficult medium to manipulate. I've seen her retrieve a bubble from the well after the crank had broken and have it follow into her kitchen. But trying to redirect a river or stop the tide would probably give you an aneurysm. I guess you already know about metal."

"Seems a combination of all of them, visualization, feeling, and knowing what's available, its capabilities, and the words." Guilder looked at Ryleigh, a quizzical look on his face. "Only a bit more. It seems to need emotion as a conduit. I'd only been able to conjure when I was extremely angry... or scared."

Ryleigh nodded, her eyes drifting down, her smile fading. "Emotion strengthens all the magics." After a moment, she came back to herself. "Anyway, the symbol needs to be conjugated to what you want done. So *judeti* modifies to *pereiti* if you demand that it moves."

Guilder raised an eyebrow. "Demand?"

Ryleigh shrugged. "Excuse me if the other magical proficiencies are more polite than Earth magic. Just try it."

Guilder sighed. "What are the rest of the words?"

"Oh, right. M*ono vala.*"

Guilder spread his hands against the rock wall, closed his eyes, and took in a deep breath. In a staccato voice, he repeated, "*pereiti mono vala.*" The earth symbol glowed a pale azure. The wall clicked as if falling past a broken cog, then stopped as the glow faded. "What happened?"

"Not sure." Ryleigh searched the stone for something she'd missed. "Perhaps it needs a push?"

Guilder slid his finger into the symbol hole, braced his legs, and repeated the words. The symbol glowed as Guilder pushed to the side. The wall shifted into the adjoining rock face, opening to a descending path beneath the mountain range.

"Well, it's about time." Shyloh smacked Ashyr on the shoulder and pushed herself upright. "Get up. We're leaving."

Ashyr yawned, stretched out his arms, and tentatively got to his feet. "What's going on?"

Guilder poked his head into the tunnel entrance and sniffed the air. "Smells like… death. Rotting carrion, something else though, beneath." He sniffed again. "Something almost… musky."

"Probably a thriving rat colony," Shyloh said, bundling up a fist full of fallen twigs.

"Rats? I hate rats," Ryleigh murmured. "Anything look familiar, Guilder?"

"Only vaguely."

"*Summoneie perjos adiuvare tegere*," Shyloh murmured as she brushed her hand across the end of the bundle. The torch ignited with blue-orange flames, settling back into a soft glow as she ducked through the entrance. "Nothing like a jaunt through a dark tunnel to jog one's memory," she said, sending a backhanded wink at Guilder as she passed.

Guilder grabbed Shyloh's arm. "Wait. There's something carved into the stone here." Shyloh waved the torch near the tunnel wall. "Beware the Jabberwock, my son!" Guilder read, tracing the chipped-out words with his finger. "The jaws that bite, the claws that catch!"

"What in the nine realms does that mean?" Shyloh squinted at the message, her lips moving as he read the inscription.

"Not sure," Guilder said.

"You wrote it, didn't you?"

"I don't think so, I'm not sure I remember it ever being there." Guilder looked back at Ryleigh. "We should be careful."

Ryleigh nodded.

Shyloh rolled her eyes. "Let's go. I'm sure between the four of us we can handle whatever's in here." She ducked beneath the entrance and headed down the tunnel.

Ryleigh followed. "As long as it isn't rats."

"What are you guys talking about?" Ashyr said through another yawn. "Damn, what stinks?"

"Nothing. Just follow the torchlight." Guilder feigned a reassuring smile as the stone entrance slid shut behind them.

CHAPTER 20
Shellrock Palace

Guilder scraped his hand along the cavern ceiling, fearing an inadvertent assault by an unseen stalactite. A cool breeze slid past as Ashyr materialized in front of him. "It seems like hours since we've seen the sky," Ashyr whispered over Shyloh's shoulder. The torchlight shone through his translucent body like an undulating prism, splitting the light into a dancing rainbow of colors before dying away as he solidified. "Guilder, how far down does this go?"

"I don't recall. A ways more, I think." Guilder stared, fascinated by the ease at which Ashyr moved around. "It's like the memory is still there, just unclear, like from a long time ago. I knew the tunnels were here, but navigating them…" He shook his head.

"Tunnels, as in multiple?" Shyloh peered behind her at the train of people following. "This seems like a single descent into the nine realms itself. Where is this leading us?"

"Eventually? Aurora's dungeons."

"Great." Shyloh turned ahead. "It'll be nice to trade the stench of death and shit for desperation and abandoned hope."

"It's strange." Guilder peered behind him, squinting through the dark at Ryleigh. "I remember these caves smelling musty. They'd always been damp, moss and mushrooms growing rampant." He slowed his pace, letting her catch up. "But never this reek. Like some kind of—"

"Abattoir," Ashyr interjected.

"Yeah."

"Are you sure your memories can be trusted, Guilder?" Ryleigh's voice, soft and thoughtful. "You said there were still gaps. Could this be one of those... times?" Her gaze followed the tunnel opening into an immense cathedral. Arching columns held up a ceiling high enough to fit a quartet of multistory taverns, with ample room to spare. A carved dome spanned the center, a hundred meters around at the very least, its oculus projecting a white beam of starlight to one side. "What is this place?"

"Shellrock Palace," Guilder said, a knowing grin plastered across his face. "The ancient rulers worshiped their gods down here. In times of war, it served as their last refuge, an ultimate means of escape if ever they needed one."

"I thought the palace was that carved out mansion behind the city," Ashyr said, marveling at the ornate engravings along the circle of pillars.

"Everyone thinks that. Everyone outside the royal family, anyway. Common knowledge of a secret temple beneath the castle defeats the purpose of having the secret."

"Where do these doors lead?" Shyloh asked, throwing a shoulder into the meters-high double door at the opposite side of the chamber.

"Most of the exits lead to traps," Guilder said, fiddling with a shining black disk embedded into one of the archway columns. "Bottomless pits, some with iron pikes, or worse."

Ryleigh craned her neck, peering at the carved reliefs in the dome's interior. "What could be worse than falling into a pit full of pikes?" She squinted at the stained glass at the apex of the dome.

"Shyloh, give me your torch." Guilder stretched out his arm as Shyloh joined him near the center of the room. "Worse than pikes? I've heard of a room where the fall is so long that you can feel the air get warmer as you plummet." Guilder locked eyes with Ryleigh, a mischievous grin growing across his face. "The spikes at the bottom are so extensive they slow your descent as you slide down their impaling shafts. If you're unlucky enough to survive, you'll hear the pit start to fill with vitriolic alcohol, the acid eating away at your flesh as you drown."

Ryleigh's eyes narrowed as her smile widened. "Just pits then?"

Guilder shrugged, his smile persistent.

"You are so full of it," Ryleigh mouthed, her eyes lingering before turning back to look up at the dome.

Shyloh handed Guilder her torch. "If all the exits lead to traps, then how do we get into the castle?"

"I didn't say all the doors lead to traps."

"Most lead to pits," Ryleigh said, tracing a finger across one of the peripheral doors.

Guilder set the torch into a sconce above the black disk. He gave the disk a slight turn. Diamond-shaped crystals embedded along the outside walls flooded the room in lavender-blue light.

"Nice trick," Shyloh said, taking in the full extent of the massive room.

"Siren's glass, right?" Ashyr asked. "Takes in any available light, magnifies it a hundredfold. Very rare and super expensive."

"Less rare centuries ago. Each of the twelve pillars has a Siren's glass crystal in it. They only need a small bit of light to spread into the whole place."

"So, what's with the beam coming from the top of the dome? Why didn't they just use that?" Ryleigh asked, strolling over to Guilder.

"That's used to find our path." Guilder moved to the center of the cavernous room. "Twelve doors. One led us here, the one still open," he pointed back the way they'd come. "One leads to the Castle dungeons, the rest to death." Guilder looked back to Ryleigh; his smile faded.

"How do we know which is which?" Ashyr asked.

"That's the tricky bit, I'm afraid," Guilder said. "The paths switch depending on ancient star charts." Guilder shifted his stance, examining the circular painting on the floor beneath the dome. "This illustration represents the night sky. It changes according to the stars' celestial locations." He pointed to one of the pillars. "The columns represent the month.

There should be marks along the back wall to indicate specific days."

"Why do the ancients overcomplicate things?" Ashyr tilted his head, studying the map. "I recognize most of the constellations. They're where they should be for this time of year, but this central figure, *Tellus*, if it represents Earth, then there shouldn't be anything orbiting it."

"I'd always taken it for Earth." Guilder kneeled next to the depiction. "The ancients were meticulous with the accuracy of their maps. I guess I'd never questioned it." He brushed away the dust from the central planet. "*Tellus Mater*."

Shyloh huffed and shook her head.

"You know what it means?" Guilder asked.

"It's Earth," she nodded. "Tellus Mater, Mother Earth in the ancient tongue, but Ashyr's right; there shouldn't be anything around it."

Guilder ran his thumb over Tellus's satellite. "Luna." He turned toward Ryleigh. "Like in your grandmother's story."

"But that's all it was, a story." Ryleigh placed her hand on Guilder's shoulder, peering down at the floor. "A fable, to teach some life lesson to children."

"Seems Luna is a popular character in old fables," Shyloh said as she followed the light beam to the far wall. "My grandfather linked her to the zombie horde. Called her *the light*."

Ashyr joined the others after exploring the room. "So, the ancients fashioned a mural according to old fairy tales, so what? How do we get out of here?"

"Maybe they're more than just stories. If the ancients knew something about Luna, knew that it once orbited the Earth, or believed it did, there'd be evidence in the old texts."

"Those texts are probably in one of Iks' neglected libraries," Shyloh said. "Not in this underground labyrinth, so stop postulating as to why and get us out of here."

Guilder took a thoughtful breath. "We have to orient the Earth to the star map according to today's date." He brushed off more dust from the central planet, placed his fingers into the uncovered depressions, and twisted. "It's stuck. Everyone off the mural."

Guilder waited until he was the only one left on the painting and tried again. Far off, gears sounded with a metal clunk, as if shifting into position. The door they'd entered slammed shut. "Mark that door!" Guilder pointed to where the tunnel had been. Ashyr rushed over to stand next to the closed door. "That exit is our negative declination. If we lose track of it, none of this will work." Guilder twisted the planet again. The room began to spin around him. Shyloh tumbled to the ground as Ryleigh braced herself against the nearest pillar. Ashyr faded to mist reflexively, needing to run to catch up to the door he was meant to have marked.

"There," Guilder pointed, as the room shuddered to a stop. "The pillar by the exit should represent the back end of the calendar. The first month in front." The group rejoined

Guilder on the map. "That's the correct day, right?"

"Yeah, but the light beam doesn't touch any of the doors," Shyloh said. The dome's oculus projected its beam to the center of one of the pillars. "You must have done it wrong."

"What about Luna's position?" Ryleigh asked. "If it was important enough to depict, it should have some relevance to the puzzle."

Guilder rotated the smaller satellite around the larger orb. The white light beam shifted in an elliptical motion between the centers of two doors.

"Well, which one is it?" Shyloh asked.

"I'm not sure." Guilder looked down at the map.

"You seemed to know before."

"A lot has happened since…" Guilder shook his head. "I may have used another trick to find the right passage."

"Use your other trick, then."

"I never had a reason to sneak into the castle, just out, and I'd always leave the correct tunnel open, never being out more than a night."

Shyloh threw her hands up. "Just great."

Ryleigh shook her head and glared at Shyloh. Guilder looked back at her, eyes questioning. "I just don't know."

"Can we at least get the exit opened again?" Ashyr asked.

"The paths switch when the mechanism is engaged." Guilder stood, brushing himself off.

"It isn't worth the risk. Until we figure out the correct path, we're stuck."

"Perfect, just fucking perfect," Shyloh said.

"Just what in the nine realms is your problem?" Ryleigh stomped a few paces toward Shyloh, her fists clenched. "Ever since we left Paracel, you've had some bug up your ass for no reason."

"I've got a bug up *my* ass?" Shyloh pointed at herself, feigning shock as she took a step toward Ryleigh. "We're trapped down here, forced to follow this lobotomized lunatic in his sick pursuit to break into his daddy's castle. Once he shows his face up there, what do you think they're going to do with us?"

"He wouldn't be lobotomized if it weren't for you."

Guilder stepped between the two, putting a hand on Ryleigh's shoulder. "Ryleigh, it's okay. This isn't the time to rehash this."

Shyloh took another step forward. "It isn't bad enough you've been trading fuck-me eyes this whole time—"

"Shyloh, that's enough," Ashyr said from across the room, distracted from his examination of the doors.

"No, I bit my tongue for this royal pissant long enough."

"You're the one who stuck him in that cave," Ryleigh screamed. "You're a damned coward for offering him up to that monster in the first place."

"Ryleigh!" Guilder hollered, regaining the group's attention. He took a deep breath and in a softer tone said. "It's all right, Ryleigh. Shyloh's welcome to her opinions." His sympathetic gaze turned to Shyloh.

The room fell silent as all eyes remained on Shyloh. Her jaw tightened, fists white, tears, streaming. "Damn you, Guilder," she whispered, turning away, wiping her face on her sleeve. Guilder watched her retreat toward the back of the room as Ryleigh stamped off in the opposite direction.

"Guilder," Ashyr called, waving for him to come over.

Guilder shook his head, glancing back to Ryleigh, then ambled over to where Ashyr was standing. "Hey," Guilder said, directing his gaze anywhere but Ashyr's face. "Thanks for... speaking up back there."

"Don't mention it," Ashyr said, going back to his study of the door. "Shyloh, she's... got a lot on her mind."

"There's a lot of that going around." Guilder glanced back at Shyloh pursing his lips. "Find anything that can help us get out of here?"

"Perhaps." Ashyr traced a finger along the writings carved into the door. "These depictions seem to be written in the ancient language, only... it's strange."

"How so?"

"They aren't instructions per se, but a story told over and over again. The same story, as if told from different perspectives. All of them, regarding Luna. Look here, *tamsoje pasiklydusi mergina.* It speaks, not of a girl, but of a body lost in darkness and a great wizard, *puikus burtininkas.*"

"What's so strange about it? It's the same story Ryleigh's grandmother told her. They're probably just decorative."

"They're not, though. The language is more historic. Not like a story, but actual happenings. It's the story I recognize as Luna's, but see this word? *Menuis*, it's on every door, taking the place of Luna from the story."

"It's just the translation for Luna, isn't it?"

"In the ancient tongue, names don't change. Guilder translates as Guilder, Luna to Luna. That's the strange part, *Menuis* translates to the moon."

"So, Luna means moon, so what?"

"Not moon, *the* Moon. These doors tell the history of an orbiting body, a planet revolving around *Tellus*, Earth."

Guilder leaned in to study the door, moving to the one adjacent, then the one neighboring. "These carvings depict the changing of the seasons." Guilder pointed at the background landscape depicted in the adornment. "This is Shellrock Mountain, snow on top and on the surrounding ground. This should be the door for the first month." He went three doors clockwise. "Yes, fourth month. Shellrock still has snow, but the trees are fuller, these small lakes depicting melted snow."

Ashyr headed the opposite way. "I think you're right. This one seems like autumn."

Guilder pointed to the other side of the room. "And summer the way we came in." His eyes darted around as he rubbed his chin in thought. "The book predicted that a shadow was cast onto Luna, changing her shape each month from spherical to semicircular and at times disappearing altogether."

"How does that help us with the pictogram?"

Guilder hurried back to the door Ashyr was studying. "The marks on the wall indicate the day, the door, the month." Guilder traced the arch around the outside of the door, a gradually disappearing circle, gone, then reemerging. "These symbols must show Luna's phases during this particular month. And today, she would be…" Guilder stopped and poked a finger at one symbol. "About half." He raced back to the central pictogram. "So, if that door is the date, then Luna's shadow would be…" Guilder squeezed the tiny satellite, sliding it into itself according to the door's depiction, the light falling against a pillar between two doors.

"I must have interpreted it wrong," Ashyr said.

"No, there's just something we're missing," Guilder said. "Something else we need to do."

"The words," Shyloh said, impatience echoing in her tone.

"What words?" Guilder asked.

"You said the paths switch magically?"

"So?"

"Then you probably need some kind of

magic word, a phrase, or something."

"Any ideas?" Ashyr fixed his gaze on Shyloh.

Shyloh huffed and sauntered over to where Guilder had knelt. She lowered herself to one knee and stared at the pictogram. "If this is Earth, *Tellus* in the ancient tongue…" She pressed her finger on the central planet, pushing it into the floor. Blue light glowed behind the circular illustration. "Then this…" she pressed the orbiting planet. "Luna," she said in a clear tone. The blue glow encircled the rest of the pictogram. "Should show us the way out."

The door where Ryleigh had been standing glowed with white light. The oculus's beam issued just above her head. She pulled at the shimmering door, revealing a stone pathway into a dark corridor. "Looks like the way out."

Guilder rushed over to Ryleigh and poked his head through the door, taking in what he could. "Hope there isn't a pit," Ryleigh whispered. Guilder turned, shooting her a snide look.

"I'll lead the way," Shyloh said, lighting another torch. "But only if you two can control yourselves until we get out from under this mountain." She passed through the door without looking at either of the two. "Gods be damned, it stinks worse than the first path."

Ashyr followed behind Shyloh, waggling his eyebrows in Guilder's direction as he passed, a cocksure smile plastered on his face. Guilder held out a hand, gifting a slight bow, as he offered Ryleigh the right of way. "Now, I kind of hope there *is* a pit," she said smiling as she passed. Guilder matched her step as they followed Shyloh's torchlight, the door closing with a muffled rumble behind them.

CHAPTER 21
Tithes to the Ageless Lord

The uppermost library of my citadel looks southeast toward the Shaman Bluffs, remnants of the Crystal Mountains at the opposite edge of the continent. I leaned against my blackwood cane, shoulders stiff, knees aching, and took in a ragged breath of brackish morning air. I've been here too long, hungry for the sights and sounds of what was once familiar and uncorrupted. The perfume of cityscapes and asphalt, the symphony of traffic and crowded sidewalks. Science and invention, without the tarnish of magic.

I stretched out my back, feeling my joints grind like coarse chaff in a dull mill. A black satin robe hung around my skeletal frame like an ill-fitted death shroud as my gnarled fingers clamp the cane's ornately carved grip, a lion's head with a scorpion's tail tracing through the silver collar and down the staff. The gold-stitched winged manticore at my back brandishes my adopted house crest. Its strength and ferocity mock my thinned, wispy hair, liver-spotted head, and the magnitude of my age. I have been here far too long.

"My lord," Iven announces judiciously as I turn from the window. "I've procured the candidate you asked for." He tilted his head in a slight bow, placing a hand behind the trailing child's shoulders. The boy, only tall enough to reach my advisor's hip, held on to the hem of

Iven's burgundy swallowtail coat, his dark brown eyes focused in childish curiosity.

I lace my hands over the grip of my cane, taking in the boy's countenance. He's small for his age, seven perhaps eight, by the lack of understanding in his eyes. Dressed in a clean white linen shirt and tan ankle-length trousers. Iven had clearly insisted on a bath, his dark auburn hair still damp, falling beyond his shoulders. His inquisitive gaze darts around the room as if in wonder at the packed shelves of countless leather-bound books. Curiosities he has yet to have experienced.

Iven's mechanical eye whirls in its socket, a sign of his frustration with his mechanical stillness. "Your Excellency?" Iven prodded. His exasperation seeps out in mock concern.

"Yes, Iven. I heard." Distant rumbles from a far-off storm sound as I took a tentative step from the window. I breathe in the smell of electricity mixed with deteriorating paper, dried leather, and stone. "Since your rebirth, Iven, you'd often had difficulty with subtle emotion. The automation confused by those few parts which remain human."

Iven breathed out a steadying sigh, adjusting his posture against the remark. "Your Excellency, may I present Eli Maerek, son of the Elder Maerek." Iven gave Eli a push toward the center of the room, freeing himself of the boy's grasp. "Bow your head, boy! You're in the presence of sovereignty." Eli bowed his head and curtsied. Iven rolled his remaining human eye, its gray-blue color stark against a red, corneal background, highlighting his annoyance.

"Maerek?" an old man's voice croaked from my lips. "Your father's a quadrant supervisor?" Eli looked back toward Iven, trembling and unsure, as a dry coughing fit followed my half-question. "His company's logging efforts—" I coughed again. "—centered on the foothills—" Straining to regain my breath. I wiped the spittle from my cracked lips, refocusing on the young boy.

Eli stood at arm's length, taking a half step back as I amble forward. "Yes… yes sir," Eli said, nodding in a tremulous voice.

"You'll address Lord Iks as my lord or your excellency," Iven corrected as his servos clicked in punctuation.

"Yes, Your Excellency, sir," Eli said, receiving another eye roll from Iven.

"It's fine, Iven." I reach a trembling hand toward the boy, his mouth agape, clearly spellbound by the frailty of old age draped in fine silk. He pops his thumb into his mouth as I run a craggy finger across his guiltless temple. "The boy hasn't enjoyed the privilege of a court education. We can forgive his lack of decorum."

I turn from Eli, ambling toward a pair of stretched leather side chairs set before the open hearth. Dropping into the far chair, I hooked my cane over the headrest. "Please." I waved Eli to come closer, covering my mouth against another coughing fit. "That will be all, Iven," I said, keeping my eyes glued on Eli while pointing a craggy finger toward the door.

"Your Excellency." Iven bowed, turned on his heels, and left the library, closing the doors behind him.

"I abhor the pomp and circumstance around this place," I said, continuing to stare at the closed doors. "Yet we all have our roles to play."

Eli gawked at the vast collection of books. Colored leather bindings with gold inscriptions along their spines, loose manuscripts of yellowed paper, and arcane tomes in exotic scripts.

"Had your father taught you to read?" I asked, remarking on his fascination.

"Hadn't much cause to sir… your lordship."

"You may call me Andorian." I offered, a half-smile beckoning him closer. "But don't let it get out. Only my closest friends may call me that." Eli stood before me, his eyes stuck on the floor-to-ceiling bookshelves. I took the boy's hands in mine, resting them on my bony knees. "I'd like to tell you a story. One that'd been written in these very books some time ago. Would you like to hear it, Eli?"

"Yes sir. Andorian, sir." Eli's gaze tentatively found mine. His voice strained as his heart pounded.

I lightly squeezed Eli's hands, focusing on his trembling eyes. "Long ago, when the world was a very different place. A better place. There was a man named Isaiah Crowley."

Eli's face relaxed, his eyes closed. "This man was a brilliant scientist," I continued. "He studied the universe, as much as science and the technology of the day would let him. One night when he was exploring the skies, he discovered a new asteroid. Do you know what an asteroid is, Eli?"

"Yes," Eli said, as if far away. His body, stiff and unsteady on his feet.

"Good." I strengthened my grip on Eli's hands, closing my own eyes. "Isaiah noticed this asteroid, deemed 2026TC, seemed different from most. He used all the scientific knowledge and instrumentation available to him, full-spectrum cameras, forward-looking infrared, gamma, and x-ray spectrometers, all leading to one undeniable fact. Do you know what that was, Eli?"

The boy remained motionless. His breath, slow and calm.

"Asteroid 2026TC bled energy. An energy Isaiah had never seen before. If he could bring the asteroid toward Earth, maybe even *to* Earth, he could study it further, and in his own way, understand the universe that much better." I took a deep, clear breath, stretched out my back muscles, my neck. Felt my limbs and joints loosen.

"Bringing an asteroid to Earth would be quite the undertaking," I continued in a sturdier, silvery voice. "He received help from the United States Military's Missile Defense Systems satellites, changing the trajectory of the asteroid so it would travel nearer to Earth." I got up, leaving the boy where he stood, my cane still hooked over the back of the chair. Sauntering over to one of the bookshelves, I slid out a random book and paged through it.

"After its slight... nudging, it took another five years to travel into Earth's vicinity. By then, it was too late. A miscalculation had brought the asteroid into a collision course with the planet. Isaiah was blamed, of course, and cut out of any further discussions of viable solutions. Endless bureaucracy and infighting led to a total lack of action. The fools continued their useless debate even after the asteroid crashed into Earth's moon."

I felt my face tighten, the pain from extreme age receding. My back, legs, and arms filled again with strength. The boy, hands still held out, motionless in front of the stretched leather chair, grayed, wrinkled, and mummified, his eyes still closed behind his lifeless face.

"The asteroid struck hard enough to shatter the moon to pieces, effectively pushing it out of its orbit and throwing several fragments into Earth's atmosphere." I snapped the book shut, replaced it on its shelf, and looked back at the boy. "For three days, humanity suffered a global panic," I said, calm, emotionless.

"Isaiah found refuge in an underground bunker, in a small town outside what the ancients called Colorado Springs, purchased after being excluded from the military's futile discussions. He prayed, in his weakness, that the damage would not be world-ending, though his computations said otherwise. As fragments of the moon crashed into the planet, leveling mountains, and effectively raising the ocean levels, segments of the meteorite fell as well. The biggest landing in an out-of-the-way town in rural Colorado. The meteorite destroyed the town, vaporized everyone, and collapsed into the bunker Isaiah cowered in."

I returned to the library window as the clouds let loose a cascade of welcomed rain. Catching my reflection in the window, I adjusted the black satin robe hanging regally around my powerful shoulders. I touched my taut face, my chest firm and muscular. My eyes, though held my age. I looked out into the gloomy sky, running my fingers through long, white hair, knowing full well it would grow out the same dark brown it always had.

"How the planet survived is anyone's guess. Every living thing on Earth should have ceased to be, and yet… Still, we are, after all, descendants of survivors." I peered back at the boy, my nostalgic smile now faded. "Isaiah didn't die, far from it. The meteorite kept him alive, somehow. Isaiah stayed trapped." The blackwood cane remained hooked to the chair. "A hundred years, a thousand? It's hard to determine how long he was down there. Not dead, but not alive. Radiation soaked into the destroyed Earth and into his body. Ultimately, he used this newfound energy, this… magic, to free himself from his bunker."

I reclaimed the cane and kneeled beside the corpse retaking its still-clasped hands. "Your life will not have been used in vain. The time of conjunction is approaching when the celestial pull will amplify my power. I will fix this. For you, young Eli Maerek. For all your kind and for all you've sacrificed." I stood and headed toward the hallway closing the doors behind me, leaving Eli alone with his books.

CHAPTER 22
The Serpent King

"So, why don't you use magic?" Guilder whispered as he matched Ryleigh's step. The tunnel leading out of Shellrock Palace proved wider than the one leading in and at least a full arm's length taller. Torchlight danced above their heads as Shyloh sped along the corridor ahead of them, Ashyr right beside her.

Ryleigh shrugged. "I've already told you." Her gaze fell to the carved rock floor as her smile diminished.

"It's just that Breya said—"

"Said what?" A sharp tone invaded Ryleigh's voice as she narrowed her eyes at Guilder.

"Quiet, you two," Shyloh said, turning back. "No telling what's down here. And we wouldn't want to announce our presence."

Guilder ran a hand along the back of his head, feeling the sweat on his neck. "She said you were… fragile."

"Breya's just an old witch," Ryleigh whispered, jaw tight and eyes downtrodden.

"It's just that you don't seem fragile, not to me. I mean, the way you handled Viviana—"

"Shut up, Guilder." She pointed her gaze ahead.

"I only thought that… your strength, I mean… I assumed—"

Ryleigh stopped. "Assumed what?" she turned face to face with Guilder. "That I magicked my way into *all* my strength?"

"No." Guilder reeled. "I didn't—"

"You're damn right you didn't." Ryleigh tightened a fist. She exhaled an angry sigh, turned, and ran to catch up with Shyloh.

Ashyr slowed, floating back to take her place. "Lover's quarrel?"

Guilder shook his head and looked away.

"She's a complex one, our Ryleigh." Ashyr stared ahead, watching the back of Ryleigh's hair bounce irritably. "Give her time. She'll open up and tell you the whole story."

"I thought she had."

Ashyr raised his brow as a tight-lipped smile crossed his face.

"You know? What happened I mean."

Ashyr shrugged. "We're her friends, of course we know. But it's not my place to tell, so don't ask."

"Then why come back here, if not to rub it in my face?"

"Only to offer a little encouragement. Besides, what else are friends for?"

"Something up ahead," Shyloh muttered behind her. "The cave's opening up. Could be a room of some kind." She examined a shoulder-high trough, a hand wide, filled with an ink-black liquid leading into the dark recesses of the room. She placed her dimming torch into the thick fluid. Fire raced around the periphery of the circular room, illuminating another cavernous chamber.

Guilder ambled in behind the rest, mouth agape at the sheer volume of space. Dragon glass pillars decorated with carved soldiers, hand to foot like a ladder holding one another up, arms skyward extending to the prodigiously high ceiling. Covering the floor, a regiment of stone Aurora legionaries in full armored regalia stood shoulder to shoulder in squadron formation. Black on black cloaks, helms, swords, and spears, waiting or perhaps guarding whatever lay beyond. Along each wall, seemingly carved from the same stone, women, children, and even animals. The glimmering firelight danced off the intricate structures as the shadows played on their features, imitating movement and false emotion from the transfixed figures.

"These supposed to represent the old gods?" Shyloh asked, examining the corner pillar nearest to where they'd entered. Adjacent to the pillar, a statue of a shrouded woman knelt next to a young child. A bearded man in leather armor standing over them, eyes fixed across the room, his sword held out in defense.

"I don't think so," Ryleigh said. "They're all so elaborate, so detailed. Does any of this look familiar, Guilder?"

"The cavern and the dragon glass pillars... yes. But all these statues are new."

"Who would possess the skills to do this?" Ashyr asked.

"Or the raw material?" Guilder traced his hands along the form of a horse, reared up on his hind legs, its rider cowering beneath. "For that matter, who would have this kind of access? We're in a secret cave under the castle. I don't know of anyone this gifted, and certainly not with suitable knowledge of this place."

"Look at this one." Ashyr stood next to the furthest pillar from the entrance, the adjoining tunnel continuing a few meters behind. The group gathered around the sculpture depicting a young man fallen onto his knees, his hood resting on his shoulders, arms outstretched toward the back tunnel, palms shielding his face. "I'm thinking these may not be carvings."

"There's a definite theme going on here," Shyloh said, looking down the mouth of the connecting tunnel.

Guilder pressed his face closer to the figure. "It looks like he's... screaming."

"This one too," Ryleigh said. Behind the hooded man, another ran mid-stride toward the opposite corner. His head turned, mouth frozen open, horror trapped in his stone gaze.

Shyloh clapped her hands together, startling her colleagues. "Okay," she said as all eyes fell on her, an impish smile poking through. "Time for a break."

"You think that's wise?" Ryleigh asked.

"About time," Ashyr said, always the quickest to forgive. "We haven't eaten since this morning. What's on the menu?"

"Meat, my fine vaporous fellow."

Ashyr's smile widened as he closed the gap between him and Shyloh. Ryleigh shook her head, retreating to a neutral corner of the room.

"You brought meat with you?" Guilder asked Shyloh, tilting his glance at Ryleigh.

"Didn't have to." Shyloh pointed to the

tunnel they'd come from. "The land has provided. All the rat you care to eat."

"I'll pass," Guilder said, wandering over to where Ryleigh sat.

"More for the rest of us." Shyloh squatted near the center of the room and gathered up a pile of brush. She plunged the end of her extinguished torch into the burning oil trough and tossed it on top of the kindling, igniting her campfire. Ashyr sat next to Shyloh, rubbing his hands together in anticipation as Guilder pushed down the rumbling in his stomach revulsion fought with hunger.

Ryleigh stared down at the floor. A melancholy look overtook her face as Guilder sat beside her. He watched Shyloh roasting a trio of plump rats, Ashyr sitting across from her, sniffing their aroma up as they sizzled.

"Sorry about before," Ryleigh said. "I didn't mean to snap, I was just…" She shook her head. "I don't know." She turned her eyes up to ward off her tears.

"Nothing to be sorry about. I shouldn't have pried. It's none of my business, anyway."

"No, that's… that's just it. I…" she looked over to Ashyr, timidly peeling a bite from his cooked rat. "I tend not to share, not about myself."

"Ashyr said that you'd told your friends. The whole story, I mean."

Ryleigh reeled on Guilder; her eyes narrowed. "Ashyr told you?" The others turned toward them, just as quickly, turned away.

"No." Guilder leaned forward. His hands folded on crossed knees. His eyes fixed on Shyloh's fire. "He said it wasn't his place."

"It isn't." Ryleigh turned her narrowed eyes toward Ashyr, who busied himself nibbling on a tiny thigh as he explored the mouth of the continuing path.

Ryleigh's melancholy returned with a sigh. "It's just that... It wasn't my most glorious moment." Guilder turned, peering toward Ryleigh as regret took over her face.

"I've only been traveling with you all for a short time," Guilder said. "I'd never expected to be part of this group, but as my memories return, I can't seem to recall ever feeling part of anything. Nothing real, at least. Plenty of fair-weather friends, sure, but never anyone I'd connected with, not on a personal level." Ryleigh turned her glassy eyes toward Guilder. "Never anyone I'd actually cared for."

Ryleigh let slip a reluctant smile. She leaned her head on Guilder's shoulder and stared back at Shyloh's flickering campfire.

After a long moment of silence, she took a strengthening breath. "There was a time I used magic. Earth magic, if you hadn't guessed." She let a sad chuckle escape, indulging in another reinforcing breath. "I was... sick, quite a bit, as a kid. My folks, they... sheltered me. I'm not sure what else to call it. They probably thought I was stupid, or weak, or at least vulnerable. Made me think I was, anyway. Even when I was older, and not as sick, I was still treated like that, as if I was weak. I felt small, useless.

"My folks weren't skilled magicians, not by any means. They didn't keep their spells from me, but never taught me how to use my powers, either." Ryleigh lifted her head from Guilder's shoulder. Her eyes explored the cavern, careful not to stop on anyone too long. "I met Breya in Gunnison when I was thirteen. Ashyr must have been ten, I guess. He was a natural, a powerful air caster, even at that young age." Ryleigh tucked her arm around Guilder's, pressing back into him as she sniffed back threatening tears. "Breya taught me how powerful I could be. And I loved her for it, but when I was at home, I was that same feeble girl everyone saw me as."

"Breya's lessens never seemed enough," Ryleigh continued. "I wanted what she had; what Ashyr had. Breya filled my head with nothing but promises and teased me with mere tastes of power. I'd do exhaustive research, beg for, and borrow anything I could get on Earth magic." Ryleigh sighed. "It was never enough. Breya and I… she… anyway, I said a lot of horrible things to her, betrayed her, I guess. And that woman can hold a grudge, that is for sure. I left to find who I thought was a stronger master. You know the rest. It was my biggest mistake in a life full of mistakes."

Ryleigh picked her head off Guilder's shoulder and scanned around the cavern. "I abandoned Ashyr when I left. He continued studying with Breya. Never held it against me either, which seems to hurt more." Ryleigh raised her voice in concern. "Where is Ashyr?"

"Uh, guys." Ashyr poked his head out of the tunnel. "You should see this."

Ryleigh hurried to stand; Guilder grasped her arm. She turned, her severe features softening with his tender gaze. "Tell me more later," Guilder whispered.

Ryleigh nodded, brushing the remaining tears from her face as they joined Ashyr and Shyloh at the mouth of the tunnel. "You found something?" Shyloh asked, ignoring Guilder and Ryleigh's proximity.

"See for yourselves." Ashyr led the way out of the dragon-glass chamber. A few hundred meters in, the tunnel forked. One path led in a noticeable upward slope, the other, narrower, continued straight through.

"From what I remember, the castle dungeons are this way." Guilder pointed to the sloping path. "Not sure I remember another channel down here."

"I figured that may be the way out," Ashyr said. "So, I took this other way just to see what was down here. Come on." He ducked, waving a hand for the rest to follow.

Shyloh grabbed Ashyr by the shoulder. "No rats," she said in a hushed voice, her finger held up to her nose as the stench of decay intensified down the narrower corridor.

"Good." Ryleigh shivered. "I hate rats."

"No, not good. In that immense room, they were abundant, only that's not the sort of environment they like. Down here, in these dark musty tunnels, they'd typically thrive."

"Meaning what?" Guilder asked.

"Meaning there's something else down here. Something predatory."

Ashyr's smile widened. "Follow me."

Another hundred meters in, the tunnel widened to a dome-covered antechamber. Smaller than the first, tight, and crowded with debris. Pillars and walls of the same dragon glass. Water dripped from the ceiling with a clocklike tone filling a small pool at the center. Near the apex of the dome, a natural fissure brought a knife blade of sunlight in. The light danced off the pool, giving the room a twilight gray sheen.

Ashyr skirted around the central pool to the back of the alcove. "Took me a while to find it. In the dim light, it blends in exceptionally well." He kneeled next to a hollowed-out petrified tree stump, peering inside. A hand's length deep bowl of charred bark had been smeared and glued together with dried mud.

"What is it?" Ryleigh put her hand to her nose. "It reeks like shit."

"Take a look." Ashyr dug his hands into the center of the stump, digging through a shallow layer of mud-caked leaves and brown grass.

"I'm not going near that thing," Ryleigh said. "Let's just go to the castle. Whatever this is, it can sit down here and rot."

Shyloh kneeled next to Ashyr.

"Are those…" Guilder squinted into the

hollow log

"Eggs." Ashyr cupped several mottled gray leather-like eggs and placed them on top of the nest. "I'm not sure from what, though."

"They're not bird's eggs," Shyloh said. "Not any bird that I know. These are soft, maybe reptilian, but I don't recognize the shell pattern." She gently lifted one of the eggs closer to her face. "Hard to tell the color in this dim light. There's a sour smell, to them, not sure if that's the nesting material or…"

"Guys?" Ryleigh said, staring above the alcove's entrance.

"Just a minute." Shyloh snapped the fingers of her free hand, sparks emanating from the tips. "I'm trying to figure out what these belong to."

"I'm pretty sure I know who the eggs belong to." Ryleigh backed to the far side of the room. Guilder followed her eye line, moving between her and the entrance, their gaze fixed partway up the wall. "And those statues in the other room, I don't think they're statues."

"Umm, you two should probably stop fucking around in there," Guilder said, cautiously pulling his sword. Its measured singing filled the whisper-quiet cavern before settling to guard its wielder.

"What are you two talking abo—" Shyloh bolted upright. She set the egg delicately back into the nest, waggling her hand to gather Ashyr's attention.

"What's gotten into all of—oh shit!"

The creature hung on the wall just above

the entrance. Her dark brown leathery skin, brindled in black, let her blend into the rock walls as if in relief. An undulating fin, scanning head to tail, trembled as she savored the air with her glossy forked tongue. Across her face, a scarred slice cut straight through her eyes. Necrotized tissue hung from the empty sockets. "I can smell you," she said in a slithery drawn-out voice. "Taste you." Each word punctuated between flicks of her tongue.

"What do we do?" Ryleigh whispered, her breath coming in gasps.

"Not sure," Guilder said over his shoulder. "There isn't room to swing a sword, and I can't work a spell without bringing the whole place down on us. Shyloh, can't you send a fireball at it or something?"

"It's a basilisk," Shyloh whispered through her teeth. "They're immune to fire, and arrows would just piss it off."

"I hear you, humans," the basilisk hissed, edging her way to the floor. Her tongue flicked as she blocked the exit. "Only some... so familiar." Its head bobbed between each of them, hovering nearer to Guilder. Her front, needle-like claws, thick as a sword hilt, matched by a mouth full of razor teeth.

"You know me?" Guilder sent a questioning look toward Shyloh. "I mean, you recognize my sent?"

"Your stench!"

Guilder stifled a cough as the creature's hot breath wafted over him with a foul acrid reek.

"Urrgot hears things, knows things."

"Guilder, we need to get out of here," Shyloh whispered.

"Wait, just wait." Guilder took a step forward. The basilisk's tongue grazed the tip of Gilder's blade.

"What're you doing?" Ryleigh asked.

"Urrgot, is that your name?" Guilder asked. "I don't recall you being in these caverns. What's brought you here, now?"

"Lured. Trapped. And only recently. Chatter of war escalates. Murmurs of Rayne's forsaken child. And prophecy."

"And what do you know of this forsaken child?"

"Only that the child was meant to have died, killed long, long ago." Urrgot's tongue brushed against Guilder's forearm. "Whispers of human concerns, rumors reignited."

"Guilder!?" Shyloh waved her hand, grabbing Ryleigh and pushing her to the adjacent corner of the room.

Guilder gestured for the others to wait. "Whose whispers, Urrgot? The king's? My father's?"

"Urrgot cares little for human concern. Urrgot only hears things."

"These whispers about a forsaken child, these are our concerns, our human concerns. We're here to avenge this murdered forsaken child." Guilder replaced his sword, moving around to where the others had gathered.

"Murdered?" Urrgot hissed, shifting her head toward Guilder's voice. "Not murdered, spared. For the good of us all, yet countless lives sacrificed before him."

"Urrgot?" Guilder signaled for Shyloh to move. "I don't understand."

"You may leave, child of Rayne. Prophecy demands it. Others stay."

"Wait, what? No, Urrgot, we all need to leave. All the humans."

"You may leave, others, penance for your intrusion."

Shyloh waved her hands at Ashyr, signaling for him to steal past the basilisk.

Guilder eyed Ashyr as he moved to slip by. "Urrgot. We can't leave anyone here. We saw your clutch. Our standoff is a stalemate. You have just as much to lose."

"Eggs infertile. Meant for sustenance, now dessert." Urrgot lunged to her right, catching nothing but mist as Ashyr slipped past.

Shyloh motioned Ryleigh to follow.

Ryleigh's eyes met Guilder's, her concern held in check. She nodded to keep the basilisk talking.

He returned her nod, urging her to be safe before turning back to the basilisk. "Who blinded you, Urrgot?" Guilder asked in a mock inquisitive tone. "Was it one of the king's men? Did they hunt you?"

"Nothing so valiant. Women and children hid with human soldiers. Many. One took my sight, not before succumbing to it." Urrgot swung around, trapping Ryleigh near the exit.

Ryleigh flattened herself against the wall,

Urrgot's teeth glistening near her face. She turned her head, clamping her eyes shut as Urrgot took in a long breath, as if savoring her scent, thick saliva dripping onto Ryleigh's cheek. "You seem… yes. Your transformation has yet to be." The basilisk tipped her head as if to bow. "My queen." Ryleigh skirted around, exiting as Guilder snuck out from behind.

The four preceded at a quiet sprint toward the alternate route to the castle. Guilder paused a few meters past the fork as the sound of talons scraped against rock. A low guttural scream, Urrgot's indignation for lost meat, echoed through the caverns. Ryleigh waved for Guilder to follow. Meeting her eyes he extended an index finger, his sword held out, ready for a quick strike. Urrgot passed into the far chamber of stone statues in blind pursuit of her escaped meal. Guilder released his held breath, nodded toward Ryleigh, and continued up the path as thoughts lingered on Urrgot's stone victims, frozen in their silent screams.

CHAPTER 23
Shellrock Castle

Guilder bumped Ryleigh from behind as the tunnel continued to darken with their ascent. "Why are we stopping?" Ryleigh whispered, shoving a spirited elbow at Guilder. "That thing could come crawling up behind us at any moment."

"That thing had suffered enough," Shyloh murmured back. "Blinding is worse than death to a basilisk. Anyway, we've run out of tunnel, there's a locked drainage grate above us. Looks to lead into a larger room."

Ryleigh shoved her way to the front of the line. "Your affinity for these monsters is going to get us all killed." She looked up, grabbed the iron lock, and pulled it free.

"They're just animals, same as any other. Survival is all they know." Shyloh pushed the grating over and lifted herself through, offering a hand to Ryleigh.

Ryleigh swatted her hand away. "Survival at the expense of everyone around them." She lifted herself up. "Sounds far too familiar to… someone… I know."

Guilder hauled himself up from the tunnel as her words cut off. They had entered the dungeons into one of several communal cells. Nearly two dozen men, women, and even a few children crowded to one side. Frozen in their final horror-filled moments. Dragon glass statues with wide-eyed faces. Some had climbed over the others in their last attempts at escape.

Necks craned back in panic.

Ryleigh skirted around an outstretched stone arm as she shifted toward the central gate. Guilder moved in beside her, leaning his hands along the crossbar to peer into the rest of the room. The chasmal stone dungeon consisted of three rows of four cells each. Burning torches scattered throughout, with a metal-strapped wooden door at the far end.

A handful of other cells were filled with prisoners, some shackled to the wall or bound to iron balls with chains. A stack of crushed straw was laid down as bedding for the lot, with a metal bucket for a toilet. They clustered together at the far corner of their enclosures, watching with fear-laden eyes and guarding their children against the four interlopers from below.

"Who are these people?" Ryleigh asked, her eyes frozen to the cell across the way.

Guilder peered inside the cell Ryleigh stared into, catching the eye of one exceptionally grimy young girl. "Any threats to the crown would usually be dealt with by execution, so political prisoners would be my guess. Some held for ransom, others... who knows?"

"Why so many?"

"That's a good question. These dungeons typically see two or three prisoners at most." Guilder scanned around the room. "There must be nearly a hundred people down here." Stealing a glance behind him, he added, "Not counting these poor bastards."

Shyloh sat against the far wall, flicking gravel down the still-open floor grate. Guilder shook his head. "I just don't get her." An icy breeze wafted by as Ashyr misted through the cell bars.

"She's all butthurt about that basilisk," Ashyr said as he went to explore the rest of the dungeon.

"The basilisk? What about all the people she'd killed?"

"That's just Shyloh," Ryleigh said, her lips pursed in irritation.

"There must have been a legion of soldiers down there, families… children." Guilder glared back toward the tunnel they'd escaped from. "What were they doing down there in the first place? And in such numbers?"

"Seems like the rats know something we don't," Ashyr said, lifting his foot as a portly brown rodent scurried past him. He stood in front of an open cell nearest the wooded door. "They seem better fit for a meal than anybody here. This cell's stacked to the ceiling with dry goods. Wheat and grain in cloth sacks. Rations, maybe?"

Sludge-covered hands reached through iron bars as the rodent sauntered past, none long enough for a clean capture. The rat toddled down the center of the aisle, edged through into the last cell, past Ryleigh and Guilder, and hopped into the basilisk tunnel. Shyloh watched the creature's hesitant exploration with an empty expression, closing the gate with a metallic crash.

Ryleigh sent an irritated hush toward Shyloh as she broke the cell door's tarnished lock. Shyloh threw her hands up in a shrug, brushing by Guilder to join Ashyr kneeling next to the reinforced door at the far end of the room. Ashyr peered through the door lock as torchlight refracted through his mist, casting rainbows throughout the dungeon. "Any ideas what we'll find on the other side?"

"Courtyard, most likely," Guilder said, sauntering up behind them. "This isn't the castle's only dungeon. There's another one on the opposite side of the portcullis and two more in the towers. Though I remember these being used more for storage."

"Three more dungeons, as full as this one?" Ashyr stood and looked around at the packed cells. "What's going on here, Guilder?"

"It's strange. Normally, the castle would be pulsing with activity. Vigilant if war was imminent, but…" Guilder peeked out the keyhole. "The courtyard should be teeming with soldiers, archers stacked along the wall, and guards posted everywhere, particularly outside the dungeons." He craned his neck around, narrowing his eyes at Shyloh. "Swarming after the racket we've made. I don't understand. Where is everybody?"

"The king's taken on a new advisor," one prisoner squeaked out in a feathery but staunch voice. The same exceptionally grimy young girl looked no more than ten or eleven, filthy from barefoot to knotted blond hair. Her face held the scar of an old knife wound below her right eye, like a teardrop dripping down her cheek. She wore a mud-caked sack dress falling just above her scabbed knees. Her exposed arms, seen clearly beneath the grime, bore multiple bite marks, from rats or other prisoners.

Ryleigh kneeled beside the girl's cell. "Can you tell us what's happened here? Why are there so many of you imprisoned here? Where are all the guards, the soldiers?"

"The Viscount Shayde, he whispers in the king's ear." Murmurs of Æthelred the Unready preceded stifled snickers from the knot of prisoners behind the little girl. Her eyes bore into Guilder, vicious, accusatory. "Ever since the crown prince disappeared." The knot of people shifted anxiously with whispers of the Butcher Prince underlining the girl's words.

Guilder stood behind Ryleigh, staring down into the little girl's ocean-blue eyes as he choked down the lump in his throat. "Wilfried Shayde? No, he's no one to my father's court, least of all a viscount." His unsteady voice prompted renewed chortles from the shadows.

"He's a spy. Shayde twists the truth, making his lies easier to believe." She stuck her tiny hand through the cell bars, beckoning Ryleigh closer. "But I know his secret," she whispered. "The Viscount is loyal to one far more powerful than any of you."

Ryleigh leaned nearer to the girl. "And what does this Shayde want?"

The girl waved Ryleigh even closer. "To

make war." Her eyes narrowed as a cobbled-together blade swung from below, meeting Ryleigh's face, skittering along her skin from chin to forehead. Ryleigh jumped back, a mark of surprise the only product of the attack. The girl held a malicious sneer, backed to the rear of the cell, and merged into a knot of prisoners.

Guilder rushed to Ryleigh's side. "What in the nine realms…" Ashyr followed. "Are you okay?"

Ryleigh put her hand to her face, looking back into the throng of prisoners. "It's fine… I'm fine. Just… help me up."

Guilder offered a hand, bringing Ryleigh back to her feet as a heavy door lock clicked open. Shyloh looked back at the three of them. "If you're done fooling around, we can go." She replaced a set of lock picks into her pocket and waved for them to follow.

The clouded morning sky cast a gray light over the open courtyard as they made their way out of the dungeon. "This isn't right." Guilder gawked at the emptiness, the abandoned battlements. "There should be markets set up, security patrols, something." He ran to the dungeon at the opposite side of the lowered portcullis and tried the door. Finding it locked, he put his ear to the door. "This one seems full, too. There's far too much prisoner chatter to have guards in there."

"Guilder, focus. We're blind and in the open here," Shyloh muttered as she and the others plastered themselves to the exterior castle walls. "You know this place, so where are we going?"

Guilder pointed to an out-of-the-way door just to the other side of the portcullis. "Servant's entrance to the main castle. If we can get the gate open, we can figure out where to go once we—"

"Archers, take aim." The call came from above, followed by a stampede of soldiers from the towered outer corners of the courtyard. Bowstrings stretched taught along the ramparts as a squad of pikemen marched in formation toward them from behind the portcullis. Shyloh nocked her own arrow, staggering her aim around to far too many targets. A wall of spears formed behind them, swords drawn in front, and countless arrowheads above.

"Fuck." Shyloh released the tension in her bow as the gate began to rise, allowing the pikemen to push forward.

"Hold!" A hand raised from behind the rows of soldiers. Archers held their aim while straightening to attention as pikemen lifted their spears, each keeping vigilant, nonetheless. The swordsmen shuffled into rank and file, presenting arms while leaving a column's width at the center of their company.

A middle-aged man marched in step between the squadrons of soldiers. Dressed in black leather armor and matching trousers, his sword remained sheathed at his hip. The gold chimera stitched on each shoulder of his azure blue gambeson mirrored the adornment at every one of his soldiers' chests.

He halted, filling in the first rank of soldiers. He gave a scrutinizing inspection to Shyloh and the rest, paying exclusive mind to Guilder. His gaze expressionless and unwavering, he clasped his arms beside him, straightened his stance, and bowed his head. "We thought we'd lost you, Your Royal Highness."

Guilder squeezed his fists tight, his jaw set. "You nearly had, General," he said as the whole of the assembled soldiers dropped to one knee.

***

"General Greymoor, I must insist, my father would want to see me as soon as possible, no matter what his schedule dictates." Guilder fidgeted on the lavish bed, blankets rising to his waist as he sank into them.

"With all due respect, Your Highness, you are in no condition to be received by the king." Greymoor stood at the far end of the room as if guarding the entrance, his arms folded behind in military fashion. "Rest assured, an assemblage is being arranged to welcome your safe return. In the meantime, I'll have attendants sent to draw a bath and have your royal mantle laid out for you."

Guilder stood, moving to the massive fireplace neighboring the overstuffed bed. "And my friends?"

Greymoor raised a comforting yet well-practiced smile. His ice-blue eyes creased at the corners, quarreling with the deep azure of his uniform. "They have been given similar accommodations."

"Where are they, General?" Guilder insisted.

Greymoor's smile faded. "The misty gentleman is roomed across the hall." He tipped his head, gesturing behind him. "The two ladies, adjacent. They have been given equivalent instruction as to their relative cleanliness when addressing His Majesty. Proper attire has been provided if it pleases Your Highness." Greymoor gave a contemptuous bow, not lost on Guilder.

"Very well," Guilder conceded with a sigh. He leaned a hand on the stone mantelpiece as he considered Greymoor's manner. "My friends and I could use some food," he said, staring into the red-orange flames. "Cheese and a bit of beef if it's available, boar if not, and Greymoor." Guilder turned a narrow eye over his shoulder. "See to it yourself."

Greymoor tightened his jaw, taking in a noticeable breath at the command. "Very good, sir. And welcome home, sir. We did miss your presence in the castle."

Guilder's eyes followed as Greymoor closed the door behind him, no longer able to hold back his venomous smile. It faded quickly as he looked around the luxurious room. The unnerving flashes of returning memories lessened in the familiar environment, though he'd expected a greater sense of home being back in Shellrock Castle. The weight in his chest, though, said differently.

So much had changed in his absence, yet

familiarity remained as tenuous as if hidden behind the tapestries, grand four-poster bed, and tableau rugs surrounding him. Had he been here at one time? This room? The recollection remained foggy.

Overfilled dungeons with massive numbers of prisoners, a blinded yet unchecked basilisk, and a stone army in the catacombs. The basilisk, Urrgot, and the army were connected, Guilder reasoned. But what led to their proximity to begin with and in such a secret place?

Then there was General Greymoor. Politically they rarely saw eye to eye, Guilder recalled, but his leeriness at their group's arrival was unexpected, and he never pinned Greymoor as warmongering, not like his father's chancellor, Eshtyn Barrows. And what of this spy the little girl mentioned? Shayde? How had someone unknown to Guilder risen so high as to be influential in his father's decisions, military or otherwise, and so quickly? Who was he and what other illicit knowledge did this newcomer possess?

"If I'm unable to get answers from Greymoor, I'll need to go directly to the source," Guilder murmured to himself, his attention pulled to the shadowed corner of his room and the trivial buzzing of a bothersome fly.

***

Guilder sprawled on his bed, a linen towel wrapped around his waist. New clothes were draped over his corner dressing table, the old ones taken to be laundered or mended, maybe burned. His bath had been warm, herbal, and so relaxing, so much different than his last. It helped ease his aching muscles and temporarily calmed the storm of memories. It failed, though, to quell the sour mix of dread in his stomach.

He stared at the ornamental ceiling, coffered in dark stained woods, moody yet inviting. The crackling fire was warm, his bed soft, rendering him drowsy as he breathed out the last of his tension. His eyes became heavy. Brushstrokes in green and blue flame caressed the back of his eyelids. Congealing. A dead tree emerged from the back of his mind, bark twisting into an old man's bearded face.

As if in the room, the lifeless tree whispered. "Struck down by the martyred."

"The martyred?" Guilder murmured in his dream. Or was he still awake, or partway between?

"Brandishing five claws."

"What five… who are you?"

"Their venom dividing the hawk."

Dried logs within the fireplace popped with growing intensity, carrying Guilder back to his room. Relinquished tension returned to his neck and shoulders, his muscles taut.

"Divided by the serpent." Guilder's own strained voice woke him from the dream. He grasped an absent hilt as he bolted to his feet, eyes open, jaw tight, teeth clenched. The green hue of an enraged fireplace echoed the fury overtaking the room.

A gentle tap on the door brought Guilder back to himself. The fire subsided, turning back to oranges, yellows, and reds. Guilder took a deep calming breath, tightened the linen around his waist, and went to answer.

"Oh... Oh my... umm, I thought... you'd be dressed," Ryleigh stammered. "The General, what's his name? He said you'd be in this room."

"General Greymoor," Guilder said, not hiding the disdain from his voice. He turned, leaving the door ajar. Ryleigh let out a sigh before entering, closing the door behind her. "Were the accommodations to your liking?"

"Uh, yes." Ryleigh stared open-mouthed at Guilder. "Yes, they're... more than adequate. Thank you." She turned her face to the corner of the room.

"It was the least they could do." Guilder returned to the bed and leaned back, hanging his legs over the side. Bare-chested, his muscles glistened from the oils added to his bath. He ran a hand over his face, shaved smooth, through his hair, slicked back and clean.

Guilder turned his gaze toward Ryleigh. "I'm glad you're okay," he said, quieter than intended.

Ryleigh shook her head, her eyes moving between Guilder's face and his flat stomach.

"That kid, I mean. The kid from the dungeon, with the..." He made a slantwise movement across his cheek.

"Oh, yeah, I'm okay." She nodded, flashing a hollow smile, her eyes falling away. "She just… startled me, is all."

Guilder's eyes followed Ryleigh as she moved toward the bed. She wrapped an arm around the nearest foot post, leaning her temple against the wooden column, and stared at his exposed thigh. Her knitted white dress accentuated her curves, stopping just below her knees, her free hand kneading at the hem, her breath shallow and rapid.

"I'm glad they found you something to wear. You look… it looks nice on you."

"The bath was nice too, warm. Yours too?" Ryleigh pressed her lips together.

"Yeah, I guess it was." He smiled, gazing into her sea-green eyes. His smile faltered, as a somber, deep-laden sadness seemed to haze over the bright mood.

She turned away, taking in the rest of the room. "Can't remember the last time I had a hot bath, a non-glamoured one anyway."

Guilder stood and brushed the edge of a finger over the back of her bare arm, bringing her attention back to him. Her skin was firm, yet soft, like soapstone or fine porcelain. He traced the outline of her ear, pushing her wavy auburn hair behind.

Ryleigh closed her eyes, pinning her face into Guilder's palm, her own holding him tight to her cheek, her chest rising with deep ratcheting breath. Guilder leaned in, pressing his lips against hers, moving his hand to the small of her back. His muscles tensed as her hands wrapped around his waist, pulling him closer.

Guilder drew back as phantom pain poked at the base of his skull.

Ryleigh's eyes remained closed, her mouth parted, breath held. "Wait," she whispered, her tongue exploring her bottom lip as she pulled him back into her. Slowly, she opened her eyes, gazing into Guilder's face. "You just need to be more—" A playful smile overtook her as she laid her hand on the back of his thigh. "—forceful."

**

Guilder lay beside Ryleigh, his head resting on his forearm, trying to regain his breath. He placed his free hand on Ryleigh's bare hip as sweat glistened off her skin. "I didn't hurt you, did I?" Firelight danced around the twisted bedclothes as the smoky-sweet Cherrywood perfumed the room. Ryleigh turned, cracking a reluctant smile, and shook her head. "It was strong enough... I mean, you were able to feel..." Guilder raised his brow, expectant.

Ryleigh's smile grew. "Guilder, shut up." She placed her hand on Guilder's cheek, then swung her legs off the bed, picking up the knitted dress from the floor. "You were wonderful, thank you."

"Won't you stay?"

"The others would talk." Ryleigh pulled the dress over her head, pushing it down to her knees.

Guilder retrieved his trousers from the dressing table, slipping them on before heading Ryleigh off at the door. "They already talk, and

I don't care. Ryleigh, I…"

Ryleigh placed her hands alongside Guilder's face, the sadness in her eyes renewed. "Guilder." She shook her head, pressing her smile tight. She stared into his disenchanted gray-blue eyes. "We can't. Not with me being the way I am, and you… being… who you are." She kissed his lips once more. The saline taste of her, sweeter than the finest wine, bitter in its longing, the last sip emanating an ache throughout his entire body.

"We can heal you," Guilder said, desperate. "The court's magicians are the best on the Continent."

"I've tried." She nodded, forcing a reassuring smile. "Breya's tried. We… she just wasn't powerful enough."

"But I have resources you never had. I can have the king's sorcerers try—"

"Guilder, I've come to terms with it. You need to as well." Ryleigh ran the palm of her hand across her moist cheek. Her smile faded, her eyes downtrodden. "I may not be able to feel much with my skin, but I feel it where it counts." Her gaze returned to Guilder's eyes. "I really did enjoy myself tonight."

Guilder nodded, offering his own artificial smile.

Ryleigh opened the door, her eyes lingering on Guilder's disheartened face. Turning, she stopped short, standing face to face with Ashyr, his hand raised in a preparatory knock. "Ryleigh? I thought this was Guilder's room.

Shyloh over here too?"

"Umm, no. Anyway... I was just leaving." Ryleigh skirted around Ashyr, hurrying across the hall.

Guilder leaned against his door, watching Ryleigh steal into her room as Ashyr misted his way inside. "Hey, Ashyr, Sorry." Guilder turned, shutting the door. "My mind's... elsewhere."

"So I've noticed." Ashyr looked around Guilder's dim, fire-lit room. "Actually, we've all noticed." He shot a knowing glance back at Guilder, then continued his exploration. "You and Ryleigh, then? You be careful with her."

Guilder grabbed a shirt off the dressing table. "Since you're here, can I ask you a question?"

"Anything, except if it's about Ryleigh."

"It's not about Ryleigh."

"Best not ask about Shyloh, either." Ashyr narrowed his eyes toward Guilder. "You and she haven't..."

"No! By the gods, no."

"Oh, good. Better to not complicate things... in that way, I mean. Anymore, at least."

"Ashyr." Guilder's jaw tightened. "I just wanted to ask how you use your powers." His face softened as he came back to himself, his irritation forgotten. "How do you turn into mist and disappear and all that?"

"Oh, well, I guess in the same way you know how to walk around without having to think about it."

"There's no incantation or formula or

something?"

"Not really, more muscle memory than anything." Ashyr misted over to the window and gazed out at the starlit sky. "Some air spells cast similar to the other elements, conjuring up windstorms, a tornado if the casting is powerful enough. Not really my style, though."

"Can you show me?"

Ashyr glanced over at Guilder, who'd sat turning the dressing chair toward the window. "Can you show me how you make your heart beat? Or force your lungs to transfer oxygen to your blood? Make your liver do... whatever a liver does?"

Guilder shrugged and shook his head.

"Same thing. I can't teach you something I've been doing my whole life. It's something I wasn't taught how to do."

Guilder nodded as he recalled his dream. Five claws. *Does that mean the five of us?* Including Breya? Or something less tangible? His gaze faltered as the thought mixed with mild disappointment.

"You could watch me, though." Ashyr continued to stare out the window. "Maybe you can figure it out on your own."

A knock at the door brought Guilder from his thoughts. "Good, you're both here." Shyloh barged into the room as soon as Guilder opened the door. "Where's Ryleigh? She should hear Ashyr's report before we strategize."

Ashyr exchanged a knowing look with Guilder. "I think... she needs her rest."

"Strategize for what?" Guilder leaned against the bedpost, his arms laced in front of him. "I'm recognized as the crown prince. You're all protected under the throne."

Shyloh shook her head and glanced over to Ashyr.

"Maybe not as protected as you think," Ashyr said. "I think it's time you told him, Shyloh."

"Tell me what?"

Shyloh pursed her lips, narrowing her eyes at Ashyr. "Just give the report," she said through clenched teeth. "We don't need to complicate things more than they already are."

"Shyloh," Ashyr prodded, taking a seat on the windowsill, his arms crossed, mirroring Guilder's doggedness. "Tell him or I will."

"He doesn't need to know."

Guilder alternated his glance between the two. "Know what?"

Ashyr strengthened his insistent look.

Shyloh leaned against the back wall, resting her hand on the doorknob. "Fine!" Her gaze sought anything that wasn't the two others in the room. After a cleansing breath, "While you and Ryleigh were off screwing around with that Fae queen, I headed to Byzantium."

"We were acquiring Ashyr's cure, not screwing around."

Ashyr huffed. "Shyloh, just tell him."

"I'm trying! Stop interrupting." Shyloh turned back to Guilder. "I'd only ever met my contact in Byzantium. He referred to himself as the Scarecrow Man." She took a deep, purging breath. "I'd been on that side of the border enough times to know this guy didn't fit in. His clothes, his mannerisms, even the way he looked down on everybody, screamed something was off." She shook her head. "But I didn't care. He had the job I was waiting for. The contract hit for you. It didn't take much to find out who he really was, Wilfried Shayde."

"But Shayde's just a low-level politician, an ineffective one from what I remember."

"Not from what I've heard," Ashyr said. "Seems like the political gig was just a cover. I was poking around last night, eavesdropping on a shadowy conversation with him and some guy named Barrows. This Shayde character's all over whatever going on here. Ask me, he's a spy."

"Order of Mstovaris," Shyloh added.

"How'd you know that?"

"Tattoo along his spine, centered at the shoulder blades. A woman, waist-deep in a pool, and reflected as a skeleton. He tries to hide it, just not very well."

"Probably the reason he's advanced so quickly in the political world."

Guilder shook his head. "I've only heard his name around court. I'd never met him myself. Chancellor Barrows, though. He's my father's top advisor. What was Barrows doing conversing with this Shayde?"

"And in shadowed hallways besides?"

"I only caught the tail end of their conversation, but from what I gathered, this Barrows guy's got his own agenda in their upcoming war. Shayde, on the other hand—"

A delicate knock sounded outside Guilder's door. Shyloh stepped back along the wall as Ashyr faded into the shadows. "Guilder?" Ryleigh opened the door and peeked her head into the room. "I wanted to talk about what I said before."

"What was it you'd said?" Shyloh came out from the corner shadows, a wicked smile plastered across her face.

Ryleigh narrowed her eyes and sighed. "Ashyr, you can come out too. I know you're here." Her stare remained on Shyloh as she swung the door shut behind her.

"We were… having a meeting," Ashyr said.

"Without me, I see."

"We'd just started." Guilder shifted his gaze from Ryleigh to Shyloh. "Haven't actually gotten to anything important yet."

"Shyloh's tangled in a conspiracy with spies and some Barrows character," Ashyr added.

"By all the gods, you're not in league with Eshtyn Barrows again, are you?"

"I'm not," Shyloh said. "I swear."

"How do you know Eshtyn Barrows?" Guilder asked, looking back at Ryleigh.

Ryleigh knotted her arms in front of her. "He's a lowlife arms dealer. Sometimes meets his contacts at the Marked Oak."

"You let him deal inside your bar?" Ashyr shot Ryleigh an incredulous look.

"His gold is good, so stick your judgments."

"Apparently, he's also the royal

chancellor."

Ryleigh looked at Guilder, her eyes wide. He nodded. "Well, shit."

"Barrows meeting with Shayde outside the castle walls is pretty suspect," Guilder said. "Probably won't lead to anything good."

"And who's Shayde?" Ryleigh asked.

"The piece of shit who wanted Guilder to disappear," Ashyr said.

"True enough," Shyloh said. "But Shayde was only the handler. He didn't back the bounty." She glanced over at Guilder. "I think the king did."

"I don't believe it." Guilder shook his head. "Can't believe it. I'm the crown prince, my father's only heir. Why would he want me dead?"

Ashyr eyed Shyloh, then Ryleigh. "The prophecy," they all said in unison.

Guilder shot a questioning look between Shyloh and Ashyr. "You think that prophecy refers to me? You all are as crazy as Breya with this stuff. It's all mystic nonsense."

"Maybe not," Ashyr said. "You do have an affinity for magic."

"It's not the prophecy that's important," Shyloh said. "It's what Lord Iks did because of it. Every newborn boy in each of the three kingdoms was murdered. Every boy but one."

"I'm a year removed from that tragedy." Guilder's face took on a stern look. "I told you, I'm not him."

"If Guilder's father protected him from

the Iks Massacre all those years ago, why the change of heart now?" Ryleigh asked.

"I'm telling you," Guilder bellowed. "I'm not the one from that prophecy."

"Pressure from Iks?" Ashyr suggested.

Shyloh narrowed her eyes at Guilder. "Or maybe you weren't the savior King Rayne hoped for."

"Gods be damned!" Guilder slammed his palm into his chest. "I turned one during the year that massacre happened." He looked toward Ryleigh, eyes softening.

Ashyr tilted his head, his eyebrows raised. "There's a mural in my room mapping out the Rayne family line. The entry with your name, Guilder, it's the only one without a date. Looked as if someone burned it off."

Guilder fixed his gaze on Ryleigh. "Then I've led us to our deaths."

"Maybe." Shyloh nodded, turning her attention to Ashyr. "You find out anything else useful?"

"Castle seems to be on some sort of modified lockdown. The king's still here, sequestered in his chambers with only a skeleton crew of military left."

"Where did they all go?" Ryleigh asked.

"The tunnels," Guilder said. "If troops were sent out to fortify the front lines and the rest were sent to Shellrock Palace…"

"This is going to be a short war," Shyloh said.

"I overheard chatter about a bunch of VIPs called to the Black Tower. Shayde and

Barrows plan on traveling together alongside a legion of Auroran soldiers."

"That's practically all that's left." Guilder paced across the room, stopping in front of the fireplace. "Protocol would send General Greymoor out shortly after. Near fifty legions in Aurora's standing army, gone, and my father's top advisor, his highest-ranking general, and a spy whose loyalty is still unknown are beckoned to the black tower. Leaving the castle and the royal family unprotected." He stared at the orange-red tongues leaping from their wooden borders. "This could be the opportunity we need."

"The only opportunity we need is to get our asses out of here," Shyloh said. "I wasn't hot on coming here in the first place—"

"—And you've made that abundantly clear since we left Paracel." Ryleigh took a threatening step forward.

"Listen." Guilder turned his gaze toward Shyloh. "I don't expect you to forgive me for what I did to your parents. But what you'd done in the name of revenge has changed me."

"Guilder." Ryleigh held her hand out to him.

"No, Ryleigh, this needs to be said." He turned his gaze to Shyloh. "Guilder Rayne died when you left him in that cave. I'm not the same man I was. I remember him, more as if in a dream, but I *have* changed."

Shyloh crossed her arms, avoiding Guilder's stare as she sniffed back her emotions.

Guilder looked at Ryleigh. "I can't do this without you."

She nodded.

He turned back to Shyloh. "Whether I'm this prophesied one or not, stopping whatever Shayde and Barrows are up to, and finding out who's behind them is my one priority. And…" He shook his head and sighed, his eyes imploring. "I'll need all the help I can get." Guilder extended his hand to Shyloh. "Will you help me?"

Shyloh took a cleansing breath. Glanced at Ashyr, then Ryleigh. "It's probably suicide."

Ashyr shrugged. After a long moment, Shyloh said, "I'm done with my revenge. If the crown prince is truly dead, I guess I have little else to do." She looked into Guilder's eyes, stone-faced, then clasped his hand. "What's the plan?"

"First, I need to confront my father."

CHAPTER 24
Family of Rayne

The predawn light stole into Guilder's room like a viper seeking its next meal. He hadn't slept, as thoughts of his father plagued his mind. Was a father's love enough to betray the sorcerer Lord Iks and save Guilder's life, only to turn his betrayal back on his son? Or was it a king's love? The monarchy, no matter how feeble, must prevail. By defiance or murder, in the end, it seemed to matter little.

Guilder stared distractedly out the window at the city of New Aurora below. The absence of early morning commotion, or the scents he'd so vividly described to Ryleigh, even the lack of chimney smoke throughout the various districts of the city proper, suggested a dead city. Dead to them at their approach days ago, now surreal with the fresh sunrise. The dark blues of morning were pockmarked with a skeleton crew of city patrols, their lanterns weaving throughout the city, assuring the life of the city remained subdued.

Shellrock seemed to hold few allies. Barrows, Shayde, what conspiracies did they contrive? And where did General Greymoor's loyalties lie? With the king? With himself? Confronting any of them seemed a far-flung aim from where he stood. Then there was his father. He'd never been one quick to wage war. King Æthelred the Unready, the moniker earned in hard-fought debates about such things and, at times, with his own son. Had this been the response to his absence? The Byzantium's woman's death? Guilder touched the base of his skull. "I can't even recall her name," he whispered.

A scarcely heard knock carried Guilder's mind back to his room. He turned as the door unlatched, shooting a glance at his sword propped against the dressing table. A petite figure edged herself through the slight crack, silently closing the door behind. Dressed in a jade housecoat accented in gold lamé, her movements were light yet particular. She turned, seemingly startled by Guilder's presence, though a grateful smile peered out from below her hood.

"Guilder," she whispered as she purged the space between them, wrapping her arms around him and pressing her still-cloaked cheek to his. "I'd feared the worst."

Guilder endured the embrace, breathing deep the woman's familiar scent; winter lilac, reminiscent of mountain rose with hints of vanilla. She pulled back, holding his face in her tender hands. Copper hair streaked with wisps of white peered out beneath her hood as pale pink lips splashed a porcelain smile over alabaster skin. Tears fell from her gemstone-green eyes as she lowered her hood and took in her son's appearance.

"Mother, it's been an exhausting journey. More so, over the last few days." Guilder forced a smile through the deluge of emotion. "I've missed you more than you can possibly imagine."

The queen held up a cautious finger. Returning to the door, she peered out and whispered to an unseen someone. Closing the door quietly after, she hurried back to Guilder and slapped him full-bore across his face. "Damned fool of a boy! Over a month you'd been missing."

Guilder stroked a hand across his stinging cheek, his neck, mouth held agape. So much had happened in such a short time, it was difficult to fathom. "Æthelred sent out seekers to no avail." She took a seat on Guilder's bed. "I'd even sent my personal guard, not that you'd deserved it. Everyone came back wanting." Her eyes bounced from Guilder to exploring the room. "So, what was it this time?" Her gaze rested high in a shadowed corner.

Guilder leaned beside the hearth, his arms crossed, and stared at the floorboards below the queen. "Someone set a bounty to have me killed."

He glanced up, his mother's face fixed on him. "They obviously were wholly inept at doing so," she said.

"Æthelred… Father, he…" Guilder crossed over to the bed and sat beside the queen. He slumped over, knotting his hands, and stared into the fire. "Did my father try to have me murdered?"

"Dear boy." The queen kneeled below where Guilder sat. "Dear, dear boy." She took his hands in hers and looked into his eyes, her face now soft, compassionate. "Æthelred would never, could never."

"There seemed to be a prophecy... around the time of my birth... the Necromancer, Lord Iks—"

"Don't trouble yourself with the prophecies of dead men. You're home now. That's all that matters."

"I am glad to be home." Guilder forced a smile. "It's just so... coincidental."

"I told you not to trouble yourself." She motioned for Guilder to help her up. "Damn these old knees and this drafty castle!" He stood, helping her to her feet. "You do seem different, Guilder. Calmer, less... I don't know... impertinent."

"I feel different. Mother, I've..." Guilder widened his smile, clasping her hands in his. "I've made new friends."

"That... ensemble accompanying you?" The queen's eyes drifted to the door, the shadowed corner. "They... shall be... heralded as heroes." Her gaze returned to Guilder, along with her plastic smile.

"They helped me. Some more than others."

Guilder's chamber door burst open as the queen's guard rushed into the room and dropped to a knee. "Apologies, Your Majesties. The king approaches."

The queen turned back to Guilder, reseating her dagger into a hidden sheath beneath her cloak. "I shouldn't be here, not without permission. Æthelred..."

Guilder eyed the corner, which mesmerized

his mother. Only the buzzing of a trapped fly, its delicate iridescent wings buzzed as it struggled against a spider's web. Such a peculiar thing to hold her attention. "The garderobe," Guilder said, his attention shifted. "You can listen from there."

"Return to your post, quickly," the queen told the guard as Guilder held open the door to the adjacent room, closing it as a pair of guards entered. The queen's guard stood resolute, meeting their bewildered stares with brazen steadfastness. All three stood at attention as heavy footfalls echoed from the hall. King Æthelred Rayne stopped in the doorframe, two other guards halting behind. With a frustrated sigh, he eyed the unexpected guard. "Natasha, I know you're here. Come on out." As if hiding her petulance, the queen eased back into the bedchamber. She pulled back her hood, standing resolute, her face unyielding. "You three are dismissed."

"Your Majesty," the tallest of the three guards said. "With strangers in the castle, I must insist—"

"Wait outside the door." Æthelred gestured a finger behind him, his gaze fixed on Guilder.

"Your Majesties." The three guards bowed before leaving.

Genteel blue-gray eyes stood in stark contrast to Æthelred's stern face. Hardened by an imperial beard, gray more than black, his brushed-back hair bore the circular indentation of a weighty crown. A green velvet robe, collared in white fur, wrapped around his bulbous frame. More apt for nightwear than trudging around the castle, its sweeping hem skirted the floor as he glided forward, grabbing Guilder's jaw to manipulate his face in examination. "Did you think you could monopolize this time with him, Natasha?"

"No, Your Majesty." The queen curtsied, her eyes downcast.

Guilder watched their exchange, questioning what had happened in his absence to warrant such formalities between them.

"Where've you been, boy?"

Guilder held his breath as he felt the room's temperature drop. "It's a long story, Father. Perhaps you should sit."

"Pathetic child, I asked you a question."

Guilder eyed the waning fire, his mother's expectant eyes. "I escaped a memory eater's cave." He straightened his stance and chanced his father's gaze. "It… she took—a lot from me."

"And yet your life is still your own," the king said, his voice softening. "Gods be praised." Æthelred paced to the dressing table, picked up Guilder's sword, and ran a thumb over the chimera crest at the hilt. "Many times, I'd warned of nefarious deeds emanating from shameless acts."

"It wasn't like that, Father."

"Wasn't it!?" Æthelred's gaze jumped, meeting Guilder's. "Did you not just say your mind was no longer your own?"

Guilder let out a frustrated sigh. "Father,

I—"

"Save your excuses. I've no time for them." Æthelred echoed Guilder's sigh, returning the sword to its place. "Much has happened in your absence. These last few weeks have seemed a century." The king stood, turning his attention back to Guilder, eyes flicking to the queen. "Assume your duties when you see fit. I have a war to prepare for." The king turned his back, reaching for the door.

"But he's only just been rescued."

"Rescued?" The king turned, eyes narrowed at his queen. "We'd been led to believe kidnapped, executed even. His selfish callousness led to—" Æthelred clenched a fist at his mouth, seeming to hold back his rage. "His blatant disregard for duty resulted in an enactment of war, one that I've been unsuccessful to quash despite the aid of my top advisors. Damn that grizzled Necromancer." Æthelred shook his head. "His endless, tiresome decrees, the sanctimonious prick." He stepped toward the queen; finger held out in blame. "You bent my ear with this assassination prattle. You and that warmongering brother of yours, Barrows."

"Wilfried assured me—"

"Wilfried?" The king sighed. "The only people who'd want our son dead are the gambling hall masters after I'd cut off his allowance." Æthelred stared into Guilder's eyes. "If he'd had any sense for his royal station, he'd have stayed in that cave and let the memory eater take what was left of him."

"Æthelred!"

The king's cemented glare remained on Guilder. "Leave us." His eyes flicked to the queen. "Natasha."

"Æthelred, please."

"Guards!"

The three castle guards entered the room and stood in formation, hands clasped behind them, awaking in anticipation of their next orders. "Escort Her Majesty back to her chambers."

The queen's personal guard stepped forward. "As you command, my lord."

The queen lifted her chin and strolled past her guard without a word. Her guard turned to follow. "Assure they arrive unencumbered," the king ordered. A second guard snapped to attention, turned, and followed the other two. A nod to the remaining guard saw him retake his position outside the room.

Æthelred took a long, calming breath. "She's been… difficult as of late." His tone seemed weary, as his eyes remained on the door. His face softened as he turned back toward Guilder.

"Father, I'm not sure I understand what's happened here." Guilder remained standing, his hands clasped behind him, mirroring the guards' posture, and stared over the king's head. "Has so much changed in such a short time?"

"More than you know." The king stood at Guilder's shoulder, gazing out his window at the rising sun. "Quite a bit in the last few weeks.

More in the last couple of months. You'd been kept out of some of it. Been the catalyst for most." He grunted scornfully. "Wasn't hard given your... appetites." He took a second deep breath. "You'd never been one to take your station seriously."

"I'm sorry, Father."

"Sorry?" Æthelred rounded to Guilder front. "And what exactly are you sorry for? Your absolute indifference to any of our subjects? Your selfish lecherousness, childish drunkenness? Or your unrepentant cruelly in starting a war by murdering your betrothed!"

Guilder stood, choking on the recitation of his life before the memory eater.

"I can scarcely fathom where the depths of your hatred originate."

Guilder clenched his jaw as Æthelred studied his face. Finally, he shifted toward the bed.

"The Byzantium people's ways are not our own and our tumultuous relations have a history beyond even me." The king peered over his shoulder, lowering his voice to a scornful whisper. "A marriage pact may have breached the gap between our two countries." He shook his head. "Sparked trade, seeded understanding, and perhaps, given time, solidified my legacy beyond Æthelred the Unready."

"Father, I—"

"Tell me something, Crown Prince." The king turned, stretching out his back before clutching a hand to the bedpost. "Was the

Byzantium girl so much of a burden to you that you'd risk both our lands?"

"I recall her beauty. The soft features of her tawny skin and champagne-colored eyes. The slight waviness of her deep black hair. She was sure-eyed with a bow, deadly when mounted, and never shy as a fire mage." Guilder shrunk in his bearing, his head heavy with shame. "Her competitiveness filled me with so much rage, chiefly when she'd best me at archery or riding. I see now she was only seeking common ground, but I still felt the tightness of hate, like a vice around my chest." Guilder felt the tears prickling behind his eyes as he looked up into his father's face. "I hated her for who she was… and for being better than me."

"Tell me this. Why, in all your loathing of her, did you kill the horse?"

Guilder's gaze fell. His lips moved in pantomime as the words stuck to the back of his throat. Finally, he whispered, "Because she loved him."

With a deep breath, Guilder straightened his stance, wiped his moist cheek, and ventured a look toward his father, meeting the king's narrowed eyes.

"A memory eater, you say?"

Guilder lowered his gaze in affirmation.

Æthelred's harsh expression faded with a calming breath, replaced by something more akin to exhaustion. "In the last few years, it seemed a rarity that your bed would get used. More often laid up in the local bars and brothels with those dubious, fair-weather friends of yours. Most of which fled the city shortly after you were proclaimed missing, out of some cowardly fear of being accused, and I'd wager for apt reasons."

Guilder straightened his stance, clasping his hands behind him. "They'd look all the more guilty for their cowardice."

Æthelred nodded "That they did." He again took in Guilder's presence, this time with a questioning gaze. "You do seem different. More… internal, thoughtful… respectful even." Guilder reasserted his stance. "Don't get me wrong, it's a welcomed change, mind you, but…"

"My former, self-indulgent life ended in that cave, father. I'd found true friends, rediscovered magic, and parts of myself that I didn't know. It's seemed a renaissance of sorts."

"And your memories of before? They've fully returned?"

Guilder offered a reluctant nod. "For good or ill."

"Magic." Æthelred sat hunched over Guilder's bed, his hands beside his hips. "We'd done our best to keep you from magic."

The harshness of age, of his station, showed on Æthelred's face. "An impossible task, granted…"

"It seems to come naturally, most anyway."

"I'm sure it does. There had been a prophecy. Some fool monk speaking against Andorian Iks."

Guilder stepped over to the fire. "So I've been told."

"You fell within the Necromancer's edict. All born within that year were to be forfeited or face his wrath. We only saw one course, a sacrifice for the greater good."

Guilder turned a questioning eye toward Æthelred. "But I'd always understood myself too old."

"That was your mother's idea. The gift of a lie. She thought that if you were ignorant of your true birth year, you'd never let slip the truth. She'd burned the date from our family tree herself."

"But if you'd decided to hold to the edict, how am I still here?"

"For many years, we had in our employ a royal healer. An obstinate young woman, Oriel, or something. I believe her name was."

"Breya." Guilder shook his head, letting a smile escape as he sat next to his father.

"Yes. You know of her?"

"Somewhat, I mean, I thought I did."

"The queen couldn't stand her. Begged me to send her away, but she was a brilliant healer and one I'd difficulty letting go. In secret, I entreated her to hide you. After a year she'd bring you back, insist you were in your third year. No one questioned it. Who'd dare? Your mother was told the deed was done, the edict, satisfied. She mourned for you that whole year. Her grief somehow turned to rage when you were returned to us. Natasha insisted Breya be publicly hanged for abducting the crown prince." Æthelred shook his head. "I banished her instead. Much to your mother's ire and my own dismay. It's her you need to thank. Her willingness to put herself in danger to save you, then be punished for her efforts."

"She never said anything."

"She was always one to keep her secrets and ours, it seems. The whole sordid affair changed Natasha. She held on to her anger, letting it fester. She distanced herself from me, spoiled you, and took to scheming with the like of her brother, Barrows."

"It seems my entire existence has led to nothing but chaos."

"The crown breeds it, not you. Chaos is an unfortunate byproduct of rule. This war began far before you killed that poor girl. Pieces placed well before your lack of discretion, that time itself refuses to remember. I'd never been one to hold to prophecy but… If that memory eater has truly changed you, maybe you are the one it spoke of." Æthelred chuckled. "My five-clawed chimera. If you're ready to be the king you were always meant to be, prove it by achieving what I've obviously failed to do. Bring order to this continent before chaos eats us all."

***

Guilder sat on his bed staring at the window as he listened to the clunking of his father's armored guard fade down the hallway. He'd brought his friends into his castle, into danger, and for what? His own hubris? But what was the alternative? Byzantium? Foxgate?

Despite prophecies or bloodthirsty mandates from paranoid, power-hungry lords, his actions alone had started a war. As the future king, it was his charge to end it. By any means. "Ashyr, I know you're there. The least you can do is help me figure this out."

"You're good," Ashyr's disembodied voice said. "Most people can't see me misted out in front of a window." He lowered himself from the sill and crossed to the dressing table as the remainder of his ethereal form coagulated.

"You snuck in when the queen's guard escorted her away. The morning light flickers when seen... through you. Good try, though." Guilder attempted a smile, which faded quickly. "You pick up anything from all that?"

"Daddy's ear seems to be more than just bent. Pinned, I'd say. Surrounding himself with a court of militant advisors while agreeing to an all-out war on the ostensible reason of a broken union?" Ashyr shook his head. "He didn't seem too choked up about you being gone, though."

Guilder went back to stare out the window. "A bitter heart buried deep in stone seems a king's way. It's all a façade, though."

"Like dear, queen mum?"

"Yeah." Guilder tilted his head, puzzled. "Something's off about her. She seemed... fidgety. Like she was being watched." Guilder looked back at the spider web in the corner.

"Or wearing a mask?" Ashyr added. "I've heard some humans can glamour, half-humans, anyway."

"She's pureblood. In that, you can be

assured. But father mentioning her and Wilfried Shayde together doesn't sit well." Guilder brushed away a drip of sweat from his temple. "Her brother, Eshtyn Barrows, can't be trusted, that's for certain. I need to find out what's going on with her. Can you steal into the war room? Gather some intel on father's battle plans?"

Ashyr nodded, turning toward the fireplace, the flames reaching high into the chimney flue.

"Even with the security detail Barrows took, there should be at least a full legion of soldiers patrolling the castle. Another two throughout in the city." Guilder ran his hand across his chin. "Why are they down to less than a skeleton crew?" His eyes rested on Ashyr. "Find out where all the Auroran troops are."

"Sure can."

"I'll go see if I can have another chat with the queen. One a bit less… monitored."

Ashyr's stare dwelt above the fireplace mantel.

"What?"

He tilted an ear at the chimney. "You hear that?"

Guilder shook his head and turned back to the window, deep in his thoughts, as he wiped his damp forehead with a loose sleeve. "Probably just the winds blowing across the chimney."

Ashyr steamed at his shoulders, his neck.

He backed further into the corner of the room, away from the increasing fireplace flames. "No, it's like scratching from inside the brickwork."

A thin crimson leg poked out from beneath the mantel, leaving the stone hearth blackened and chard. Whip-like antenna followed, scanning across the mantel, and reaching into the room.

"What in the nine realms?" Guilder said, joining Ashyr along the back wall, his gaze glued to the flaming creature emerging into the room.

"Impossible," Ashyr whispered.

"I'll distract it. You get out."

"No need to tell me twice." Ashyr slid his way around toward the door. "You handle an *Ōmukade* before?"

"Never had the pleasure."

The creature poked out its bulbous head, crimson like its forelegs. Saucer-like milky-black eyes scanned the room as a pair of black-tipped pincers stretched out into the widening space. Its segmented body landed several more pairs of legs on the stone hearth as it crept onto the plank wood floor, scorching holes with every step. What seemed the majority of its body, its innumerable legs, remained inside the chimney.

"I'll get Shyloh," Ashyr said, finding the door locked. "She'll know how to handle that thing."

"Palace guards could be helpful." Guilder kept his eyes on the flaming centipede, the Ōmukade, as Ashyr misted through the crack beneath the door. "You talk?" Guilder asked, affording a glance at his sword near the dressing table in the room's opposite corner. "Beasts like you seem to be mighty chatty when they want to be."

The Ōmukade reared its head, skirting the rest of its massive length into the now sweltering room. Its antenna whipped about, eyes considering Guilder who held his hands out, fumbling for the right magical phase. Saffron-orange magma spit out toward him from the creature's mandible-bracketed mouth. Guilder crossed his wrists, his hands splayed. Steam mixed with the increasing smoke as he redirected the lava into the shadowed corner of the room and the metal fly still lingering about. Window glass exploded outward from the creature's heat as shouts from the hallway captured the Ōmukade's attention.

Guilder slid his way toward the window as plate armor clashed against the bedroom door. The creature squared up to this new threat. Guilder lunged for his sword, only to be pinned between the wall and the dressing table by a flaming leg. The searing needle-like limb bore into his abdomen like the tip of a dagger fresh from the blacksmith's forge.

Guilder stretched for his weapon, screaming in pain as armed guards broke through the door. Liquid flames spewed onto the incoming soldiers, boiling them inside their armor as Guilder clutched the sword hilt. A downward swing severed the Ōmukade's leg. Bright, fire-red blood oozed out, setting more of the wooden floor ablaze. Guilder plucked the claw from his stomach, tossing it aside as he skirted around the growing flames.

Shyloh skidded to a stop outside the room. "Gods be damned!" She threw her arms up, redirecting a fresh stream of magma around her. The wall behind turned black, an oblong patch left uncharred where she stood.

Guilder readjusted his grip on the sword, jabbing deep into the creature's back end only to watch the steel glow red, then orange. Saffron-colored blood gushed from the wound, catching flames as it oozed down the creature's back. The Ōmukade spun its head, whipping its antenna toward Guilder, hitting him square to the chest, shoving him out of the castle's upper window.

Time slowed. Multiple arrows pierced the creature's neck, liquid flames bursting forth, catching the buried arrows aflame. Shyloh leaned out the window. Her expression, bleak as her eyes met Guilder's, Ashyr materializing behind her. Blue sky shone through wispy clouds overhead as Guilder plummeted toward the courtyard. Shyloh and the window sped further out of reach. Calmness overtook him. The wind rushing past his ears faded as he closed his eyes, content with the inevitable. A deep breath in, then… nothing.

Part III

Mourning the Dead Earth

CHAPTER 25
The Iks Meteor

Eshtyn Barrows leaned forward from his pillow-laden seat, waggling his finger between his two riding companions. "If this dark sorcerer thinks he'll continue to have the power to summon us at his whim while insisting on staying neutral against Byzantium's treachery, then he's a bigger fool than I've been told." He reached into his breast pocket, produced a silver flask, and added a splash of spirits to his cup before sipping the steaming honey tea.

"Mind what you say near the citadel, Chancellor," Wilfried Shayde said. "Lord Iks pits spies against his own spies and our mounted guards all have ears."

"You ought to know," Barrows muttered between sips, narrowing his eyes at the scarecrow of a man sitting across from him.

"I also wouldn't ignore the rumors of his affinity for necromancy. I'd hate to see dear old dead granny, or the long-buried family hound come back to repay you for your sour commentary."

Barrows dismissed Shayde's warning with a wave of his hand as the twin black towers loomed over the convoy like a dagger thrust into the earth's heart. The Sal Flats had already bled beyond Southfork's borders into the foothills beyond, forming a cracked skin of white, circling outward from the monoliths. The troop of cavalry guards galloped beside the train of carriages traversing the salt road, the rear gates of the largest of the twelve cities not half a dozen kilometers behind.

"You need to mind Shayde's warnings, Eshtyn." General Greymoor pried his gaze from the window. "You may have the ear of the king, but he has an eagle's view of the entire playing field." He tightened the knot of his arms, his face a desert of emotion as his glance landed on Shayde. "Ignore his cowardice, but mind his words."

"Tactless as ever, General." Shayde returned the insult with a sneer, his frown returning as he turned into his corner.

"Your self-indulgent bickering is meaningless," Barrows said. "And how are you even here, Greymoor? Your orders were to follow behind, not accompany the foremost party."

"Lead from the front, Chancellor, not the shadows."

Barrows narrowed his eyes. "Shayde, this political scheme of yours had better bear fruit, or I'll have you standing ahead of Greymoor's army ordering the initial charge."

"We'd just as well give up," Greymoor said, turning back to stare out his window.

Barrows pointed a warning finger. "We are at the precipice of war, General. Byzantium's spies have been privy to the decay of the Auroran throne far longer than its sovereign would ever admit. Your soldiers grow fat off their idleness and wasted salaries as our enemies accumulate south of the Bulwark Divide. The crown prince's return changes nothing and kowtowing to this wizard is only a waste of resources. The time for action is now!"

"Past more likely, but I agree," Shayde said with a cross look at Greymoor. "However, obtaining Lord Iks' blessing on this... military endeavor will ease the transitions after our victory, lending credence to the legitimacy of our... imperialistic coup d'état."

"Fucking politicians. Peacetime not the best environment for your back alley dealings, Barrows?"

"Peacetime is fine for farmers. But real tradesmen need to tickle demand when the stock is in excess." Greymoor shook his head. "You should be thanking me, General. If it wasn't for my back-alley dealings and silver tongue buried deep in Rayne's ear, you'd have nothing but plowshares to arm your troops with." Barrows turned his attention back to Shayde. "Byzantium's council seems to request their lord's permission whenever they need to shit, but usurp the remainder of the Southern Continent and Iks' summons becomes an inconvenience for us all."

"Æthelred's hesitancy has already put us at a disadvantage. These delays will have us buying bread with Byzantium coin before the year's end," Shayde added, scowling at Greymoor. "The Auroran sewers even now bloat with Æthelred's likeness across on his own worthless currency."

"What Iks demands is irrelevant to our side

of the continent," Barrows continued. "We should steal into the crown prince's chambers, bash the royal bastard's head in, and spike the Republic's flag through his bloody corpse. Get this war started right."

"Something Greymoor could have done instead of escorting him and his compatriots into the castle." Shayde pursed his lips, turning his gaze back to Barrows. "Instead of expanding the kingdom, he'd rather our heads be staked to Aurora's overthrown castle wall. Or was that your plan all along, General?"

"Fuck you, Shayde! You scarecrow looking—" "—Myopic single-minded child!"

"Shut the fuck up, both of you!" Barrows screamed. His pudgy finger again pointed at Greymoor. "The Order of Mstovaris has declared the monarchy dead and Byzantium's council experiment has proved less than effective. Iks may hold sway in both republics, but his power is still limited. Dispatch enough fire-wielders and even his asinine black castle will burn." Barrows cleared his throat as the others turned back to their respective windows. "You'll have your war, Greymoor. So, play your part like the good soldier you are, and keep your loyalist mouth shut! Understand?"

Greymoor's narrowed eyes remained on Shayde before turning to stare out the carriage window. He released the tension in his jaw nodding as his sigh fogged up the glass.

"And you!" Barrows swung his finger toward Shayde. "Try not to piss yourself when we meet with Lord Iks."

***

Like war drums thundering before battle, my blackwood cane beat out every other step as I progressed through the hallways of the citadel. The household staff pilfered only the slightest of glimpses as they bowed with my passing, seeing my transformed body spry and erect. My renewed face, taut yet fixed and resolute. For months, I'd isolated myself in a study of the Tessermancy spell, the precise timing and body positions, the proper pronunciation of each magical word, intending to undo my transgressions upon this world. Their gawking only served to further stoke the flames of irritation for this tiresome assembly. The dogmas of these phantoms will be remembered by no one.

A reverberating thunderclap filled the crowded hall as Iven gaveled his ceremonial mace, depicting the Iks house manticore. A golden, roaring lion's head adorned the top while a green-black scorpion's tail spiraled down its ironwood staff. As I entered, he announced my presence with all the formality given to a feared sovereign, yet as I gazed out into the sea of faces, all I saw was contempt.

The crowd bowed their respects regardless as I took my seat atop the dais, Iven standing at my side. The receiving hall boasted crystal chandeliers etched in gold, reflecting the cloud-filtered sunlight from its high windows. Arched, hand-carved oak doors to the back reaffirmed the house crest while white marble enveloped the walls, spilling onto the floors and echoing the chatter of its occupants. Elegant tapestries softened the din while depicting centuries-old battles, lost to all memory but my own.

Dressed more for a grand gala or ball than a diplomatic congregation, the countless representatives of each territory stood separated, leaving an ironic, widespread aisle and volleying glares of disdain between. War, at its core, is an act of will. The force of one party to compel the other to bow to their will. Magic, it seemed, had done nothing to quell human's affinity to force their will on others.

Iven gaveled his mace off the stone floor. "Representative Eshtyn Barrows, Lord Chancellor of the Kingdom of New Aurora in the matter of the Republic of Byzantium's claim of the interregnum of the Aurora throne."

"The throne has not been left vacant!" Barrows roared. "The crown prince survives, despite Byzantium treachery." Greymoor placed a hand on Barrows' shoulder, pulling him back from his forward step.

"You will address this court, Representative Barrows, in the appropriate manner," Iven rebutted. "Or you will not address the court at all."

I fixed my stare on another of Barrow's faction, a scarecrow of a man, his attention shifting everywhere but the main performance.

"If it pleases your lord." Barrows bowed again, regaining his composure. "There is no interim in Aurora. King Æthelred Rayne III's heir went missing, presumed dead. While it is true the king's health had been in question, it has considerably improved, now that the crown prince has returned, unharmed."

"His lordship recognizes the continued sovereignty of Æthelred Rayne," Iven said.

"Æthelred the Unready," someone shouted from the back of the crowd, snickers and murmurs erupting behind Barrows.

Iven gaveled his mace, quieting the crowd. "Æthelred Rayne is the acting sovereign in the Kingdom of New Aurora," he said with an irritated staccato. "If the Republic of Byzantium has issue with this, then they should take it up with the acting king."

Barrows schlepped forward again, aiming a portly finger at Iven. "What I don't understand is why I have to address this insult to my king with a humanoid automaton instead of the lord of this house!" Greymoor stepped up and whispered into Barrow's ear, effectively pulling my attention to his continued tirade. "Don't tell me to calm down. I know damn well how to address this court."

Barrows turned back to the dais. "The Republic repeatedly has eyes on Æthelred's lands. They see him as weak, claiming he is again without any legitimate heir, regardless of the crown prince's return. Their armies have readied for an illegal war demonstrating their continued subversion and betrayal to this court. This issue cannot be defused when the crown prince's actions have been the sole reason for the dispute."

Barrows scratched at the back of his hand, shifting his pointed finger in my direction. "You are the only one holding to peace on this continent. Why we've had to travel here, with full entourage, to ask permission for anything mystifies me to no end."

Greymoor sighed, shook, and lowered his head.

I tightened my grip at the end of the armrest, disconcerted by Barrows' continued outburst.

The scarecrow man's eyes widened as he gazed at the back of Barrow's neck. Turning toward Greymoor, he whispered into his ear before both men took a step back.

"Byzantium will not reconsider this invasion with a simple recognition of your authority," Barrows continued. "When they usurp Æthelred Rayne's half of the continent, adorning the castle walls with his subjects' heads only to seat their own false king on the throne, they will then come west, for your citadel!"

Iven gaveled his mace. "Representative Barrows. You will conduct yourself in the appropriate manner—"

"I'm not talking to you, abomination," Barrows screamed, pointing back at Iven and scratching at his lower arm, at his neck.

Greymoor's mouth slacked open, reaching a tentative hand forward, pulling it back at the scarecrow man's insistence.

"If you will not intervene in arbitration of

this charade, then the throne will need to—" His last words choked as his throat closed off. His eyes watered as he glared down at his hands. His arms welted with growing hives. He felt his face, his neck, masses of carbuncles emerging beneath his skin. Barrows fell to his knees as pus burst through his trousers, staining the white marble a cloudy red and yellow. He ripped open his tunic, already wet with blood and discharge, his chest, covered in ulcers as his skin boiled from beneath.

My irritation with pointless disputes swelled like Chancellor Barrow's bloated form. My gaze fixed on his pleading eyes ultimately forced shut by the spreading sores. I remained unmoved by his choked screams for mercy, the crowd's mingled gasps, or Iven's questioning glances. Barrows raised a bulbous arm as black-purple bruises splotched across his skin. Milky discharge, akin to tears, dripped into the growing mess below, as he forced a final whimper through his blocked esophagus before exploding into a puddle of blood, bones, and yellow foamy secretions.

The crowd took a collective jump back from the oozing remains. The foul stench of rancid alkali permeated the room. "His lordship will reconvene the assemblage after a short recess to... cleanse Representative Barrows from the chamber floor." Iven motioned toward the standing guard to clear the room as I rose to take my leave, the alternating click of his metal limb tailing me into the hallway.

"My lord?" Iven called, catching up as I

plodded my way toward the uppermost library. "My lord, if I could be so bold as to say that was ill-advised."

"Which part?"

"You know to what I refer," Iven said. His tone remained soft and unexpectedly understanding.

"He insulted you, Iven. He insulted this house, which means he insulted me." I turned onto the spiral staircase as metal fingers clasped my shoulder. I turned, my foot atop the first stair, and looked back at my servant.

Iven stared at me. "Reminiscing about a foregone past again?"

"I always feel nostalgic after a reaping. You know this."

"The young Master Maerek was an offering, his people understand—"

"I don't mean that. The boy's energy was necessary for what's to come. But it drains me, my essence. Like trading a part of my soul for his life. An unequal trade if ever there was one." I turned to glance up the staircase, yearning to lose myself in my studies. My troubled gaze returned to Iven. "All that's left is this feeling of… emptiness. A longing for something I can no longer touch. Something beyond myself."

"I'm not sure I understand, sir."

"No, no, of course you don't, old friend," I said with a feigned smile. My thoughts raced as memories intermingled with present realities. Too long I've lingered here, accumulating knowledge like dusty tomes abandoned on overtaxed bookshelves. Lacking the will to act.

Iven took a heavy breath, his internal clockwork echoing his discontent. "Rest assured, sir, that I am here to facilitate your every need, including this longing, as you call it, for your dead past. The historical projections you've gifted me are at your disposal at any hour."

"The gesture, Iven, is always appreciated. Though simulated archives will never be the same."

"It is a great deal safer than your current... obsession, and if I may speak freely... I must say, less taxing."

I nodded, a touch of a smile encroaching on my face. "You're right, as always."

"As you say, sir."

"I should save my power anyway," I said with renewed vigor. "The alignment will be here in another month's time. Then all of this, all this death and destruction, will be forgotten."

"Reversed, sir. Reverted to its natural order," Iven corrected.

"Of course. You're right, Iven. You're always right." I looked back at my creation, eyeing him like a well-trained pet. "I've made somewhat of a mess out there, haven't I?"

"Only politically, I'm sure, no more. Aurora will likely be energized by the Chancellor's death, more than likely ending whatever stalemate has forestalled their own actions against Byzantium's mobilization. With your permission, we can offer our consideration for a defensive position, in secret, of course.

Offer compensatory troops to bolster their efforts for a quick resolution. Any thoughts of a sustained war with New Aurora will be put on hold with the added backing of your lordship. Byzantium will need to consider reparations to the citadel for the insult." Iven's aperture whirled open and refocused. "In your own way, sir, you've truncated a war we knew was inevitable."

"A secondary intention, I assure you. But not so unfortunate as first surmised. What of Rayne's heir? Has our emissary in New Aurora failed so decisively?"

"It appears so, my lord."

"Unfortunate. Send a legion of our soldiers to fortify the New Aurora armies with a message of our intent to their commanders. General Greymoor should still be in the citadel. Offer him my personal condolences. And to our failed emissary, send our normal reaction." I placed a hand on the automaton's shoulder. "I'm always thankful for your guidance, Iven, and your friendship. I want you to know that."

Iven clenched his jaw, fighting those circuits which removed any liberty he once had. "It's the purpose you'd restored me for, sir." Fighting, even after all these years.

"I suppose so." I stepped off the stairs and turned to look into Iven's mismatched eyes, clasping him fully. "Though, when the time comes, and the Tessermancy spell is complete—" I choked back the unexpected sentiment knotted in my throat. "I will be sorry to see you go."

"The conjunction will give you the strength needed," Iven said with a sigh. "And with your success, I won't ever have existed."

CHAPTER 26
Escape from Shellrock

Darkness. Silence. If there were ever a sense of nonexistence, Guilder had found it. He floated, weightless, though without fear. Unsure if his eyes were open or if he was sitting or standing or... He listened as his breath became the only sound, his heartbeat, the only thing felt. The chill started at his feet, crawled up his legs, and into his core. It spread over his body like sweat icing over, forming a new skin, a protective shell.

He turned his head and saw a ruined planet drifting in blackness, green flame encapsulating the sphere, dust trails, like tendrils, lagging behind. Guilder drifted, incorporeal. The ensuing cataclysm's sole witness. The planet burned, turned red, liquefied, then cooled. Rivers of molten rock formed like veins, hills grew to mountains, erosion carved out canyons like a sculptor chipping away stone, forming recognizable features, a face.

Eyes of blue water opened behind widening sea caves, staring into Guilder. Depressions and valleys sat in judgment. The dead planet, now a detached old man, its features so like his father's, as time sped by faster than light. Guilder felt the pull of the planet, unseen hands beckoning him closer. He crashed through the grating atmosphere like a comet, an asteroid plummeting into the heart of the planet until smashing into fertile ground. Guilder crawled out of the impact crater into a furrowed field, weak and exposed from his tumultuous passage.

At the center of the field sat a gnarled oak, its branches, lush and green, unfurled in the sun. Familiarity grew as Guilder approached, warming his chest and shoulders, his extremities. He'd known this tree, seen it burst into green flames, assimilating his father's face.

A young man sat beneath the tree eating a crisp red apple, its juices dripping down his chin onto his white tunic. Guilder staggered forward, listless. "Hello?" The man ignored his approach. "Hello?"

"Fate is a wicked mistress," the man with the apple said before taking another bite.

"I don't understand?"

"Neither will you... until the end." The apple man raised an eyebrow. "Perhaps not even then."

"Who... do I know you?"

"No. But I know you."

"Who am I... to you?"

"A thorn, nothing more. No one of any consequence."

"Then why are we here?" Suddenly exhausted, Guilder fell to his hands and knees.

The apple man looked up into the tree's branches as if considering his question. He looked back at Guilder, took another bite, and smiled.

"Why don't you answer?"

"The answer has already been determined." The apple man's smile faded. "Otherwise, there'd be no reason for you to be here."

"I still don't understand?"

"Neither will you..."

"Until the end. Yes, so you've said."

"Your father was much the same," the apple man

said before taking a final bite.

"You knew my father?"

"Once, maybe. But only as much as a god knows an ant."

Guilder narrowed his eyes with a quizzical look. "Who are you?"

"Prophecy becomes bothersome when it stands in the way of ambition." The man tossed his apple core aside and wrapped his hands around Guilder's neck. Guilder clawed at the man's hands as they tightened around his throat. Green flame erupted around the two of them, engulfing the tree, the field, the apple core. "I killed this world... once," the apple man said with an apathetic expression. "You are powerless to stop its rebirth."

"Who... are... you?" Guilder croaked as he pried the apple man's hands from his neck, stepped back, and kicked him square to the chest, sending him flying into the charred oak. The tree loosened from the ground, exposing the under root as it fell. The apple man picked up the bulk of the tree, flinging it into the air and out of sight. He readied himself for another attack, then stopped, lifted as if from a string tightened around his neck. Dark red blood stained the front of his tunic as a sword tip pushed out from his chest. He looked at Guilder with wide-eyed bewilderment, then fell to his knees.

"Who are you?" Guilder asked, standing over the apple man.

"Guilder." The answer came from nowhere, or everywhere. Saplings began sprouting from man's limbs, his back, his head. Guilder stared in disbelief as the body was swallowed into the earth, a mature oak growing where the apple man knelt. Ryleigh's motionless

body rested against the newly formed tree. Her eyes stood open, yet vacant. Guilder kneeled beside her. "Guilder?" the voice said from nowhere, Ryleigh's lips moving in pantomime. "He's awake, go find Breya."

"Ryleigh?" Guilder questioned the lifeless body, tears blurring his vision. Her head snapped toward him, eyes yellowed and bloodshot, teeth bared. "What are you?!" she screamed before darkness again overtook him.

"Guilder?" a more tender voice asked, accompanied by a cool hand against his cheek. "Guilder, please come back to me." He opened his eyes as Ryleigh's smiling, tear-filled face hovered above him.

His returned smile deteriorated to a grimace as the ache in his body flushed over him. Guilder propped a sore arm behind him struggling to sit up as he lifted his shirt to inspect the burn wound below his chest. "What happened?" he asked, as Ryleigh aided his efforts.

"We were hoping you could tell us." Shyloh stepped out of the corner shadow into the light of the fireplace.

"You've been unconscious for nearly three days," Ryleigh said, her eyebrows raised in concern. "We saw you thrown out the window by that monster."

"By that Ōmukade," Shyloh corrected, prompting an exaggerated eye roll from Ryleigh.

"Three days?" Guilder marveled, lowering his shirt over the palm-sized yellowed bruise. "It seemed only moments ago. I was... lost in my dreams."

"More fire-scorched trees?" Shyloh asked.

"Yeah. But there was something else, someone… else. A man, young. He spoke of fate." Guilder shook his head. "I don't know."

"Dreams can be quite powerful, Guilder," Ryleigh said. "Divining, even."

"All clairvoyance aside, I'm not even sure how I survived."

"I know how," Ashyr said from his window seat, a coy smile on his face. "You turned to mist."

"No." Ryleigh shook her head. "Not possible. You'd always said it wasn't something that could be taught."

"I'm not sure it can. It's like teaching your heart to beat, or your lungs to breathe." Ashyr's eyes met Guilder's. "After you… exited the room. I stole out to the courtyard. Figured there wouldn't be enough left of you to fill a bucket, yet there you were, flat on your back on the stonework. You'd resolidified all except your eyes. I couldn't believe it." Ashyr flashed a wide smile. "I was like a proud parent."

"Ashyr," Ryleigh said. "Focus."

Ashyr shook out his smile. "Right. Well, once you'd gathered yourself, we had you moved here."

"Why didn't you tell us you could mist?" Ryleigh asked.

"He didn't know," Shyloh said. Guilder peered up at Ryleigh and shook his head.

Ashyr glanced over at Shyloh. "He's the one the prophecy spoke of. He controls all five virtues of natural magic."

Shyloh stared at Guilder, eyes questioning.

"He did take to fire-wielding pretty quickly," Ashyr said enthusiastically. "And the metal spells with the faery, none of us knew those."

"You did get us through the underground cavern," Ryleigh said. "Only an earth caster can work those spells."

Guilder swung his legs off the bed and stretched out his back. "If you're referring to that tired prophecy about Iks, we've been through that, I'm not the one it refers to."

The three looked at one another. "You'd said you were too old; we know. Prophesy can be fraught with inaccuracies." Shyloh said lowing her gaze.

Guilder turned back to Ryleigh as she pressed her fists to her hips. "Typical, Breya leaves out the important bits and only says enough to keep your interest up. Manipulating witch."

"The prophecy mentioned something about a devourer of light…" Guilder said.

"Missing from the sky, the hawk devours the angel of black light," Ashyr recited. "Struck down by the venom of the martyred lion, brandishing his five claws. Alms to the Earth, stolen, then returned. So shall the martyred strike back, devouring the hawk. Or something like that."

"But what does it mean?" Guilder asked.

"It's widely believed that Iks is the hawk that destroyed whatever this angel of black light is," Shyloh said.

Ryleigh moved to sit next to Guilder. "Could it refer to Luna?"

"The Luna from those childhood fairy tales?" Guilder asked.

"Or Earth's missing moon from the pictogram under the castle," Ashyr said.

"Iks destroyed Luna?" Ryleigh questioned. "But how? He can't be that powerful. Can he?"

"Maybe he is," Guilder said. "But Luna must have been destroyed centuries ago. There must be more to it."

"It goes on to say that a lion will strike, brandishing five claws," Ashyr continued. "Meaning the five natural elements of magic."

"And you all believe that I'm this lion?"

"It does say a martyred lion," Ryleigh said. "You'd said yourself you'd changed after that cave. The old Guilder left to die?"

Guilder nodded.

"And the alms to the earth have to refer to the Zombies that were 'stolen' from their graves, then returned when you killed that Faery queen," Ashyr said.

"But he hasn't *mastered* any of the elements," Shyloh said. "Certainly not aquamancy."

Guilder raised his hand in front of his face. Touched his thumb and middle finger together as he closed his eyes. He pulled his hand forward. A bead of sweat dripped sideways from Shyloh's brow and floated toward Guilder as if on a string. He opened his eyes, calm, effortlessly he held the drop in midair. "The prophecy doesn't seem to call for mastery, only aptitude." Guilder flattened out his hand. The droplet fell onto the corner of his bedding and absorbed into the silk sheets.

"Guilder fitting the prophecy only confirms Iks' ultimate involvement in a greater conspiracy," Ashyr said. "We'd already known it was his edict that had all those children killed, so he must have accepted the divination as truth, but it doesn't explain the bounty for Guilder now or the attack in his room. Iks can't make a creature like that just materialize. There must've been someone inside the castle controlling it."

"The Ōmukade was afraid," Shyloh whispered, her arms remaining crossed, eyes inquisitive. "He was defending himself the only way he knew how."

"Well, someone put it… him in a position to attack Guilder." Ryleigh said. "Shayde, maybe?"

Shyloh shook her head. "Shayde's plans seem to be more political than anything, plus I think he's a gelding."

Ryleigh threw her hands up. "For Gaea's sake, Shyloh."

"A what?" Guilder questioned.

"Someone who can't use magic," Ashyr explained. "Or never learned. Calling someone a gelding is extremely derogatory." He looked back at Shyloh. "It also infers they're untrustworthy and up to no good."

Shyloh raised an eyebrow.

"He did contract you to kill Guilder," Ryleigh added.

"Your ineptness regarding that is extremely appreciated," Guilder said, aiming a smile at Shyloh.

Shyloh nodded with a timid smile of her own. "Shayde was only the intermediary. Someone above him put out the hit."

"So, if it isn't Iks and it isn't this Scarecrow man, who's connected enough to get that Ōmukade into my room?"

"Connected and powerful," Ashyr said. "Took the three of us, plus another six royal guards, to bring that thing down."

"Him," Shyloh corrected. "He was male."

"Does it really matter?" Ashyr shot back.

"Male Ōmukades are typically smaller than the females, they aren't even native to this continent." She looked back at Guilder and dropped her eyes. "I guess... I guess it doesn't matter."

"How did it... he get here, Shyloh?" Guilder asked.

"He shouldn't have ever been here." Shyloh came to the foot of the bed, wrapping her arm around one of the posts. "Their fire can only be sustained in the southernmost desert environments of the Frisian Continent. Euraillian Island, most commonly. If he were suspended in that chimney as a trap for you, then it would have taken an extremely robust spell to hold him. Unnatural magic like that takes skill."

A clanging knock on the door stole the

attention of the room. Ryleigh peered out and sighed before opening the door. "Apologies, ma'am, to you and your party, but I have a message for Crown Prince Rayne." The armored soldier held a letter-sized parchment in one hand, his helm tucked under his arm.

"What's the message?" Ryleigh asked, holding her ground.

The soldier cleared his throat and stiffened his posture. "It is a message intended for the crown prince and of the utmost importance. Again, ma'am, my apologies."

Ryleigh peered back into the room. Guilder nodded at her to allow the soldier in. She stepped away from the door, letting it swing fully open.

The soldier stepped in, eyed Ryleigh as he passed, then dropped to a knee with a clang. "Your Highness, I have a message from the king, to be given to you in private."

"I trust those in this room further than anyone in this castle." Guilder pushed himself to stand. "Rise and give me your message."

The soldier rose, looking around at the others in the room, and again bowed his head. In a whispered voice, he said. "The king wishes to meet." He held out the slip of yellowed parchment. "This will show you where and when." He lifted his head to meet Guilder's stare. "There are those in these walls, my lord, who wish you harm."

"That has become undeniably apparent." Guilder studied the parchment. Written in his father's hand were the words *Lost Magics*, followed by the number 137. "Messenger, what has occurred these last few weeks to make it so unsafe for me here?"

The soldier looked back toward the door where Ryleigh stood, her arms crossed. In the same hushed tone, he said, "No, my lord, only in the last few days." He hesitated, taking in a ratcheted breath. "I should not be the one to tell you this, my prince, but... the queen... she's distraught over Chancellor Barrow's... passing at the hands of Lord Iks. We received word only this morning that your father has been left with new counsel. General Greymoor hastens to the front, leaving the newly appointed chancellor, Wilfried Shayde, as his majesty's sole advisor."

"Oh fuck," Shyloh said.

"Indeed," the soldier responded. "My lord, Councilman Shayde has escalated a war your father hoped to quell."

***

As the others prepared for a stealthy departure from Shellrock Castle, Guilder entered the neglected octagon-shaped room depicted on his father's note. Ornate hardwood bookshelves stood empty, books replaced by cobwebs and dust as they fanned out to each corner from a centralized rotunda, the domed ceiling mirroring that of the forgotten palace.

The back walls flaunted depictions of the various ruling houses residing in the known world, the winged manticore of House Iks holding the most prominent position. An iridescent dragonfly for the faery clans of the marshlands to his left, and Allenrude Byzantium's Kraken beside them. Once the southern coast turned to a republic, Byzantium no longer used the Kraken as representation, preferring a flag depicting a kusarigama, a weapon consisting of a billhook chained to a heavy iron weight, encircling a pair of clashing swords. Their new crest was unsanctioned, according to Aurora, so Allenrude's Kraken remained, at least in Shellrock's empty library.

The Mist Mages of the Crystal Mountains were depicted by a silhouette of a dragon with its black wings splayed out, and a single emblem for the entire Frisian Continent. The Frisian's Ifrit, a kind of djinn fire demon, didn't represent any house, only the continent itself. The names of its ruling clans were ignored for reasons Guilder could only guess.

Guilder trailed his hand across the wood scroll adorning the untidy shelves as he moved along the aisle representing the Rayne monarchy. At its end, engraved into the back wall, was a fire-breathing chimera. A formidable beast with a lion's head, the body of a goat, and a dragon's tail. The image depicted the creature in battle with a diminutive soldier in the foreground, though it was unclear who would be the victor.

Guilder turned to the right-hand aisle. Near the bottom shelf, shadowed behind the ornate lip, lay a thin, sea-blue journal. Guilder removed the lone book, turned to the 137th page, and read the handwritten spell aloud. "*Nuzvesk elia sagma.*"

Behind the wall sounded a heavy cluck, the disengagement of a door latch. The chimera depiction split, tracing along the side of the beast and the warrior from top to bottom, candlelight shining around its contours. He pushed the creature-shaped door open and tentatively peered inside.

His father sat alone at a humble desk, a leather-bound book open in front of him, and two wooden chairs placed at the desk's front. The stone floor was covered in a threadbare rug, its faded design matching that of the chimera-carved door. Along three walls were more bookshelves, cobwebbed and dusty, yet a scarce number of books filled their racks.

"Father?" Guilder ventured as he entered. The door closed behind him with a soft click.

Æthelred looked up from his reading, offering a troubled smile. "Guilder. You'd received my message, good."

"Yes, but…"

Æthelred held out his hand, offering Guilder a seat. "We have much to discuss and, sadly, little time." He closed his book and leaned back, resting his arms along his sides. "You have questions, I'm sure. Ask."

"Why was I spared?" Guilder's raised voice echoed in the chamber, lending weight to his question. "The mandate from Iks; why was I the only one saved?"

"Why indeed? You were the crown prince, yours would not be the fate of peasants."

"That is not an answer."

Æthelred's eyes fell from Guilder's face. "Through my own folly, then. A king's hubris." He took a deep breath and looked back at Guilder, tears welling up. "Your mother and I... we'd lost three already to stillbirth. I'd prayed to all the gods, old and new, for an heir. Just one, so the monarchy could continue. When Lord Iks enacted his edict, you had only just been born."

Æthelred leaned forward, his breathing long and heavy, eyes downtrodden. "Understand, the want for a child was strictly my own. I loved your mother, but she... had ulterior plans and the Barrows family were never satisfied with a dukedom. Their want of the throne was unending, and ever since I allowed your Uncle Eshtyn into the castle... well." He sat back in his chair, resting his hands across his stomach. "I believe he'd been poisoning her against me for some time."

"The birth of a legitimate heir, my birth, halted their plans?"

"Only temporarily. In secret, they hoped for another stillbirth, I'm certain of it. Schemed all the more after. The Iks mandate was a convenient alternative to regicide. Their family crest would be kept clean while humbling themselves to that dark sorcerer. You lost six cousins to their cowardice."

"If the Barrows family was so keen on my death, why was Iks never informed I'd escaped his mandate?"

"One final courtesy of Breya Oriel. With her aid, I'd fashioned a potion." Æthelred's gaze fell as he seemed to shrink into himself. "I gathered the entire Barrow family together." He sat up straight, his face hardened in his conviction. "And as their king, ordered them to drink. The poison was painless, or so I'd been told. Eshtyn survived, somehow. I gave him a seat as an advisor to buy his silence. To the queen, I offered Oriel's elixir. It erased her mind and made her... susceptible to suggestion. She was told you were stillborn. Breya took you away until a later, agreed-upon time."

"But didn't that raise further questions? Where I'd come from or why Breya took me in the first place?"

"It did. A warning Breya was adamant about reminding me." Æthelred's gaze fell, turning vacant. "The queen, I feel, could never justify the disparities she saw about you, her family, her other... inconsequential beliefs. They soured her mind against me. Deciding to banish Breya instead of executing her was the last straw. She turned to that Necromancer looking to gain power in other ways. She was already a formidable sorceress, mind you. Yet she became consumed as Iks promised to bolster her magics."

"She was a fire wielder?"

"Among other things. Iks taught her how to corrupt her flame, use it in unnatural ways."

"And what was the price for this training?"

Æthelred refocused his gaze on Guilder, a prideful smile overtaking his melancholy.

"You've become wise from your travels. You'll make an admirable king."

"What was the price, Father, for my mother to become a puppet to that…monster."

"Only that she bear no children."

"Yet here I sit."

"Yet here you sit." Æthelred nodded.

"Was she the one who had me put in that memory eater's cave?"

"As an exercise to right a wrong, she felt done to Lord Iks, yes. But I have it on good authority that your uncle backed the compensation. Used one of our own spies to contract the bounty."

"Wilfried Shayde?"

Æthelred stared at Guilder, a quizzical look across his face. "Clever. Shayde's known to be…discreet. I can't say who he got to do the deed, but—"

"That part I know. What about the Ōmukade in my room?"

"What she's done to you is no longer of importance. I'll deal with it, personally."

Guilder's jaw tightened as he gawked at Æthelred. "You'll have her killed?"

"Worse, I'm afraid. To avoid any scandal, I'll need to end her myself. I might not be the keenest of aquamansers, but not even an accomplished fire wielder can evaporate a trachea full of wine."

Guilder's stare persisted.

"I loved her, once. But her siding with Iks makes her a liability, at the least, dangerous at most. It's…unfortunate. I'll incriminate one of the republic prisoners and finally put some legitimacy to this war."

Guilder looked into the king's eyes, shaking his head, dejected. "This whole thing is madness. You'll destroy the whole eastern continent. Is this Barrow's advice? Shayde's? War at all costs?"

"No. This war was inevitable. With your disappearance, Byzantium saw the crown at its weakest. They plan to unite the continent under their council's rule, destroying this kingdom, the monarchy, and your legacy with it."

"Father, we have to stop this. What of Lord Iks? Do we not give our tithe to him to prevent this very thing? To be the buffer against these confrontations? Have you looked outside your own castle walls? Aurora has been left empty. Shayde's brainwashed you."

"My mind remains my own."

"How am I to trust that?"

Æthelred rose from his chair, rounded the desk, and kneeled at Guilder's feet. "Guilder, my precious son. After Natasha failed in her attempt to kill you, Shayde advised me to finish what his assassin could not."

"So, you've brought me down here to do just that."

"No." The king stood, moving to the back of the room. He pushed against a panel, revealing a hidden doorway. "This path leads to the exterior of the castle. The forest narrows are beyond. I've had word sent to your friends to meet you at the forest edge." Æthelred retrieved a scroll from his desk and handed it to Guilder. "That scarecrow's whispers may have started this war, but I was the one who brought us to the brink. Take that to the Byzantium council. It requests a stay of battle. Maybe some compromise can still be found."

"Why not take it yourself?"

"I'd be dead as soon as I crossed the Bulwark divide. Be assured, Guilder, the Necromancer's reach is deep, and there's no doubt he's buried his talons in Shellrock… Byzantium as well." Æthelred clasped Guilder's shoulder. "No, now is the time to show Aurora's strength, as paltry as it may be. Peace-mongering is better left to the shadows. Now go."

Guilder held out his hand, grasping Æthelred's forearm. "We will see each other again."

"This war was my doing, by my indecisiveness and… my arrogance. I deserve whatever fate the gods deem worthy. Your fate lies elsewhere. Go now, before you're discovered."

"Thank you, Father."

"Thank me by saving our kingdom."

CHAPTER 27
Journey to Byzantium

"Guilder?" Ryleigh reined in her horse, slowing to match Guilder's plodding speed. "Guilder, you haven't said a word since we left Aurora. Is everything, I mean, are you... all right?"

Guilder stared a dozen lengths ahead as Shyloh charted their way through the rocky bluffs along the western coast of the kingdom. "My father... I'm not sure. He was always critical of war, constantly preaching in opposition to any hostility with Byzantium, with Iks, even. Said that our differences would eventually be the bridge to understanding. It infuriated me. I thought it made him weak. At the very least, I couldn't see the sense in it, not before."

"And now?"

"Now, there seems to be a fervent ambition for the opposite." Guilder turned his gaze toward Ryleigh. Concern bordering on dread sat heavy in his chest. "Those same infuriating feelings are still there, but... for different reasons." Guilder spurred his mount, narrowing his distance to Shyloh, Ryleigh following suit. "Father seemed torn in a way I'd never seen, remembered, anyway. I feel there's an unknown influence at work here."

"You mean this Shayde character?"

"Maybe. But I think it goes further than him. Shyloh said he was in some secret order?"

"Order of Mstovaris." Shyloh said, craning her neck back from her fidgety mount. "They're a secret guild of spies or assassins or something. A radical offshoot of the Trades Commission pushing their agendas into the political realm."

"Seems like they've succeeded, at least in Aurora," Guilder said.

Ryleigh narrowed her eyes at Shyloh. "And how is it you know so much about this secret order?"

"Wyrmlen spouted off about them in one of his drunken stupors. Apparently, he had wanted into their little club but got denied. I just happened to be lucky enough to be in earshot."

"Lucky." Ryleigh snickered. "I'll bet."

"I asked around, afterward. For a secret society, they didn't seem keen on keeping their own secrets. Seems every cutthroat and their mother knew about them."

"So, who leads this band of spies?" Guilder asked. "Maybe we can reason with them to help stop this war, or at least barter for their assistance."

"That's one secret they do keep. Nobody seems to know who heads the order, or where they're headquartered. Instructions come from runners, wannabe recruits from outside the Trades Commission. They seem to prefer them to ravens."

"You tried to be a runner, didn't you?" Ryleigh shared a knowing look with Guilder.

"Their timelines were brutal." Shyloh

nodded, raising her eyebrows.

"Ashyr's up ahead," Guilder said. "Come on, let's hear what he's found out." Guilder spurred his steed into a trot, Ryleigh and Shyloh following behind. At their approach, Ashyr's mare whinnied out her greeting. He patted her neck as the others approached.

"What's the word?" Shyloh asked.

"Not great." Ashyr straightened in his saddle. "There's a barricade set up about five kilometers past the end of the cape. A rally station, maybe even a rearguard. Patrols ride along the edge of the forest. Anyone trekking through the narrows has a good chance of running into them. Plenty of gaps, though. Beyond that, another ten kilometers or so is the rear of the Auroran army. Tents set up for hospitals, armories, stables, that sort of thing."

"Did you happen to spot General Greymoor or any of his colonels?" Guilder asked, fighting to temper his stubborn horse's waywardness.

Shyloh leaned over and grabbed the silver mustang's reins. Pulling her close, she placed her free hand over its muzzle. Promptly, the horse calmed. Shyloh nodded toward Guilder, a snide "you're welcome" on her face.

"There's a massive tent set up a few rows in, Auroran colors flying at full mast above. Greymoor should be there. There's chatter among the lieutenants that the fighting hasn't started. Posturing, yes, but each side seems to be holding its line." A squabble of nesting sea birds took flight behind Ashyr, breaking the woodland silence and stealing the group's attention. "Not sure what they're waiting for." Ashyr turned back to the others. "But I don't see any way through the Auroran front, let alone getting into Byzantium, not now."

"We could wait till nightfall," Ryleigh said. "Sneak our way in."

"It's near a day's ride to the capital. We'd never make it without being caught by one side or the other," Shyloh said.

"Guilder and I could mist our way through with a full day's rest, maybe. Reconnaissance sapped all my strength. It was all I had to get back here without being spotted."

"I am wholly unprepared for that kind of stealth," Guilder said. Leaves rustled as a cool breeze kicked up around them. "I can go to the checkpoint alone. Demand to see General Greymoor. As the crown prince, they'd have to obey my orders."

"And what happens to the rest of us?" Ryleigh asked. "We don't know if we can trust Greymoor anymore than Shayde or Barrows. We'll have to find another way."

"I may know someone," Shyloh said. "We'd have to get closer to Foxgate—"

A trio of fully armored cavalry knights loped toward the group, their swords drawn. Guilder nudged his horse past Ashyr, holding out his hand as Shyloh readied her bow.

"Hold where you stand," the lead knight said. "We've archers trained on you as I speak. Reach for your weapons or mumble a single spell and they'll down you before you've drawn breath one." The lead knight lifted his visor. "Who are you to be snooping about in these woods, spying on...Your Majesty?" The men sheathed their swords, removed their helms, and lowered their heads.

Guilder dismounted, leaving his horse as he approached the still-mounted knights. "My emissaries and I need to speak with General Greymoor," he announced loud enough for anyone within earshot. "It is most dire that you escort us to his command tent at once."

"My lord, at once," the lead knight said. "We'd feared the worst after word of your..."

"Word of my what, Commander?"

"Well sire, we'd been informed that... spies had infiltrated the castle." The knight took in the others, his extended gaze resting on Shyloh. "Three, to be specific." He reset his helm, his comrades responding in kind. "Word was they'd tossed you from your bedroom window." The lead knight drew his sword as the other two horsemen took up offensive positions.

Guilder placed himself in front of the lead knight's outstretched sword. "Commander, do you no longer believe your own eyes?" The knight's mount wavered in its stance. "I am very much alive and not in the least under duress."

The knight held up a gauntleted hand. "Hold!"

"From what I understand, General Greymoor has less of a front and more of a field army, that's why you haven't started an attack. There is scarcely a legion at the front, so there's no affording you archers to cover your flank. You're not behind your own back line on any orders, are you, Commander?"

The lead knight grew a cocky smile. "All's true, my lord. We three've been planning our leave from this witless campaign for days. We weren't the first, neither. Happening upon you lot just sweetens the deal. I'm sure the bounty on your head's still twice that of the spies which killed you."

Guilder fixed his gaze on the knight's eyes, bringing an open palm, fingers splayed out in front of him. He closed his fist as shards of black metal burst from the earth, skewering through the lead knight's armor and one of the other horsemen. Their mounts bucked, bolting off into the wood, leaving the riders where they fell. The third horseman writhed on the ground, breathless from his fall. Shyloh jumped from her mount, grabbed the lead knight's fallen sword, and placed the tip at the fallen soldier's neck.

Guilder strode over to Shyloh's side. "Take us to General Greymoor or join your friends in their desertion."

***

General Greymoor's war room was a paltry replica of the one tucked away inside Shellrock Castle. A beat-up conference table to one side with mismatched chairs all around, a worn field desk stuck in the corner, and, at the center of the tent, a sand table depicting troop alignments of Byzantium and Aurora complete with accurate landscapes in miniature.

"I'd left instruction not to be disturbed." General Greymoor sat at the overflowing field desk, shifting documents into disheveled piles as Guilder stepped up to the sand table.

"I was told your troop numbers were marginal, but these are practically anorexic."

"Guilder... I mean m-my lord." Greymoor shot to his feet, knocking brimming papers to the threadbare carpet overlaying the earthen floor. "I'd only recently received word of your demise." He bent to retrieve the fallen documents as Shyloh and the others entered the tent. "Within the castle walls, no less." He stood, papers in hand. "And by... three... Byzantium... spies." He dropped the stack onto the desk, allowing several to fall back onto the floor.

Guilder studied the sand table, adjusting several miniature troops into tighter formations. "Your intel was mistaken. These are my friends. Bodyguards, if it pleases you. We've been sent by my father to parley with Byzantium's Council."

"Soldier, you've been privy to this?" Greymoor asked.

"Oh, we found him in the wood, behind your rearguard." Guilder turned a lopsided smile toward the knight. "With two other deserters. He... reconsidered and brought us to you."

"Is that so?"

"Aye, sir." The knight straightened his stance with a clunk of his armor.

"Then you ought to be commended, commissioned, even." Greymoor sat, grabbing a fresh parchment from atop the field desk. He quickly scribbled a note, folded it, and sealed it in wax. "See the commander of the Fifth Battalion and give him this accommodation."

"Aye, sir." A broad grin spread across the soldier's face. "Thank you, sir," he said before taking off at a trot, leaving the tent's flap unsecured.

"You sent him to the front lines, didn't you?" Shyloh said, taking a seat on top of the conference table and swinging a leg.

"I'm sure his reconsideration was not of his own accord. And I can't afford to waste any men. Coward or otherwise."

Greymoor joined Guilder at the sand table. "Friends, aye?" He looked each of them over before letting out a conceding sigh. "This whole campaign has been... unprecedented. You, showing up here now, only suits the pattern."

"General," Ashyr said from the far end of the sand table. "How do you suppose a victory over Byzantium when you seem to be outnumbered four to one?"

"My question as well," Guilder added.

Greymoor hesitated. "My lord, I can understand the befriending of your... liberators, but these are Auroran secrets known only to a very few. You sincerely trust these people?"

"With all my being."

Greymoor leaned against the edge of the sand table, scanning his model. "We'd known for some time that there was a traitor within the castle walls. Æthelred..." Greymoor clenched a fist and turned his head as if choking back some unwanted emotion. "He... came up with a plan, shared it with only a small inner circle, people we could trust, or so we thought. We'd conceal our numbers by holding back ten legions within the catacombs beneath the castle."

Guilder shot a knowing glance at Ashyr as Greymoor pointed out various locations around the map. "These we'd march along the eastern coastline, skirting the Bulwark Divide to attack their weaker flank. The skeleton force assembled here will hold their attention to the front." Greymoor looked up at Guilder. "And hopefully give them a false sense of... you know something."

"General," Guilder said. "We'd been in those caverns. Whoever your traitor is, they trapped a basilisk in with your troops."

"Blinded her after," Shyloh cut in, prompting a glare from Ryleigh. "Well, he did, the bastard."

"It may have been your troops fighting back, but she's right. There were nothing but statues in Shellrock Palace. I'm sorry, General. You have no strategy here. Your only option is to assist us in getting across the border. I'll take my father's letter to Byzantium's council and put an end to this conflict."

Greymoor hung his head, bracing himself against the sand table. "Then, truly, all is lost."

"No. My presence, along with the king's letter, *will* put this right."

"I'd received a raven from Shellrock only moments before your arrival." Greymoor stepped back to his field desk and shuffled through the mess of parchments. "Your... unexpected presence made me question its legitimacy. But if what you say of—a basilisk, was it—we may be seeing the last of the Rayne monarchy."

Guilder took the message Greymoor held out to him, tightening his jaw as he read.

"The king is dead." Greymoor bowed his head, his gaze remaining fixed on Guilder. "Long live the king."

"I'm sorry, Guilder." Ryleigh skirted in beside him, placing a consoling hand on his shoulder. "But won't this only add legitimacy to your claims that this is an unjust war?"

"Let's hope." Guilder nodded. "The four of us will continue to Byzantium. General, can you forestall your troops' advancement?"

"There's more."

"How could there possibly be any more?" Shyloh said, her hand thrown up in frustration.

"With the king's death and the rumors surrounding your assassination, the queen has declared sovereign leadership over Aurora. She's taken control of the war room and ordered our initial attack to commence immediately."

"But what of the king's inner circle?" Ryleigh said. "Don't you still hold influence? Barrows may be a warmongering bastard, but you, General—"

"Eshtyn Barrows was killed by Lord Iks."

Ryleigh threw up her arms. "Gods be damned." She slunk over to the conference table and fell into a chair beside Shyloh.

"I was, unfortunately, present when it happened, as was Shayde, so you can be sure, as her only remaining counsel, the queen has been informed."

"What purpose did it serve for Iks to kill Barrows?" Guilder asked. "He has no stakes in this war. If anything, I'd think he'd be against it."

"He hasn't backed either side. To him, this conflict is illegitimate."

"Yet he's allowed it to happen without even a word?"

"Regardless of that Necromancer's stance, I believe this hurried advancement is fueled by the queen's grief."

"And whatever secret aims Shayde is harboring," Ashyr said.

Greymoor nodded.

"Tasker, you know my mother has no legal claim to the throne. As a direct order from your king, hold your line. Do not advance on or into Byzantium-controlled land. Will you comply?"

"I will, Your Majesty, but—"

"We can still stop this war if we can get to Byzantium's capital. How do we get to the front, General?"

Greymoor stared at Guilder for the longest time. Finally, with a deep breath, he said, "I can't spare anyone to accompany you."

"You needn't bother."

Greymoor nodded. "South of Foxgate, there's a narrow stretch of land which leads into Byzantium. There's a ferryman, ten kilometers southwest of here who, for a price, will see you across. I have a few men stationed there." Greymoor quickly scrawled a note and handed it to Guilder. "Give them this and they shouldn't offer any trouble." He grabbed Guilder's hand and set in a small satchel of coins. "For the boatman." Greymoor returned to his field desk and sat heavily in the chair behind. From the bottom drawer, he produced a crystalline decanter and cleared a space to fill an accompanying glass. "After you reach the other side, you're on your own."

"Thank you, Tasker... General Greymoor. You've served your station with honor."

"To your success, my king." He raised his near-overflowing glass and downed it in one gulp. "Resupply tent's next one over." He refilled his glass, rising it as before. "May the gods see you to your rightful end." And downed it as before.

As the group left the command tent, Guilder hesitated. He stepped over to Greymoor and his half-drunk decanter and seized a blank parchment from the top of the desk. "I'd ask you for one last favor, General." He scribbled a note, letterlocked, and sealed it in wax. He pressed his ring into the wax and handed it to the General. "As soon as you can spare a man, see that this gets delivered."

"It will be done, your majesty. But, may I

ask, who is so deserving of your correspondence at this late hour?"

"Someone I own my life to."

CHAPTER 28
Coin for the Ferryman

"I didn't see any guards, Auroran or otherwise," Ashyr said, solidifying next to Shyloh as she busied herself dousing their morning campfire. "Did Greymoor say how many he'd sent to protect one old ferryman in his rickety old shack?"

"He didn't." Guilder sat on a nearby fallen tree, running a sharpening stone along his sword's blade. "Just that he sent a team to protect the inlet below Foxgate."

"They probably deserted like those dipshits we ran into at the edge of the western bluffs," Shyloh said.

Ryleigh lay restless in her sleep next to Guilder. His gaze lingered over her, concern poking at him like an entrenched splinter. "We shouldn't assume anything. Let's be wary from here on out. The last thing we need is to be caught by surprise and be strung up in some out-of-the-way dungeon."

"You mean, again?"

"Mmm, why are you guys talking so loud?" Ryleigh rolled toward the still-smoking remnants of their fire, squeezing her closed eyelids tight. "It can't be morning already."

"Afraid so," Shyloh said. "Ashyr's back from reconnoitering the boatman's docks, so we broke camp."

"If you can call it a dock." Ashyr plopped down next to Ryleigh as she sat up, stretched her neck, and attempted to come back alive.

"Not sure those rotted timbers would hold Guilder, let alone all four of us."

Guilder stood and sheathed his sword. "As long as his boat gets us across into Byzantium."

"If you can call it a boat."

"Greymoor assured us—"

"He did, yes. I'm just saying that if this is our only way into Byzantium, we might be swimming most of the way."

Ryleigh stretched out her arms. "You guys know I can't swim," she said through a massive yawn.

"Best learn quick," Shyloh said. "Let's go before our assumed deserters decide guarding an outlying dock wasn't all that bad."

***

The sun-grayed planks of the pier groaned with Guilder's every step, drowning out the birdsong of the woods behind the water gently splashing against the pilings below. The rickety shack sat near the end, held above the water much the same way as the pier, and spanned not more than a grown man's outstretched arms. Opposite the shack, a moored fishing boat bobbed along the water's edge.

"Guilder, wait." Ryleigh closed her hand over Guilder's raised fist. "If you go pounding on this guy's door with your sword and your… royal… muscles… you'll probably give him a heart attack."

Guilder shrugged. "Step back, all of you. Give the man his space."

Ryleigh turned and raised her arm as the

door flew open. She froze as a grizzled old man stood, taking them all in. "You four are about as stealthy as an ostrich in a chicken house." He bent hand over hand, leaning on a knotty walking stick, his stringy white hair covering much of his deeply wrinkled face. Ratty, stained clothes, linen or perhaps cotton, hung off him as if on a wire hanger. His penetrating golden-brown eyes, though, held the glow of youth with a slight mixture of cunning.

Ryleigh lowered her arm as Shyloh took a step forward. "Sir, we—"

"Yeah, I know what you all want. Refugees who need to flee the country, yadda yadda yadda. Everybody and their brother. There's no boat lest ya pay."

Guilder tossed the satchel at the old man's feet. Auroran coin spilled over his oversized shoes. "Thirty to get us all across, another thirty when we reach the other side." Guilder glanced at Ryleigh looking hesitantly at the derelict boat. "The guards stationed here, where'd they run off to?" Guilder added.

"Took them across, week before last." The old man tremulously retrieved the satchel, knees cracking, careful to scoop up all the fallen coins. "Left their armor and weapons as payment." He stood, thumbed behind him to a pile of chain mail, gambesons, and leather armor tossed into the corner of his shack. A pair of uncared-for swords leaned over the pile. "S'pose we'd better get to it, then. Wait by the boat. I'll be with you folks momentarily." He slammed the door, leaving the four of them gawking in his wake.

The old man's boat clunked against the dock's mooring poles with the rhythm of a smith's hammer. More of a flat-bottomed canoe, its upswept bow and bleached driftwood scull oar gave the appearance of a beached sea dragon. "You learn to swim yet, Ryleigh?" Shyloh asked, staring at the feeble vessel.

Ryleigh shot her a scowl in return.

"Shyloh," Guilder said. "The day Ryleigh and I returned from the faery's castle, outside the Belt of Allenrude, Breya had mentioned you'd gone to Foxgate."

"And?"

"You didn't seem to recognize the old man, so how were you so free to cross the border? These blockades must have been up for months."

"Hadn't really thought about it. Just told the blockade guards I was meeting someone in Foxgate and they let me through. Same coming back."

"Could it have been Shayde's influence?" Ryleigh asked. "He's a spy; maybe he's a double agent?"

"Maybe. But he also seems to be doing a lot of his own legwork," Guilder said.

"You're saying he's not the one in charge?"

"That's exactly what I'm saying."

"So, who ultimately stands to gain from this war?" Shyloh asked. "Barrows?"

"Not as such. Least, not anymore," Ashyr said.

"If Byzantium were so willing to overthrow

Aurora, they've already missed their opportunity. Now that you'd been found alive, I mean," Ryleigh said.

"Byzantium wasn't behind the attack. They may not have known of the assassination attempt or the results." Guilder shook his head in frustration. "It all seems like posturing. The same as Aurora. But it still begs the question of who benefits?"

"I'd ask that Necromancer in his repugnant tower," the old man said as he ambled down the careworn dock.

"What's he stand to gain from this war? Either side wins; they're likely to go after him next," Ryleigh said.

"That godless sorcerer's got something up his sleeves for this upcoming conjunction. I'll bet my boat on it." The old man hopped onto the stern, grabbing the sculling oar with surprising dexterity. "Everybody in, I ain't getting any younger."

"What conjunction?" Ashyr climbed into the boat, taking a splintery seat near the bow.

"There's an alignment of planets occurring, sometime in the next few weeks." Guilder followed Ashyr, holding on to the edge as the boat rocked with his movement. "It's said that magic will increase in power several-fold during these conjunctions." He placed a knee down, sharing Ashyr's seat, and glanced toward the narrow strip of land across the bay before turning to face the stern. "They occur so rarely that, well, who knows?"

Shyloh sat at the edge of the center yoke,

dipping her hand into the murky water, followed by Ryleigh taking the nearest seat facing the old man. She kept a death grip hold on the hull, her shoulders and neck stiff.

"You're suggesting this war is only a distraction," Guilder said as the ferryman cast off from the dock.

"Or a misdirection," Shyloh said, skimming her hand across the waves.

"So, if Aurora and Byzantium don't find out what Lord Iks is up to…" Ashyr said.

"What is Iks up to?" Guilder asked.

"That be the real question." The ferryman swung his oar back and forth as the inlet water calmed to a glass-like surface.

"Are we slowing down?" Ryleigh asked, panic evident in her voice. "Why are you slowing?" Guilder glanced over the side, at the ripples of wake skirting by. Ryleigh stood bolt upright, the old ferryman's shirtfront caught in her outstretched arm, feet dangling a meter off the stern.

"Ryleigh!" Guilder shouted. "What in the gods' names has gotten into you?"

"Who are you?" Ryleigh sneered. "*What* are you?"

"Put him down! Ryleigh!" Ashyr misted to the opposite side of the boat, pulling at Ryleigh's arms as the ferryman's limp white hair flashed brown.

"I'll ask one last time. What in the nine realms are you?"

"He's a changeling," Shyloh said, still

bobbing her hand in and out of the water.

"I resent that title," a noticeably younger voice came out of the old ferryman. "Changeling denotes that I only mimic children." His old, crooked stature uncurled, legs wrenched backward, shoes rounded out to hooves as a much younger part human part animal emerged dangling from Ryleigh's grip. "I prefer Skin-walker. It has an... ominous tone that... I don't know, I just like."

"And this is your true form?" Ryleigh set the no-longer old man down. "A faun?"

"My preferred form, yes." His carob brown hair still fell below his shoulders, though now with a youthful natural curl. The stained linen shirt gained a suitable fit, though his pants had transformed to woolly thighs with the same color hair. The fur of his lower legs was more trim as they tapered significantly into suitable-sized hooves.

"Their kind never remembers their true form." Shyloh sat up, shaking her dripping hand over the side of the boat. "Hi, Pik. Long time."

"How've you been, Shyloh?" Pik brushed off his furry thighs, his narrowed eyes never leaving Ryleigh. "Made some new friends, I see."

"Some newer than others."

"You know this... creature?" Ryleigh retook her seat, again with the same death grip on the sides of the boat.

"Remember, I said I may know someone who could get us into Byzantium's capital?" Shyloh held her palm toward the faun.

"Everyone, meet Pik Clawhart. Pik, everyone."

"Pleasure," Pik said, acid dripping from his voice.

"What's with the old-man disguise?"

Pik retook his station and started paddling again. "Things started getting a bit hot in Foxgate with the war and all. Thought I'd venture down the coast for a little fresh air. I happened upon the old geezer's cottage stinkin' like human jerky in a well-used sewer, poked my head in, and found him half eaten by rats."

Ryleigh shook her head. "For Gaea's sake."

"Still, can't let a good hovel go to waste and the pay of a ferryman ain't nothin' to sneeze at. Regular coin, peace and quiet."

"So, you've retired?" Shyloh asked.

"Now I wouldn't say that." Pik's crooked smile grew over half his face.

"Good, because we need a meeting with Byzantium's Grand Council."

"Not enough gold in any of your pockets, old friend."

"Can you at least get us to the capital?" Guilder asked.

Pik licked his lower lip and glared at Guilder. "You know, as I hear tell, there's still a pretty substantial bounty on your head, Your Majesty."

Ryleigh tensed.

"Settle down." Pik lowered his gaze to Ryleigh. "I know I'd never survive taking you all at once. And dumpin' you over the side gets me no proof of anything…"

"Just tell us what you want already," Ryleigh growled.

"Seeing's I can't collect the bounty the old-fashioned way. Perhaps your lordship here would pay the equiv—"

"Done," Guilder said.

"Wait... what?"

Shyloh chuckled and went back to staring into the water. "The deal is struck, old friend. Byzantium for gold."

"Shit." A dazed look of bewilderment overtook Pik's face. "I should have asked for more." He pointed a bobbing finger at Guilder. "A pardon. I need a pardon from Aurora as well."

"You'll get your gold. After we're behind the walls of Byzantium's capital." Guilder turned to watch the approaching narrow strip of land, its sibling dock, just as dilapidated as the one they'd left.

"Say, Pik," Shyloh said, bringing her attention back to the faun. "That armor in the old man's shack, whatever happened to those Auroran guards who were supposed to be on patrol?"

Pik renewed his crooked smile and shrugged.

CHAPTER 29
The Council of Twelve

From the Personal Journals of Andorian Iks

The interpretation of the Fae lord's grimoire had been arduous at times; however, most enlightening. The Tessermancy spell, no less so. Within the amalgamation of sorcery and witchcraft lie elements of science; chemistry mixed with alchemy, incantation, and ritual pantomiming physics. All these, intensified by cosmological forces. Years of study have unlocked the how and when but have yet to answer the question of if.

I confess I do not understand my hesitancy. I have lived more lifetimes than I am due, steadfast in the belief that I have corrupted this world with my ambitious study of these unnatural powers. Wanting only to unlock further secrets to a larger universe, I coerced the asteroid and its strangeness to this planet.

I'd known for some time that its magic had supplanted human evolution, though I was a fool to ignore that knowledge. Having instead chosen my studies, mistaking them for wisdom, only to let it eat away at me like an addiction. This forgone conclusion can only lead to extinction as the availability of limitless power has removed environmental stresses, causing humanity to regress with its use. I can only hope it is not too late.

Should this spell, this chaos, be unleashed to reorder the world to its rightful symmetry, or is the universe fated to drown in its own madness? Irony, it seems, remains the bedfellow of providence. Magic applied to cure the world of magic. If successful, the means to this end will usher in a return to sanity, without magic, without chaos. And if failure should abound, magic, along with everything else, will still cease to be.

Iven has remained the closest thing to an ally I have known, yet I see within him the same torment I grapple with. His struggles have led him down the alternate path. It is my belief that he no longer shares my vision as once he did and wishes instead for this world to remain. Perhaps even under his rule, within a sort of shadow régime. His consorted efforts have said this much. Within his conditioned restraints, both mechanical and biochemical, his designs forbid him to hinder my ambitions directly, yet he has conspired to undermine me in other ways.

This war, for example, its preludes, have again reclaimed the darkened hearts of humanity. For insult or land or power, it has always been the same hubris. Whether it be Iven's gambit or his Order of Mstovaris, it matters not. The keys to their successful stratagems are safe within my grasp and their war's outcome will be moot.

Despite these current distractions, I must remain vigilant. The spell is ripe for its inaugural casting, and I remain at my fullest potential. Afterward, this tainted world will cease to be. Forgotten, an unprecedented fiction apart from my own experience, should I survive. If not, I consider my sins absolved.

"Guard!" The door opened tentatively as my reticent sentinel entered the library. A slight bow conveyed his enduring willingness to obey, a lesson well learned. "Summon Iven and bring tea." He offered another bow before closing the door softly. I strolled over to the Fae text, rereading the entirety of the spell, losing myself to time in indulging my anticipation.

"Your lordship?" Iven skirted through the door, followed by the mute guard carrying tea service. "You summoned."

I stared at the guard in his preparation. Loyal, even after taking his tongue. Perhaps the most loyalty I'd seen. "Guard, what is your name?" He looked up in mid-spoonful, first at me, then at Iven.

"Maerek, my lord," Iven answered for him.

"Like the boy?"

"An uncle." As a good manservant should, Iven knew everyone on his staff by name. I nodded. Feeling all the more alone, or was it shame? The epoch of time and corruption of power had muddled them into obscurity. "Leave it, please."

Maerek rose with uncertainty in his eyes.

"Return to your post." He bowed as before and turned to leave. "And, Sir Maerek," I added before he left the room. "Your loyalty to me will be richly rewarded." A hint of a smile left his lips before closing the door once more.

"How may I be of service, my lord?" Iven stood with his hands locked behind him. Arrow straight, his eyes peered just over my head.

I pointed at the tea service. "If you'd be so kind."

Iven sighed. He took the pot in his metal hand, holding it as if presenting a gift. Soon steam began billowing from the spout. He poured a single cup and regained his former position. "The time of the conjunction is upon us." I stood unmoved from behind the Fae text.

"You'll see preparations are made."

"As you wish, my lord, but—"

"Iven," I shifted my gaze to the automaton. "You *will* make sure that my efforts have not been in vain."

Servo motors whirred persuasively, countering his tick of hesitation. "As always, my lord. My efforts will mirror your own."

***

Ashyr misted his way back to where Guilder and Ryleigh crouched, observing the third checkpoint they'd run into in so many hours. The sequence seemed well rehearsed between Pik and Shyloh. Following Ashyr's reconnaissance, Shyloh, dressed in a confiscated officer's uniform, and Pik, morphed into the form of a seemingly well-known commander, would dismiss or release or otherwise get rid of any soldiers before they took control of the checkpoint. Ashyr would retrieve Ryleigh and Guilder when the coast was clear.

"Ouverridge should be another ten kilometers or so," Shyloh said as they headed west from the last checkpoint. "Greymoor was right, sending us south. Avoiding Foxgate saved us a ton of trouble."

"We'll need to change our strategy if we hope to breach Ouverridge's wall," Pik said, still in his Byzantium soldier form. "These checkpoints are one thing, but getting this lot into the city proper is quite another."

"We could try the 'captured spy' routine," Shyloh said.

Pik narrowed his eyes and pursed his lips.

"Don't you think the spy maneuver is a little on the nose?"

"Why not use what works?"

"How often have you two done this?" Ryleigh asked.

"A few." Pik flashed his half smile.

"You can't guarantee I won't be recognized," Guilder said.

"Good point. Any ideas for your boy's famous face, Shyloh?"

"Still working on it."

"Could you show me how you…" Guilder bobbed a finger in Pik's direction.

"What? Shapeshift?"

Shyloh sighed, pursing her lips like a disappointed parent.

"I'm pretty adept at magic," Guilder said. "If you show me, maybe I—"

"Look, kid, humans aren't made for therianthropy. Your bones and… shit are way too ridged. Anyway, stick with the natural magics you're good at. Learn a few of the unnatural ones if you want, but leave the rest to those of us who can't do much else."

"I don't understand."

"What's not to understand? You humans can set villages on fire, summon monsters from thin air, or shoot lighting out your assholes." Pik shook his head, holding his gaze anywhere but on Guilder. "While we non-humans are limited to a simple glamour or disguising ourselves as some nobody."

"I didn't…I didn't realize."

"Don't worry about it, kid. The ones that have power never notice those that don't." Pik hurried his pace to catch up to Ashyr while Shyloh showed to match Guilder's.

"Sorry about him, he's... sensitive."

"Evidently, I have more to learn."

"That you do."

"What happened that he can't remember his true form?"

Shyloh took a deep breath, staring sullenly at Pik near a dozen paces ahead. "Changelings... excuse me, skin-walkers, gain their abilities in infancy, typically their earliest shift comes within their first few months. Inadvertently, of course, changing their appearance to mimic their parents or favorite toy, a doll perhaps. Since they're so young, they haven't developed the mental resources to remember form to form. Essentially, they forget their original appearance and have to... settle."

"Is he right, though? I mean, is it a skill humans can't learn?"

"Not sure. Pik's the only skin-walker I'd ever met. There don't seem to be many of them around."

***

Entering Ouverridge was easier than any of them could have predicted, even one with Guilder's notoriety. Republic gold, Auroran gold; it didn't seem to matter. It all spent the same.

The interior of the city was similar to the exterior, only slightly more organized. Tents lined the street along the wall for several blocks, with throngs of refugees meandering about, seemingly from all corners of the southern continent. Small towns and homesteads, a smattering of Auroran citizens, even some faery folk. With their queen gone, Guilder assumed there was chaos all across the moors.

Beyond the tents sprawled a thriving market. Live chickens clucked around their for-sale signs, fresh fish and regional foods sizzling on makeshift grills alongside herbs, spices, rolls of the softest fabrics, cashmere, and treated pelts. The perfumed scents, so reminiscent of Shellrock City's markets, Guilder couldn't help but marvel at the similarities. He'd even recognized some of the delicacies, candies, and baked goods he'd only thought made at the castle. Further in, storefronts advertised fine jewelry, dresses, leather goods, weapons, armor, and even a bank.

Guilder purchased some skewered quail and fried bread, Auroran staples along with curious Byzantium fare, braised squid, and rambutan jellies, for all to try. He shared half a honey cake with Ryleigh and candied fruit with everyone else.

"It's funny." Pik leaned into Guilder as they progressed into the city. "How your people bow their respects and yet flee your lands in droves."

"They're just frightened. For themselves, their families, of war."

"Of their butcher king."

Guilder's smile only reached one side of his

face. "I'm not the same man I was, Pik."

"Truly? Shyloh told me about the memory eater, but princely words mean little to people outside castle walls."

"You're saying real change comes from action."

Pik stopped, still in his Byzantium soldier's form. "I'm saying those people who prostrate themselves to you don't hear the whispers inside a war room. They see the results of those meetings destroy their lives."

"Pik, this isn't the time." Shyloh grabbed Pik's arm, attempting to pull him onward.

Guilder's smile vanished as he stepped close to the disguised soldier. "I'm here trying to stop that from happening."

"Guys." Ryleigh placed her hand on Guilder's shoulder. "We're attracting some unwanted attention." Guilder peered behind him as three Ouverridge guards emerged from the crowded marketplace.

"Trying and doing are two entirely different things." Pik's voice intensified as the guards trotted toward them. "What exactly have you done, Your Highness? For anyone?"

"Captain? Is there a problem here?" the lead guard asked Pik as he scrutinized Ryleigh's attempt to hold Guilder back.

"Yes, Sergeant." Pik's gaze remained glued to Guilder's narrowed eyes. "These folks think to induce a disturbance by evoking Prince Rayne's name, even impersonating the Butcher's likeness." Pik's sneer accompanied a wink. "Arrest them."

The city guard secured Ryleigh and Shyloh's hands behind them with leather straps, buckled tight.

"What are you doing? No. Keep your hands off them." Guilder fought off the lead guard's restraints. "Pik, you know exactly who I am."

"Captain?" the lead guard questioned.

Pik took a step toward Guilder, face to face, sneering up at him, waving a low hand at the shadowed corner behind. "Of course I know who you are, Your Majesty." He turned away, eyeing the lead guard. "You're anarchists, charlatans who only wish to sow discord and disrupt peaceful commerce."

Guilder clenched his jaw as the lead guard restrained his tightened fists behind him. "Take them for processing, Captain?"

"No. Take them to the capital building. I'm sure the grand council would enjoy a meeting with the infamous Crown Prince Rayne."

The two other guards chuckled nervously. "Sir," the lead guard said. "That's hardly protocol for this type of—"

"Sergeant. In these uneasy times, an example needs to be made of these…people. The council will know the correct course of action. Now secure them properly and prepare to move out."

***

"In these uneasy times?" Shyloh whispered toward Pik. "Laid it on a bit thick, don't you think?"

"You work with whatcha got." Pik leaned over to Guilder, cutting his still-bound hands free. "We good, big guy?"

"You know, Pik." Guilder kept his gaze fixed on the twelve marble seats in front of him. "If I hadn't changed so much in these last months. I would have simply cut your head off and taken your boat."

Pik feigned a weak chuckle. "Ah, well then, thank the gods for your miraculous... change of heart."

"We'll see."

"Pik," Ryleigh cut in. "What happened to Ashyr?"

"What? He isn't here?"

"Stop fucking around, Pik," Shyloh said. "You got us here, now let the rest of us in on it."

"This is, well... really... This is the extent of it. You wanted to see the council." Pik held his hands out toward the empty dais. "I give you the council. Ashyr, I waved off when we were screwing with those guards."

"What in the nine realms for?" Ryleigh asked in her most intensive whisper.

"In case this all goes pear-shaped."

"Pear-shaped!"

"I assume he'll meet us back in the city."

"If any of this goes wrong," Guilder said, "he's going to be waiting a long time."

Trumpets sounded beyond the wings of the dais as a dozen white-robed individuals paraded, six from either side, onto the stage. They sat in unison on the stone seats, raised hoods obscuring the eyes, shadowing the contours of their faces. Guilder took a step forward and cleared his throat. "I am Guilder Æthelred Rayne, first of my name, Royal Knight of the Noblest Order of Cañon and king of the Southern State of Aurora. Recognize me as such."

"This council recognizes King Guilder Rayne," the central figure said. He was a broad-shouldered man, dark umber skinned with a triangular jawline.

To his right, accompanying him in the central seats, a petite, olive-skinned woman. Her wide jaw bracketed scowling garden-pink lips. "Recognize you we do. However, is it not your mother who claims the Auroran throne? In your stead, no less."

"My mother's claim is false. She is misled by disreputable counsel and…" Guilder choked back the tightness in his throat, his chest. "Distraught by the passing of my father, her husband."

"Distraught?" said another woman furthest to the end. "She is downright emboldened."

"Has she not also lost her brother to Lord Iks?" inquired another councilman.

"She has, but—"

"And who is this entourage you've gathered?"

"Are you here to legitimize this war?"

"Or fight against your own mother?"

"Are you here as an assassin, Butcher King?"

The barrage of questions made Guilder's head spin before silence abruptly fell over the council chamber. The twelve hooded figures stared at Guilder, anticipation masking their faces as to his response. He allowed himself a centering breath as he scanned across their half-hidden faces. "I come not as an emissary of my mother, not of war, but of self-sacrifice. I come as a changed man, humbled and apologetic for past offenses, a harbinger of peace and understanding. I have seen little of your cities, less even of your people. But what I have seen reminds me much of Aurora.

"Our similarities outweigh our differences. As king, my father failed to propagate peace over the Southern Continent, and my mother in her grief has taken us to the brink. An all-out war between our two countries will destroy us all. I fear I've been the genesis of this discord. I am here in an attempt to right this." Guilder drew his sword and laid it across his off hand. He held his arms out to the dais, and dropped to his knees, placing the sword on the ground as he bowed. "The Crown of Aurora humbles itself before the Grand Council of Byzantium. Please forgo this war for the sake of both our countries."

Murmurs emanated from the dais. Mutterings of "vote" from some, grumbles from others.

"Rise, King Guilder Æthelred Rayne, first of your name," the broad-shouldered central figure said, effectively silencing the din of the others. Guilder rose, retaking his previous stance. "This council shares an equal voice in matters of governance. Unlike your... disrupted monarchy. As such, a vote has been declared. By a show of hands, how say you to an armistice with the Kingdom of Aurora. All in favor."

Six hands raised, accompanied by a call of yea, including the councilwoman to the right of the broad-shouldered man whose hand remained at his side. "The vote has concluded in a tie," he said. "No action will be taken."

"No action," Shyloh said from behind Guilder. "But you have to stop your armies."

The twelve council members rose in unison. Ryleigh grabbed Shyloh's arm, pulling her back to where they'd stood. "Guilder?"

"The council has voted," the broad-shouldered man said. "By our grace, you and your party may return to Aurora. A courtesy denied your betrothed, her death at—" He raised a tight fist, squeezed his eyes closed before releasing a held breath and readdressing Guilder. "Retake your throne and call a halt to this conflict from your own country." The council members began filing out the same way they'd come in. "Be thankful for this mercy, young King Rayne."

Guilder lowered his head as the last council member left the dais.

"Well, what in the nine realms do we do now?" Shyloh asked. Ryleigh laid a hand on Guilder's shoulder as he sheathed his sword, meeting his disconcerted gaze with consoling eyes.

"We go back to Aurora," Guilder said. "Retake the throne."

"Guys?" Pik said from behind them.

"And I'm sure your mother will gracefully step down," Shyloh said. "She's probably the one who called that Ōmukade down on us."

"Shyloh," Ryleigh warned. "Have some consideration."

"Umm, guys?"

"Shyloh's right. We should have never come here. I was better off staying at Shellrock waiting for the inevitable."

"Guys!" Pik bellowed. Guilder and the others turned to see the olive-skinned woman standing next to Pik. Her hood remained, covering most of her face as her garden-pink lips turned up in a cautious smile.

Guilder wiped the sweat from his forehead with the back of his hand. "Councilwoman."

"Your Majesty," she said with a slight bow.

"These are my friends. Shyloh Erbus, Ryleigh Marlow, and… Pik."

"Glad to ah… make your acquaintance," Pik said.

"And your vaporous friend floating outside the capitol building?"

Guilder smiled uneasily. "Ashyr, Ashyr Oriel."

"Oriel? As in Breya Oriel?"

"Her younger brother. You know Breya?"

The councilwoman lowered her hood, exposing a surprisingly youthful face. Pulled back into a thick braid, her wavy black hair was accented with a thin gold chain looped over her forehead. A teardrop-shaped jade pendant hung at the center, drawing only the minimalist attention away from the slender black sutures stitching her eyelids closed, sufficiently blinding her. "Breya's an old… associate," she said.

"Damn, that witch gets around," Ryleigh muttered, breaking the stunned silence of the others.

"That she does."

"How can we be of service, Councilwoman?" Guilder asked.

"The sorcerer to the north, Lord Andorian Iks, I believe to be behind most of what has befallen your kingdom. Here, too, I fear his influence pollutes this chamber. There is more to this war than is readily apparent. Even to my fellow council members."

"I can't say I agree with your council's decision but—"

"This chamber has been impotent of decision for some time. Its alderman most of all." The councilwoman angled her face in Guilder's direction. "Since his daughter's inopportune death in your kingdom."

Guilder averted his gaze, feeling the tightness grow in his chest, and swallowed the lump formed in his throat.

"His leniency seems unprecedented but, I suspect, may serve ulterior motives. Many of our more articulate members have been silenced, either by our alderman or other unseen forces, ultimately leaving the council out of fear for their own safety."

"What benefit could Lord Iks gain with half the continent embattled?" Shyloh asked.

"Of that, we're not entirely sure. However, threatening letters and chance encounters in our own streets, strangers dictating outcomes of secret upcoming votes speak of shadowed plots of a would-be puppet master. Those who've refused met with… unfortunate tragedy befalling not only them but their families. Understand, I want only what's best for our people. A continental war would serve them no good. Those of us who remain true to the council's purpose believe that Lord Iks has set this war in motion as a mere distraction against his furtive plans. Consequences of which be damned."

"We'd come to that same conclusion," Shyloh said, prompting a sour look from Ryleigh.

"What is it you propose?" Guilder asked.

"A secret accord. Succeed in removing this threat to both our nations and I'll do everything in my power to convince the rest of the council to consider peaceful negotiations."

Guilder narrowed his eyes. "You take a risk going against these veiled threats and the council's vote."

"Those will be my demons to slay. Hurry, you scarcely have time to delay."

Shyloh began heading for the chamber door, the others holding fast. "What is it that you fear Iks is planning, Councilwoman?" Ryleigh asked.

The councilwoman let out a ratcheting sigh, turning her chin as if listening for eavesdroppers. She lowered her voice to a whisper. "My own sources report he's occupied with a spell called Tessermancy, time magic. Given his reputed power, this spell could potentially wipe out all existence."

CHAPTER 30
A Boat Returning North

The rays of Wellingrey Lighthouse rolled over the North Sea like the ardent swing of a golden sword. A predawn fog obscured the salient coastline of its wielder less than a nautical mile from their anchored ship and a mere twenty kilometers from the edge of the Sal Flats. The steep cliffs and rocky coast refused any port built along its shores. As if the land itself conspired against the way forward.

"Glad to be back?" Guilder asked as Shyloh strolled up behind him. "In the northern continent, I mean." The *Belledragon* was not a fast ship, even with its cargo hold close to empty, taking nearly a full day's journey from Foxgate.

"The North never held any sentiment for me." Shyloh leaned against the taffrail, looking out into the fog. "If anything, it feels like a step backward." Wellingrey's light swung around, attempting to slice through the haze above their heads. "You buying anything that councilwoman said? Time magic and all?"

"She was holding back, I'm sure of it. If there's any truth to the sorcerer's manipulation of this war or this Tessermancy spell, we need to confront him and soon. Greymoor will hold per my directives, but I can't speak to Byzantium's armies."

"You're right," Ashyr said, sauntering up to the two of them. "About the councilwoman holding back, not that other stuff. Ryleigh filled me in on what happened."

"Can't sleep either?" Shyloh asked.

Ashyr shook his head. "Pik snores louder than a banshee after a reaping."

"How's Ryleigh doing?" Guilder asked, turning to face him.

"Once we anchored, she finally fell asleep."

"Boats and her don't get along," Shyloh added with raised eyebrows.

"She's spent much of the journey hugging a bucket," Ashyr said. "Face down on the floor of her cabin. I wasn't aware she had that much food in her until it started coming up."

"She'll be all right once we're back on solid ground." Guilder furrowed his brow. "Ryleigh's strong, she'll have to be. Captain says we'll need to anchor here and let the morning sun burn off the fog," He gazed skyward as a shooting star painted the fog a crimson red.

Shyloh turned toward Ashyr. "That councilwoman somehow knew you were skulking about town. Find out anything interesting?"

"Well, while you all were screwing around, I did do some digging of my own." Ashyr grew a boastful smile. "Apparently, Lord Iks collects a tithe from Byzantium. I'm pretty sure he gets one from the Trades Commission as well."

"That's nothing new," Guilder said. "Aurora sends him previsions twice a year. Grain, lumber, and sometimes a monetary contribution to keep the peace on the northern continent. It's been a longstanding tax on our kingdom."

"Sometimes it's more than a monetary tax, though." Ashyr shook his head. "At his last assemblage, he insisted on taking one of the Trades Commission's people. A boy was given as tithe. A northwestern quadrant supervisor's boy by the name of Maerek. Eli, I think it was. Allegedly, he drains these children to sustain his own life."

Shyloh scrunched up her face. "Drains, how?"

"Not sure, but it seems after young Eli was tithed his father, on a calm, clear night, requisitioned a fishing boat and trolled out into the northern sea never to return."

"What does that have to do with the councilwoman we spoke to?" Guilder asked.

"One guess as to what your mysterious councilwoman's name is."

Guilder pursed his lips, his jaw tight. "Maerek."

"Young Eli was her nephew, and her younger brother was deemed lost at sea."

"So, this mission is more personal than altruistic. She willingly sends us into danger to keep herself politically distanced?" Guilder slammed a fist into the taffrail. "Damn her manipulations."

"Manipulating or not, if this was all a plot to keep everyone occupied, it's an extreme distraction," Shyloh said. "If this Tessermancy spell is as dangerous as the councilwoman claims—"

"Tessermancy? As in time magic?" Ashyr asked. "That's powerful Fae sorcery. I mean, Earth-shatteringly powerful. There's a reason those spells have never been conjured, should never be conjured."

"All the more reason to confront him before it's too late." Guilder watched a blue-green shooting star race across the fog-covered darkness, its light blurred by the mist. "All signs seem to point back to his citadel. Both my father and the councilwoman said as much."

"I always thought that growing salt leach couldn't be natural," Shyloh said. "You think he truly incited this war? Byzantium's council seems to. Half of them, at least."

"My father was always one to avoid war. It can't be a coincidence that at the end of his reign, he'd start one." Another blurry shooting star streaked across the sky. "Ever since I escaped that memory eater's cave, I've felt... hunted."

"Before, even." Ashyr pointed a snide smile at Shyloh, who returned it in kind.

Guilder nodded, his expression remaining dire. "The Faeries, Yelrem, their psychotic queen, and even that jackass from Gunnison; what was his name?"

"Who, Wyrmlen?" Shyloh asked. "He's just a brawler with a title."

"He did hold a knife to your throat," Ashyr said.

Shyloh waved the notion aside. "Wyrmlen didn't know you from anyone."

"The gate guard in Paracel knew me."

"True. If that fossil knew who you were, others might of as well." Shyloh pursed her lips and sighed. "Point taken."

"And what about that Ōmukade inside the castle?" Ashyr said.

"The basilisk, too. My father had no knowledge of either."

"General Greymoor didn't know about the basilisk, that's for certain," Ashyr said. "Sure changed his battle strategy once he found out."

"The Ōmukade would have been no small feat," Shyloh said. "Whether he was trapped there or…"

"You thought of something?" Guilder turned his gaze toward Shyloh.

"Not sure. What if Shayde—"

"Is this boat ever going to stop rocking?" Ryleigh said as she ambled her way toward the others.

"Not much longer," Ashyr said. "A bit further up the coast and we can take the dinghy ashore. Stock up in Westcliffe or Silverton."

"Wonderful, another boat." Ryleigh hunched over, wrapping her arms around her stomach.

"Should you even be up here?" Shyloh asked. "You look terrible."

Ryleigh shot a tight sneer at Shyloh. "I hate boats."

"The lower decks are better for fighting off seasickness." Guilder stepped closer to Ryleigh, his hands supporting her at the shoulder. "By the gods, you're cold… Let's take you back to your room and get you warmed up."

"I'm fine!" Ryleigh pushed Guilder's arm away. "I mean... I just... needed some air." She wobbled to the railing, bracing herself as she looked over the misty water. "I'm fine, really. What were you all talking about?"

"About how everyone's out for Guilder's blood," Ashyr said with a wide smile. Guilder shook his head as the others gawked at Ashyr, brows lowered and faces flat.

Ryleigh shook her head and glared at Shyloh. "If we're assigning blame, I'd throw some at that shape-shifting friend of yours."

"Pik? No. He may be a bit brash at times, but he's on the level."

"The fuck he is! After what he pulled in Ouverridge? He'd have us in a Byzantium work camp if it wasn't for Guilder."

"I don't think…"

The heavy clicking of the anchor being weighed sounded off the starboard bow, followed by several blasts of the ship's foghorn.

"Where is Pik, anyway?" Guilder peered up into the wheelhouse. "He can't still be sleeping, not after that." The captain sent a puerile wave back as the ship lurched forward.

"Ryleigh, why don't you go back down to your room," Ashyr said. "We'll come and get you when we've anchored again."

Ryleigh clutched the ship's railing, her head hanging over the side. "I told you I'm fine," she said before a gush of brown-black bile splashed into the sea below.

***

"Westcliffe would have gotten us there faster," Shyloh said as they crested the final hill before the descent to the Sal Flats. "There wasn't even a decent livery in Gunnison. We'll be riding plow horses against veteran Dragonaught troops before we even get close to Iks."

Plumes of black smoke rose against the early dawn, kilometers east of where Guilder stood with the others. He pointed to the horizon before staring down into a deserted Gunnison. "Any idea about what that's all about?"

Ryleigh shook her head. "Not sure. Something's up, though. The city gate's open with no guards." Its streets seemed abandoned. No movement whatsoever. Even the chimneys refused to offer any signs of life. Several kilometers beyond the rear of the town, precariously leaning to one side, and surrounded by a sea of white, was a lone rickety building. "And those assholes never moved my bar."

Guilder started down the hill toward the town. His grip firmly attached to the hilt of his sword.

"At least they didn't demolish it for the wood," Ashyr said with a pat on Ryleigh's back.

Shooting stars glowed red against the cloudless orange and yellow sky as Guilder and the rest cautiously moved through the empty streets. Vacant storefronts, boarded-up houses, and not a sound say for a paltry breeze gave a ghost-town feel to the whole settlement.

"Stables are empty too," Shyloh said, returning from a few blocks over. "It's going to be a rough trek across the flats without horses."

"Maybe Pik can change into a horse," Ryleigh quipped. "Pull us in a carriage or something."

"Doesn't work that way, honey. Strength doesn't grow with me, unfortunately, and you seem a few stone heavier than the rest." Pik narrowed his eyes, pointing toward the boarded-up Trades Commission building. "I think someone's trying to gather your attention."

Through the cracked door, a nervous hand waved them forward. Ashyr misted his way quickly onto the weathered porch, the hand ducking back inside just as quick. As the rest joined Ashyr, the door swung open. "Get inside, all of you, quick." Wyrmlen swept his arm, coaxing them in as he peered up and down the streets, swiftly closing the door as noiselessly as he could.

The far wall of the office held a row of three empty jail cells, each with a cot. A feather pillow at its head, and a folded wool blanket at the foot. As if familiar with the place, Shyloh ambled over to the sidewall where hand-sketched wanted posters were tacked, haphazardly overlapping one another. Oversized keys, locks, and chain-linked shackles filled the opposite wall, behind a paper-strewn, tattered work desk with two mismatched wooden chairs set in front.

"Hey, Ashyr. Your reward doubled since we'd been here last."

Ashyr joined Shyloh, scanning over the posters. "Damn, I'm worth twice that, still."

"Could you two be serious for once?" Ryleigh scolded.

"What's happened here, Wyrmlen," Guilder asked. "Where is everyone?"

"That damned sorcerer, Andorian Iks, happened." Wyrmlen sat behind the desk, reached down, and yanked open one of the bottom drawers. "Bastard sent his entire force out to shutter all the towns." He clunked down a brown wine bottle on top of the desk, next to his tin cup. "Started at Crestone a day ago, came south, where Truegate challenged them." He shook his head, filling the cup near to overflowing, and gulped down its contents. "Dragonaughts nearly destroyed the whole town, taking out a third of my Trades officers." He filled the cup again, coughing as he did.

"We saw the smoke as we approached," Guilder said.

"Did you now." Wyrmlen hesitated, then nodded, taking another drink. "Leafside and South Fork got the hint. By the time they marched through here, people had boarded up. I sent any remaining men ahead, those that stuck around anyway, to help prepare the rest of the towns, warn them not to resist."

"Why is Iks sending his troops here? Now?" Ryleigh asked. "There'd always been an understanding between us."

"Have you looked at the sky lately? That sorcerer is attempting some major spell."

"The meteor shower?" Guilder said. "That's from him?"

Wyrmlen nodded. "Something to do with time, if you believe the rumors. Probably wants to annihilate us all. Started soon after the Dragonaught entered Crestone. It's no coincidence, I'm sure of it. Apparently, he doesn't want anyone interfering. Not that anyone would be fool enough."

"Well, we're here to interfere," Shyloh said, taking a seat on the corner of Wyrmlen's desk.

Wyrmlen scanned the group before taking another drink. "You five think you can take him on, you're welcome to it." He drained his cup, stashing it and the bottle back in the drawer. "Only reason I pulled you in here is I didn't need anyone drawing those monsters back this way. If you were smart you'd dig in and cover your heads like the rest of us."

"That's starting to sound like a good alternative," Pik said. "Look, guys, I didn't sign on to fighting elite soldiers or homicidal wizards, especially Lord Iks—"

"Who's this, then?" Wyrmlen asked. "You picking up strays again, Erbus?"

Pik leaned across the desk, morphing into Wyrmlen's form. "Just looking for my next opportunity, Officer."

Wyrmlen jumped back, reaching for his knife.

"Everyone, just relax," Guilder said. "Pik, leave him alone."

Pik righted himself before morphing back into a faun. He meandered to one of the jail cell cots and plopped down with his arms tucked behind his head.

"Officer Wyrmlen, with Iks' troops dispatched his citadel is ripe for assault. We could use the Trades Commission's help to stop whatever he's planning, and maybe rid our continent of his influence once and for all."

"We're not fighting for some kingdom to rule, *your majesty*. My men are already deployed to our northern cities. The more people we get hunkered down, the fewer lives are lost. And judging by how fast the Dragonaught marched through Gunnison, they're most likely nearing Crestone by now. I can't spare anyone."

"Then come with us," Guilder insisted. "Even one additional blade will help."

"Forget it. If the Dragonaught return, someone needs to be here." Wyrmlen sighed. "But… if you're all set on this suicide mission, I'll fix you up with some horses and a coach."

"I'll stay here if it's all the same to you," Pik said from his cell. "Fight the potential fight instead of the inevitable one."

Wyrmlen pointed to the back of the room. "Take him with you or it's no deal."

CHAPTER 31
Assault on Iks Tower

Guilder stared into the cloudless midday sky. Oncoming thunder, lightning, a rainstorm, something, anything besides a perfect autumn day seemed more appropriate. Bright red streaks of light painted the sky like claws ripping across a field of pale blue. They ascended to an out-of-sight point far above the citadel, racing from all sides, all corners of the globe.

The horses' nervousness turned to fear nearing the edge of the tiltyard, bucking their refusal to go any further past the circular pad of cobblestone extending from Iks' black towers. The citadel's main parapet stood raised; at most a kilometer from where they'd disembarked, with two lone individuals waiting patiently in front. "Only two guards," Pik said, jumping down from the coach seat. "Maybe this won't be a total massacre after all."

"If Iks held back only two guards, they're probably his best," Shyloh said as she unharnessed the horses.

Ashyr helped Ryleigh out of the coach, a coughing fit doubling her over as he did. Guilder followed, placing a hand on her back, his other firmly gripping his sword. "If you're not up for this, Ryleigh—"

"Don't even!" Ryleigh held up a warning finger.

"Sick or not, she chose to be here, just like the rest of us," Shyloh said with a slap to the horses' hindquarters, sending them on their way.

"You all chose to be here?" Pik said. "I was coerced. Shanghaied, even."

Shyloh narrowed disapproving eyes at Pik. "Ryleigh's the strongest one of us. She'll take out the two stragglers, no problem."

Ryleigh shot a sideways glance at Shyloh. "Umm, thanks?"

"Leave it to Wyrmlen to be the opportunist in our absence," Ashyr said, handing Ryleigh a diamond-etched metal Bo staff. "He cleared out the Marked Oaks' weapons room for us."

"Most of my booze too, I'd think," Ryleigh said as Shyloh grabbed a recurve bow and full quiver from Ashyr.

Pik retrieved a field glass from beneath the driver's seat and scanned the entrance of the citadel. "Those two don't look like guards. One seems part mechanical and the other's just some scrawny, scarecrow-looking guy."

Shyloh finished adjusting her quiver before grabbing the monocular off of Pik's face. "Scarecrow-looking… in all the realms of hell, what is Wilfried Shayde doing here?"

"Shayde? He should be back at Shellrock Castle," Guilder said.

"Let me see." Ryleigh adjusted the eyepiece as she peered at the citadel. "Master Lusoren?"

"Your old earth mage teacher?" Ashyr said. "Iks killed him. Didn't he?"

"Apparently not. Looks like he got his eye replaced, among other things." Ryleigh handed the field glass to Guilder. "This isn't going to be as easy as we'd hoped."

"Anything in that trunk for me?" Pik asked as Ashyr continued to rummage around in the back of the carriage. "You all thought this would be easy? To gain an audience with Lord Iks, it would take like… a committee of gods to achieve, let alone wanting to confront him."

"A pantheon." Ashyr held out an eight-flanged mace for Pik. "A group of gods is called a pantheon."

Pik held a blank stare at Ashyr. "Well, of course it is." He took the mace, his arm dropping with the weight. "You know what? Fuck it!" Pik's form grew into a colossal monster with the body of a man and the head of a bull, a minotaur with dark-hued skin and sable mane differing from his faun shape only in size. Pointed horns and upturned tusks made for a menacing appearance as he laid the now undersized-looking mace across his muscular shoulder.

"Thought you said changing form doesn't affect your strength," Ryleigh said, her narrowed gaze fixed on the citadel.

"It doesn't. Never said I wasn't strong to begin with and if I gotta do this, I'm doing it with style."

***

Guilder drew his sword, holding it out. He stood a pace in front of the rest, a duel's length from the two barring his way. "I am King Guilder Rayne of Aurora, and I demand words with this citadel's lord."

"Queen Natasha Rayne-el-Shamshyr, formerly of the Frisian Continent, is now sovereign over Aurora," Shayde said as if announcing her presence. "You forfeit your claim by your absence."

"By my death, you mean. You must be her gelded advisor, Wilfried Shayde. What stock do you take in recommending this war to the grief-stricken queen?"

"The Order of Mstovaris' means will always justify its end."

"I told you he was with the Order," Shyloh whispered. Ashyr shook his head.

"And what end is that?" Guilder asked.

"The same end your queen hopes for, as well as Byzantium's impotent council. Peace under one rule."

"Mstovaris' rule?"

"That outcome remains to be realized."

"Master Iven Lusoren!" Ryleigh stepped up next to Guilder, her Bo staff clicking off the cobblestone below. "Our Order was meant to temper this continent's skirmishes. Why stand against us now?"

"Dare you utter the name of the Fallen Star? An Order that saw you exiled for your arrogance."

"My arrogance?!"

"A trait, I see, that still possesses you." Iven shook his head. "More's the pity. The Order is no more, as Lord Iks has promised to exorcise this world of its vises. Shayde and I may have differing goals, but our task remains the same."

Shayde extended an arm to his side, palm open toward Guilder, his other pointed in the same direction. He arched his outstretched arm, ending at the opposite shoulder. "Your death, Prince Guilder Rayne, will put an end to a much-doted-on prophecy." He brought his palms together, centered at his chest, his lips moving in a droned incantation as salt-laden dust and soot began swirling around him.

"Oh, shit," Shyloh muttered.

Guilder turned his chin to the side, eyes remaining on Shayde. "What?" He glanced over at Ryleigh. Her breath came quick, teeth clenched. She leaned forward, muscles tight, pushing on her staff, cracking the cobblestone. "Shyloh? What's happening?"

"He's a summoner," Shyloh finally said. "And we are totally fucked."

Ryleigh bolted forward toward Iven as the particulate began to solidify around Shayde. Guilder pointed his sword forward. "To the citadel!" he cried, rushing headlong toward Shayde.

The others followed a pace behind. Shyloh's bow stretched taut, arrow strung. Pik held his mace high, nearly above his horns. They stopped short, Shyloh taking aim as Ashyr misted across the field to Ryleigh's side. Already engaged with Iven, Ryleigh swung her staff down, blocked by Iven's metal arm. Ashyr held out his daggers for a quick strike, misting out as a chest-size cobblestone splashed through his body.

Guilder swung his sword, aiming downward at the crux of Shayde's neck. His strike stopped, cutting partway through a black-gray talon. The creature's clawed hands fused into two massive wings wrapping around him like a leather shield, a white reptilian sail bristling on its back.

Pik gawped, open-mouthed, at the creature now fully materialized around Shayde. "What in the nine realms is that?"

Shyloh remained frozen, her arrow left unfired. "A wyvern," she said in a quivering voice. "He summoned a damned wyvern."

Its spear-tipped tail stretched into the air, smashing down where Shyloh and Pik were standing, missing the two of them as they circled back to Guilder.

"She's vulnerable at her underbelly," Shyloh yelled toward Guilder. The wyvern beat its wings and lifted off the ground, sending gale-force winds all around. "Attack her from beneath. Do your spiky thing, like with the korrigans."

"There's nothing here but salt!" Guilder said, his arm raised, shielding himself from the winds. "I can't just chuck our weapons at it, hoping for the best! Is it immune to fire?!"

"Resistant, yes. To most natural magics!"

Pik charged, horns down, at Shayde. Knocked aside by a rear claw, his mace took much of the blow as the wyvern jerked back its appendage.

"Is it resistant to arrows?!"

Shyloh shook her head, smiled, and nocked an arrow, sending it flying toward the creature's neck. Its wingbeats sent it off course.

Guilder jumped back as another tail strike landed in front of him. Shyloh circled to the front, sending arrows arching toward the wyvern's face, eyes, and gaping mouth. One found its mark, embedded in the roof of the beast's mouth. The creature let out a defining scream before breaking the shaft in half with a snap.

Pik recovered his fallen mace as Guilder sprinted toward him. Across the tiltyard, Ryleigh's old master had fallen to his knees as she mercilessly beat her Bo staff against his metal arm. "You think you can get me on top of that thing?"

"I did something to the underside of its foot." Pik gestured to the wyvern's under-tucked near leg. "But, I think, Shayde—"

"Don't think. Just get me up there."

Shyloh moved to the far side, dodging the creature's snapping jaws, recovering arrows as she went.

Pik scanned over the creature. "Okay, follow my lead." He took off at a dead sprint, Guilder a few steps behind. Pik skidded to a halt, dropping to one knee, arching his back, horns and mace held upwards.

The wyvern's clawed foot dipped tentatively toward Pik's makeshift caltrop as a pair of arrows pierced through its opposite wing. Guilder planted his boot between Pik's shoulder blades, springboarding himself onto the creature, burring his sword into its massive upper thigh.

Scrambling onto its back, Guilder removed his sword to the high-pitched foghorn of the wyvern's screams. He shifted for a downward strike into the creature's wing joint. The wyvern bucked, sending Guilder tumbling out over its wing. He jabbed his sword into the leathery skin, slicing through all the way back to the cobblestoned ground, severing its front claw. The limb vanished to dust and smoke.

Guilder peered beneath the creature. Shayde rose from his knee, a dark red stain growing at the hip as wyvern blood rained over the cobblestones. The creature flapped its wings, taking awkward flight in defense of its master. Pik stood next to Shyloh, breathing heavily, resting his mace on his shoulder. Shyloh loosed more arrows, strayed by tempests of the beast's wing beats.

"Ashyr!" Guilder yelled across the yard. "Stop fucking around and get over here!"

Ryleigh's old master had recovered, putting some distance between him and Ryleigh as he held Ashyr by the neck. Ashyr misted out of his grasp to Guilder's side. "How's she doing?" Guilder asked, his eyes fixed on Shayde bleeding at his hip and down his arm.

"Holding her own. She's starting to tire, though. She'll need some help."

"We need some help! You see that prick underneath this thing? Think you can get to him?"

"Not a problem, boss."

Guilder sprinted toward the head of the wyvern, drawing its deft, dagger-filled mouth as it stomped, thick talons smashing the surrounding cobblestones. Ashyr rushed in the opposite direction, misting in behind the creature where the wind was a mere squall.

"Get ready!" Guilder yelled, pointing his sword at Shyloh as he rounded to their side. "Aim for Shayde!"

"What do you think I've been trying to do?!"

"For Shayde! Aim for Shayde!"

Shyloh nocked another arrow, taking aim as Ashyr misted in behind Shayde, slicing his throat with his dagger while plunging another into the side of his ribs. The wyvern shrieked all the louder, fading to black smoke as Shyloh's arrow found its mark at Shayde's temple.

Pik aimed his mace at Guilder. "I was trying to tell you—"

"No time. We need to help Ryleigh."

Guilder sprinted to the other side of the tiltyard, the others following in his wake. Iven backed up, scanning the new arrivals, holding Ryleigh's Bo staff in front of him. Guilder helped Ryleigh to her feet, pointing his sword at the automaton. "He got my staff," Ryleigh said, breathing heavily.

"You okay?"

"Yeah, I'm tougher than I look."

The rest caught up, arching around Iven.

"Surrender," Guilder said. "We don't want to fight you."

"Are you kidding?" Ryleigh said. "What do you think I'd been doing all this time?"

Iven stood up straight, resting the end of the staff on the cobblestone ground. "I cannot allow you to interfere with Lord Iks' plans."

"And what plans are those?" Shyloh asked.

Iven smiled. "To purge this world of all it has become."

"Your Order was formed to fight against tyranny," Guilder said. "Why help Iks now?"

"The natural order of life has been corrupted. Do you not see it? Magic has infected this world, been allowed to fester and grow gangrenous. My lord has shown me a different world. A world of science." Iven brought his mechanical arm up in front of himself, as the aperture holding his eye adjusted. "A world without sorcery. Painful though it was, it is, at its core, pure."

"Magic has always been a part of our world. It gives us control over our environment. It gives us meaning. Iks has no right to take that from us."

"How fitting that a would-be king should find meaning in control."

"Enough of this." Ryleigh charged toward Iven, fist brought back for a decisive strike.

Iven held the Bo staff in front of himself, manipulating Ryleigh into the air like so many rocks. "Your ire had always been your weakness," Iven said before slamming Ryleigh down into cobblestones and tossing her to the far side of the courtyard.

"I guess the deliberation is over," Pik said, turning toward Shyloh. "Cover me."

Pik lowered his horns, taking off toward Iven at a dead sprint. Shyloh nocked an arrow, letting it fly over Pik's shoulder, a second right on its fletching. Iven deflected the arrows with his staff, sending splintered shards bursting behind him. A leap and downward thrust brought Pik's head into the ground, tilling up cobblestone as he came to a halt.

Guilder and Ashyr rushed Iven from either side. Like a stone rag doll, Ryleigh was tossed toward Ashyr, his daggers misting out just before her body flew through him, knocking him back several paces.

Guilder's sword met Iven's Bo staff with a clang, sparks exploding around them as Pik lifted to his hands and knees, only to be met with a titanium boot to his forehead. Pik lay at Iven's feet, unmoving, as Guilder pushed off Iven's staff, giving leave as Shyloh loosed several more arrows.

Iven deflected two of the arrows just as before. The third buried itself into Iven's remaining human shoulder. He pulled it free with a sickening squelch of tearing flesh, cracking the shaft in two as he raised an open palm.

Loose cobblestones rose around him. Clenching his fist tight, the cobblestones burst apart, forming rough-hewn rock blades. Guilder prepared for another strike as Iven jabbed the end of his staff into his gut, stealing his breath. Iven thrust his fist forward, sending the blades scattering in all directions.

Several rock knives flew through Ashyr as he misted in evasion; a final one drew blood. He dropped his dagger with a clang to grab his injured shoulder.

Ryleigh batted knives away, rushing back toward Iven as Shyloh nocked another arrow. She dodged to the side, narrowly avoiding one knife, drawing again as a second passed between the bow and its taut string, severing her lower arm just above the elbow. The bowstring twanged as the bow clattered to the ground. Shyloh clasped her upper arm, dropping to her knees.

"No! Shyloh!" Guilder swung his sword in a high arch. With a snapping ping, he shattered a rock knife into dust, while a vein of blue light etched itself along the sword's shaft. Ryleigh turned and glanced at Shyloh. Gnashing her teeth, she picked up speed toward Iven. Guilder did the same, diving for Pik's unconscious body, tumbling away just as Ryleigh's fist connected with Iven's jaw.

Pik drunkenly shook his head, shrinking down into his faun shape. "Did we win?"

Guilder steadied himself, his eyes firmly attached to Iven, his dangling jaw sparking as he attempted to reattach it. "Not yet. You and Ashyr help Shyloh. Ryleigh and I will finish Lusoren."

Without a word, Pik was up, waving for Ashyr and heading toward Shyloh as Guilder ran toward Ryleigh.

"What's up with your sword?" Ryleigh asked, picking up the fallen Bo staff.

"Not sure. Something Breya did back in Paracel."

"Damned witch can't keep her magic out of anything."

"You will not stop him," Iven said, his jaw continuing to spark with each word. "The Tessermancy spell is too powerful. *He* is too powerful."

"What is this Tessermancy spell?" Guilder asked. "What is Iks attempting to do?"

Iven again surrounded himself with fallen cobblestones. "He means to revert this world to what he's known. Cleanse the corruption and all who'd come out of it. Failing that, he will destroy everything. One way or another, the virus that is magic will cease to be."

"That means you'll die along with the rest of us," Ryleigh said.

"The end of my pain and torment will be my just reward as glorious oblivion greats us all."

"I'll show you oblivion." Ryleigh leaped up, thrusting the end of the staff toward Iven's chest, stopped by a shield of rock quickly assembled from the surrounding cobblestones.

Guilder followed Ryleigh's lead, striking downward to Iven's shoulder. Meeting rock armor, another sickly ping, and a blue vein spreading to his sword's tip.

Guilder and Ryleigh stole a few steps back as Iven continued adding stone shards to his expanding armor. Soon, where Iven once stood, a golem of rock took his place. Its red glowing eyes mirrored Iven's mechanical form as its bulk lumbered forward.

"Any ideas?" Ryleigh asked taking another step back.

Guilder followed. "I assume Lusoren's still at the center of that thing?"

"Good assumption."

"Let's see that staff of yours." Ryleigh held up the Bo staff, leaning one end on her shoulder, the other pointing out in front. Guilder concentrated on the end of the staff, clenching his fist, and mouthing silent words. He tightened his fist as the end of the staff began to glow red, twisting and constricting to a sharp point. "Aim for the center. I'll distract him."

Ryleigh nodded, trotting off a few more paces for a running start. Guilder raced to the side, the golem's sightline following him. He hiked his sword up gripping it above the hilt and tossed it straight at the golem's head. It batted the sword away like a bothersome fly, sending it skittering across the cobblestones.

The golem took a lumbering half-step toward Guilder as Ryleigh leaped into the air with a guttural scream, hurling the now javelin at the apex of her leap. Guilder drove his hand forward as if grabbing the javelin in midair, thrusting it forward, and burying it partway into the golem's armor.

Ryleigh's continued leap slammed her feet into the end of the javelin, sending it completely through the creature's chest. She rode Lusoren's momentum backward as loose rocks fell around him, landing beside him before Ryleigh yanked the javelin out, leaving a sizable hole in Lusoren's chest.

Guilder retrieved his sword and joined Ryleigh, putting a hand on her back as they stared down at Lusoren. "You won't win," he said, coughing out a mouthful of blood. "You can't. The prophecy, my prophecy, predicts your defeat."

"So shall the hawk be divided by the serpent, buck, and lion," Ryleigh recited. "You know as well as anyone that divination is fraught with inaccuracies."

Guilder glanced down at his sword, turning it over as blue spiderwebs glowed along the blade. "The interpretive nature alone," he said as Iven coughed up more blood, his head lolling to one side.

"I fucked up, guys. I mean royally, fuc—" Shyloh winced, clasping her stump of an arm as Ashyr tightened a torn piece of cloth above where her elbow should have been. Her detached limb lay where it fell, still clutching the broken bow.

"Stay still," Ashyr said in a quiet, reassuring voice. "This needs to be tight or you'll bleed out."

Ryleigh stood, javelin in hand, looking into the citadel as Guilder kneeled next to Shyloh. "How's she doing?" he asked Ashyr.

"I'm right here, you ass," Shyloh said through another wince.

Ashyr raised his eyebrows and tilted his head as he concentrated on bandaging Shyloh's wound.

"I see that. And I'm glad for it." Guilder put a hand on Shyloh's outstretched leg. "We're heading back to Gunnison, get you the attention you need."

"No! We have to go after Iks now!" Shyloh took in a sharp breath letting it out in a sigh. "Those Dragonaught bastards could be marching back here at any time."

"She's right," Ryleigh said, turning chin to shoulder. "This may be our only opportunity to get to Iks."

"You go," Pik said as he tore off more strips of cloth to hand to Ashyr. "We'll take care of Shyloh." He looked at her, weary, concerned. "I may know someone in Gunnison, if not, Silverton."

"Those Silverton sawbones wouldn't know where to put the leaches." Shyloh chuckled, grasping her shoulder with a tight grimace.

"Okay. Ryleigh and I'll catch up with you soon." Guilder nodded. Shyloh offered a breathless nod back. He gazed up at Pik, determination set in his eyes. "Get her there quick."

"Consider it done." Pik tapped Ashyr on the shoulder. "When you're finished, hook me up." Pik strolled a few paces behind them, his face already beginning to elongate. His arms and legs turned white beneath the knee, growing feather-like hair as they lengthened. He widened his shoulders as his sturdy back leveled out. A massive bay-colored Clydesdale took the faun's place, trotting in a circle, looking as if he were trying out this new form.

Ashyr helped Shyloh to her feet, slowly moving her to the abandoned carriage outside the ring of cobblestones. He situated her inside before dashing back toward Guilder. "Don't worry about Shyloh. She's gotten through worse."

"Really?"

Ashyr's pained smile faltered. "No, not really. But we'll get her through just the same." He held out his open palm. Guilder grabbed his wrist. "You are the one prophesied, I know it."

Guilder nodded.

"Save this world, Guilder, and give him hell, Your Majesty." Ashyr's face widened in a genuine smile. He picked up Shyloh's severed limb, wrapped it in the remaining bandage, and sprinted back to the carriage.

Guilder grasped the hilt of his sword as he joined Ryleigh at the open portico. "I knew he could do a horse," she said, leaning her javelin against her shoulder.

Guilder pointed his gaze above. "Not one of his favorites, I guess." The late afternoon sky still endured its inverted drizzle of shooting stars. Far off, at its apex, a spherical dust cloud took shape, monstrous yet out of focus. "I'm glad you're here with me, Ryleigh." His gaze dropped to the entrance of the citadel. "There's no one I'd rather have fighting by my side."

Ryleigh turned to meet Guilder's eyes, his

cautious smile. She sighed. "Save the sentiment. There's work to do."

Guilder nodded, drawing his sword. "Ready?"

"Ready." And they headed into the citadel.

CHAPTER 32
Moon Rise

"Gods be damned, this Lord Iks is well read." Ryleigh grabbed a book off a random shelf from the third library they'd come across since entering Iks' labyrinthian citadel, each bigger and more elaborate than the last. "Listen to this: *The creatures the common people have deemed faery are, like most of the fauna in this land, evolved, or, rather, mutated from a base order.* Who is this guy?"

"A powerful sorcerer we shouldn't underestimate, from my understanding." Guilder peeked around the next corner, sword at the ready. Its blue veined glow had taken over much of the blade, offering a dim but welcome light in the growing twilight. "Way's clear," he said, waving for Ryleigh to follow.

Ryleigh shook her head. "No guards, no servants, just endless staircases, stretched-out corridors, and countless libraries." She replaced the book on its shelf. "And all these manuscripts seem written in his own hand. Narcissistic bastard."

"We'll keep searching, but we're running out of time. His forces could be marching back as we speak."

"We must be halfway up this damned tower by now and seen nothing." Ryleigh meandered around the corner, nearly running into Guilder as he slunk his way along the wall. "He could be anywhere, and we'd never find him."

"We'll find him. We have to."

"Maybe he isn't... even... There!" Ryleigh took off at a sprint, past Guilder, and around the next corner.

"Ryleigh!" Guilder hurried after her. He'd seen it too, a shadow, just beyond the corners. He turned down the next corridor as the shadow slithered around the next, Ryleigh only a stride behind. "Ryleigh, slow down!"

"We need to catch him and get the hell out of here."

"He's purposefully leading us deeper into this maze, getting us lost." Guilder slowed to a stop. "Separating us." He sheathed his sword, catching his breath before slinking around the next corner. At the end of a short hallway, the space opened to an immaculate foyer. A crystalline chandelier bathed the room in a soft golden light as an open-hearth fireplace blazed, warm and inviting.

A centered grand staircase led Guilder to a pair of splayed open, steeple-topped doors flourishing the house's manticore crest, a scorpion tail encircling its roaring lion's head, leading to a sizeable circular terrace. Guilder turned his gaze upward to the pinks and violets of twilight continually scratched by the occasional stain of red. Ryleigh stood near the far edge as Guilder joined her, gawping into the early evening sky, its unfamiliar glow from a ruined orb floating just beyond the horizon. Its yellow-cream surface crackled around orange-red seams, like a net thrown across its surface. Shooting stars continued adding their mass as they pummeled against it while silent blue lighting flashed between a massive split at its center. Every second threatened to fracture the whole in two as a wispy dust trail followed its steady rise above the eastern bluffs.

"Luna," Ryleigh whispered.

"She's beautiful," a voice sounded from the far edge of the rounded terrace.

Guilder spun, pulling this sword, holding it double-handed in front of him. Ryleigh turned, lowering her gaze, javelin in hand.

"Not as beautiful as I'd remembered... still, it's good to see her retake her rightful place."

"You need to stop," Guilder said. "Whatever this is."

Iks ignored him, staring at the cracked satellite in awe. "Her absence has denied this world a guiding beacon." Iks lowered his gaze, leaning heavily on his blackwood cane. "Against the darkness, against the malevolence that took her from us." He looked between Ryleigh and Guilder. "That further poisoned us."

"Byzantium and Aurora are on the brink of war!" Guilder yelled. "This continent will see nothing but death! You have the power to stop them, stop... this."

"It is a paradox, humanity." Iks took a few tentative steps forward. "No matter how much humans change, how much magic has changed them, their world, their drives, their... essence remains exactly the same."

"Do you not hear me? The kingdoms no longer seek your endorsement. When a victor is declared, they *will* march on your citadel."

"I only sought to eradicate that paradox from this world, the human reverence for absolute power." Iks' gaze remained transfixed on Luna. "Your war, it seems, was both inevitable and irrelevant."

Guilder craned his neck behind him. The foreign satellite cast its fractured luster over a misleading night as shadows scurried to long-overlooked hiding places. "What exactly have you done?"

"The spell was meant to revert the world to a time without magic, to bring back a semblance of what was." Iks ambled closer, smiled, his eyes sunken and bloodshot. "Failure has again damned me to a cursed existence." His gaze, blank, passing through them, beyond them. His gaunt face and thin frame betrayed Guilder's expectation of the powerful sorcerer.

The sorcerer's smile faltered. He straightened his stance, focusing on Guilder. "This world, it seems, has clung to this false gift. Humankind's greed and its voracious desire for unrestricted power have always been and remain its most fatal weakness. I've tried to understand it, remedy it, exorcise it, yet repeatedly I've failed. This world's addiction remains." Iks peered back into the sky. "All I've accomplished is to illuminate it."

"Guilder," Ryleigh said, her eyes trained on Iks. "We need to finish this. Whatever spell he's started has clearly driven him insane."

"Can't you see?" The sorcerer's smile returned as he raised a finger skyward. "It is already done. The spell, though not reversing time in its entirety, has granted me the means to amend my mistakes. If I can't undo the meteor's influence, I will end it and start the world anew."

"Enough of this." Guilder stepped forward, sword at the ready. "Lord Andorian Iks of the Northern Continent, surrender for your own safety and the good of this world. You'll be granted amnesty—"

"You've cast a spell of unbreaking." Iks stared at Guilder's sword. The spiderweb of blue glowed throughout the entirety of the blade. "No, not you. One more… powerful." Iks raised a hand from his cane, spreading his fingers as Guilder's sword burst into shards, scattering fragments along the ground.

Guilder stared thunderstruck as he clutched the bladeless hilt.

Ryleigh took off toward Iks. "I'll finish this."

"Ryleigh, wait!"

Iks returned his hand to his cane as Ryleigh trotted toward him, javelin at the ready. Her movement slowed. Iks muttered noiselessly, holding out a finger as if in defiance. Ryleigh's knees buckled as the floor cracked beneath her. The javelin clanked to the ground. "Guilder?"

"It doesn't need to end this way." Guilder held out his hand, pleading. "Lord Iks, please."

Ryleigh dropped to her forearms, the ground continuing to crack beneath her. Finally succumbing, her body slammed onto the terrace's floor. Head immobile, her creased face turned to the side. "I... I can't breathe."

"It is inevitable, her death. She will be the harbinger of this world's destruction."

Guilder clenched a fist to his side, focusing his gaze on Iks. "The prophecy foretold the end of *you*." Mist formed along Guilder's upper arm. "Release her. While there's still mercy within me."

"It cannot be stopped. And Iven's prophecy merely predicted his own end."

"Consider yourself warned." Guilder thrust his arm forward as mist solidified and bolts of blue-tinted ice flew toward Iks.

Iks raised his staff. The ice shattered like glass off an unseen shield, his likeness shimmering behind.

Ryleigh caught a fractional breath. Guilder turned his gaze toward her as fragments of broken tile jetted to the perimeter of the terrace. Terracotta knife blades flew from all sides, passing through Guilder's body as he turned to wispy smoke.

He floated to the far side of the terrace, extending the distance between him and Ryleigh. Iks raised his staff again as an opaque black bubble encased Guilder. The bubble slammed into the floor, shattering to pieces as Guilder's increased weight cracked more of the earthen tiles.

"You've become a formidable sorcerer," Iks said, his breath coming heavy. "Despite my efforts to the contrary."

Guilder circled around Iks, each step

cracking the tiles beneath less and less.

"Queen Natasha el-Shamshyr was ambitious in her lust for power."

Guilder clenched his jaw. "Do not invoke my mother's name."

"She refused, though, to kill her son. Even when it was the only thing I asked."

Guilder raised his arm. The words, like wild beasts, circled inside his mind. Blue-green fire rained over Iks as he lowered his arm. He whipped his cane around, redirecting the flames, sending them back toward Guilder. Crossing his arms, Guilder split the wave of fire to both sides, letting it careen off the edge of the terrace.

Thunder clapped above him as bolts of white lighting stuck Guilder, wrenching out a guttural scream as he dropped to his knees.

"Guilder," Ryleigh begged through gasping breath. "Help… me."

Guilder remained on his knees, breathless. His clothes smoldered from the lightning strikes, sweat pooling on his forehead. "Please, release her. I beg of you."

Iks cocked his head. "You're much more like your father. Where your mother was ambitious, your father's fear kept him stagnant. Too circumspect, I think."

Guilder held out his hand, pressing his thumb and forefinger together. "It wasn't fear that held him." Iks clasped a hand around his throat as Guilder pushed himself to stand. "Or his prudent analysis of impossible situations."

Ryleigh sucked in an audible lungful of air, coughing, already on her hands and knees. Iks struggled to regain his breath, gurgling on the water stuck in his throat.

Ryleigh stumbled over to Guilder as he held the tiny bit of water steady. "Do it, Guilder, drown him, finish it."

"Of the many things I'd learned from my father, mercy was one of them." Guilder snapped his fingers. Iks coughed out the stuck water. "I learned that in my second life."

"What?" Ryleigh said. "No, he's trying to destroy our world. He tried to kill me and you're letting him live?"

"He's the reason I've become who I am. If it weren't for his influence, I'd simply be one more tyrant in this world." Guilder turned his sympathetic gaze toward Ryleigh. "He gave me a chance to be better. I'm repaying that influence."

"Hasn't he done enough to our world?!"

Iks pushed himself back up on top of his cane, coughing out any watery remains.

Ryleigh narrowed her eyes at him. "If you won't kill him, I will." She hiked her javelin over her shoulder, took a heavy step forward, and hurled it toward Iks.

"Ryleigh, no!"

As with the fire, Iks stretched his arm back, curving the weapon around. He thrust his arm forward, speeding the javelin headlong, piercing Ryleigh center to her chest, felling her where she stood.

"Ryleigh!" Guilder gnashed his teeth as he

glowered at Iks' bent and depleted form. Bringing his fist in front of him, he splayed his fingers as fragments of his broken sword flew toward Iks, piercing him from all sides. His blackwood cane fell into the bloody pool beneath as the sorcerer's wrecked body crumpled to the floor.

Guilder rushed to Ryleigh. Black-red blood seeped out of the thumb-sized hole in her chest, past the edge of the javelin's staff, staining her soapstone neck. He grabbed the staff, Ryleigh's hand meeting his. "No, leave it," she said, breathless. "I... finished...I finished what I came here for." She coughed, splattering more blood onto her face.

Guilder attempted to clear the blood from her wound. "I'll get you back to Gunnison. Breya can heal you, somehow, I'll...I'll get you back."

"Guilder." Ryleigh lifted her hand to his face. "I lived to avenge what Iven did to me. What Iks did...to you, it's done."

Guilder held her cold, stonelike hand to his cheek. "But, there's so much more we…"

"Yes, there's always more to do. At least…" She coughed up more black-red blood. "At least you helped me remember what it was like…" Ryleigh's head slumped over. Her arm went limp in Guilder's grasp. Her breath stopped, eyes distant as if taking in the newly risen moon.

CHAPTER 33
Mourning the Reborn Earth

"Wyrmlen, while we appreciate you putting us up, there is such a thing as decorum," Breya said as her heavy footfalls sounded inside the hotel room. "Can't a woman perform major surgery without being disturbed for even a minute?" Falling silent as she opened the door, her gaze scoured over Guilder, the carnage that remained, her eyes flicking between him and Wyrmlen. "Ryleigh?"

Guilder only shook his head. He hadn't the words. None that wouldn't decisively crush him right there in that unfamiliar hallway.

"Come... come inside." Breya shook her head as she gazed into the all too luminous night sky. She stood aside as Guilder ambled through the doorway, Wyrmlen directly behind. "Not you." She held out her hand, pushing Wyrmlen back into the hallway. "You, go... assume your duties watching out for Dragonaught, or whatever."

Wyrmlen took another step back, smiled, and nodded before turning to go. "And hey, thanks for bringing him," Breya added, shutting the door quietly after.

"Well, don't you look like last place in a bar fight." Shyloh sat in her underclothes, legs thrown over the side of the room's lone bed. Her hair, wet from a bath. The tub, set near the blazing fire, remained filled with bloodied water. Her arm, what was left of it, was bandaged up to the shoulder in what looked like torn bedsheets. Pik steadied her as she wobbled, attempting to stay upright. "Where's Ryleigh?"

"Don't mind her," Breya said, placing a hand on Guilder's shoulder. "She's so doped up on wood rose tea she won't remember what year it is, let alone any conversation."

"I so will," Shyloh said through a yawn. Pik helped her lie down and covered her with a worn blanket before soft snores began filling the room.

Guilder slid a chair out from beneath the modest dining table and sat heavily, his shoulders rounded, eyes distant. "I… I wouldn't mind some tea myself." He lifted his sad gaze toward Breya.

Breya smiled sympathetically. "Sure thing, sweetie. Will do." She swung a kettle back over the fire and busied herself mixing herbs in her mortar.

"You going to tell us what happened?" Ashyr sat at the corner writing desk. Metal parts, screws, and tools bordering the edges. He picked up a screwdriver and adjusted what looked like a wrist joint before glancing up.

"Ryleigh, she…"

"He doesn't have to tell us anything," Breya said, emptying the contents of the mortar into a cup. "Not right now, anyway."

"No, it's… it's okay, Breya," Guilder told them what transpired after they'd left. How Ryleigh had fought bravely, ferociously. How Iks had killed her even after being shown mercy. How she died with honor, having considered her revenge complete after defeating her ex-master, Iven Lusoren. Why it had taken the better half of the morning for Guilder to arrive at Gunnison. Carrying Ryleigh's body across the Sal Flats to bury her in still-fertile soil.

"It'll be at least another generation before the salt overtakes that hill." Guilder wiped his cheek, smearing the dirt and blood around before taking the steaming cup from Breya. "She overlooks the whole township from there. On quiet nights she'll hear the North Sea, its serenade of crashing waves. Even the soft glow from Wellingrey can reach her when the moonlight doesn't drown it out."

"It sounds like a lovely resting place, dear," Breya said. "Drink your tea and I'll draw you a fresh bath."

Guilder nodded. "Thank you, all of you. If it wasn't for… all of your… Words seem to elude me." He shook his head and breathed deep. "Iks is gone. His mark left shining down on our world, a world… suddenly smaller from those we've lost. We must endure. Peace is even more important now, in this my father was right." Guilder took in those present, the friends he'd made. "I will bring peace to this continent, and beyond, this I promise you."

Pik leaned against the far wall, his eyes closed. Breya nodded, continuing to heat water for Guilder's bath as Ashyr lowered his head back into his work. "We are nothing without our word."

***

"Breya, please. I need your counsel on these matters." Guilder leaned back into his father's war room chair tossing more parchments onto the pile strewn across the lengthy table. Each report, a different view of the state of the continent. "Wyrmlen and his Trades Commission have done their best to quell the initial panic, but that Tessermancy spell did some significant damage. They're lending aid while spreading word about what Iks had done, the cracked moon and all."

"Truth seems a safe route," Breya said. "Folks'll still take it as allegory. They need it to be symbolic somehow. Otherwise, they can't wrap their heads around it."

"You have a suggestion?"

"Light from the darkness, or some such shit. I don't know, hire a playwright."

Guilder took a deep breath, dragging his palm across his temple. "Peace with Byzantium is tenuous at best, their council remains in stalemate, and our forces are worn thin with so many searching for any remaining Dragonaught soldiers. We've been able to recruit a handful of deserters, but several pockets remain loyal to Iks' cause, whatever that remains to be. It's already been three weeks, and I'm still not sure where to start. And since you refuse to accept a position, I have no advisors."

"Probably because all your dad's toadies got themselves killed." Breya propped her legs on top of Shellrock Castle's massive war room table as she packed tobacco into the end of a long Churchwarden pipe.

"General Greymoor continues to send ravens from the field. Hardly a position to give advice on matters of state, though."

"Greymoor's a single-minded idiot. All he knows is war and without it, he's useless."

"Well, if we don't get this madness under control soon, his uselessness may not last for long." Guilder slouched into his seat at the table's head and sighed out a long breath. "With my mother seeking asylum in her home country, there's now the matter of the newly opened land bridge between here and the Frisian Continent."

Breya lit her pipe, puffing white smoke out the side of her mouth. "Who knew the fractured remains of Luna were sunk at the bottom of the ocean?"

"Who indeed." Guilder narrowed his eyes questioningly at Breya. "Now that she's whole again—"

"Whole-ish."

"The lowered ocean levels offer more opportunities for trade but increase problems of national security. When the land bridge stabilizes enough for travel, we're going to be faced with a logistical nightmare." Guilder shook his head at the pile of correspondence scattered across the war table. "Increased volcanic activity, quakes in the Crystal Mountains, sightings of dragons... *dragons,* Breya. Ravens arrive by the hour reporting more destruction, damn that sorcerer and his magics."

"Iks stole from Gaea," Breya said puffing out curls of smoke. "She's pissed and showing her rage. Bet you'd wish you'd stayed in Da'Kar's cave; let her feast on those juicy memories, instead of enduring all this political drivel."

"Would've been easier, yes." Guilder sat up, tenting his arms beneath him as he met Breya's smoky gaze. "Breya, I need an emissary on the Frisian Continent. My mother, undoubtedly, will try to poison any relationship with their government. I need someone I can trust who can take care of herself."

Breya's unblinking gaze held Guilder expectant as she exhaled a long stream of smoke.

"You don't have to answer now," Guilder amended before taking a soothing breath. "Regardless, Breya, I'm glad you came."

"Well, if it wasn't for your raven, I wouldn't have been in Gunnison for Shyloh. Not sure how you'd expected me to rally that fool Wyrmlen and his Trades Commission cronies, not after they all went and got their asses handed to them by the Dragonaught."

"It was a calculated risk. If we'd fallen…" Guilder choked back the emotion. "If we'd failed at the citadel, Iks still would have needed to be taken care of. I figured an army, even a small one, could have finished the job. After we'd taken the fight out of him, at least."

"No offense, Your Highness, but it seems to me that Iks was severely weakened from casting that time spell of his."

"None taken, and you're probably right."

"It's the only reasonable explanation that you beat him at all."

"We were lucky, I grant you."

"I mean, hell, Iks was a prodigy when it came to magic, a true genius of our time. A Tessermancy spell? Are you shitting me?"

Guilder glared at her over-exaggerated awe.

"You'd been just a baby compared to him…"

Guilder let slip a laugh. "Baby or not, you've been an exceptional help." Guilder's smile faded. "Iks said he wanted a world without magic Any thoughts on why the spell failed?"

"Using magic to erase magic?" Breya shook her head. "Can't be done, it's like unthinking a thought. Iks was a powerful sorcerer but a spell to reverse time would need… his power tenfold, at least."

Guilder nodded. "Breya, how did you know? About my sword, I mean?"

She shrugged. "I don't know. I assumed a big strapping lad like yourself knew only how to hack and slash his way through a sword fight. Figured a simple spell of unbreaking couldn't hurt."

"But, that's not just a simple—"

Breya raised a finger. "Simple, for some."

Guilder's smile returned. "Fair enough. But I still need a representative. Someone who'd leave the politics out of it, someone I can trust."

"Trust indeed. Can't say I don't appreciate

the pardon. Paracel had gotten a bit… curmudgeonly, but a pardon with a caveat isn't much of a pardon."

A knock on the war room door stole their attention. "A… lady… here to see you, your Majesty." The guard said before Shyloh pushed her way inside.

"You're damned right I'm a lady, you glorified doorstop." Shyloh slammed the door behind her. "Guilder… oh, I mean Your Majesty." She gave an abbreviated bow, her gaze shifting. "Breya."

Breya puffed out more smoke as she waved her hand, dismissing Shyloh's brazenness.

"I was told Pik was here."

"He requested a job where he could stand around and look important. I told him he could be a glorified doorstop."

Shyloh pointed back to the door. "Oh, that was…?"

Guilder nodded.

"Nice disguise. Ashyr around?"

"Leading the discussions with the Trades Commission about getting into the citadel. The books Iks… collected belonged to each of the three continental kingdoms, maybe beyond. Wyrmlen suggested peaceful negotiations with Byzantium. Could bridge some gaps between our two counties as northern lands are returned to their original owner. How's the new arm?"

"Well enough, I suppose." Shyloh twisted her mechanical arm around. Skeletal in appearance, it clicked softly as she flexed each finger. "Can't feel a damned thing, though. Hard to fire a bow, sharp edges fray the string."

"Partly why I sent for you." Guilder gestured at a wooden case sitting at the edge of the war table.

Shyloh stepped up to the case, fumbling with the latch on one side. Inside was a new bow, skeletal like her arm, and made of the same lightweight metal. Two round discs at its ends connected a braided string between.

"My engineers assure me the pulley system will reduce draw weight by nearly ninety percent and give you at least another hundred meters on your shot."

Shyloh took the bow from its case, testing out the string. "Braided metal?"

"Carbon fiber. Something the alchemists have been working on for some time. Not sure how they make it. Breya helped, too."

"I put a spell or two on it, simple ones, you know, for old time's sake."

"Meaning what?" Shyloh loaded an arrow and pulled back the string. The arrowhead glowed red, discoloring the shaft as she released the tension. "Nice."

"It won't break, either," Breya said. "Of course, given your proclivity for destruction…"

"I'll take extra care with it." She replaced the bow in its case. "There was something else you wanted, Your Majesty?"

"One other thing, I've sent a raven to General Greymoor. In three days, you're to start your tutelage under his command, Leftenant General Shyloh Erbus."

***

Six days later, far off to the north, in a dark corner of the glamoured castle of Mistfall, Lord Cirrus Yelrem looked up as a soft knock stole his attention away from his writing. "Enter."

"My lord." A tall fey soldier stood in the doorway, fully armored, helmet in hand. "You wished to be informed when the last of the citadel's books had been procured."

"Excellent. Had you encountered any resistance?"

"None to speak of. Our rearguard reported Auroran emissaries in South Fork. Possibly bartering rights from the Trades Commission for spoils of the citadel. A similar scene in Gunnison, only…"

"With Byzantium."

"Yes, my lord."

"It was to our advantage that the Trades Commission so quickly cordoned off the citadel, don't you think, Captain?"

"Aye, sir." The fey captain stood up straighter, eyes peering over Yelrem.

"This tentative peace between the humans will not last. Shortened still when they begin to blame each other for the absence of certain manuscripts."

"If I may, my lord, the…scout from Shellrock has returned."

Yelrem sighed, set his pen down, and folded his hands. "Show her in."

A young blond girl sauntered past the fey guard and stood at Yelrem's desk, meeting his gaze. She looked no more than ten or eleven, wearing a white chiffon dress, her bare arms, pale against the gold belt at her tiny waist. Her face held the scar of an old knife wound below her right eye as if she had an everlasting tear dripping down her cheek.

"Why go to the trouble of reclaiming the majority of the citadel's libraries when we have no use for them?" the girl asked, unprompted. "No fey can work those spells."

"Captain, you're dismissed." The Fey guard turned, closing the door behind him as Yelrem addressed the little girl. "All that is about to change." He rose from his seat, scanning a finger across a newly filled shelf. He removed a notably battered manuscript and took it back to his desk.

"Andorian Iks may have been one of the most disturbed humans I'd ever had the displeasure of knowing," Yelrem said, "but, at his core, he was a prolific sorcerer. Probably the most powerful this world has ever seen." He sat paging through the beginnings of the manuscript. "The evidence, if you hadn't noticed, hangs over this planet nightly. Reminding us, by its blinding light, that with his death he takes with him magics no one will ever be privy to again."

"I still don't understand your need for his books," the girl said in her feathery but staunch voice. "Our queen is dead. There's no one with magic enough to… You know something."

Yelrem waved his hand in dismissal. He pulled a letter-locked page from the bowels of his desk, unfolded it, and fit it into the grimoire as he shook his head. "I mourn his lost magics, is all," he murmured.

A hint of a smirk pressed against the girl's scar. "And of our queen? Do you mourn her as well?"

With pursed lips, he smoothed the creases from the newly fitted page. "What Iks gifted Viviana rotted her far beyond her undying skin, but her power won't die with her." Yelrem stood, closed the book, and returned to the shelf. "The gift of undying endures in another." He said, sliding the book back into its place. "Our queen is dead, long live the queen."

END

Acknowledgment

When I began my writing journey way back in 2006 I wrote primarily science fiction and horror. I wrote to release the stresses of being a US soldier, being away from my family and most of my support. I wrote for my own mental health, and I wrote often, nearly every day, and whenever I had a spare minute.

After a long, fifteen-year hiatus, where my hundreds of handwritten pages were placed in a box not to see the light of day, I began writing again. This time not, not for escapism, but to tell a story. One that I would want to pick up and read. The result, after a short nine months of, again, writing nearly every day was a complete manuscript weighing eighty thousand words. This still as yet unpublished manuscript, although generally readable wasn't nearly the polished novel I knew it could be. Fast forward another year and thousands of hours of writing later and I have a file full of unfinished yet pliable manuscripts. *Mourning of Lost Magics* and *The Change Paradox* being the first two published.

The Change Paradox was my attempt to write a time travel novel that made logical sense according to contemporary science. I'd done tons of research to familiarize myself with physics, theoretical or otherwise, and philosophies about time travel and the likelihood of its existence. I'm happy to report, and somewhat let down that time travel's existence is as yet negligible. The concept, however, fits my idea of what kind of writer I saw myself as, a science fiction writer.

My wife Tanya, who has given her unflappable support to my writing, asked if I'd ever considered doing a fantasy novel. Although she enjoys my other writings when she reads for herself she reads fantasy fiction akin to Sara J Mass or Laurell K Hamilton. I said I'd give it a try however it might end up darker than she's used to. She shrugged, told me to give it a shot, and *Mourning of Lost Magics* was born.

Although there is a strong fantasy flavor to *Mourning* I tried to convey where the magic had come from putting it into a category of Science Fantasy a real and growing genre in the deep down the rabbit hole of fantasy fiction. Tanya got her fantasy, and a sequel now in progress, and I kept a toe in the science fiction realm. I can only say, now at its completion, it was a joy to write.

I cannot thank Tanya enough for her support and love throughout my continued writing journey. I could always call myself a writer but without her, I could never have called myself an author.

I also need to thank Lisa for being my patient and understanding writing partner as she scribbles out my writer foibles and attempts to hammer me into a coherent writer. And Nicole for continuing to agree to be my first and typically best bata reader.

I'll also need to mention the Wisconsin Writers Association and their programs to level up writers of all levels and my writers' group for the comradery, laughter, and their continued support and guidance.

Born and raised in rural Wisconsin, Steven started writing science fiction and fantasy while in the military. With a background in Psychology and Mental Health, his life's work has been the study of the mind, behavior, and those particular occasions when differing minds and alternative behaviors do not coalesce. Steven's writing attempts to capture the truly remarkable way humans interact and represent that humanness played out in the extraordinary.

Steven is a member of the Wisconsin Writers Association, has attended their sponsored Novel-In-Progress Bookcamp and Writing Retreat, and has been a part of a local writing group for several years. He is married to his best friend and sole inspiration Tanya, the love of his life, a kind but demanding critic, and the only person he writes for intending to impress. She is also his biggest support. With a love of cooking and travel, they live in a semi-rural town with their dogs Amber, a young-at-heart rescue, and Jax a playful ball of puppy-like energy.

Visit the author's website at
www.swstrackbein.com

Milton Keynes UK
Ingram Content Group UK Ltd.
UKHW010817241123
433194UK00004B/291